Louisiana
Lament

JULIE SMITH

A TOM DOHERTY ASSOCIATES BOOK
NEW YORK

LOUISIANA LAMENT

A Forge Book
Published by Tom Doherty Associates, LLC
175 Fifth Avenue
New York, NY 10010

www.tor.com

Forge® is a registered trademark of Tom Doherty Associates, LLC.

ISBN 0-765-34466-1
EAN 978-0765-34466-3

First edition: July 2004
First mass market edition: July 2005

Printed in the United States of America

0 9 8 7 6 5 4 3 2 1

To Uncle Harris and all the Harris kids—
Debbie, Bink, and John

And to all their kids—
Ben and John McGonagil and
Erinn, Jenny, and Matthew Harris

And, as always, to Lee Pryor

Acknowledgments

All my thanks to Greg Herren, Kathy Perry, Betsy Petersen, Win Blevins, and Lee Pryor for editorial aid and comfort, to Hurricane Carol for the use of her name, to retired Captain Linda Buczek for police procedure, to Carol Gelderman for UNO expertise, to Bethany Bultman for biker advice, and especially to Gregory Holt for menhaden lore.

In addition to advice about the world in general, I often turn to friends for a better understanding of my characters. In this case, I must thank Michael Stoehr for his thoughts on the strangeness of love and seduction, and Rosemary Daniell (both in conversation and in her wonderful book *Confessions of a Female Chauvinist*) for insight into Famous Southern Poets.

Finally, I'd like to thank my Pete's drinking buddies: Kathy Perry, Mary Bode, John O'Rourke, Ken Cunningham, Tommy LeFort, and Iva Jean Graff for their companionship and hospitality.

Chapter One

The glad tidings had barely arrived: On this particular autumn day, early in the twenty-first century, New Orleans was not going to end up in Davy Jones's locker.

The weather service claimed that under certain unfortunate conditions—all of which had been present for hours—the river would flood, the lake would flood, the land bowl between them would fill, and the city would sleep with the fishes. But Hurricane Carol had just veered to the west, sparing The City That Care Forgot, as has every major storm since Betsy in '65. The early-October near-miss was getting to be almost as much a New Orleans tradition as termite swarms on Mother's Day.

But you never got used to trying to decide whether to build an ark or not.

Everyone who could afford to had left town. Those who couldn't had spent the early morning praying to Our Lady of Prompt Succor—or at least St. Expedite—for a quick fix.

Now that it was granted, Carol was still moving slow and dumping rain by the barrel. The city, unlike its usually playful self, was shrouded in a pall of gray. It was going to be this way all day, and maybe the next.

The schools were closed, and so were the city offices, but there was still power, and the phones worked. It was business as usual for many, if you didn't count the apocalyptic rain and the snarled traffic.

Both Talba Wallis and her boss, Eddie Valentino, were among those who'd decided to play Russian roulette. But Talba had arrived at E.V. Anthony Investigations, not flushed with the triumph of having guessed right, but late, soaked, and out of sorts. Normally not a pessimist, she actually uttered the old Dorothy Parker line when the phone rang: *What fresh hell is this?*

"Talba?" said a voice she didn't know. "Talba, it's Janessa."

"Who?" she asked, in the confusion of the moment.

"Janessa." Long pause. "Janessa ya sister."

Janessa, her sister. Whom she had seen exactly once in her life. Who had let it be known she wanted nothing to do with Talba. And who, today of all days, was on the other end of the line. Talba hadn't come close to assimilating this when Janessa spoke again. "I got a situation here."

"What kind of situation?"

"Bad. Real bad. Can you come on over here?"

It didn't occur to Talba to panic. She barely knew the girl. "Janessa, what's going on?" she asked calmly.

"I'm on Philip Street, just off St. Charles." She gave Talba an address on the river side of the avenue, in the Garden District, not at all the type of place Talba would expect to find Janessa. The Garden District was old, white, wealthy, stuffy, and way, way out of her sister's range of experience, Talba would have guessed. Janessa had impressed her as a young woman who'd stick pretty close to her own neighborhood, and this wasn't it.

"So, Janessa . . ." She was about to repeat her question when her caller hung up.

Well, hell. When she first found Janessa—which hadn't been all that easy, even for an ace PI and acknowledged computer genius (acknowledged by herself, at any rate)—she'd opened herself up to this. She wanted to help the kid, right? Apparently, that was going to require going out in the pouring rain. She selected an umbrella from the agency stand (the office manager, Eileen Fisher, kept a handy supply for days like this) and told Eileen she had to go out.

She drove her old Isuzu to the distinctly upscale, slightly familiar neighborhood, found a parking place, opened the umbrella, and stumbled to the address Janessa had given her, which she hadn't remotely recognized. She stared in surprise at the nineteenth-century mansion, realizing she'd been there before, as a guest. But unless her sister was making house calls these days, she couldn't see Janessa there.

Janessa was still a manicurist, so far as she knew, and the lady of the house certainly had need of manicures. Allyson Brower generally looked as if she spent about fifty percent of her time getting ready for fabulous parties, and the other fifty percent giving them. The latter part was more or less accurate.

It was one of these that Talba had attended a couple of months before.

She climbed the few steps, but she had no time to ring the bell. The door swung open on a young girl so vastly changed Talba wouldn't have recognized her on the street. Though her job was grooming other women, the Janessa Talba knew didn't go in much for grooming herself. She was overweight and unkempt, or had been.

This Janessa still had some meat on her bones, but her hair was now woven into gorgeous braids—probably extensions like Talba's. She wore jeans and a T-shirt, but somehow, the outfit seemed carefully chosen, certainly carefully fitted. It flattered her full figure.

"Janessa?" Talba blurted. "You look terrific."

The girl pulled her inside, shut the door quickly. On closer inspection, she didn't look terrific. She looked scared to death. Her face was tear-streaked and grayish. Talba spoke again. "What is it? This is Allyson Brower's house, isn't it?" She swiveled her head to get her bearings, and gasped when she saw a gun, water dripping from it, on a console table in the foyer. A long-haired cat lapped at the little puddle the drip had formed. Under Talba's gaze, the cat dropped heavily to the floor.

Janessa moved toward the gun, but Talba thrust out an arm to block her. "Wait. What's going on here?"

"*You* take the gun. Somebody might be in the house."

Talba's scalp prickled. She hated guns worse than some people hated rats. She dropped her dripping umbrella and frantically grabbed for her cell phone. Janessa groped her forearm. "Ya can't call the po-lice."

Fighting panic, Talba threw the door open and tried to speak calmly. "Janessa, let's go outside. If you've got a prowler, we don't need to be in the house."

Janessa peered anxiously in the opposite direction, then back at Talba. "No, I think it's all right. I already checked."

"What is it, then?"

Janessa glanced once more at the gun, and seemed to come to a decision. "Come on." She turned and walked away, leaving her sister soaking and confused. Talba found her cell phone—into which 911 had already been programmed—and followed anxiously through the center hall and kitchen, into a loggia, and out to Allyson's luxurious patio and swimming pool, the setting for her over-the-top parties, which were quickly becoming famous in a city with a lot of competition.

It wasn't so festive at the moment.

A woman—almost certainly Allyson—was floating face-up in the pool, hair swirling about her head. Her blue eyes were open and staring. But still as marbles. She was dressed in sandals, capris, and a blouse tied at the waist. Her face was white as wave-froth.

To all appearances, she was dead, and had been for hours.

But she didn't look as if she'd drowned. Talba had never seen a bullet wound up close, but the perfect round hole, dark with blood, in the woman's left forehead had to be one. Blood had stained her lemon-colored blouse—but not badly. If she'd bled a lot, the water had washed most of the gore away. Talba really hadn't known Allyson well (and hadn't particularly liked her) but there was something so sad about this used-up object, bereft of animation and joy and hope, that tears sprang to her eyes.

And then panic seized her. "Is that Allyson?"

"She dead, ain't she?"

She had to be, but maybe there was a chance. . . . "Help me get her out of there."

"Already thought of that," Janessa said. "How we gon' do it?"

It was a reasonable question. The Wallis girls were African American, Talba from an extremely modest background. Though they'd grown up separately, Talba hadn't had the benefit of swimming lessons at a country club and she doubted Janessa had, either. "Can you swim?" she asked. Miserably, Janessa shook her head.

"Did you shoot her, Janessa?"

"No!"

"Who did?"

"I ain' know. Found her like this."

Panic continued to surge like current through Talba's body. That gun was between them and the door. "Come on. We've got to get out of here. The killer could still be in the house." She darted into the kitchen, through the house, and back to the foyer, Janessa running after her. Talba breathed a sigh of relief, seeing the gun still dripping on the silver-leaf table. The door remained open, and rain was beating in. She didn't know which was worse, venturing into the storm or staying inside.

Janessa put a hand on her arm. "I think we okay. I took the gun, looked in every room. Nobody here." She pushed the door closed, fighting the wind and rain. "I wait right here for you and nothin' happen. We all right, I think. What we do now?"

Talba put the phone to her ear.

"Who you calling?" Janessa asked.

"Nine-one-one."

Her sister looked horrified, but made no move to stop her.

"I need an ambulance at 1321 Philip Street," Talba said into the phone. "There's been a shooting." She hung up before the dispatcher could ask any questions. The first thing was to get some help for Allyson—in the unlikely event she wasn't beyond it—the second to get a friend on the scene. She had one who worked Homicide. She dialed information, got a number for the Third District, and asked for Detective Skip Langdon. "She isn't in at the moment," a cheerful voice told her. A male one that obviously belonged to a morning person. "May I take a message?"

"It's an emergency."

"You want her pager number?"

Talba took it, left a message, and sighed, knowing she'd have to wait for a call-back. She turned to her sister. "Okay, Janessa, we've got a minute, but that's about all. Let's make it count. What the hell are you doing here?"

"I work here," the girl said sullenly. "I'm a artist now. We paintin' a marsh in the bathroom."

Allyson and her wall paintings. She'd had three or four two months earlier and must be adding more. "Go on."

"I came in for work, found her like this. Called you."

"That's it?"

Janessa nodded.

"Well, where the hell did the gun come from?"

"Found it by the pool."

"By the pool."

"Right on the edge. I'm lookin' in the pool, lookin' at the gun, tryin' to figure out if I'm seein' right, and I hear a noise behind me. So I pick up the gun and turn around."

"Pointing the gun?"

Janessa smiled. "Yeah, but it's just Koko. She jump off the kitchen counter."

"The cat?"

"Umm-hmm. But now I'm good and scared. So I take the gun, run across the patio callin' for Rashad, but he don' answer. Rashad live in the carriage house on the other side of the pool."

"Okay." Rashad? Right now last names were the least important part of the story. Thankfully, she heard sirens.

"I open the door, he ain' there. Then I'm real scared. Scared of who's in the house, but even scareder of the po-lice. Shit! *Can't* call the po-lice. For all I know they toss my ass in jail, throw away the key. Finally, I think of callin' you." She gave Talba a sullen look. "Coulda just ran. I'm tryin' to do the right thing here." She reached in her pocket and pulled out her own cell phone. "Then I take the gun, look around the house, call you while I'm lookin'."

"Oh, man." *The police are really going to buy that one*, Talba thought, wondering what to make of it herself. The siren had grown steadily louder, and now an ambulance stopped in front of the house. Talba glanced at the gun again and breathed a sigh of relief.

Two paramedics rushed in. She directed them to the pool, instructing Janessa to stay by the door and wait for the police. A pair of uniformed cops were running up the walk when she got back, grim-faced in the downpour. *It's starting*, she thought.

They were out of time.

Please, please let Skip call back, she prayed, and another district car arrived. Two more cops made the mad dash up the walk. Talba explained the situation quickly. "Is there anyone else in the house?" the short white one asked.

Talba shook her head. "We're pretty sure there isn't. My sister checked before I got here."

Two left to make sure. The women led the second pair out to the kitchen, where they could see the paramedics trying to fish Allyson from the pool. Before they started firing questions, Talba tried to take control. "I'm a PI. My sister found Ms. Brower in the pool and called me."

They turned quickly to Janessa. "Why'd you call your sister? Why didn't you call the police?"

The girl shook her head, apparently too intimidated even to speak.

Her eyes darted toward the window, then back to Talba, terrified. One of the officers noticed and spoke to the other. "I'm going outside."

The remaining one said, "Is there somewhere we can go to sit down?" and Talba realized that, in some way she'd missed, he'd been ordered to keep an eye on her and Janessa. Getting no answer, he said to Janessa, "Do you work here?"

Janessa nodded. Still not talking.

"Where we can go to talk?"

Janessa thought a moment. "Library," she said, and led the cop and Talba into a small, comfortable room lined with books and equipped with an antique sofa (the one uncomfortable touch), as well as a couple of wing-back chairs. The two women took the sofa, the cop one of the chairs.

Janessa had evidently been doing some thinking. She answered the question on the table. "I ain' know what to do. I call Talba 'cause she a detective."

"PI," Talba said again. "I work with Eddie Valentino. You know Eddie?" In New Orleans, it was always best to get your bona fides on the table; it made for friendlier treatment. Apparently, this guy hadn't heard about it.

He ignored her question, instead introducing himself as "Officer Lambert," and asked for the women's names and addresses. Lambert was in his thirties, white, and a little pudgy. Talba thought he seemed tired, but perhaps that was just the weight of the job.

The taller and better-looking of the two—the one apparently in charge—was a brother. He returned shaking his head. Talba was pretty sure what that meant.

Janessa said, "Miz Allyson dead?"

Both cops ignored the question. "You say you work for her?"

Janessa nodded.

"What's her name?"

"Allyson Brower. I'm doin' some paintin' for her."

The black one spoke. He was still standing, wet and dripping, obviously uncomfortable. "Why don't you tell us what happened here?" He didn't introduce himself, but his name tag read THOMPSON.

"I ain' know!" the girl whined, and Talba winced. "All's I know is, I come in this mornin' and found her in the pool."

"How did you get in?"

"With the key in the fake rock outside. Usually Rashad lets me in, but he ain' here. See, I went out to find him and—"

"Back up a second. Who's Rashad?"

"He live in the carriage house. Over there—on the other side of the pool."

"Did you check to see if he's there?"

"Yes sir. He ain't. See, I come in, everything real quiet, holler for Rashad, don't get no answer, you know? Then I go out to find him, find her instead. I start screamin' and screamin', bang on Rashad door, even open it, holler for him—he ain' there. Then I holler for Carmen and Austin, but ain' nobody answer. I'm gon' tell ya somethin', it's spooky as hell in this big ol' house. I want to go outside, but it's rainin' so hard—and anyway, *she* outside. So I just try to keep calm, and think who'd know what to do. And I think of my big sister, Talba."

Thompson said, "Carmen and Austin?"

"Carmen the cleaning lady. Austin Miz Allyson son. He visitin'."

"And neither one of them's here?"

Janessa shook her head. "Pretty sure they ain't. Call Talba." She shivered. "Spooky in here."

Talba noticed she'd left out the part about picking up the gun and searching the house.

The doorbell rang, and Thompson strode to answer it. He let in two men pushing a gurney. *Coroner's deputies*, Talba thought helplessly. *Skip Langdon, where the hell are you?*

She tried her theory out on Thompson when he returned. "Was that the coroner's office?"

As if he hadn't even heard, Thompson turned to Janessa again. These guys were obviously graduates of the we'll-ask-the-questions school of police work. She wondered if it would have been different if she'd been Eddie—her thoroughly plugged-in boss—and was sure it would have. By now, he'd no doubt have figured out he knew both these cops' dads from high school. They'd be afraid he'd call their mothers if they weren't polite to him.

Thompson said to Janessa, "When did you last see Ms. Brower?"

"Last night. She made supper for Rashad and me. See, I was working late and I heard Rashad and Allyson talking. He all upset about somethin'—yellin', kind of—so I came out to see what was the matter and she huggin' him. I look closer and I see he been cryin'. I don't say nothin', see, I'm real embarrassed, and I'm about to go back in the bathroom and do some more work when he see me, and he push her away, kind of. Miz Allyson say, 'It's okay, Janessa. Rashad's just had a disappointment, that's all. I'm 'bout to fix him a snack. Why don't you join us?' Just like I'm some invited guest. Rashad say, 'Sure, Janessa, you been workin' hard. Come on, have somethin' to eat.' So Miz Allyson, she fix us some grilled cheese sandwiches. Rashad, he a poet, ya know?"

She looked sideways at her sister, and suddenly something clicked with Talba. "You mean Rashad Daneene?"

Janessa seemed excited. "You know him? You know Rashad?"

"I've met him a few times. At open-mike readings." And in this house.

"See, my sister's a poet, too," Janessa said, and Talba could have sworn there was pride in her voice. "The Baroness Pontalba? You heard o' her?"

Thompson and Lambert shook their heads, Lambert with a little half smile, as if to say, "Are you kidding? Heard of a *poet?*" Talba was used to that sort of thing.

Janessa didn't seem to notice. She said, "There's this real pristijis writing school—"

Talba struggled with that, then realized the girl had said "prestigious."

"Hollywood? No, just Holly, maybe. Somethin' like that."

"Hollins," Talba supplied.

"Tha's it. Well, Rashad didn't get in. That was the disappointment. See, Miz Allyson, she help writers. She famous for it—tha's how Rashad come to be livin' in her carriage house. He take care of things for her—fix things, weed the garden, do a little paintin'. He the one hired me here, to help him paint a couple rooms. He do things for Allyson and she let him live there for free. So she tryin' to help him get into Hollins and they both real disappointed he didn't make it. That's what the whole thing was all about."

Lambert said, "How did you find out about all that?"

"They told me while Allyson fixin' supper."

"And what happened afterwards?"

"Well, I went back to clean up, put things away, and Allyson, she tryin' to cheer Rashad up. She put on some music, be dancin' with him. So I come out, all ready to go home, and they say, 'Come on, dance with us.' So we all dance a little, we drinkin' a little wine, and Austin come in."

"Austin."

"Allyson son, the one visitin'. Well, he come in and he have a fit. He say, 'What the hell goin' on here?' something like that, and his mama say, 'Come on, Austin, let's dance. It's a beautiful night to dance.' And he say again, 'What the hell goin' on?' 'Bout then, we catch on, he really mad, maybe drunk or somethin'. Allyson say, 'Oh, Austin, it's so sad. We feel bad for Rashad, 'cause he didn't get into Hollins. We chasin' the blues here. Playin' music, gon' wake up to a bran' new day. Come on, get yaself a beer and join us.'

"Well, Austin, he ain't havin' none of it. He say, 'Mama, whatcha doin' dancin' with the *help?*' Jus' like that, like he might as wella said the 'N' word. Well, Miz Allyson shocked. You can see it. She say, 'Austin, I didn't raise you to be rude in front of my frien's. You apologize right now.'

"Instead, he say, 'You gon' get yaself in trouble this way. Ya don't know nothin' 'bout half the people ya hang with. Don't know whatcha doin' three-quarters o' the time. Ya just a ole drunk broke-down whore.' Well, then that really starts it, they yellin' back and forth, callin' each other names, then Miz Allyson say, 'You ain't never gon' get a penny of my money!' and Austin, he just stalk off. To his room, I guess."

Lambert and Thompson were clearly riveted. Talba was more or less on the edge of her chair as well. But Janessa quit talking, seemingly just as her story was getting good.

Thompson crossed his legs, making an obvious effort to control himself. Finally, he said, "Then what happened?" Speaking softly, drawing it out, as if he didn't much care, just asking to be polite.

"Well, I got real embarrassed and left."

"Just like that?" Lambert blurted. "Without saying good-bye?"

"No, suh. I say good-bye. Just say, 'Think I better go,' some-thin' like that, and Allyson say, 'Sorry about Austin. He shouldn't drink.' "

"Did you get the feeling he was drunk?"

"Couldn't tell. Coulda been."

"Where'd you go when you left?"

"Home."

"Did you stop anywhere on the way?"

"No, suh. I went straight home."

"And who do you live with?"

"That ain't your business."

Lambert looked thoroughly exasperated. "Let me rephrase the question. Was anyone at home when you got there?"

"Don't know. Didn't see nobody."

The doorbell rang again. It was a couple of male cops in suits—obviously the Homicide guys. Lambert waited with the two women while Thompson filled them in.

Out of the blue, Janessa said, "You sure could use a manicure."

Talba looked at her hands. The last professional manicure she'd had had been the one Janessa did. "Guess I could," she said. "You could paint my nails 'Professor Plum.' "

Janessa grinned. "You remembered."

It was their one common memory.

Chapter Two

Talba hadn't even known Janessa existed until a year and a half before, when she'd found out more or less by acci-dent. The younger woman was her half sister, the daughter of Talba's father, Denman Wallis, and a woman named Lura Jones, who had died soon after Janessa's birth. Learning even that much had taken hours of detective work. But Talba needed to find the girl. She owed her big-time—for something she'd taken from her that could never be returned, never be atoned for.

Finally, she traced her to Lura's sister, Mozelle Winters, who claimed to have raised her, though Mozelle didn't have a kind word for Janessa, or for Talba's father, or for Talba. Mozelle had eventually married a well-to-do doctor and Janessa'd left home at fifteen. Talba traced her to a beauty salon called Eve's Weaves, where she was working as a manicurist, living with the family of her best friend, Coreen Brown. Talba had called on her at the Brown home, talked to a woman who was apparently Coreen's mother, and learned where Janessa worked. One day she dropped by for a manicure, intending just to get a look at her sister, maybe decide what to do next, but another patron recognized her and sang out her name as she waited her turn.

Mrs. Brown had evidently mentioned her visit. Janessa knew exactly who she was, and, for reasons she hadn't mentioned, decided to be hostile about it. They talked warily with each other while they literally held hands, Janessa cutting her sister's cuticles and filing her nails. And then, in an apparent change of heart, Janessa offered to pick a special color for Talba's polish. It always made Talba smile to think of what Janessa said as she applied it: "It's called Professor Plum. Whatcha think that means?"

That was almost her only friendly remark. She had not asked Talba a single thing about herself except why the other customer called her "Baroness."

"It's my professional name," Talba had said. "The Baroness de Pontalba."

And after that, she had to deal with Janessa's disappointment that she was a mere poet and not a rapper. On impulse, as she left the salon, she'd asked Janessa to come hear her read, but the girl hadn't shown.

In the weeks that followed, during which her brother's first daughter was born, making Talba an aunt, she found herself longing to know her sister, and not just because she felt she owed her. It had something to do with a renewed family feeling, maybe; Talba couldn't really explain it.

She'd dropped by the Brown house again, called repeatedly, even ferreted out Janessa's e-mail address and tried to reach her through the Internet, all to no avail. And the next time she went to Eve's Weaves, her sister was gone.

She barely thought about her anymore.

But Janessa, she realized, had thought about her. For one thing, she'd called Talba at work. That meant she'd known Talba was a PI as well as a poet. So she'd been following Talba's career. But she'd never have called unless she was desperate.

The question was, why was she so frightened?

One of the Homicide guys, Sergeant Reuben Crockett, joined them after what seemed an eternity, during which the crime scene techs had arrived and he had worked with them and the coroners' deputies. He wasn't a bad-looking white guy, for someone in his forties, but he had a bossy manner that Talba didn't much care for. He took Janessa aside to question her, then came back to Talba, isolating her in the living room while her sister waited once again with Lambert. He asked for her story, much as the district cops had, then had a few questions of his own.

"Did you know the victim?"

"I met her once—when I came to a party here."

"Did your sister kill her?"

That one threw Talba. She didn't honestly know the answer. She finally said, "She didn't have a reason to. She was just working here."

"Oh, really? Ms. um . . ." he consulted his notes and evidently noted that there were two Ms. Wallises ". . . Janessa says Ms. Brower owed her money."

"That's a murder motive?"

"You tell me."

"My impression is that they got along."

"Does your sister have a history of violence?"

"Not that I know of."

"Not that you know of. She's ya sister, right?"

"We've been out of touch for a long time. She called me because she needed help."

Crockett stared at her. "She needed help. Usual thing would be to call the police, wouldn't it?"

Talba tried to keep cool. "Janessa's fairly inexperienced. She thought because I'm a PI I could help. I work with Eddie Valentino." She tried the network ploy again. "You know Eddie?"

Crockett's face was stony. "Yeah, I know Eddie. Look, Ms . . . uh, Talba—why do I get the impression you're leaving something out?"

How to play this? Talba wondered. Try to stop the bullying or put up with it? Finally, she said only, "I'm not leaving anything out. If you like, you can call my office and find out what time I left."

"Look to you like that woman died this morning? You're a PI. She's been dead for hours—you happen to notice how white she is? Know what we call that?"

"Lividity," Talba said. "Yeah, I happened to notice—I'm not the one who's dead here, Sergeant. She died sometime in the night. Is that what you're saying?"

"You tell me."

"I'm afraid I've told you everything I know. May I take my sister home now?"

"Now, you know better than that." He walked her back to the library and spoke to both sisters. "You two are going to have to come down and sign a statement. Lambert'll take ya. You can wait for me at the district."

"Never mind. I've got my car."

"Okay, Lambert'll escort ya."

"You know what? We're really wet. Can we go home and get changed first?"

He looked them up and down. "You can make one stop. Ya wear each other's clothes? Ya sisters, right?"

No way, Talba thought. *Uh-uh and negative. Janessa is not coming to my house.*

But Janessa said, "I got some clothes here I wear to paint in."

"And I've got a pair of sweats in my trunk."

Crockett held out his hand for her key. "Where's ya car? Lambert'll get ya clothes for ya."

Seeing the melancholy look on Lambert's face, she thought maybe it wasn't such a bad day, after all.

But of course the fun had just begun. She and Janessa were at the station for hours, repeating their stories again and again, then waiting for the statements to be typed up so they could sign them.

When they left, Crockett gave them each a card, after first

writing his pager number on it. "Y'all call if ya just happen to remember somethin', okay?"

Talba had suddenly had it with the meek act. "Are you always this patronizing?" she asked.

To her surprise, he smiled. "Always. You don't want to mess with me."

You got that right, she thought.

It was still pouring rain when they left the station. The cops had kept Janessa longer, but Talba had waited. Since Janessa had come on the bus, Talba was happy to take her home, eager to see where she lived, even more eager to conduct her own interrogation. When they were in the car, she said, "You still living with those nice people? The Browns?"

"Kind of. But I got my own apartment now, over the garage. Ain't no kitchen, but I can use the one in the big house."

Talba said, "Big changes in your life," wondering if the girl would take the bait.

To her surprise, Janessa's face twisted; she bit her lip, but a tear still squeezed out of each of her eyes.

"Not good changes?" Talba said. "You seem good to me."

Provided you didn't just kill your boss.

"I got things to tell ya."

Sweet Jesus, I'll bet you do. She waited.

"Could we get somethin' to eat? I'm starvin'."

Talba realized she was, too. Absolutely famished. They drove up Magazine to Café Roma, which was miraculously open, and for once, parking was plentiful, so they didn't have to run too far in the rain.

"Have whatever you like," Talba said when they were seated. "I'll buy. I'm the big sister." It seemed the decent thing to do, but she had the feeling she was setting an unfortunate precedent. She wasn't surprised when Janessa didn't protest.

"What do you have to tell me?"

Janessa looked at her lap. She was silent for so long Talba almost thought she'd changed her mind, but evidently she was just getting up the nerve. "I didn't call you before because I was embarrassed."

"Embarrassed? What about?"

"Ya promise ya won't laugh?"

"Sure. Cross my heart."

"Okay, look. I wadn't doin' nothin' with my life, okay? Coreen said so, and her mama, and everybody—they was tryin' to get me to get my GED, find a decent job—and I just never thought I could. I mean . . ." she stared out the window for a moment ". . . I 'bout half didn't even want to."

Talba nodded. "Lotta work," she said. "The hard part's getting up your nerve."

"Well, you helped me." The girl looked down again. "You come in lookin' so pretty and bein' famous and everything—I mean, jus' for being a *poet*—then I start readin' in the paper about ya, find out you a detective and everything, and I thought, we got the same blood! We the same. I gotta do that."

Talba's heart pounded. This wasn't exactly what she'd expected. "It pays really badly," she said, to cover her own embarrassment.

"I don't mean be a detective. I mean I thought I gotta improve myself—make somethin' of myself. But I didn't want to talk to you till I done it. I didn't feel right, see?"

"I guess so," Talba said, somewhat reluctantly. This was a reasonably foreign idea, thanks to her pushy mama, Miz Clara, who'd not only always told her she could be anything, but had more or less required her to. She and her brother, Corey, both. Corey was a doctor, the least of the three professions Miz Clara deemed suitable for her offspring. The other two were speaker of the house and first African American president. That kind of thing probably bred confidence as well as neuroses.

"So I get my frien' Coreen to help me fix myself up. I look better, don't I?"

"You look really good." Janessa was worlds away from the hostile, unkempt girl who had held her hand and applied Professor Plum. That girl had seemed without hope or dignity or pride. "What about your GED?" she asked.

"Got it!" Janessa said, and held her hand up for a high-five.

Talba smacked her palm. "All right!" She let a beat pass. "And now you're an artist."

"Oh, no, I ain't no artist! No way. But I painted all those nails, you know? I can stay in the lines real good. I was just doin' some regular paintin'—just walls and woodwork and stuff for Rashad—I mean, he hire me for Allyson—and they get this other guy, a real artist, to paint the bathroom. But he quit in the middle. Only he left this stencil thing, and Rashad figured out I could put leaves on as good as the next person if I had a pattern to go by. So that's all I been doin'. I ain't got no career yet."

"How do you know Rashad?"

Janessa smiled. It was probably the first time she had, in their brief acquaintance. For the first time, Talba caught a glimpse of the real Janessa, the one who wasn't so busy being hostile or embarrassed or both that she looked like a black cloud. She looked good—like any other young girl with a future. "I took his poetry class," she said.

Talba was just taking a sip of her coffee. Her hand jerked, and she spilled a big glop on her white shirt. "Damn!" She grabbed a napkin and dabbed at it.

Janessa was amused. "You think I'm tryin' to turn into you? Steal your identity or somethin'?"

In fact, it had crossed Talba's mind.

Janessa shrugged. "Just thought I'd try it, tha's all. Maybe see what it's all about so if I ever do come hear ya read, I won't be stupid. But guess what? I still will be. Didn't get nothin' about it. But me and Rashad, we hit it off."

Talba was still dabbing at her spot. "Where does Rashad teach?"

"UNO. Adult ed." University of New Orleans. "Real good class, too. But I like this paintin' thing. Maybe I'll take drawing next. Some kind of art."

Talba felt they were getting off the subject, whatever it was. She didn't know where Janessa was going, but to her, this conversation was about how her sister had come to find a body that morning. She said, "Is Rashad your boyfriend?"

Again, Janessa smiled. "Closest thing I got to one."

Meaning what? Talba thought. *You sleep together now and then?* She didn't ask. Instead, she said, "Where do you think Rashad is now?"

Something flickered briefly on the girl's face—fear, perhaps—and then grief took over; all-out misery. Janessa lowered her face and whispered, "I don't know. I just don't know." When she looked up, her cheeks were wet again.

"Is that why you called me? You think I can find him?"

"No! Why you say that? I never even thought of that till you said it just now. I call you 'cause I thought you'd know what to do."

Uh-huh. "Do you think Rashad killed Allyson?"

Janessa hit the table with her open palm. "Why the hell he do somethin' stupid like that?"

Talba took a leaf from Crockett's book. "You tell me."

The girl calmed down. "No way. No way in hell Rashad kill Miz Allyson. She a bitch, but he love her; he crazy about her. But . . . *you* know."

"No doubt. But fill me in, just in case."

"Well, he black and he missin', ain't he? What you think them white po-lice gon' think?"

"That 'missing' part's a little sticky," Talba mused.

"Well, you a PI. You could find him." Janessa spoke so wistfully that Talba was inclined to treat her gently.

"Uh—Janessa. Do you really think that's what he'd want? If he's missing, it must be because he has a good reason." *Like he's running for his life.*

Janessa thought about it.

"Look," Talba said. "Let's give him some time to think it through and come in if he wants to. I could get him a lawyer if that's what he needs."

Janessa picked at her napkin, apparently still thinking.

"Let me take you home and let's wait a day or so. I'll follow up with my police sources."

"Okay." Janessa spoke regretfully, obviously disappointed.

"But, listen, Janessa—you did right to call me. If the police come back at you, don't try to handle this on your own. Call me again, okay?"

Janessa was silent.

"I'm not taking you home until you promise."

"Okay. I promise." Her voice said she'd as soon bite into a cyanide capsule.

On the way to Mystery Street, where Janessa had her garage apartment, they spoke little. Talba felt it best not to push.

She thought about her own odd encounter with Allyson Brower.

Chapter Three

The invitation had come through a friend, Mimi Dirr, who knew everybody in literary New Orleans, but it hadn't been Mimi who called. Talba wasn't sure who had, if the woman had even given her name. She had said, "Talba? I got your name from Mimi Dirr. Allyson Brower's giving a birthday party for Hunt Montjoy, and we wanted to make sure and invite you. Can you give me your address?"

Who Allyson Brower was didn't seem to matter at the moment. This sort of thing happened in New Orleans—and elsewhere, she assumed. One person supplied the list, another gave the party. Mimi Dirr really was her friend, so that was okay, and Hunt Montjoy was a name to conjure with, an extremely well-known poet whose one novel, a period piece about a lynching in Mississippi, was something of a classic. In its day—about twenty years ago—it had won a Pulitzer Prize.

He was no friend of Talba's. They'd met twice, perhaps, and she'd felt a distinct coolness from him. Or maybe that was giving herself too much credit. More likely, he was simply indifferent, too secure in his own greatness to have time for a little-known poet, particularly a young, female black one. Now, maybe if she'd been blond and adoring . . .

But she wasn't, and they hadn't hit it off. She hadn't particularly liked him, but she was flattered to be invited to his birthday party. In retrospect, she couldn't deny it. Hunt Montjoy, whatever you thought of him personally, was an undisputed icon. This was an honor, or so she construed it.

Hunt was born in mid-August. Apparently pursuing an astrological theme, the invitation made reference to a gathering of "Literary Leos." Talba showed it to her boyfriend, Darryl Boucree, a high school English teacher who taught Hunt Montjoy's work to his deeply apathetic students.

"Humph," Darryl sniffed. "A little on the self-conscious side."

"Makes *me* a little uncomfortable," she said. "Think we ought to skip it?"

"Hell, no. Look at this address. At the very least, we'll get to see a beautiful house and the food'll be good. You can get all tarted up like a baroness."

Talba was famous for her flamboyant performance costumes. "Wonder who the hostess is?" she said.

"Allyson Brower." Darryl shrugged. "Don't have a clue."

She took out her cell phone and dialed Mimi Dirr. "Mimi? Talba Wallis. Who's this Allyson Brower?"

Mimi took a moment to answer, finally said, "Oh, the Leo lady. Some friend of Hunt's, I guess. You know Burford Hale? Burford called me and asked who to invite."

Talba didn't know Burford, either, but what the hell, it was a party, and New Orleans loves nothing more than a party, particularly in near-dead August, when most people who can afford it have gone somewhere cooler.

For the occasion, Talba chose a leopard-print, toga-like creation with matching scarf, worn as a turban.

"Ah. Literary leopard," Darryl had said, getting it instantly.

"Meow," Talba replied.

The outfit proved a prophetically appropriate choice. Whoever Allyson Brower was, she'd pulled out all the stops with the jungle theme, even constructed a palm-thatched structure on the patio as a dance floor. She seemed to have borrowed every lion picture, poster, and sculpture the city had to offer.

Flanking the door was a pair of crouching lions resembling the ones at the New York City Public Library, and just inside the entry was a stuffed lion's head mounted on the wall, a large tiara perched on its head.

"Queen of beasts?" Talba inquired.

"Meow," Darryl replied.

Tropical plants had been artfully placed to give a jungle effect, populated by the occasional non-feline beast lurking in the foliage—a giraffe here, a zebra or antelope there, mostly of carved wood, either borrowed or purchased from a dealer in African arts and crafts.

A chamber music group played in the living room, the pianist seated at what evidently was Allyson's own Steinway. Lavish arrangements of exotic flowers sheltered the ceramic and bronze and carved lions that frolicked on every surface.

In the formal dining room, a huge bronze lion served as the centerpiece of a gorgeous spread from a catering service called Food for Thought, which Talba might have thought had been chosen for its name, except that its product was superb. The wait staff wore the usual black and white, with one exotic touch—leopard-print gloves that matched Talba's outfit.

No sooner had Talba and Darryl passed through the door than a waiter appeared with a tray of champagne, another with one of hors d'oeuvres. The man who met them was small and neat and white, sporting a moustache so carefully trimmed he resembled a colonel in a '40's movie. He wore an impeccable white linen suit. "Burford Hale," he announced.

Talba introduced first Darryl, then herself. No sooner had she said her name than the man bowed over her hand. "Ah, the Baroness de Pontalba. It's an honor to have you here." He turned quickly to a woman at his left. "Do you know Lena Krause? Very very up-and-coming short story writer. We're expecting great things from Lena."

Lena was a short white woman in a full black lace skirt and a corset, which had to be giving her heat rash. "And how do you know the guest of honor?" Talba asked, to get the conversation started.

"Me? I've never met the man," Lena admitted. "I don't know a single person here." She snagged a crustacean from a passing waiter. "Good shrimp, though."

"Come on," Darryl said. "Let's go get a gander." And so, with Lena in tow, they made their way through Allyson's vast, beautifully decorated, momentarily over-lioned house, snacking and drinking and talking with friends, of whom quite a few had turned up. Talba counted fourteen fellow poets alone, including a couple she met for the first time that night. One of these was a handsome young man named Rashad Daneene, whom she had heard read once or twice.

Rashad had a slender, open, slightly chiseled face, and short, fashionable dreads. He was flirting with one of the waitresses, a breathtaking blonde at least a head taller than he was. "Do you know the hostess?" Talba had asked him.

He gave her a warm smile. "We've been best friends for at least fifteen minutes. Tall lady with, kind of, uh, bangs."

It wasn't much of a description, but when Talba and Darryl finally tracked her down, Talba saw what he meant. She had thick, highlighted brown hair, unremarkable in itself, but she wore it in a kind of exaggerated Louise Brooks style that framed a face just a little too perfect—and a little drawn. Perhaps, Talba thought, Allyson had had a nip and tuck too many. She wore a tie-dyed silk dress in shades of taupe and fuchsia— stunning, Talba thought, and told her so. "Oh, thanks," she said, as if the compliment barely registered. "Have you met Hunt yet? Let me find him for you." And she was gone.

After waiting a decent interval, Talba and Darryl determined she wasn't coming back, and moved out to the patio, which had also been jungled within an inch of its life. As they stepped out, Darryl was nearly decapitated by a giant, low-flying butterfly. "Now that," he said, "is one gorgeous swimming pool."

It was particularly gorgeous at the moment, full of orchids floating languidly to the strains of a five-piece rock band. "Want to dance?" Darryl asked.

"What?" Talba shouted back.

They decided, on grounds of not being able to hear themselves think, to go back inside and find some food. In the dining room, Burford Hale was consulting a piece of paper and surveying the guests. "Ah," he said, and strode over to Talba. "Baroness. May I borrow you for a moment?" He offered his arm, escorting her to the library, where a photographer Talba recognized was taking a picture of Hunt Montjoy and a haughty brunette, a biographer who taught at Tulane.

"The Pulitzer twins," Hale said with satisfaction.

"I beg your pardon?"

"That's Bethany Felter with Hunt. Her history of the yellow fever epidemic won the Pulitzer a few years ago. Can you wait here a minute?" It was clearly an order.

When the session was done, she chatted briefly with Sue Reissman, the photographer, while Montjoy and Felter carried on an animated conversation about the virtues of North Carolina in August. Talba had no doubt what was in store, but she wished she'd been asked. Reissman worked for the *Times-Picayune*.

Long after the Pulitzer twins had excused themselves and Talba and Reissman had run out of chitchat, Burford Hale returned with a well-known male romance novelist, and asked Talba to pose for Reissman with him. Or rather, jockeyed her into position and posed her himself, arm around a man she'd just met.

When she returned to Darryl, he was applying himself to a plate of lamb chops so tiny they made perfect finger food. "What was that all about?" he asked.

"Picture for Sue Reissman. You know her? She takes all the stuff for the *T-P*'s society column."

"Oh. Guess I didn't make the cut."

"Royalty only," the Baroness said, with the uneasy feeling that there was truth to that assessment.

Hale seemed to be working double-time. A beautifully dressed woman Talba recognized as the owner of Food for Thought wandered among the guests, looking focused and a little nervous. Talba had seen her supervise a party only once before, a wedding for four hundred guests.

"There's Tasha, the caterer," she said to Darryl. "She's got almost as much staff here as Allyson has guests."

"Whoever Allyson is," Darryl replied. After that they made it their mission to find out.

Mimi Dirr just shrugged. "She blew into town a little over a year ago, bought this house, and started giving parties. The literary festival's dying to get her on the board."

"Made a small contribution, did she?"

Mimi smiled wryly. "A biiiig contribution."

Burford Hale appeared again. "Mimi, do you know where Anne Rice is?"

Talba gasped. In New Orleans, Rice, though a mere writer, was a bigger celebrity than the actor Nicolas Cage, who owned a house on Esplanade.

"And how about Nicolas Cage?" was the next thing out of Hale's mouth. "Their assistants promised they'd be here."

Mimi said, "Well, it's a pretty hot night. Maybe they just—" but Hale bustled away before she could finish, a panicked look on his face. He was back in a moment, once again consulting his cheat-sheet.

"Baroness, do you know Barbara Osborne?" He named the

most important poet in New Orleans, a woman who'd won international awards; an idol of Talba's, actually.

"Sure, I know Barbara."

"Can you find out why she didn't come tonight?"

"I could ask her." *And I might if you gave me a few pounds of emeralds. And hell froze over.*

"I'd appreciate it," Hale said, and left again.

Darryl asked her once more to dance, but after a few minutes, they were both dripping with sweat. "Let's go home," he said, "and try to figure this thing out."

"Counting musicians," Talba mused, "There were definitely as many staff members as guests."

"And I *didn't* count the lions," Darryl replied.

Two days later, Talba got a call from Burford Hale. "Baroness, darling, I was wondering," he drawled, "what did Barbara Osborne say?"

Talba was baffled. "Barbara? About what?"

"About why she didn't come to the party."

"Gosh, I'm so sorry; I forgot to ask her." *And why would anyone care enough to follow up?* she wondered. Especially someone who wasn't the hostess.

The next week, they read about the party in the *Times-Picayune* society column, which pretty much portrayed it as a be-there-or-be-square kind of event—and did run Talba's picture. But nowhere did the writer give a clue as to who Allyson Brower might be, or why she'd given a birthday party for Hunt Montjoy.

Chapter Four

Eddie Valentino was wondering just where the hell Ms. Wallis had got to when she swanned in dripping wet and demanded an audience.

"Must be serious," he said, "when the Baroness herself comes crawlin'."

She set her rain-soaked butt on his other chair. "It is serious. I spent the morning watching the cops fish a body out of a swimming pool."

That stopped him cold. For a moment he just sat there trying to get his mouth to close. Finally, he said, "Ms. Wallis, Ms. Wallis. Fulla surprises, as usual." He looked at his watch. "How 'bout the afternoon?"

"The cop shop."

Eddie sighed. "Nobody we know, I hope?"

She frowned, trying to figure out what he meant.

"The floater."

"Oh. Not really. I mean, I met her once, but that's not the issue. Somebody I know called me over there. Found the body and called me instead of the cops."

He didn't like the sound of that at all. "And who might that someone be?"

"My sister."

She was trying to shock him. Or maybe she wasn't—she had a way of doing it without trying. "Didn't know ya had a sister," he said uneasily.

"Neither does Miz Clara. I think she might be about to find out."

"Half sister? Is that what ya sayin'?" He liked correcting her, for once. She had a college education and never let him forget he didn't.

She nodded. "Yeah, half sister. My dad's kid. I didn't know about her myself till about a year and a half ago. I've seen her exactly once before in my life. Tried to get in touch many times, but she didn't want anything to do with me. Then she finds this body, freaks out, and calls me."

"Or, anyway, that's her story," Eddie finished for her.

"You got it."

"Well, ya got me interested." He leaned back and picked up the phone. "Eileen, bring us some coffee, would ya? Me and Ms. Wallis are 'bout to have a nice long talk." He folded his hands on his chest. "Shoot, Ms. Wallis, and ya don't have to take me literally."

It took her about half an hour to unfurl the story. When she got to the part about the gun, he said, "Uh-oh."

"Uh-oh is right," she said miserably.

"Keep goin'." He gave her the get-on-with-it sign.

The second thing he didn't like was the part about Rashad being Janessa's boyfriend. He raised an eyebrow.

"Yeah," Ms. Wallis said. "If Janessa didn't do it, sounds like he did, doesn't it?"

Eddie shrugged. He'd worked way too many cases to jump to conclusions. "Now, hold ya horses, Ms. Wallis. What ya think his motive might be?"

"I don't know—crime of passion or something. Maybe he and Allyson had a fight—simple as that."

"Ya think ya sister did it?"

"Of course not. Why would she?"

"She's a temporary employee, right? And obviously this Brower broad had some money. Maybe Brower caught her stealin'."

"Eddie, come on."

"That's how cops' minds work, Ms. Wallis. They've gotta think of every contingency. Let me give you a little lesson about how the police work. They've got three suspects right now, and ya sister's number one, especially if that gun turns out to be the murder weapon. She *says* there were two other people there, but no one's around to say yea or nay—so they've got only her word. With her prints on that gun, she's in it big-time. They're gonna try to find those two guys to eliminate her as a suspect. But if they can't do that, they're gonna try harder and harder to build a case against her."

Ms. Wallis actually appeared chastened—a wholly new and, in his opinion, utterly becoming look for her. "But . . . she wants me to look for Rashad. She thinks they're going to think he did it."

"So she says."

"I was thinking I might do it. What do you think?"

The thing was to be calm, Eddie told himself. If he came down too heavy too soon, that would clinch the deal—he'd never get a minute's work out of her till she'd run the thing into the ground. He executed his famous shrug. "Her money's as good as the next client's."

"EdDEE!" she barked. "You and I both know she hasn't got any. She wants me to work for free."

He leaned forward and fixed her with a boss-stare. "Well,

that's another animal, idn't it, Ms. Wallis? Whatever happened to 'no tickee, no washee'?"

"For heaven's sake, Eddie, I don't even know what that means."

"Well, let's try it another way. 'Course ya shouldn't do it. When ya gon' do it, for one thing? I need ya here."

"I knew you'd say that."

"Well, why'd ya even waste my time?"

She fidgeted, which wasn't like her. "I don't know. I didn't feel like keeping it from you, that's all."

"Uh-oh. There's more, isn't there?" The office phone rang, but he ignored it.

"Not exactly."

"Eileen, get the phone, will ya?" he shouted. He turned back to Ms. Wallis. "Ya do think ya sister did it. 'Zat it? Then we *would* have a *pro bono* mess on our hands."

He had meant to be stern, had just been thinking out loud, but suddenly she was smiling, practically hugging his neck, and he saw the trap he'd fallen into. "Eddie, baby, you're a prince!"

"I'm not ya damned baby!" He was seriously pissed at himself, and Eileen had to pick that moment to poke her head in.

"Talba, it's for you. Says she's ya sister."

"Hoo, boy," Eddie said. "Go on. Take it."

He listened as she picked up the phone. "Janessa? What's up?"

Ms. Wallis listened a few minutes, saying hardly anything except, "Oh, shit," which made him wince. He hated it when women cursed.

Finally she hung up and turned to him. "They've got her back at the Second District."

"That was damn quick. They must have found something— like a witness."

"She wants a lawyer."

"Have they arrested her?"

"I don't know. I didn't ask. All she said was, they came to her house and got her. She freaked out."

"And called you. She got her sister's brains, anyhow." He sighed. "I guess we better get Angie." His daughter was a criminal attorney.

He picked up the phone.

"Tell her I'll meet her there," Ms. Wallis said.

"What for?"

"Like I said, the kid's freaked."

The Second District, housed in a ramshackle old building on Magazine Street, resembles a police station of a century ago. Aside from computers, it contains almost no artifacts of the late twentieth century and, due to lots of dark, lustrous wood, has an unexpected homey feel about it. Talba took along the book she was reading (*The God of Small Things*—prose, but food for the poetic soul) to keep her busy while she waited for Angie Valentino to work her magic. When her cell phone rang, she was almost reluctant to answer. But she did and she was glad: it was Skip Langdon, finally returning her call. "Baroness. What's up?"

"I called to report a murder. Think nothing of it, though—I made do with nine-one-one."

"A murder. What the hell happened?"

In her mind's eye, Talba could see Langdon in her office at the Third District, probably wearing pants a little too short— Langdon was six feet tall—and some kind of T-shirt that didn't quite match. She wasn't known for her fashion sense. But the detective was a big, good-looking white cop with hair so curly some of her relatives might also have been Talba's.

They'd met on a case and hit it off.

"Relative of mine went to work and found the lady of the house floating in her pool with a bullet in her head. Called me instead of the white po-lice."

"Uh-oh. What kind of relative?"

"My little half sister—love-child of my daddy's. Miz Clara doesn't even know about her."

"Did she do it?" Langdon might be her friend, but she was still a cop.

"So far as I can tell, she doesn't have a motive. But they've got her down at the Second District. Took our statements, let us go, then came back for her. Like, almost immediately."

"Oh, man. They must have gotten something. Who caught the case?"

"Guy named Crockett. Kind of a bully, seemed like."

"Reuben Crockett. At least he's not a racist. Could be worse. He's actually a pretty good guy."

Crockett hadn't seemed like a good guy to Talba. "Listen, I really appreciate your calling back. Janessa's scared to death."

"Let me know if there's anything I can do." Langdon rang off, leaving Talba to her reading.

It was over an hour before Angie Valentino came out of the room where she'd been with Janessa and Crockett. Talba drew in her breath—Janessa was with her. "She's not under arrest?"

"You kidding? Aunt Angie's here."

Janessa pouted. "Well, they gave me that 'you-got-the-right' shit. And you ain't my aunt, okay?"

"You're walking out of here, aren't you?" Angie snapped.

Talba said, "You guys need a playground monitor?"

Angie and Janessa glared at each other. Best to separate them, Talba thought. She said, "Come on, Janessa. I'll take you home. Thanks, Angie."

"Bring her to the office. We have to powwow."

Janessa seemed to have disappeared into herself. Once in the car, she folded her hands over her chest and bowed her head, as if she intended to sleep. *Poor kid*, Talba thought, and finally said, "I'm sorry you had to go through that."

And Talba heard some faint gasps, as if the girl was crying quietly.

Janessa's shoulders started to shake. For a while she didn't speak, and when she did, she screamed. "I hate that bitch!"

"All, right, out with it. Why would you hate Angie?"

"She ain' act like she on my side."

"Well, she is. She got you out, didn't she?"

"I hate everybody! I didn't do *nothin'* and they say I kill Cassie and Allyson!"

Talba couldn't believe she'd heard right. "What'd you say?"

Janessa didn't answer.

"Janessa, who the hell's Cassie?"

"Allyson's daughter. They say I was jealous of her and Rashad!"

"Wait a minute—there was another body in that house? What are you talking about?"

"Oh, hell, I don't know. I only know what Ms. Hotshit Lawyer tell me. I ain' know what happen to Cassie. All I know, she dead, too." Janessa started to cry. "I wouldn't do nothin' to Cassie. She always real nice to me."

"Well, what's this about Rashad? He was involved with Cassie *and* you?"

"They say Cassie with Rashad. Say I got mad, kill Cassie, then kill Allyson."

"That doesn't make sense."

"Yeah. Why would I kill Allyson, too?"

"They were just trying out a theory."

Janessa didn't answer. Deciding silence was the best course, Talba kept quiet till they were in the office, where Angie was drinking coffee with Eddie.

Eddie stood up to greet the newcomer. "Janessa. Real glad to meetcha. I'm Eddie Valentino."

Janessa didn't offer to shake hands, but Talba could see her thawing a little. Eddie was good with people.

"Eileen!" Eddie called. "Can you bring in a couple of extra chairs?" He went to help Eileen, and then waved to the sisters to sit. Janessa dropped heavily into hers, like a sulky kid. She fixed Angie with a hostile stare. Talba figured Janessa was intimidated by her. The lawyer was dressed in black, as always, and she was sleek and commanding—sleek dark hair, sleek body, sleek outfit—like she was born to win in court. Other lawyers found her scary; why not Janessa?

Eddie said, "Ladies, can I get you anything? Coffee?"

"Sure," Talba said. Janessa shook her head, determined not to speak.

Eddie called Eileen again for coffee. "Janessa? Ya sure?"

Janessa didn't answer.

Eddie said, "Ya look like ya sister a little bit. You as smart as she is? 'Cause Ms. Wallis is the brains of this operation."

Talba would have given anything for a tape recorder.

He hadn't finished laying it on. "We can't do anything around here without ya sister. If you're as smart as she is, we're gonna get ya out of this with no problems. Now Angie here, she's my daughter. Did ya know that?"

Talba saw the girl do a near double-take. Evidently it hadn't occurred to her that the self-contained Angie was anybody's daughter.

"Yep. And she's smarter than ol' Eddie is, too. We've got us a reg'lar all-girl band here. Ms. Wallis is about the best detective in town—little inexperienced, that's all—and everybody knows Angie's the best lawyer in the parish. You do what she says and we're gonna get to the bottom of this thing."

Janessa spoke directly to Eddie. "I ain' like her."

"Yeah, that's what she tells me. Talk to me. Why don't you like my little girl?"

"She too tough."

"Tough is good. Tough's what you want in a lawyer."

Janessa almost looked as if she believed him. Talba had to hand it to Eddie—he could charm a cobra.

"Well, I'm not tough in this office," Angie said. "That was just for the cops. It's a game, Janessa. I needed you to stay really quiet in there so you wouldn't say anything they could use against you. We didn't know each other and I wanted to get you out as quick as I could. Now that we're out of there, we can let down our hair. Let's just talk, okay?"

"Ain' got nothin' to say."

"Okay," Angie said. "I'll start. Miss Janessa's in a heap of shit."

"Angie, for Christ's sake!" Eddie cried.

"Dad, I'm a *lawyer*, not a Sunday school teacher."

Here we go, Talba thought, but Janessa giggled. Maybe things were looking up.

Angie uncrossed her legs and recrossed them the other way. "Look, here's the story. Jimmy Giarruso went to notify Brower's daughter, and, while he was banging on the door, this big, half-drowned cat comes up to the door like he thinks he's going to be let in. There's also a soaked newspaper lying on the ground. At first, Jimmy just figures Cassie isn't home, but then he thinks, 'Who would leave their cat out in a near-hurricane?' Anyway, for whatever reason, he looks in the window and sees the body of a young woman in the living room. And he tries the door and it opens."

"Wait a minute," Eddie interjected. "How'd he know she was dead?"

Angie made the *who-knows* sign. "Christ, Dad, I don't know. Maybe he did and maybe he didn't. Maybe there was blood. Anyway, he thought she was in distress or deceased, and it turned out to be the latter."

"Umm, umm." Eddie said. "Was she shot, too?"

"They wouldn't say. Only told us that much to have something to bully Janessa with. But then Crockett, the Homicide guy, took me aside and made the old plea for a plea. Said they had evidence Cassie was involved with Rashad, and Janessa's already admitted she was. That tells you what their theory is."

"I'm kind of curious," Eddie said. "About how they worked the mother into this."

"Exactly what I asked him. You know how it is—they've got a million theories. Maybe Janessa killed Cassie, then went back to confront Rashad, and Allyson was killed in some kind of struggle. She and Rashad could have fought, and Allyson tried to intervene—"

"You *bitch!*" Janessa shouted. "Whose side ya *on?*"

Angie flared, but Eddie patted air. "Now, honey. She's only repeatin' what they told her. Ya gotta think like they do; that's what makes a good lawyer. Ya gon' be okay with that?"

Janessa settled back in her chair and nodded. "I'm sorry." Talba had seen it before. Eddie had a way with kids—and a kid was probably what Janessa was to him.

"Go on, Angela," he said.

"Well, what they found—the evidence that makes them think Rashad and Cassie were an item—was a book. Seems Rashad's a poet and this was a book of his poems—with a mushy inscription to Cassie."

"Where'd they find it?"

"Hell if I know. Crockett's not the kind of guy that gives away anything he doesn't have to."

"Reuben Crockett?" Eddie said. "That who ya talkin' about?"

"You know him?"

Eddie was tapping his lips with a forefinger; he seemed to be thinking. Scheming, Talba thought. "Reuben and I go way back," he said. "Cassie was definitely murdered?"

"Oh, yeah," Angie said. "Your buddy Reuben was real clear about that."

"Well, how about murder–suicide?"

"I brought it up, too, and he said no way in hell Cassie killed herself. So I said Janessa found the gun on the side of the pool, so maybe it happened the other way. Allyson kills her kid, maybe in a fight about Rashad—maybe she didn't like her dating a black guy—and then goes home and offs herself in a fit of remorse."

Janessa sulked. "Miz Allyson wasn't like that."

Angie turned on her. "Now that is *exactly* why I told you to shut up in there. You were undermining your own case. It's to your advantage for them to think it's murder–suicide. Don't you get that? You've got to trust me to know how to deal with these people."

"Bitch," Janessa mumbled.

Talba said, "Rashad's just as good a suspect as Janessa is."

"You shut up about Rashad," Janessa cried. "Rashad didn't do nothin'!"

"How do you know, baby?" Eddie asked gently.

"Just know."

"Because you know more than you're telling us?"

"No! Told ya everything. Austin musta done it."

"Well, he might have," Eddie said. "He might have. Baby, is it true what they're sayin'? Rashad ya boyfriend?"

"Rashad and Cassie was *friends*. That's all."

"How about Rashad and you?"

"Well, I like him a lot."

"And what else?"

"We hang out together, tha's all."

Talba said, "You told me he's the closest thing you have to a boyfriend. Is that what you told the police?"

"They ax me was I sleepin' with him. It's disrespectful."

"Are you?" Eddie asked.

"That ain't ya business."

"Janessa, this is a murder case. Talk to us."

Janessa looked as if she might cry. "He's not my boyfriend. Okay?"

"Let's move along," Angie said. "Tell Dad and Talba what you told the police before I got there."

"Told 'em what I tol' y'all—ain't their business. Then they ax me where Rashad is. I say I don't know. They ax do I know Cassie involved with him; I say she ain't. Then they ax me who his frien's are. I tell 'em, then they go back to the other thing. They get all nasty, try to bully me and stuff. So I say I ain't tellin' 'em nothin'. This goes on for a while, and I cry and yell and stuff and I say they can't talk to me that way and they say I'm in big trouble. So I say, am I under arrest, and this one dude, Sergeant Crap-it, he say, 'Okay. Read her her rights.' And some other one do. I know I got a right to a phone call, so I call Talba." She shrugged. "That's it."

Eddie said, "What did you say when they asked who Rashad's friends are?"

She shrugged again. "I tol' 'em."

"How about if you tell us?"

"I don't know 'em all. But he live with his brother, Marlon, before he come stay with Allyson; I tell 'em that. I know Marlon pretty good. He work for Miz Allyson, too; her and her other daughter, Arnelle. Rashad got lots of poet frien's, too. And Hunt and Lynne."

"Hunt Montjoy?" Talba asked. "He was a friend of Hunt Montjoy?"

"Yeah. Like he Allyson frien'. Mr. Montjoy try to help him. He got a teacher like that, too. Wayne. I ain' know his last name."

Talba said. "Who's Lynne?"

"Mr. Montjoy's wife."

"Do you know the Montjoys?"

"Seen 'em at Allyson's, tha's all."

Talba was curious about something. "Didn't the police ask you about Austin?"

"Oh, yeah. Ax the same things—did I know his frien's? But I didn't. Hardly know Austin, he just there a few days."

"Where does he live?" Angie interjected.

"Don' know."

"Okay," Eddie said. "Tell me the truth, Janessa. Did you kill Cassie?"

"Whose side *you* on?" Janessa snarled.

"Come on, baby. You know we're on your side—all three of us. We're gonna get you through this." He glanced ever so briefly at Talba, but it was long enough for her to see that he'd come to a decision. "I promise you, ya not going to jail if ya didn't kill anybody. I just want to hear it from you—did you kill Cassie?"

Janessa leaned against the back of her chair, squaring her shoulders as if to show she understood the seriousness of the situation. "No, sir, I did not," she said.

"Did you kill Allyson Brower?"

"No, sir, I did not."

"That's all we need to know then. See how easy that was? That's all we need to know. We're gon' get you outta this. I promise."

Janessa said nothing.

Eddie stood and offered his hand. "Shake on that?"

Gravely, Janessa stood and shook his hand. Talba could have kissed him.

"Take Janessa home, will ya?" he said. "She's had a rough day."

Talba could see Janessa falling a little bit more in love. "Come on, kid," she said, and Janessa said, "I'm not your kid."

The rain was falling more gently now, and the evening seemed almost peaceful. On the way to Mystery Street, Talba focused on her driving, wanting for a little while to forget Janessa's troubles. But when they arrived, her sister said, "Just because he gave Cassie his book, that s'posed to mean he was in love with her?" Her voice was furious. "He gave me one, too."

Talba was jolted. "Who? Rashad?"

"You want to see it? Here, I'll show you." And she ran up the steps.

Chapter Five

Talba arrived home to find her mother in a black funk. Miz Clara, who cleaned houses for a living, had evidently been home for quite a while. She'd changed into a pair of clean sweats and put on her old blue slippers. Instead of "hello," she said, "Some girl call for ya. Say she ya sister."

Uh-oh. Talba had never thought Janessa would call the house. She kept her voice casual. "Did she leave her name?"

"Jocasta. Somethin' like that."

"Janessa, maybe?"

"I guess." Miz Clara's sulky voice matched her don't-mess-with-me face.

"When did she call? Am I supposed to call her back?"

"Few minutes ago. Say she call tomorrow. Sandra, what's goin' on here?" Her mother used the name she called her daughter instead of the one Talba had chosen for herself. Neither one was her given name, which was never mentioned within the family.

Talba considered whether it was possible to protect Miz Clara from finding out about her father's love-child. Too early to tell, she decided, and took the coward's way out. "I never mentioned Janessa?"

"No, you did not. Who this girl is?"

"She's just somebody I know." Talba looked at her watch. "Mama, Darryl's due here in ten minutes and I'm not remotely ready to go out. Did she leave a number or not?"

"Say she call tomorrow." Her mother was simmering with suspicion, but the mention of Darryl's name kept her from pressing the issue. Darryl Boucree, Talba's boyfriend, was the best thing in her daughter's life, so far as Miz Clara was concerned; she wasn't about to stand in the way of progress.

Talba went off to get out of her white shirt and blue skirt, her invariable work outfit. Before getting her PI license, she'd done time as a temp, and she couldn't see putting money and energy into snappy work clothes. Her performance clothes, the ones she wore when she assumed her poet persona, the Baroness de Pontalba, were the very antithesis of low-profile. Thus she had a closet full of glamorous flowing garments, with a few generic work outfits squished into a corner. The latter worked just as well for a PI as a temp—she was always professional, never memorable.

She peeled off her disguise, slipped into the shower, and on emerging, selected a T-shirt and black jeans from yet a third stash of clothes, the ones she wore "to slop around in," as Miz Clara would say. As she dressed, she heard Miz Clara entertaining Darryl, the sullenness now gone from her voice, replaced by a birdlike quality it acquired only in Darryl's presence. Even if Talba hadn't adored him, she'd have had to keep him around to retain her mother's approval. Miz Clara had only contempt for her previous boyfriend, didn't think much of poetry as a profession, and the PI field appealed to her only when her daughter got her name in the paper. "Waste of a perfectly good education" was a phrase Talba had heard more than once. But she considered Darryl on a par with a Harvard MBA.

By the time Talba had her lipstick on, Miz Clara had Darryl eating leftover gumbo. "Mama! You always do this. How do I get him to take me out to dinner if he's already eaten?"

"Nobody said you can't have some."

"I want to go to Mona's."

Darryl stood and gave her a kiss. "Hello to you, too, Samantha Spade. It was just a little taste."

Resigned to spending the evening by herself—or maybe secretly happy about it—Miz Clara held the door for them. "Y'all have fun, now."

"I'll be home early, Mama." Talba and Darryl often had short dates, since Darryl had a love-child himself—the troubled (and in Talba's view, bratty) Raisa, whose mother had custody but who nonetheless spent a good bit of time with her father. So they went out on weeknights just to have time alone together, even though both had to get up and go to work the next day. For Darryl, being a teacher, these were literally school nights, and for Talba, there was often literal homework.

Since Miz Clara tended to cook Southern—and so did nearly every restaurant in New Orleans—Talba liked the Mideastern food at Mona's in the Faubourg Marigny for a change. It was a bit out of her neighborhood, but that was a good change, too.

"Remember that party we went to at Allyson Brower's?" she asked when they'd ordered their chicken schwarama.

Darryl laid down his menu. "I heard about her on the radio," he said softly. "I was going to tell you if you didn't know. Sad, sad thing. And that poor daughter of hers."

"Yeah. Real nasty thing." Talba paused for a minute, trying to figure out how to tell the rest of it. Finally she decided simply to plunge in. "Listen, there's big news—really big news."

"I'm bracing myself."

"Are you ready for this one? My sister, Janessa, discovered Allyson's body."

"Janessa," he repeated. He squinched up his eyes in disbelief. "You mean you finally heard from her—after all this time?"

The case was confidential, but Talba never stood on ceremony—when she needed to talk with Darryl, she did. This was something she really had to run by him. She told him what had happened, having to stop about every two seconds, as he peppered her with unbelieving questions. When she got to the part about Janessa calling her house, he said, "Oh, boy. What'd you tell Miz Clara?"

"Nothing yet. What do you think I ought to do?"

The chicken came, and he speared a bite. "You want my honest opinion?"

"That's why I asked."

"You've got to tell her. Did you give Janessa your home number?"

Talba tried to remember. "You know, I don't think so. Uh-uh. I'm sure I didn't."

"Okay, she's going where she hasn't been invited—it won't be the last time."

Talba sighed, thinking that she herself should break the news, not Janessa. Not at all a pleasant thought. Miz Clara could be a terror under the best of circumstances, and her least favorite subject was her late husband, Denman Wallis.

During dinner, she and Darryl spoke of almost nothing but the case—not too romantic, but then they'd see each other on the weekend. When she kissed him good night, she said, "I'm reading at Reggie and Chaz on Friday—usual open-mike thing—" Darryl had seen it a hundred times"—so why don't you and Raisa bond that night? And I'll see you Saturday."

"Counting the minutes," he said, but she could tell he was relieved.

"However, don't forget what's important."

"And that would be?"

"*I* am a baroness."

"Pardon me. Counting the minutes, *Your Grace*."

She went to bed early, intending to call on Marlon Daneene first thing in the morning. One of the things Eddie had taught her was that the best time to get people at home is before they go to work—and before their defenses go up. She had a fairly recent address on the river side of Magazine Street, in the Irish Channel—that is, for Marlon and Rashad, before Rashad moved in with Allyson. With luck, Marlon was still there.

Miz Clara was sitting at the old black-painted kitchen table, reading the *Times-Picayune* when Talba bustled in for breakfast. Her mother was still sulky and silent, and wasn't about to relinquish the front section, but looking over her shoulder, Talba saw two familiar faces: Allyson Brower (the picture was one taken at the literary lion party) and Cassie Edwards. And suddenly a picture came to Talba—of Rashad at Allyson's party, talking to that beautiful blond girl. It was Cassie.

She had been wearing the white shirt and black skirt of a catering employee. Talba wondered whether her mother had gotten her the job with Food for Thought.

"Terrible thing," Miz Clara muttered. "Mother and daughter murdered. Mmm. Mmm. Mmm."

The reality of it had only just begun to hit Talba the night before, when she told the story to Darryl. It *was* a terrible thing, but she felt more sadness for Cassie than she did for Allyson, perhaps because Allyson had seemed so much more like a character in a play than a real person. She wondered what Cassie had been like.

"No one's gonna get us, Mama," she said. "We're too mean to die."

To her surprise, Miz Clara cackled. "You got that right. Mmm, mmm."

Talba gulped some coffee, hopped in her old Isuzu, and pulled up at Marlon's house shortly after seven. It was half a double shotgun, shabby and ordinary. She wondered if he lived there alone.

The young man who answered the door was still in his underwear, hiding behind the door to preserve a little modesty. "Marlon Daneene? Hi, I'm Talba Wallis. My sister Janessa's a friend of your brother's."

"Janessa?" he said. "I be knowin' Janessa."

"She asked me to come see you. Could I come in and talk to you?"

"You mind waitin' a minute?"

"Not at all." Definitely not if that meant he was going to put his pants on.

A moment later, his place was taken by a woman about her own age, but heavier. No, pregnant, she realized, seeing that the woman's white T-shirt was caught on a melon-shaped shelf. Her hair was clipped close, almost as short as Miz Clara's. Evidently she was getting ready for motherhood. But maybe not, because the 'do suited her. She had a well-shaped head and gentle features set off by gold hoop earrings. "Marlon's gone to put on his clothes," she said. "I'm Demetrice."

Talba repeated her spiel.

"Come on in," Demetrice said. "You seen Janessa? I mean since—you know."

"Yes. She was the one who discovered Mrs. Brower's body. Did you know that?" She'd managed to read enough of the article over Miz Clara's shoulder to know that the paper had described the discoverer only as "an employee."

"We thought it was. Had to be either her or Carmen." She led Talba into a thoroughly chaotic kitchen, and asked if she wanted coffee, which Talba accepted. Another of Eddie's tricks was to take refreshments when they were offered so you'd have an excuse to stay till you'd finished.

She'd only had time for a sip when Marlon rejoined them, in jeans and extra-large T-shirt, though his build was slight. He was a light-skinned man, lighter than Rashad, but not nearly so attractive as his brother, who managed to have that poet's . . . what? Not sensitivity, exactly. Perhaps alertness would describe it; Rashad had seemed a lot more alive than his brother.

And no wonder, Talba thought. Marlon was about to have more responsibility than he probably bargained for at his age. He poured himself a cup of coffee and said, "Let's go in the living room." He glanced at the cluttered kitchen as if he was slightly ashamed, but the living room wasn't much better. A woman's shoes were still on the floor, where Demetrice had probably removed them while watching television. Various shirts and jackets had been left hither and yon, and mail, both opened and sealed, had been left unattended, scattered on the floor and various other surfaces. Demetrice didn't seem like much of a housekeeper.

Marlon sat in a recliner and Demetrice on the shabby sofa, probably in their usual places, leaving Talba a straight-backed dining room chair that looked out of place in the room. "Janessa's worried about Rashad," she began. "The police are looking for him."

Marlon nodded. "They were here last night."

"She wants me to try to help him. Find him if I can. I've got a good friend who's a lawyer."

Demetrice said, "Wonder if he just got fed up with that Allyson bitch."

Marlon started. "Demetrice, what you talkin' about? You know Rashad ain' done nothin'."

"Rashad and Allyson didn't get along?" Talba interjected. "I had the impression they were pretty tight."

Demetrice sniffed. "That woman the devil. Cheated people; wouldn't pay 'em what she owed 'em. Rich bitch. She wouldn't pay *Marlon*. Wha's up with that?"

Talba turned to Marlon. "You worked for her, too?"

"Yeah, I'm a painting contractor. When she started doin' work on her house, Rashad brought me in to help her. Both of us work there—other guy quit, she was so hateful."

"What other guy?"

"The one doing the murals. Doug something. He quit, Janessa say she could finish the marsh scene. She pretty good, too."

"Wait a minute. What order did all this happen in? Rashad knew Allyson and got the painting job, is that it? Then he brought you in?"

"Yeah. He bring Janessa in, too. She wasn't no professional painter or nothin', but she real careful—real good at doin' trim. He know her from poetry class."

"That's what she said."

The mention of poetry seemed to have triggered Marlon's memory. "Wait a minute. You a poet, too! You the one they call the Baroness—Janessa always talkin' about ya."

Janessa's secret life, Talba thought—the one where I exist. "That's me. I even met Rashad once—at a party at Allyson's."

Demetrice rolled her eyes. "Her and her damn parties."

"I thought I saw Cassie there, too. She worked for the caterer, right? I forget her name."

"Tasha. Yeah, Cassie work for Tasha."

"Were she and Rashad involved?"

Marlon and Demetrice looked at each other and seemed to hesitate. Finally, Marlon said, "Think they was just friends."

"How about Janessa and Rashad?"

"Oh, no, uh-uh," Marlon said. "I'm not goin' there. She ya sister."

"Listen, both of them could be arrested for murder at any minute. I think we'd better get some things out in the open."

Again the couple looked at each other. Finally, Demetrice shrugged. "I don't know. You know, Marlon?"

"I ain' know," he said. "I don't think so."

"One police theory is that Janessa killed Cassie because she was jealous of her."

"That's plain ridiculous," Demetrice said.

"Why do you think so?"

"Well, why she kill Allyson, then?"

"Good point," Talba answered absently. She had spotted a picture of an older woman on the mantel. She seized on it as a lead-in to what she really wanted to know—where Rashad was hiding out. "Excuse me, is that your mother on the mantel?"

Silence for a moment. Finally, Marlon spoke. "Tha's my mother. Mine and Rashad's."

"I was just wondering if she lives in New Orleans."

Marlon's eyes squinched up like that didn't compute. "Mama been gone a long, long time."

"Oh. Is she . . . uh . . . did she . . . ?" Talba couldn't get herself to say the "D" word. "Would Rashad know where she is?"

This time the silence was even longer, and once again Marlon broke it. "Rashad ain't with her. She gone."

Talba could feel him closing down. She tried changing the subject again, "Well, both you guys live here. Bet you grew up in New Orleans."

"Chippewa Street." Marlon smiled at the memory.

"In that case, might Rashad be with relatives?"

Marlon shrugged, a possible "yes" in Talba's opinion. Suddenly she realized she hadn't asked the obvious question. "By the way, have you seen him?"

Demetrice snorted.

Marlon was getting angry. "Hell, no, we ain't seen him! Don't you think we'd have him out here talkin' to ya, we had him stashed somewhere? Like we told the po-lice, we ain' know where he is."

"Okay, look, I understand. I'm just worried about him, that's all. I was hoping you could tell me a little about him."

Marlon waited awhile before he spoke, but this wasn't like his other hesitations, which had seemed to Talba more like decision-making. This was more like gathering his thoughts. He sat forward on his chair and set down his coffee cup before he spoke. "I'm real proud of Rashad," he said, speaking very deliberately, like a man being careful not to make a mistake. "He mighta messed up some when he was too young to know no better, but he real deep. Rashad ain' nothin' like me, nothin' like our mama and daddy—he put himself through UNO, and he a published poet. Now he 'bout to go get a master's degree. Very unusual young man. He love to read, love to study. He makin' a real good life for himself. Ain't no way he'd kill Allyson Brower, and he *sure* wouldn't kill Cassie. Rashad ain' got a mean bone in his body.

"And he love those women. Both of 'em. Really love 'em."

Demetrice said, "Humph."

Talba smiled at her, unsure how to take that. "You have a different opinion?"

"Not about Rashad," Demetrice said. "He move out so I could move in when I found out I'm pregnant. He do anything for the family. Real, real fine young man. What I got a different opinion about's Allyson Brower—different from Rashad, I mean. I know she help him, I know he like her, but that woman a bitcharama! She don't like the way a room look, she make Marlon do it over, tell him it's his fault, *she* never approve that color. Then she only pay him for one time. *And* she make him pay for the paint she pick and then turn against. She got all the money in the world, but she try to cheat folks just tryin' to make a honest livin'. Marlon need the job. Ain't nothin' we can do about it."

Talba turned back to Marlon. "Made you pretty mad, I bet."

"Now wait a minute here! You tryin' to say I kill that bitch? Ain' worth my time, Miz Baroness. Demetrice and me, we Christians. We know how to live with folks like that. You just gotta turn the other cheek, keep goin'. Hurtin' nobody ain' worth my time."

"I'm sorry," Talba said. "I didn't mean that at all. I was just thinking that if she made you mad, she might have upset a lot of people."

Marlon picked up his cup again, through with heavy emotion. He leaned back in his chair and opened his legs wide, the picture of relaxation. "She mighta'. She sure mighta'. But that little Cassie, she sweet as pie; wouldn't no one harm Cassie."

"'Cept maybe that bitch of a mother," Demetrice muttered.

"Uh-oh. Sounds like they didn't get along."

"Allyson just as mean to Cassie as everybody else."

Talba thought briefly of asking how Rashad had "messed up" when he was young. But she couldn't risk making Marlon angry—not until she had more information.

"Well, I'm going to try to find your brother and do what I can for him."

"We sure appreciate that," Marlon said.

"Got any ideas about where to look for him? Maybe I could ask his close friends. Y'all mind giving me a few names?"

"Cassie was a good friend. Lotta poets, but I don't know 'em. Funny thing about Rashad—" Marlon smiled to himself, apparently trying to comprehend his mysterious brother. "He hang with white folks."

"What white folks?"

"Writers, I guess. He want to be a writer, people he'p him, he stay friends with 'em. Hunt and Wayne probably his closest friends."

"Hunt Montjoy, you mean?"

"Yeah. Him and his wife. Wayne was his teacher at UNO—Wayne Taylor. They real tight, too."

Talba had heard of Taylor. He was the author of two or three historical novels and a cop movie—not the sort of writer considered "literary" by the likes of Hunt Montjoy. Neither was Rashad, for that matter, but he might have raw talent—and he was young. Montjoy probably enjoyed playing the mentor.

"Did y'all know Allyson's son, Austin?"

"No'm. Sure didn't. Know her second daughter, though—I done some work for Miz Arnelle. Now she a nice lady."

"Did Rashad know her?"

"Oh yeah. He work for her, too. But not like he knew Allyson and Cassie."

"Well, thanks, y'all. I've got a few places to look, so I'll go do it. Just one more question—any other relatives I should know about?"

Marlon spoke quickly. "We got a grandfather in a nursing home. Humph. Like to see Rashad hide in a nursing home."

"That all?"

He shrugged. "All I can think of right now."

She had been meaning to ask about Rashad's messing up as a kind of Colombo exit, but at the last minute, she changed her mind. There was probably another way to find out, and she didn't want to alienate these people. Besides, something else occurred to her that she hadn't asked.

She was on her feet and heading for the door when she said over her shoulder, "I almost forgot—does Rashad have a girl-friend?"

She couldn't see if the couple exchanged glances again, but once more, no one spoke for a moment. "Don't know of no-body," Marlon said.

"Don't think so," said Demetrice.

Suddenly Talba saw something she couldn't believe she hadn't seen before. The close friendships with women that didn't seem to be sexual, the helpful older woman in his life. She wondered if she dared, and decided, *Why not?*

"Is he gay, by any chance?"

Big mistake. Marlon flipped out. "You callin' my brother a faggot? Who the hell ya think ya are, comin' here, saying crazy things? You get on outta here! Just get out, now."

On the whole, Talba thought, it might have been better to inquire into his brother's youthful indiscretions.

She sighed as she got back in her car, feeling slightly defeated, but wondering if she'd hit a nerve. Maybe Rashad *was* gay—which might open up a whole new realm of people he could be staying with.

But that was for later.

The name Hunt Montjoy had come up twice, so she'd have to go see him. But somehow the idea of bearding such a personage at seven-thirty A.M. was too daunting to contemplate. She decided to go back to the office, have another cup of coffee, and tackle Rashad's book of poems.

Chapter Six

Eileen Fisher had put the *Times-Picayune* on her desk, and Talba read the murder story first. In black and white, Cassie's murder, with details of Cassie's life, seemed more horrifying as Cassie began to be real to her. Yes, she'd worked for a caterer, but she was pursuing her dream of acting as well. She'd majored in drama at Tulane, taken part in student productions, and played minor roles in various productions at Le Chat Noir, the city's current hot venue for local playwrights and directors. The picture of her that ran in the paper—probably one of her publicity photos—was heart-stopping. She looked almost ethereal—blond and delicate, with the kind of crinkly hair that managed to be thick and gauzy at the same time.

She hadn't been shot like her mother. She'd died of multiple stab wounds. Talba shuddered and thought: *Enough.*

She set the paper aside and examined the book, which was none too originally titled *Laments.* It was a booklet, really, rather crudely self-published, meaning it was made up of half-size computer pages bound in a red cover. The title wasn't particularly promising, but looking through it, she saw that it was fairly apt. It was obvious immediately that Rashad, unlike many of the city's African American poets, wasn't especially political. As she wasn't either, she took that as an encouraging sign. Many of the poems were indeed laments, as are so many poems and stories, she thought. She turned to the one entitled "Parents."

Parents
Mama so beautiful, Mother so scary,
Mother with the silver flash,
Mother with a need to bash—

And Daddy so gone.

Which one o' you
Gon' tell me what to do?

Which one o' you keep me off the streets
Keep me little-boy-sweets
Keep me out of jail
Keep me out of hell?
How many parents does it take
To make me straight?
How many parents does it take
To seal my fate?

I'd like to know where my candy is.
I'd like to know where Santy is
Hell, I'd like to know where Sanity is;
Sanitation is;
Sometimes even
Where habitation is
Hope it ain't where
Degradation is.

I'd like to know
Where my parent is
Who my parent is
What my parent is
I'd like to know
Where my childhood is
What my vilehood is
Where the wildwood is

I'd like to know
If I did right
By all
Of y'all.

That's what
My fascination is.

Talba didn't care for it—too easy, too many rhymes, too ob-sessed with being clever and sounding like a rapper. But it had something—she had to give it that. Maybe an overweening self-involvement, but then whose poetry wasn't self-involved? It made her look at her own work and wonder if that was how a reader saw it. She couldn't tell how honest the poem was, what it really said about his parents, or what his "fascination" really was. Was he just rhyming for the sake of rhyme, or was this a central theme in his life?

And then there was the "Mama" figure. The mother in Mar-lon's photograph wasn't beautiful at all. Truthfully, she was plain at best and she looked mad at the world. But what-the-hell, she thought, every kid gets to idealize his mother.

Talba paged through the book. There was a poem about Rashad's grandfather, which she skipped, and one entitled "Cassie." That one she wanted to come back to, but she looked first to see if she could find one titled "Janessa."

She didn't. If there was one, it might be disguised, but at the moment she didn't have the patience to read them all trying to find out. She turned back to the one called "Cassie":

> ### Cassie
> *Fairy princess girl who work in the kitchen*
> *Fairy girl got all the men itchin'*
> *To take off that white dress*
> *Take hold of them white breasts.*
> *They don't see the heart*
> *Underneath them cantaloupes*
> *Can't take part*
> *In nothin'*
> *Underneath their gropes.*
> *Wake up, girl,*
> *And get you some glasses.*
> *Write your own world*
> *And give your own classes.*
> *Get out of the kitchen,*
> *Get out of the bed,*
> *Get your own thing goin'*
> *Or you gon' be dead.*

She had to wonder what the gang at the Second District made of that one—yet surely even a cop couldn't construe it as a threat. Unless, of course, the poet imagined that he was the only one who could see through to the princess's true heart; that he was the prince who deserved her, and if he didn't get her no one would. Talba figured a clever D.A. could make that argument. But from the two poems she'd read, it seemed to her that Rashad didn't go in for a lot of metaphor; to her mind, the two poems were basically prose in rhyme.

But she could be wrong. Did he mean literally dead or figuratively dead? Figuratively, she thought, since there were no references to drugs or guns. And if that was the case, he was capable of figures of speech; it was just hard to tell when he was using them.

That "fairy princess" thing, for instance—did it mean Cassie was an other-worldly beauty or was he using the term "fairy" to mean homosexual? Maybe Cassie had been a lesbian; or possibly a fag hag.

This train of thought, she decided, was better suited to the classroom than a murder investigation. When you got down to it, the words didn't really tell her much about Rashad's impression of Cassie, but the poem had a feel to it. To Talba it felt like a lecture; from a friend, maybe, or a brother.

She checked the time, thinking perhaps it was time to clear her head with a little computer research. It was nearly a decent hour. She was about to background the Montjoys and head to their house when Janessa called.

"Talba?" her sister said. "I've changed my mind. I don't want y'all to take the case."

Talba sighed. She had an extremely high-maintenance client on her hands. "Why not?"

"Y'all get me off, they jus' gon' blame Rashad."

"I'm not even going there, Janessa. You wanted help, you've got it."

"You can't do that; I know what I want. I'm firin' ya."

Talba wondered briefly what was going on. Maybe Rashad had come to her to hide him.

"You heard from Rashad?"

"Rashad? No, you?"

"He doesn't even know us—we couldn't have heard from him. I just thought you might have."

"Oh, man, don't I *wish*."

She certainly sounded believable. All the same, a little surveillance work on Mystery Street might be a good idea. "Look, Janessa, in that book you gave me—did you read the poem about Cassie?"

"I read all the poems."

"What did it mean to you?"

"Meant what it said. Cassie wanted to be an actress. Rashad thought she was throwing herself away, working for that caterer."

"Just wondering. Did he ever write a poem about you?"

"Me? Why would he write a poem about me?"

"A lot of the poems are about women."

"He musta' wrote 'em before he knew me."

"Yeah, that must be it." In fact, it might be. "Listen, you can't fire us, so don't even try, okay? And by the way, Janessa, you can call me on my cell phone but not at my home." She hung up before her sister had a chance to answer.

Her mind had switched back to Rashad. She rummaged through the book again, still trying to get a handle on him—who he was, what his poetic goals were, how he saw the world. When Talba wrote poetry, she tried to tell stories, which interested her at least as much as images. Wordplay she cared for not nearly as much, finding it shallow. Rashad seemed to live for it, and mostly he seemed to like rhyme.

She turned to the poem about his parents, noted again that, in it, he claimed to have told her exactly what he was all about:

> I'd like to know
> If I did right
> By all
> Of y'all.
>
> That's what
> My fascination is.

The earlier words in the poem tugged at her memory: *sanitation, habitation, degradation.*

Was the last verse just an easy rhyme or did it mean something? She looked to see if Rashad's mother was mentioned in any more poems, and saw that she'd missed one, entitled "Mama."

> ### Mama
> I'd do anything for you.
> And I did.
> You kept me sane
> When life was a bane
> You made up for
> The other one.
> What's done
> Is done—
> But for your beauty
> And your love

> *I did my duty*
> *And maybe above.*
> *Because you were there*
> *I came to care*
> *Because you care,*
> *And that is so rare*
> *I had to dare.*
> *It was only fair.*

That one made Talba wince. She wondered if it was an example of his early work. She looked to see if there was a comparable poem about his father, but didn't find one. Okay, the boy loved his mother. She wondered if Marlon was lying—if Mama really was out of the picture.

Sighing, she put the book away, backgrounded the Montjoys, and went out to beard them.

The background check had turned up little new material besides their address. Like Allyson Brower, they lived in the elegant Garden District. For a guy who'd grown up in the backwoods of Alabama, Hunt Montjoy evidently had grandiose tastes—or maybe Lynne did. She was his fourth wife and the one he'd been with longest. Their relationship was in its twelfth year, but if Montjoy was living up to his reputation, she was by no means his only woman.

Everything Talba'd ever read about the poet made her dislike him, and meeting him hadn't helped. He struck her as your classic Ph.D.-totin' Bubba, with grammar as bad as Janessa's, drinking prowess on a par with Hunter Thompson's, and feminist sensibility resembling that of Norman Mailer, on whom he probably patterned himself, consciously or not. (Though if questioned on the subject, he'd probably call Mailer a "Yankee Jew pansy.")

A lot of his poems were about nature and hunting and guns and sex. She'd never read his novel.

The house was a monster—a double-balconied Greek Revival classic with a garden Martha Stewart would have loved. Either they had a gardener or Lynne, a successful interior designer, had exterior skills as well. Talba couldn't picture Bubba-the-poet pruning roses.

Lynne, whom she recognized from Allyson's party, answered the door herself, looking at Talba as if trying to figure out what the maid's daughter was doing on her porch. "Mrs. Montjoy? Hi, I'm Talba Wallis, a friend of Allyson Brower."

Lynne was still in her robe, but her blond hair was combed. The robe was cut so low that Talba could see collarbone. This was a very thin woman. "Omigod!" she said. "Poor Allyson."

"Yes, ma'am. Terrible."

"We're destroyed about it. Is there something I can do?"

"I was wondering if I could talk to you about her. I'm, well, I'm looking for Rashad . . ." she fumbled for Rashad's last name, but evidently she didn't need it.

"Rashad? Is he all right?"

"Actually, we're very worried about him. A friend of his asked me to try to find him and I thought I could talk to you about the situation."

"Oh." She hesitated, but in the end didn't want to be seen as not doing the right thing. "Well, come in. Do you mind waiting while I get dressed?"

"I'd be happy to." Talba followed her through a period living room that showed little imagination but a lot of money, into a less formal room with windows on a side garden.

"I'll just be a moment."

Talba surveyed her surroundings and saw that the room— quite a pleasant one, painted coral with white trim—doubled as a semi-library, though Talba was willing to bet there was a real library somewhere in the house. This was just a sitting room with a wall of bookshelves. The furniture was covered with chintz, the antiques good (to Talba's unpracticed eye), and or-chids bloomed on a huge coffee table as well as on some of the bookshelves. It was probably the place where the Montjoys had cocktails at night, perhaps read the paper on Sunday, and it made Talba thaw a little. Surely people who spent time in such a pretty room had something to recommend them. Having noth-ing better to do, Talba went to the bookshelves and began read-ing titles. There were a lot of gardening books, many on orchids, and the kind of oversized coffee-table books picturing gorgeous homes you'd expect a designer to have. There was popular fiction, too, including quite a few mysteries, but no po-etry that she could see and none of the weighty authors she imagined Hunt Montjoy reading. So maybe this was mostly Lynne's room.

Lynne Montjoy reappeared, dressed in flowered capris and a brown tank top, her makeup freshly applied. Seeing her visitor examining her books, she started, making Talba feel guilty.

"Sorry." Talba gave her an apologetic grin. "I'm a big reader."

"Would you like to sit down?" Lynne's tone was glacial. Talba wondered if she had something to hide, or just felt invaded.

"Thank you." She lowered herself onto the flowered sofa; Lynne took a chair, and Talba noticed it wasn't a wing-backed chair. There wasn't a single one in the room, which might make it unique in the Garden District. "I think we met at your husband's birthday party." Lynne remained expressionless. Her face looked slightly pinched, her body a little undernourished. Talba'd wondered if she drank. "I'm a poet," she continued, "but my day job's this." She produced her PI license, nestled in its own leather case with a badge offered for eighty dollars from the state board. Eddie had scoffed, but Talba had to have it. She loved the badge for itself alone, and also because she had a theory that it would make people talk—they'd look at it quickly and think she was more official than she was. "Rashad's family and friends hired us because they're nervous. They think that because he's black, and he was there alone with Allyson . . ."

Lynne looked embarrassed. "I understand."

"The problem is, no one can find him right now."

"Oh, no. First Cassie and . . ."

"Yes, it's scary. Have you heard from him in the last couple of days?"

"Well, no, I don't think so. I mean, he's really my husband's friend, but he hasn't been around."

It was the opening Talba wanted. "Is there any chance I could talk to your husband as well?"

Lynne shifted her body; Talba wondered if the mere mention of her husband made her nervous. "I don't know," she said doubtfully. "Morning's his writing time. Hunt always says if you can't say it by eleven A.M., you had nothing to say, anyway."

"Oh, really?" Talba asked, trying to sound innocent. "You mean, night people can't be writers?" *Forgive me, Eddie*, she thought, knowing it was unprofessional; she just couldn't resist.

Somehow the question seemed to increase the woman's nervousness. "I . . . well, I never thought about that."

Talba had brought up the subject for no other reason than to be impertinent, but Lynne's reaction had actually told her something—that either she had no sense of humor and no imagination or she was so thoroughly dominated by her husband she never questioned him.

Talba went back into detective mode. "Well, if he could spare a moment I'd appreciate it. You're really the perfect people to talk to because you were friends with both Rashad and Allyson—Cassie, too, I gather."

Lynne brought her index finger to her mouth, bit down on a fingernail, and finally seemed to realize what she was doing. She withdrew the finger and stared at it. "Not Allyson so much," she said. "We've always been a little puzzled by her. She hired me to help her with her house. Did you know I'm a designer?"

Talba nodded.

Lynne shook her head a little, looking as if she didn't know how much to say. "I can't say that I . . . really got along with her. I know Hunt thought the world of her—in the abstract, I mean. She did a lot for young writers, but . . ." she paused ". . . she kept telling me what to do."

"She was a woman who knew what she wanted," Talba prompted.

"No. No, it wasn't that. It was her style, if you will. She treated me . . . well, rather like a servant."

And I'll just bet you weren't used to that, Talba thought.

"I really didn't know what to think."

"Did she treat everyone like that?"

The question seemed to take Lynne aback. While she considered it, Talba said, "I was thinking of Cassie."

Lynne looked relieved. "Cassie. Yes. I think it would be safe to say she was quite downtrodden by her mother. Cassie was the kind of girl who lights up a room. You never saw such a beautiful girl, and her mother just . . . I don't know, Cassie was the one who got lost."

Talba felt lost herself. "I'm not sure what you mean."

"I mean, within the family. Every now and then, one child just seems to get lost. Do you know what I mean?"

Talba was pondering the question when Hunt Montjoy lumbered unannounced into the peaceful room. "Who is this, Lynne? Why do we have a visitor before eleven-thirty?"

The great man wore a pair of faded black sweats with a new-looking Auburn sweatshirt. His brown hair was disheveled and dirty; his craggy face heavy and jowly, covered with stubble. Talba thought him one of the most repellent individuals she'd ever seen—yet apparently women fell down and worshipped him. White ones, she supposed, wondering what on earth they were thinking.

Talba remembered what Lynne had said about his writing schedule. She stood and offered her hand. "I'm terribly sorry if I've disturbed you, Mr. Montjoy. I'm Talba Wallis." She waited a moment. She'd met the man at least five times, but she saw not a spark of recognition. Reluctantly, he took her hand, but released it almost immediately, as if it disgusted him. She went through her whole PI speech again, even showing her badge, but leaving out the poet part this time. It was too embarrassing under the circumstances—she'd been at the man's birthday party, for heaven's sake.

Nervously, Lynne tried to fill in what they'd already covered. As she talked, Hunt threw himself into one of the non-winged chairs, so Talba sat back down as well. Not waiting for his wife to finish, he said, "It's obvious what happened, idn't it? Ought to be obvious to anybody. Bitch killed Cassie. They argued, she killed her, killed herself. Open and shut. Good little book for my buddy Wayne—'cept maybe too simple-minded even for him."

"Why do you think that, Mr. Montjoy?" Everyone else called him "Hunt," but something told Talba he'd respond better if she feigned a little hero worship.

"They were always arguing, that's why. Allyson wouldn't leave the poor girl alone."

"Arguing about what?"

"What the hell does it matter anyway?" he exploded. "Thought you were here about Rashad."

"We're worried about him. The police think he might have killed them both."

"Rashad wouldn't hurt a fly. Doesn't have a lick of talent, God help him, but he's harmless as a newborn chick. And you can quote me on that."

It occurred to Talba suddenly that he had been drinking, despite the early hour. How else to explain the fact that she'd just become a reporter in his eyes? She tried throwing him off balance. "Was Rashad involved with Cassie?"

"Cassie? That little . . . *pissant* involved with Cassie?" Talba had the distinct impression he'd been about to say "nigger" or perhaps, given the way the two words started, "pickaninny," and then thought better of it. He was so offensive in any case, she wondered why he bothered to censor himself.

"The police think he might have been," she said calmly.

"Well, he wasn't. No way, José."

No way, José. Terrific phrase for a Pulitzer Prize winner. "Do you know Janessa? Might he have been involved with her?"

"Janessa? Who the hell's Janessa?"

"You remember, Hunt," Lynne said. "The painter. The talented girl who took over when Doug quit."

"You mean the black chick with the big ass? Uh-uh. Rashad wouldn't look at a girl like that. No way, José. Now, how do I know? Because he had a crush on Cassie the size of a mule's hard-on. Any idiot could see it from two miles away. Allyson was probably jealous as hell. Bitch!"

Talba was wondering if it was time to leave when he said, "You know she owed Lynne money. Lots of money."

His wife said, "Hunt. Please."

"Stupid phony bitch. Acted like she owned the city. Nobody in New Orleans ever saw her until a year and a half ago—she just blew into town and—"

"Like Gatsby," his wife said. She turned to Talba. "You know the novel? *The Great Gatsby*?"

Talba decided not to be offended—another of Eddie's lessons. "Indeed I do," she said, and then to needle her host, she added, "but I never saw what was so great about him."

"Gatsby is the quintessential twentieth-century American," Hunt said dreamily, as if he were lecturing a class. "The American dream personified. Gatsby is who we are and who we deserve to be. God help us."

"In the end, he turned out all right," Talba countered, paraphrasing the book itself, again to annoy him, but she kept talking to prevent further literary exegesis. "I never made the Gatsby connection with Allyson." She was surprised that she hadn't.

"Didn't you?" Lynne asked. "Oh, yes, Allyson was the female version. The mansion, the parties, the way she thought she could buy anything . . ."

"Lynne, for Christ's sake," her husband said. "You don't know what you're talking about."

Lynne looked hurt. "But I thought—"

"Lynne, shut up."

Talba changed the subject quickly. "How about the rest of the family? Did either of you know the other two children?"

"Not Arnelle," Lynne said. "She wasn't around much. But Austin . . ."

"Now I like Austin," her husband said. "Redneck through and through."

"Apparently Allyson threatened to disinherit him."

"Hmph. No surprise there. She was probably ashamed of him."

"Well? Would he kill her?" *Might as well go for broke.* "Is he the type who'd kill his mother?"

"Never know what a redneck'll do," Hunt said. "I oughtta know."

"Well, let's get back to that Gatsby thing."

"Let's don't."

"I was just wondering how Allyson did it—I mean how does someone go about something like that?"

Both Montjoys looked blank.

"She collected celebrities, that's obvious—I was at the party she gave for you and it looked like a literary festival."

"You!" Hunt didn't even try to keep the derision out of his voice. "Hey! You're that poet gal."

Normally, Talba would have done her stage trick—"*I* am the Baroness de Pontalba"—with emphasis on the "I". But she was too intimidated to do it now—and it took a lot to intimidate her. She only nodded and moved on. "What I was wondering—how did *you* meet Allyson? She had to have had an introduction."

The Montjoys looked at each other. "Through Rosemary McLeod," Lynne said finally. "They were in business together when Allyson first came to town. Don't know how *they* knew each other—I hear they were girlhood friends, but poor Rosemary's . . . well, at any rate, they had this little catalogue thing.

They were trying to sell New Orleans art and they wanted to offer my candelabra."

"Your candelabra," Talba said.

"I'm a metal worker, you know—you've never seen my candelabra?" She looked around, as if scanning for an example. "I must have rearranged things—I used to have some in here. At any rate, they're my trademark. I didn't want to sell them that way, of course, but we got to talking—Allyson was a big talker—and she invited us to a party." She sighed helplessly. "So we went. And then we were obligated to her."

"Ensnared," Hunt said.

"Then I ended up working with her, and we couldn't seem to get away. But it wasn't all bad. I found her fascinating, frankly."

"Why the hell would you say that?" her husband demanded.

"That Gatsby thing. I mean she really had no pride. I've even heard she—"

"Lynne, please!"

Talba could have killed him. She had the feeling she'd just missed out on something juicy.

"What about Rosemary? I'd like to talk to her."

"Oh, she's very ill now," Lynne said quickly, but Hunt roared, "What is this, anyhow? I thought you were here about Rashad."

Talba was a bit undone. "I am," she said simply. "Do either of you see him as a murderer?"

"Absolutely not. He's a dear, sweet, sensitive child."

"No way, José. Doesn't have the balls."

"I read the poem he wrote about his mother."

Neither one of the others spoke. Talba wondered if they'd even read it. "Might he be with her?"

Hunt shrugged. "Who the fuck knows? I'm going to Pete's." And he got up and strode out of the room.

As if nothing had happened, Talba turned to Lynne. "When you were talking about Allyson-as-Gatsby, you were about to say something . . ."

"I was?"

"Something you'd heard."

"I'm sorry. I don't have the slightest recollection what it was."

"Because I heard something about her, too. I heard she paid

to get people to come to her parties."

"Well, she certainly never paid us!"

"No, you misunderstand. I meant that she hired someone to get the guests there." It wasn't exactly a shot in the dark—it was based on the mysterious phone call she'd gotten from Burford Hale after the literary lion party.

"Oh, really? I think I have heard something of the sort. But what kind of person would do a thing like that?"

At the moment, Talba thought, *a dead one*.

"Do you know Burford Hale?" she asked.

"I've met him a few times, at Allyson's—he was close to her, I think."

"Her boyfriend?"

"Don't know. I don't know anything about her personal life."

Talba sighed. "Hale was arranging for the pictures at your husband's party."

Lynne only shrugged.

Talba had a strong urge to leave the woman's company. "Well, thanks for your time," she said, too abruptly. "Here's my card. Feel free to call if you think of anything that could help Rashad."

Chapter Seven

Eddie hated to admit it, but he knew he couldn't blame his daughter for this one—or his wife, or even Ms. Wallis (whom he preferred to blame for everything). Janessa had done it to him. He had a weakness for kids in trouble, and this one was such a deer in the headlights, he didn't even care if she was guilty, he felt like helping her. Besides which, he was going to in the long run anyhow—Ms. Wallis was going to make his life miserable until he gave in, so he might as well save them both the trouble. Furthermore, Janessa was going to give Angie a ration of trouble, and that ought to be fun to watch.

Then there was the case itself—something was very rotten in

Denmark, and he was intrigued. Whatever had happened here, it wasn't your average everyday street corner shooting. The connections he had in New Orleans, one phone call would probably tell him whether the thing was really worth pursuing. He looked up the number for an old buddy, Mike LaBauve, who was on Major Case Homicide, out of headquarters. All the homicide cops were pals; LaBauve ought to be able to find out what was going on and LaBauve owed him for keeping quiet in a little matter involving LaBauve's son a few years back. That one had worked out—the kid had straightened out and become a lawyer. If you could call that straightening out.

He placed his call, asked his questions, hung up, and waited. LaBauve called back within the hour. "EdDEE! LaBauve here. I got what you need. First, of all, Allyson's kids all had different names from hers—got it from the maid, Carmen Sandoval, who Crockett located from a phone number on the refrigerator."

Eddie interrupted. "Where was Sandoval yesterday?"

"Day off because of the hurricane. She's worked for Brower for a year or so, no record, looks clean. She left at three P.M. Monday—didn't see that scene ya client described."

"Anybody have a sheet?" Eddie had given him a list of names he wanted checked.

"Allyson and her three kids are all clean—that's Arnelle Halston, by the way, and Austin and Cassie Edwards. The other two have records. Janessa Wallis got popped a couple of years ago for possession of marijuana. Nothin' much there. But Rashad Daneene's kind of interesting. He's got a juvenile felony record."

"For?"

"Now you know I don't have access to juvenile records."

"Come on, Mikey."

"Sorry, Eddie. No can do."

"Damn."

"Yeah . . . Don't know why they coddle these kids. Okay. On to the mother-daughter murder act. Strange one. Real strange. First of all, victims were killed within the same two-hour period—so close together the coroner can't tell who bought it first."

"Damn again."

"Yeah. If the same guy did 'em both, the order would help a lot.

By the way, Crockett knows damn well why I was axin' questions. He *wants* you to know this stuff. He thinks he's got a pretty good case against ya client and he damn well wants ya to know it."

"Give me the bad news."

"They haven't done the autopsies yet, but some things are pretty obvious—the daughter was stabbed five times with a kitchen knife. Downright puke-inducing."

"Mmm, mmm. Crime of passion, sounds like. But what makes it bad news? My client's prints on the weapon or somethin'?"

"I haven't got to the bad news yet. No prints on the knife. But they found ya client's prints on that gun."

"Big hairy deal. She admits she picked it up."

"Well, this part ya didn't hear from me—Crockett doesn't even know I know. It had Brower's prints on it as well. Could have been suicide. Crockett's got to take that one real seriously, because of a few other things I found out. Guess what they found at the daughter's house?"

"I give up, Mikey. Come on."

"They found signs of a struggle at Cassie's—big struggle, like two people got into a fight. You follow?"

"She was stabbed five times—stands to reason there might have been a struggle."

"Yeah, well. They found two wineglasses in the living room. Like Cassie had a drink with her killer. Sure enough, one had Cassie's prints on it. The other had the mother's."

"So what's the theory? Allyson kills her daughter, then just splits—goes home and offs herself?"

"Yeah, could be."

Eddie wasn't convinced. "Was the gun Allyson's?"

"Uh-uh. Here's the interesting part—it was her daughter's."

"Oh, right, the gun was the daughter's. Okay, let me see if I follow you. The evidence suggests the mom comes over, has a glass of wine and fights with the daughter, gets so mad she kills her. Then she looks around for the gun—which maybe she knows about—so she can off herself. And she goes *home* to do it? Why didn't she just do it there?"

"Yeah, why didn't she? Makes you kind of think it didn't go down that way, don't it? Like maybe Cassie has a fight with somebody else who stabs her and wipes the prints off the knife, and that person gets the gun, goes over to Allyson's house, whacks her to make it look like murder–suicide, and puts Allyson's prints on the gun."

"Oh, real likely. Big hole in it, anyhow. How'd Allyson's prints get on the wineglass?"

"I get the feeling Crockett thinks the perp might have planted the glass."

"Doesn't make sense. I mean maybe, if the guy was wacko—*really* wacko. But who'd be that crazy?"

"Maybe somebody who'd vacuum the floor and all the furniture? Like, to get rid of fibers?"

"Oh, man. That clears my client right there. Case Crockett hasn't noticed, she ain't no master criminal."

"Well, I think he's got somethin' else. He only told me what he wants ya to know, but here's what *I* know—he's pretty sure ya client did it. He's holdin' something back, waitin' to spring it on ya."

Eddie was barely listening. "How about that book of poetry—where the hell was it?"

"Lyin' on the table. Plain as day."

"You smell a setup there? How about prints on the book?"

"Lots of 'em. But anyone could have touched the book—I mean, if she just had it out on the table, people could've come in and picked it up—like while they were waitin' for her or somethin'. So what ya think? Think the mom got upset 'cause her daughter was screwin' a black kid?"

Offhand, Eddie didn't—not after she read her own son out for being rude to the same kid.

"Tell you what," LaBauve said. "I kinda don't buy it. I like Rashad."

"Yeah," Eddie said. "I think I do, too. Hell, it sure ain't Janessa. All Crockett's got is the book and some can-o'-worm prints. That's nothin'." After he hung up, he reflected that juries had convicted on less. He got himself a second cup of coffee. About the time it was starting to kick in, Ms. Wallis turned up.

"Janessa's in love with you. Feels real sorry for you, having a daughter like Angie."

"I liked that kid from the get-go."

"Well, I'm not sure I like her."

"Ms. Wallis, there's some funny stuff goin' on here. Some real funny stuff."

When he had run it down for her, she said, "Come on! Nobody really tries to frame anybody. It's just too—*television*."

"Wrong, Ms. Wallis. People do it all the time. Usually, just as badly as this guy did."

"So you don't think it's Janessa. You said 'guy.' "

"Figure of speech, Ms. Wallis. But matter of fact, I don't. I like Rashad, but I sure as hell don't rule Austin out. If Janessa's telling the truth, Allyson threatened to disinherit him the same night she died. Maybe he figured he'd get rid of her before she did it, whack Cassie, too, so he could have it all."

"You forget, there's another daughter. Arnelle."

"What do we know about her?"

"Christ, Eddie, we just got the case. It's not even ten o'clock, and I've already done two interviews. When was I gonna background anybody?"

"Would you mind not swearing?"

"Right. 'Scuse my French. I'll go do the whole bunch of coconuts right now."

"Wait a minute. What'd ya get from the interviews?"

"Bottom line: Rashad's a saint, but nobody's seen him. Details at eleven. But I've barely scratched the surface here. His brother and his pal Hunt say he hangs with poets. I've got a reading Friday—open-mike thing with a whole lot of poets. Maybe I can pick up something there. Oh, that reminds me—check this out." She reached into her bag and pulled out a scruffy paperback book.

"*Laments*," she read. "By Rashad Daneene. Self-published, probably. Janessa gave it to me."

"The kid's got it bad. Maybe she's not sleeping with him, but she's got a crush."

"I wouldn't argue with you there." She opened the book to the title page. "It's got an inscription: *To my new friend, Janessa—I look forward to getting to know you.* Think that qualifies as mushy?"

She left without waiting for an answer.

But she was back in less than two hours, and her entrance, as always, reminded him of a squall at sea—not exactly dangerous, but the boat tended to heel. She didn't breeze in, she blew in on a gust of energy he envied. If she didn't have such a gorgeous voice—she could have made a fortune doing phone sex—he probably couldn't have handled it.

"What is it, Ms. Wallis?" He wondered if he sounded as tired as she made him feel.

"Got some great stuff on Allyson. Also everyone else, but Allyson's the best."

"Well, what's the Number One Rule of being a great detective?"

She smiled at him. "You mean a paid detective? In this case, it doesn't apply, *but*—" she held up a finger to keep him from protesting—"I did background the client."

It was something they always did in this office and always would. You had to know who you were dealing with—and whether they were solvent.

"Of course, I backgrounded Janessa when I first found her, but unfortunately I didn't get anything new. She was raised by her mother's sister, Mozelle Winters, who didn't have a lot of use for her, and a couple of years ago, she moved in with a friend named Coreen Brown and her very nice family on Mystery Street. For a while, she worked as a manicurist. After that, there's nothing—this painting gig of hers doesn't exactly show up online."

"Well, I got somethin' on her." It pleased Eddie to one-up her. "She's got a drug record."

Ms. Wallis laughed in his face. "I can't wait till I have your connections. I have to depend on rapsheets.com."

"Hold it. Slow down. Did you say 'rapsheets.com'?"

"Swear to God. But I never know if it's accurate. Couldn't find Janessa on it. Anything serious?"

"Hell, no, 'scuse my French. It was pot. They should legalize the stuff, ya know?" He said the last part to get a rise out of her, but she only raised an eyebrow.

"Anybody else got a sheet?"

"Only Rashad. It's a juvenile felony record—for what, I don't know."

"Uh-oh."

"Uh-oh's right. Sure would like to know more about that one. Hit me with Austin Edwards." He wondered if the name would throw her, but she didn't blink—somehow, she'd figured out Allyson's kids' names on her own.

"He seems like a drifter. He's lived in various little towns in Louisiana—Dulac, Port Fouchoun, Little Lake, Delacroix, Cocodrie."

"Hmph. Fishing towns. That might tell us something."

"His last known address is in Morgan City, but he's not there now. And he doesn't have much of a credit record."

"Ya can't get credit records online. That much I know."

Again the raised eyebrow. "If you say so. It looks like he doesn't buy much, with one notable exception—he's got a Harley."

"Allyson Brower's kid drives a Harley?"

"Top of the line. Seems like he's the rebel in the family. Arnelle used to work for a TV station, but now she's married to a Metairie internist, guy named Halston. They've got stuff in the stock market—that can't be good."

"Meaning they might need money. Did Allyson really have any, or was it all smoke and mirrors?"

Ms. Wallis put her chin in her hand and gave him a half smile. "What an interesting phrase. More or less describes her life, as far as I can see."

"Ha! I smelled it. She was a con artist."

"That I can't tell for sure. But she sure did have a gift for reinventing herself. She was born Alice Rivers in Petal, Mississippi, the daughter of an electrician. Her mother was a clerk in a store in Hattiesburg—guess the family didn't have much money and Mom had to supplement it. However, Alice was quite beautiful, and reasonably smart, I guess. Only thing was, with the family being of low social status, she missed out on all the big honors, like Homecoming Queen—evidently that kind of thing went to the sleek country-club types."

"Ms. Wallis, stop. Don't tell me ya got all that online."

"Hey, Eddie, I'm a detective, remember? Once I had Hattiesburg, I sent out a few e-mails. Funny thing about e-mail—you know how road rage works? People think they're anonymous because they're in a car. E-mail's the same—anybody'll tell you anything. You should try it some time."

"Who could you possibly know in Hattiesburg?"

"You mean who in the white community? See, that's the beauty of e-mail. You don't have to know anybody. For all they know, I'm just a freelance reporter doing a story on her murder."

Eddie sighed, exasperated.

"Well?" she said. "Who's the one who taught me to lie?"

"All right, all right. Go on."

"Okay, she went to the University of Southern Mississippi right there in Hattiesburg. She couldn't get into any of the fancy sororities, but she traded on her beauty, and in college she did better than in high school. That taught her that she needed a larger canvas, and here's where it gets interesting. She went to New York to be a model, and ended up a call girl."

"You couldn't possibly know that!" Even LaBauve had missed it.

"It's a matter of record—she was arrested once, working for an escort service; there was a newspaper story about it. Seems like she saved her pennies and managed to put herself through fashion design school, and actually worked for a couture house for a while, apparently as a saleswoman. And then she met a man."

"Who?"

Ms. Wallis consulted her notes. "Richard Peters, if it matters—he came from a wealthy family and didn't seem to have to do too much for a living, but he was a theatrical producer of sorts. Knew people in the arts. They got married, but not for long. Had one child, Arnelle Peters. He's dead now, but I don't know if he left Arnelle any money. Anyway, since he's gone, people were willing to talk. A woman who worked at the couture house said she thinks Peters beat her—Allyson used to come to work all bruised up. She must have used that to get some coins out of him, because somehow, when she got divorced she managed to leave New York with a chunk of money. She moved to Tallahassee and opened a boutique featuring her own clothing designs."

Eddie was bemused. "Why Tallahassee?"

Talba had considered that. "Pretty hard to get the 'why' in three hours, but I've got a few thoughts. It's a college town— she probably sold her clothes to sorority girls with money. I don't think that's the only reason, though. I think she wanted to go back to school herself. Because here's an interesting thing— she got a master's in English lit while she was there. Also in Tallahassee, she met and married Harry Edwards, a country club type–insurance man. Probably dull but solid."

But Eddie was stuck on the previous fact. "English literature? The ex-call girl?"

His associate raised both eyebrows. "Go figure. But put that together with the kind of people she knew in New York, and the kind of life she lived there—and here, too, for that matter."

"Hold it," Eddie said. "What do we know about her life in New Orleans?"

"I'm getting to that. Anyhow, she had two kids with Edwards—Austin and Cassie. But, always keeping her eye on the prize, about fifteen years into the marriage, she met Charles Brower, a banker from Mississippi. She left her husband to marry him, and moved back home. But not to Hattiesburg—to the Delta.

"Unfortunately, that marriage didn't last too long, either. Brower died about two years ago, apparently leaving her quite a chunk of money."

"She does seem good at chunks of money."

"Notice I said 'apparently.' The jury's still out on that."

Eddie nodded. "Keep going." '

"She became sort of a local Auntie Mame up in the Delta, and it looks like she was more or less run out of town about a year ago. Too many affairs with other people's husbands."

"Whereupon she moved her operation to New Orleans."

"You got it. The original Merry Widow. I know she gave big parties, but there's a lot I don't know. I didn't want to go e-mailing around town—any more is going to require actual legwork. But I found out she used to be in business with a woman named Rosemary McLeod. Don't know what happened to that. Also, I did make one or two phone calls."

"Did she own that house in the Garden District?"

"She did buy it, but she had a horrible credit record. Really miserable. Also a reputation. She owed a lot of people money, including Janessa, probably. Also, she bought lots of clothes, but she was the sort who'd take out a ball gown on approval and return it in a week."

"Meaning?"

"Well, one saleslady saw her picture in the paper, wearing a dress she'd returned."

Eddie exploded. "God, I hate people like that!"

"I know what you mean. I've got a feeling this might be the

tip of the iceberg." She shrugged. "But I guess she was really nice to Rashad."

Eddie got a glint in his eye. "Wonder if he was her lover."

"Ewwwww. She had to be almost sixty."

"Whaddaya mean? Sixty's a great age."

"I'm not kidding, Eddie, you really should try that e-mail thing."

"Yeah, and I should exercise an hour a day. Ain't gonna happen, Ms. Wallis. Ya got two more days on this. That's all."

She looked about as worried as a drunk on a Saturday night. Probably thinking, *Two more days, sure.* "I'm about to go see Arnelle; she might know where Austin is. And I've got a bunch more leads on Rashad."

"Make 'em count, Ms. Wallis, make 'em count. Full report later, okay?"

Chapter Eight

Actually, she'd lied to him about two things. First of all, rapsheets.com didn't even have Louisiana in its database. Second, she'd gotten the clothes-on-approval story from a good friend who worked for Saks and had a friend from Hattiesburg. One phone call and she had enough of Allyson's background to check the rest out for herself. But what it really told her about the killer she wasn't sure.

A man who'd murder his mother and sister for their money would have to be desperate, stupid, on drugs, crazy, or some combination thereof—and somehow, she thought if any two of those were true, Austin Edwards would already have a pretty nasty criminal record. The fact that he didn't made her lean toward the conclusion the police had probably already reached—either Rashad or Janessa had committed the murders, or they'd done it together.

Probably Rashad—especially with that suspicious juvenile

felony. Too bad for Janessa's love life, but better to find out your man's a killer than to rot in jail yourself.

She steeled herself to visit Arnelle Halston, cordially hoping Halston's husband wouldn't be home—Talba'd had quite enough fun couples for one day.

The Halston home was in Metairie, a suburb located in Jefferson Parish, and a whole different animal from New Orleans. Whereas the city has a distinctly foreign flavor—kind of Caribbean/Mediterranean with a big African influence—Metairie is unequivocally American. Especially old Metairie, a haven for rich white folks. It could have been an upscale neighborhood anywhere if not for its denizens' Southern accents. Even these weren't particularly New Orleans, tending toward the smooth rather than the rough, like Eddie's.

The Halstons' street was a perfect place to raise kids, lined with pretty (though not grand) houses with nicely kept lawns, some with toys and bicycles scattered randomly on them. A Lexus was parked in the Halston driveway.

Tentatively, Talba rang the bell, wondering if it was too soon to visit someone whose mother had just been murdered. But the woman who answered looked a good deal more harried than bereaved. She wore neat cotton bell-bottoms (from Banana Republic, was Talba's guess) and a tight-fitting white cotton shirt nipped in at the waist. It was a good outfit for making funeral arrangements—brisk and efficient. And not unlike Talba's own. Arnelle's highlighted hair was shoulder-length and parted on the side. Like Lynne's, her face was slightly pinched, perhaps with grief, yet her makeup wasn't smeared. If Arnelle had cried for her mother, she'd moved on.

"Mrs. Halston?" she said, and introduced herself, adding, "I knew your mother, and I'm terribly sorry for your loss. I really hate to bother you today, but I'm trying to help find Rashad."

Halston seemed puzzled. "Rashad? He isn't here."

"No, ma'am, I didn't think he would be." It was against Eddie's principles, but she decided to tell the truth. She absolutely couldn't think of a plausible lie (poor lying was her worst failing as a PI). "I'm a private investigator hired—well, to look into the deaths of your mother and sister."

"Really? Who are you working for?"

"E. V. Anthony—it's a very old and respected firm. My boss is a former Jefferson Parish deputy."

"I was actually wondering who your client is."

"I'm sorry, but that's confidential. But I know you want to get this cleared up and I wonder if I could ask you a few questions."

Halston's face changed—from what to what, Talba couldn't be sure, but she thought something like determination was what she saw now. "Come on in," Halston said, and stepped out of the doorway. "It'll be a break from making phone calls."

Talba entered a cool room painted a soothing khaki green, with framed prints of two huge magnolia blossoms hung over an ivory sofa that looked expensive—and a little too fussy. A glass-topped coffee table was surrounded by chairs covered in a gold-and-ivory stripe. Two handsome long-haired cats were taking their ease on it—one black, one white. A very restful room, she thought—and one that took no chances. The carpet was beige.

"Koko! Blanche! Off that sofa now!" Halston gave each a little nudge on the rump, and each dropped grumpily to the floor. "Cassie's and Mom's cats," Halston explained. "You wouldn't want one, would you?"

The animals made Talba smile. "Somehow, I'd expect Koko to be brown."

"No, the black one's named for Koko the talking gorilla. Whoever heard of a brown cat? And you can guess who Blanche is named for—she was Cassie's."

Remembering that Cassie had been an actress, Talba wondered if she'd ever gotten to play Blanche Dubois.

Halston had already lost interest. She offered coffee.

Talba realized suddenly that the Montjoys hadn't offered any. But Arnelle was a "nice lady," according to Marlon. "If you're having some," she said.

When Halston had returned with a silver tray incongruously bearing two hefty mugs, she said, "I just called a friend and checked on your firm."

"I hope he or she gave us a good reference."

"He not only gave the firm one, he singled you out—said you'd been in the news quite a few times."

"Eddie's the brains—I'm just a junior-grade detective." She was trying to establish rapport before starting in on her questions, but Halston had an agenda of her own.

"You're working for my brother, aren't you? He's probably trying to put this thing on Rashad."

Talba was nonplussed. "I can't say who I'm working for."

"It's just like Austin to do something like that."

She could only mean one thing. "You think he did it?" Talba blurted. "I mean, you think he, uh . . ." She couldn't bring herself to say, "killed your mother and sister."

"Isn't it obvious? He's disappeared, hasn't he? But you know where he is, and you're going to tell either me or the police." She picked up a cell phone lying on the coffee table. "Which will it be?"

"Mrs. Halston, I have no idea where your brother is. I can tell you this—" She wasn't sure she should. "We're not working for him."

"Good. Then work for me. I was going to hire a PI anyway. I need to find Austin."

"I'd like to find him too, but—"

"Why are you looking for Rashad?"

"We think he may know something about what happened that night."

"Well, if he does, he's in danger. Austin's not a very nice man. He'd sell him out as soon as look at him. I never understood what Rashad saw in him."

Talba remembered her suspicion that Rashad was gay. She said, "Are you saying Austin and Rashad have a relationship?"

Unexpectedly, Halston laughed. "Not like you mean, I guess. My brother's not gay and I don't think Rashad is. But they're friends—or they were."

"I understand Austin said some rather insulting things—"

"That's what I mean—that's the kind of person Austin is. Do you want the job or not?"

Talba was flabbergasted. The woman was a powerhouse. "I'm a little overwhelmed."

Again, Halston laughed. "Am I coming on too strong? Old habits die hard. Before my marriage, I was in television."

"Oh, yeah. You were a station manger." Talba remembered it from her background check, but Halston had quit twelve years ago.

"I never got over having authority." She sat back, trying to make herself look less threatening. "If I had kids, I'd probably treat them like employees. But I couldn't have them—so for the past few years, I've been a really hardworking volunteer. I can put together a fund-raiser like nobody's business, and I love doing it. It was time."

"Time for what?"

"To give back." It was a phrase Talba hated. That, and "make a difference." She hoped Halston wasn't going to trot that one out.

But the other woman had already moved on; she was a veritable mistress of forward motion. "Look, the reason I'm jumping on this is, I'm in danger."

"You mean from your brother? Because he wants your mother's money?"

"He's desperate for it."

"Well, he can't think he could get away with it. Wouldn't it be just a little obvious?"

"I'm not the kind of person who takes chances." Talba had seen this before—a machinelike efficiency combined with a near-paranoia. The woman would make a fantastic detective.

"Well, I really don't know if we can take the case." She knew perfectly well they couldn't. "Of course I'll talk to my boss about it. But frankly, maybe you don't need to hire us. I think you and my client have the same aim here. They want to find out who . . . uh . . ."

". . . killed my mother and sister." Apparently Halston, for all her pushiness, wasn't an iceberg. Her face pinched in just a little more, and she seemed to wince as she said it.

"I couldn't say it," Talba said. "You're a brave lady."

"Not really. I didn't care much for my mother, and my sister was lost to me anyway."

Talba revised her opinion: maybe she was an iceberg. But then she saw silent tears running down Halston's face. As if in sympathy, Blanche jumped up on her lap. Absently, Arnelle stroked the cat. "I don't know why I said that. It's true, but they were my family, and I guess I loved them. I mean, Cassie, anyway. She never had a chance, the way Mom treated her. But Austin's scum. I'm sorry—I just feel so disoriented. You'll have to forgive me."

"Of course. But what did you mean about your mother? How did she treat Cassie?"

"Like dirt. She tried to control Cassie's whole life. She

thought Cassie existed for nothing but doing her bidding . . . and poor Cassie didn't have any resources. She didn't know how to protect herself. With Mom, it was all about *her*. She had to have everyone's attention all the time, and she was completely ruthless. She'd do anything to get what she wanted. She was jealous of Cassie. She hated her. In my heart, I really believe she hated her."

"Jealous of what?"

"Of Cassie's beauty. The way people liked her. The attention she got. Mom wanted that for herself. And so she denigrated her. She told her she was ugly and worthless . . . I should know. She told me the same things. But I'm the oldest. I knew how to stick up for myself."

"One of the scenarios the police are playing with is murder–suicide. From what you're telling me, it sounds possible."

"Mom would have never killed herself. It's that simple. If she killed Cassie in a fit of rage—and believe me, she was capable of it—she'd rationalize it. She'd sit on Death Row for twenty years proclaiming her innocence."

"I'm wondering why you said Cassie was lost to you."

"Mom had ways of turning people against each other. She'd say things to Cassie like, 'Your sister says you're disgracing her—ruining her stick-in-the-mud Metairie life with your sluttish behavior.' You see what I mean? That way she got us both at once. A few zingers like that and Cassie didn't trust me. Wouldn't have a real relationship with me at all. And it wasn't only a few zingers. She did that right to the end."

Talba was so greedy for answers to the questions Big Sis was bringing up, she hardly knew where to start. "What sluttish behavior?" she finally asked.

"You're not getting this. I don't even know what Cassie's life was like, except miserable. It was *Mom* who said that. She said I called Cassie a slut by calling her one herself. Do you know how evil that is?"

It occurred to Talba that two could play at that game. Maybe Halston was running the same con on her. For the moment, she decided to play it as if Halston were straight. Who knew? She might be.

"And she never paid people what she owed them. She was always getting them to work for free."

"I've heard that once or twice already."

"From Lynne and Marlon, I bet. She owed both of them boocoos of money. And of course, she just cultivated Lynne to get to Hunt."

"Hunt?"

"She fancied herself Ms. Literary Belle of the Ball. All that help for writers—what did it cost her? Nothing! But she thought it made her look like a hero—and boy, did she want to look like a hero."

"But . . . why did she do it? Did she want to be a writer herself? I know she had a master's in English. Did she think Hunt could help her get published?"

Halston heaved a massive sigh. "Who knows? With my mother, nothing was ever simple. Mostly, I think, she was just a groupie; an arts groupie." She spoke as if that were worse than being a thief.

"Okay, let's recap here. You think Austin killed your mother and sister. Why?"

"To get our money, of course."

"But Cassie's murder was a crime of passion."

"Or it looked that way."

"Look, Mrs. Halston. It's obvious you don't like your brother."

"My half brother. Cassie was only a half, too—but I'd claim her."

"Let me be blunt—what's so bad about him?"

"He's a bum. A motorcycle bum. And a druggie."

"He's never had a drug arrest."

"Maybe not in this state."

That stopped Talba. "You're saying he has been arrested?"

Halston shrugged again, impatiently this time. "I really don't know. I've barely seen my brother in ten years. Family occasions; small talk—that's it."

Talba did the math—Austin couldn't be older than thirty. "You mean since he was twenty?" she said.

"My mother kept me up to date."

Yes, but she was an unreliable reporter, Talba thought. *That is, if you're telling the truth.*

"Well. If you weren't in touch with Austin, how did you know he and Rashad were friends?"

Here, Halston softened. "From Rashad. He thought we should reconcile. He's such a sweet boy. He and Marlon painted my house for me." She swept an arm to indicate their work, startling the cat on her lap.

"Well, at least we're on the same team here. Can you help me find Rashad? Where should I look?"

"You could talk to his grandfather. He loved his grandfather. And his aunt."

"I didn't know he had an aunt."

"Oh, yes, she raised him."

"His mother didn't raise him?"

"No, I think she abandoned the family or something."

"His father did, too, if you can believe his poems. But they don't say anything but nice things about his mother."

"Well, you know boys and their mothers. He probably worships her image or something."

"Do you know the aunt's name?"

"I'm sorry, I don't." She looked at her watch, as if she were ready for the interview to end.

Talba was, too. "Okay, I'll look for your brother," she said, figuring she'd have to, since he was a friend of Rashad's. "But not for money—just as a part of my investigation. Do you have any idea where I should start?"

Halston thought about it. "What I don't know is where he lived or what he did for a living, if anything. I got the impression from Mom it was pretty much nothing. Why don't you try biker bars? Or opium dens? By the way, you didn't say whether you want Koko or Blanche."

"I'm thinking about it," Talba said.

When she saw Talba to the door, she got close enough that, for the first time, Talba realized something she hadn't before— Halston had been drinking.

Chapter Nine

"Oh, man, oh, man, oh, man." Ms. Wallis had her hand on her forehead as if it hurt. "These people are screwing with my head. I think I need a drink—they've all had one."

She had just outlined her three morning interviews—not a bad day's work, Eddie thought—but he wasn't sure he made more sense of it than she did. The redneck biker was friends with the sensitive African American poet whom he had insulted; Allyson Brower could have killed her daughter, but not herself; Rashad was pretty much a saint, but his biggest supporter thought he didn't have a lick of talent. Allyson reminded people of some character in a book. And on and on. He wondered if he should check out that book.

"Ms. Wallis, you might be better off sticking with your infernal damn machines."

"Yeah, Eddie, I'm starting to think so, too."

"Oh, cheer up. Let's go get a po' boy."

"I'll gain ten pounds."

"Well? Did ya have lunch?" Women, he thought. All they ever thought about was their weight. Ms. Wallis sure as hell wasn't getting a drink—not in the middle of the work day. Not until he had this thing with that poor kid Janessa straightened out. "Ya like shrimp, right? Seems like I remember that."

So she went with him to Mother's for a po' boy, while they planned out how to get this thing off their backs. He had a Ferdie (roast beef and ham), she had shrimp. For someone worried about her weight, she was doing all right for herself.

"Ya got mayonnaise on ya chin," he said. "Look, I'm gonna help ya out with this thing."

"Eddie, what is *wrong* with you? Are you planning to cut my salary or something?"

"We got other cases to work on. Kinda thing pays the rent,

know what I mean? Takes both of us to get rid of this loser, we both gonna work it. Ya heard from ya sister?"

"Oh, yeah. I forgot to tell you. She fired us."

"Whaddaya mean she fired us?"

"I mean she tried. I told her she couldn't."

"Ah, well. Guess ya right. We don't straighten it out now, they'll arrest her and we'll have it on us for years. Now, listen to me. We gotta figure out who's the key to this. Not necessarily who the shooter is, but who knows something—who can get us there the fastest."

"It's not like I didn't spend half the day trying."

"Don't be petulant. It's unbecoming." At her look of surprise, he said, "Caught ya, didn't I? Ya didn't know I knew that word. Okay, ya tried. Who is it?"

"Well, it could be Arnelle. That one's the biggest can of worms I've run into in a long time."

"She's tellin' the truth about her mother, it could explain everything."

"What kind of everything?"

"Everything about her. The mom's a fruitcake, the daughter's a worse one." He shrugged. "Don't worry about her for now. If she's it, Austin's gonna know. That might be why he split. Tell ya what. I'm gonna take him on as my personal project. He's a biker, right? I got a feelin' you're not the right person to send into biker bars."

"I wouldn't dream of entering one. *I* am a baroness."

"Yeah, and I'm George W. Bush. Tell ya what else I'm gonna do—I'm gonna work on this Hunt Montjoy character. I don't mean to be sexist or anything, but that one's a man's job."

"You got that right," she grumbled. "He thinks women belong in the bedroom unless they're his wife. In which case, they're supposed to be out making a living to support him."

"Ya think Lynne's the one bought the big house in the Garden District?"

"If poets made any money, would I be a PI?"

"You know you love it," he said. "He hangs at Pete's, right?"

"He said he was going to Pete's. I thought he meant a friend's."

"Maybe. My guess is the bar—fireman's hangout. His kind

of place, right? I'll check it out. And maybe I'll go see Marlon, too." Her face had settled into something like a pout. "What's wrong?"

"I feel like you're dissing me. Like I didn't do anything right."

"For chrissake, you got your period or somethin'? I'm trying to help out here." He didn't wait for an answer. "Look, you check out Janessa's house. Wonder if she tried to fire us because Rashad's turned up there."

"I thought of that."

"I'm sure ya did, Ms. Wallis. I'm sure ya did. And read those poems some more. Maybe you'll get some more ideas. Maybe they're all lyin' about the mama leavin' the family. The way ya described that one poem, sounds like he's a real mama's boy. Maybe he does know where she is—and she's taking care of him."

"Yeah," she said. "Yeah. Something might be funny about that. So you want me to stay on Rashad, right? And you'll take Austin?"

"If it's not too sexist or racist or anything."

She made another pout.

"Oh, stop being so defensive," he said.

"Politically correct, that's all."

"Well, it ain't cute. You buying lunch or am I? You can if you want—to show I'm not sexist."

"Oh, hell," Talba said. "Let's flip a coin."

Eddie sighed. "How many times do I have to tell ya I hate it when women swear?"

"And that's not sexist?"

He shrugged. "I guess I'm buyin', then." In fact, she didn't require him to be politically correct, which was one of the things that made it possible for him to work with her (that and her voice)—since as a matter of fact, she was not only black and female, making two strikes against her, but also young and well-educated, making four. In his opinion, he handled all that pretty well, and when he didn't, she didn't rag on him too much about it. But the swearing really did get to him.

He paid for lunch and as they made their way back to the sidewalk, she said, "Rashad's got another friend. Writer named Wayne Taylor. You want to talk to him—being a man and all?"

"Naah, you're the literary light. He's probably queer or something. I wouldn't know what to say to him."

He'd expected at least a small rise, but she didn't bat an eye. She was getting so used to him it was hardly any fun to kid her anymore.

Talba felt groggy from getting up early, and also from the shrimp po' boy. The last thing she wanted to do was another interview, so she took a ride out to Mystery Street to check on Janessa, on the way using her cell phone to call Wayne Taylor at UNO. A voice message said he'd be in class from one to three and in his office from three to five.

She had plenty of time.

She easily located her sister's little garage apartment and listened for a moment at the door. Hearing nothing, she knocked and waited. After a few moments, she knocked again. No one answered.

Well, she thought, *I tried*. She picked up some much-needed coffee at the CC's on Esplanade, and, taking it with her, she drove to UNO.

UNO was a public commuter college, with very few dorms, though it drew graduate students from all over, kids who just wanted to spend time in New Orleans. But, so far as Talba understood it, the undergraduate program was pretty utilitarian; most kids were there for a chance at an education that wouldn't ruin their families financially.

Its lakefront campus was sprawling and surpassingly ugly. It had been built in that most egregious of architectural eras, the fifties, and there were no trees big enough to soften the effect of the concrete and brick boxes that passed for buildings. But, since it truly was right on the lake—one of its boundaries was the levee—there was often a breeze blowing. Despite its ugliness, she liked the no-frills feel of UNO. Her fantasy was that its students were more interested in an education than in football and beer, and she figured you might as well have fantasies.

Talba had made no appointment with Wayne Taylor, and since she was taking potluck, she figured she'd have to wait till he could get to her. She had a plan to amuse herself in the meantime. Nothing, she figured, impressed an author like seeing his book in someone's hand—she could buy one and read it while she waited.

Since the campus map didn't mention a bookstore, she found the library, asked around, and learned the store was housed in the University Center. She got directions and headed over. To her surprise, the store seemed almost luxurious. A salt-and-pepper mix of students was killing time between classes, shopping not only for textbooks, but for the requisite T-shirts, sweats, Teddy bears, and greeting cards that every campus bookstore seems to carry these days.

She stepped up to the counter. "Where would I find something by Wayne Taylor?"

"Taylor?" The clerk was a young, caramel-colored man in dreads and spectacles He was cute. "Crazy Wayne Taylor?" The young man's face lit up with recognition and the delight of a man who knew his job. "God, he's a wild man. Just a sec, let me get you something."

She waited until he returned with two paperbacks, one sporting a swastika on the cover, which the clerk was studying. "Love story," he said, "set during World War Two. It's called *Death Angel*."

Talba winced at the triteness of the title. "How about the other one?"

The clerk turned it on its back. "This one's set in New Orleans. In Storyville. Not bad—you might like it." Storyville was the erstwhile red light district at the edge of the French Quarter. "But I think his real talent's screenwriting."

"Okay, I'll take them both." She had a pretty hard-and-fast rule never to read any book with a swastika on the cover—she found Nazis simultaneously boring and horrifying—but the point was to display, not read it.

As he rang up the purchase, the clerk said, "Did you ever see *Blue City*? Great cop movie."

"His only claim to Hollywood fame, right?"

"He hasn't had a picture in a while, but he's still writing. Good teacher, too. I took his screenwriting class last year."

"You're a regular fan," Talba said. "But I'm wondering something—why did you say he's a wild man?"

"You've never taken a class from him?"

"Nope. Never have."

"If you had, you'd know. Wayne's classes are *not* ordinary classes. You don't know about him? People who aren't even registered go just to watch the show."

"No kidding."

The guy shook his head. "Have to be seen to be believed, man. Can't even be described."

"Oh, yeah? He's in class now, according to his voice message. Where do I find him?"

"Hmm. Not so sure. Want me to call the office for you?" He made the phone call, and in a moment, she was running across campus as if starring in a late-for-class dream.

The class was in progress, but no one seemed to notice as she slipped in and joined a group of standees against a wall. She figured these were the drop-ins the bookstore dude had mentioned. A student, a short white girl in a buzz cut, short lavender overalls, and a green T-shirt was standing before the class, addressing Taylor.

"You framed her, man. That was the lowest of the low."

Talba was taken aback. This was way too much like real life.

Taylor was pale and sweating, as if he were being grilled by police instead of a kid with no fashion sense. "I didn't frame her. The monster did."

"But you knew exactly who killed William—and you didn't even speak up. You just let them hang her. You're a turd."

"Thank you, Miss Brockman," Taylor said, and the girl went back to her desk. "Will anyone else speak for Justine?" No hands went up. "No? Okay, then. How about me? Isn't there anyone who'll speak for Victor?"

"You're a turd!" Ms. Brockman shouted. "And the worst kind of coward. You just burned rubber when you saw you'd fathered a monster—like some guy who gets a girl pregnant and disappears on her."

It occurred to Talba that the work in question must be *Frankenstein*. Taylor must have set up some kind of mini-drama in which he was playing the part of Victor Frankenstein as a device to discuss the book.

"Come on," he said. "I'm not all bad. Doesn't anybody have a good word for me?"

A kid in the back stood up. "Well, that was a good thing you did, not to let the monster have the bride."

"But I had to abort her to pull it off. Is abortion okay with everyone in here?"

For a moment, no one said anything. Finally, Ms. Brockman shouted, "You should have aborted the monster, too. He turned out the way he did because you deserted him. Just like a kid whose mother's a teenage crack whore's going to be a mini-gangster by the time he's two and a half."

"Because no one will love him, you mean?"

"Hey, that's what abortion is all about—not bringing kids into homes where they're not wanted. Kids who don't get love grow up to be monsters. Literally."

A neat black girl rose, with straightened hair and a gold cross around her neck "I'm sorry. In the sight of God, abortion's never right."

"Oh, really?" Taylor said. "Well, what do you guys think about cloning?"

Dead silence. Even Talba didn't see where he was going with that one.

"Was it okay for me to make the monster in the first place?" Taylor asked.

"It was against nature," the Christian girl said.

"What about those guys cloning horses and sheep? Think people are going to be next? Maybe in twenty years, if you're rich and you never want to die, you can just get cloned and live forever. Hey, you can even get cloned when you're twenty-five and never get old. Is that against nature or not?"

"Apples and oranges," said a nerdy white boy. "Cloning's science." True to stereotype, he had greasy hair and wore glasses.

"What I did was science," Taylor said. "What's the difference?"

The boy who answered looked like a jock. "You made somebody really, really *ugly*, man. Your kid was so ugly even Lacy Brockman wouldn't date him."

Titters rippled, but no way was Ms. Brockman going to take that. "Fuggeddaboutit, Boudreaux! I stick to girls—weeds out swine like you."

The girl who stood next wasn't large, she wasn't stout, she

wasn't heavy-set; she could only be described as fat. "You know, there was nothing wrong with that monster when he was born—he was a perfectly nice person until people turned him into a murderer."

"How so, Ms. Weber?" Taylor prompted.

"They were mean to him because he was ugly. We put too much emphasis on physical beauty in our society."

A black boy stood, one who possessed quite a bit of physical beauty, in Talba's opinion. "He wasn't just ugly, he was different."

"Good, Mr. Jackson! You want to carry that point a little further?"

"Like, maybe, I'm different from you."

"We're talking about racism, I take it?"

"You got it," the student replied.

"Interesting point. About that different thing. About how people shunned him and he started killing them—even people he didn't even know—out of pure rage. What does that remind you of?"

"Columbine," the nerdy kid said. "I can see doing that."

"Okay. All right," Taylor said. "Look at all the issues we've covered." He started writing on the board—ABORTION, CLONING, COLUMBINE, BODY CONSCIOUSNESS, SOCIETAL VALUES, RACISM, NATURE VS. NURTURE, ORIGINS OF CRIME—speaking each word or phrase as he wrote. He turned back to face the class. "Anybody still think *Frankenstein* is irrelevant? I believe the phrase Mr. Jackson used at the beginning of class was 'just some musty old ghost story.' "

For a moment, the class was silent again, trying to decide if the performance was over, when a loud voice spoke from the hall. "Wait a minute! Stop! Nobody ever spoke for me." And in strolled—or rather, in shambled—the monster himself, moving in the crablike fashion of everyone who'd ever played him in a movie. "I've killed better kids than you for a helluva lot less." He had a great, gravelly voice, prompting one student to yell, "Hey, it's Robert De Niro." But in fact, Talba recalled, De Niro had looked like himself in his version. This monster wore the classic bolt-head look from the original.

"No, it's not," Ms. Brockman countered. "It's Boris Karloff."

"Shut up," the monster growled. "The name's Bundy. James Bundy."

A few people got the "Bundy" part and cracked up, but most were still too stunned to react.

Taylor opened his arms for a big hug. "Son!" he cried, starting towards the monster.

"Too little too late, Vickie boy. I want you to feel my pain." James Bundy raised both arms as if to attack the professor, who cringed appropriately, but at the last second, the monster turned to the class. "Hey, let's take a vote—you ignoramuses think I should kill him?"

A few shouted, "Yeah! Waste him!" but someone, probably a shill, Talba realized later, yelled, "Who ya callin' ignoramuses?" which provided the opening James Bundy was looking for. Next followed a pointed but amusingly phrased lecture on how he, who wasn't even human, had never had anyone to love him, nor any school to go to, had nonetheless managed to teach himself to read and had educated himself "like Malcolm X in his prison cell," and could quote whole sections of Goethe, Plutarch, and Milton. After that, he proceeded to lay a little *Paradise Lost* on them, and then to ask how many of them had even read it. Zero, it turned out, and Taylor's point was made.

The session wound up with a few more remarks about the relevancy, both of *Frankenstein* and of popular culture in general, and in the end elicited wild applause, in which Talba joined happily. She could honestly say it was the most enjoyable class she'd ever attended—and she'd always been bookish.

Once it was over, she resumed Plan A, making her way to Taylor's office after a brief stop in the ladies' room. When she arrived, the door was already closed. She knocked, and was told to come in. Taylor sat at his desk; the nerd from class lounged in the other chair. "Yes?" the professor said.

"Sorry to interrupt. I wonder if I can see you next."

"Wait outside," he said curtly.

She sat on the hall floor to examine her purchases. *Death Angel* she hardly glanced at. The other book was called *Mahogany Hall*, which she recognized as the name of a historic bordello run by a black woman named Lulu White—probably one of the city's first successful African American businesswomen. The ragtime pianist Spencer Williams, composer of "Basin Street Blues," had played there often. But the story's hero was neither Williams nor White. The jacket copy said the book was about a young white man who'd been taken to Mahogany Hall by his father, for what some men seemed to think of as their initiation into manhood. In fact, the boy was changed forever, but not exactly in the way his father had imagined. Instead, he fell in love with the demimonde and became a newspaper reporter who chronicled the city's criminal underbelly, unwittingly turning up skeletons in his own family's closet.

A pretty good story, Talba thought. She had time to read about twenty pages before the door opened, the white kid came out, and Taylor summoned her, frowning at seeing her sprawled on the floor.

Taylor was about five-ten and exceptionally slim, which gave him a youthful look belied by the white in his sandy hair. She put his age at about forty, slightly younger than Hunt Montjoy. His hair was cut short, but you could see that it wanted to curl. He had hazel eyes and smile lines, and he wore a striped shirt and a tie. Very correct for a place like UNO. Aggressively white-guy, which wasn't Talba's thing. Still, there was something about the agile way he moved that was very attractive—sexy, even. Talba guessed he was pretty popular with the female students.

He looked at her in a puzzled way, trying to place her, perhaps, not yet ready to admit her to the inner sanctum. "What can I do for you?" he asked finally, electing not to introduce himself. He probably thought he was supposed to know her.

"Sign my book?" she said, and drew a smile. "Make it, *For Talba, to whom I poured out my soul*."

"Oh, really?" The professor's smile disappeared.

Talba held out her hand and introduced herself. "I'm Talba Wallis. A PI, I'm afraid."

Taylor took her hand but he didn't seem happy about it. "Hunt Montjoy warned me about you."

The more he didn't smile, the more she did. "Thought he might have. But I don't bite. Really. And I think you're a good writer. Also a terrific teacher. I just caught your *Frankenstein* class."

He let his teeth show again. "Okay, okay. Flattery gets you an 'A.' Come on in."

"Wish I'd known it was that easy when I was in school. I could have made my mama so happy."

She followed him into his lair, and saw that, to her surprise, it was carpeted and cheerful, with natural light from a wall of windows opposite the hall. Bookshelves loomed behind his desk, and lined the wall across from the windows. A metal cabinet rested against the fourth wall. There were no pictures, but then, there was no room for any. One green plant thrived on a ledge by the windows. More would have looked better, but then Taylor was a guy; probably no one had told him. Except for his desktop, the cubbyhole was surprisingly clear of papers, but she figured the cabinet was stuffed with them.

He waved her to a chair, apparently through with the pleasantries. For the first time, she noticed a tightness around his mouth, as if he were a lot less relaxed than he'd first appeared. "Hunt said you were asking questions about Allyson and Cassie. Damn, what a waste! This whole thing's hit us all like a sledgehammer. Hunt's been drinking all day, I guess. He called me from Pete's."

"Pete's? The bar?" She could get that much for Eddie.

"Yeah. Wanted me to come join him." He paused, grimacing. "Like some of us don't have to earn a living."

"Hunt's . . . uh . . ." she left a nice long pause ". . . quite a character."

"He's not at his best when he's drinking." Quickly, Taylor changed the subject. "He said Rashad's disappeared."

"I understand you're one of his best friends."

Taylor nodded. "I've tried to be. The boy's had it rough, and he's got talent—which is also rough but it's there. He's quite brilliant, really—his true genius hasn't begun to be tapped. Have you read his poetry? If you want to understand Rashad, read his poetry."

"I've read some of it. The piece called 'Cassie' was pretty interesting."

Taylor reached for something, an imaginary coffee cup, Talba thought. It was a nervous gesture, the pocket-patting kind an ex-smoker makes. "They were close," he said.

"As in dating?"

Taylor seemed to be considering. "Well, I don't know. I don't think so, but . . ."

She gave him a moment and finally interjected. "What?"

"I was just thinking of this other girl. Kerry."

"What about Kerry?"

"Look, everybody loves ole Hunt, and he's my buddy, okay?"

Talba nodded, wondering where on Earth he was going.

"He's a great guy, and one of our finest writers, but he sure leaves a lot of feminine flotsam in his wake. You know about that, right? It's anything but a secret." Again she nodded, and Taylor continued as if, having done his duty to his buddy, he was free to speak. "Well, it's this way—Rashad always felt sorry for them." He looked at Talba narrowly. "You may have gathered Hunt's a bit of a racist. Did that make you wonder why he kept Rashad around? If you want to know the truth, he's cleaned up quite a few of Hunt's messes. Kerry was suicidal. Really. I hate to say it, but Hunt must have really worked her over—and I don't think she was that stable to begin with. Rashad nursed her back to health, literally. He even moved in with her for a while." He shrugged. "The crazier they are, the better he likes them."

Talba thought about what he was implying. "You're saying *Hunt* was involved with Cassie?"

Taylor looked surprised. "Uh . . . I thought . . ."

He had thought she knew it. "Are you saying he was, and it was common knowledge?"

Taylor's face was flushed. "No, I'm not saying that. I'm just saying Cassie was a little emotionally unstable; therefore, Rashad would have been attracted to her."

"Do we know for sure he isn't gay? Does he actually have sex with these broken wings?"

"We haven't discussed that particular matter, Ms. Wallis. All I can tell you is that he falls in love with them. Hunt said there's another girl involved in this mess—the one who found the body."

"He told me Rashad couldn't possibly be involved with a girl like that."

Taylor allowed himself a smirk. "She must be unattractive then. That's the yardstick by which he measures all women."

That annoyed Talba. "She's African American and she isn't thin. Is that your idea of unattractive?"

Taylor grunted, maybe in disgust. "We're not talking about me. We're talking about Hunt. Here's what I can tell you—if she's crazy enough, Rashad's probably involved with her."

Talba felt as if she was getting a handle on Rashad's sexuality, at any rate, which meant she might be able to rule out gay love nests as possible refuges for him. "Let me ask you something, Mr. Taylor."

"Wayne." He crinkled out a smile, having regained his composure. She had the distinct impression he was trying to be ingratiating.

"Wayne. I'm wondering if you've heard from Rashad since all this happened."

"Me? No, he hasn't called. Why?"

"He's got to be staying with someone. So far, his brother and his best pals—of whom you're supposed to be one—don't know where he is."

"Well, he has stayed with me. He had to give up the place he had to move in with Kerry—and after that, he moved in with us for a while, until he found that duplex with his brother."

Something about the "us" surprised her—Taylor wore no wedding ring. "You and your wife?" she said.

Taylor nodded.

"She must be pretty understanding if she lets your students stay with you."

Again he nodded, not really addressing what she'd said.

She tried for one last tidbit. "Well, if Rashad didn't go to you, and he didn't go to Hunt or his brother, where would he go?"

Taylor pinched the end of his nose, as if the stimulation of mild pain could help him remember. "His grandfather's in a nursing home. So I guess his aunt's his closest relative. You might try her."

The aunt again. "Okay. Do you know her name?"

"Sorry, I don't."

"Well, I won't take up any more of your time, then—except for one little thing." She held out *Mahogany Hall*. "You forgot to sign my book."

On the title page, he wrote, *For Talba Wallis—a Baroness in detective's clothing*.

She read it in surprise. "I didn't know you knew about that."

"You know that poem, 'I Am Like a Cat'? I teach it."

"What? You *teach* it?" She had no idea her work was being taught at the university level. "I just conducted an interview with a man who teaches me?"

He stood up and held out his hand. "I admire your work very much."

"You have got to be kidding."

"It couldn't be more true."

She left feeling all the wrong stuff—utterly disconcerted, and more or less walking on air. And slightly in love with the man.

Maybe it hadn't been such a bad day after all. Still, she was exhausted.

Chapter Ten

Any hopes she had of a quiet evening were destroyed the minute she opened the door and smelled chicken frying. Miz Clara didn't fry chicken just for herself and Talba.

"Sandra, where you been?" her mother sang out, her words more upbeat than accusing. She was happy.

Talba looked at her watch. It was barely five-thirty, an hour before she normally returned. "Mama, I'm early."

"Well, good. Corey and Michelle are coming over. You can make a pie or somethin'." Talba's brother and his wife, she meant. There'd been a time when Talba didn't really get along with them, but that had changed with the arrival of their baby, Sophia Pontalba. Both she and Miz Clara doted on the kid, and if Michelle was coming, Sophia was—Michelle was an ardent breast-feeder. With her niece in the house, Talba really couldn't say she was too tired to participate.

She changed into jeans and went into the kitchen. "It's October," she said. "How about gingerbread?"

"Mmm. Gingerbread be good."

Talba whipped up the confection and retired to look at a few of Rashad's poems before the onslaught. Instead, she found herself seated before the computer, trying to locate Rashad's aunt. Marlon was listed, along with a Walter Daneene, whose number she wasted no time in dialing. But it had been disconnected, and there was no new number.

She flipped quickly through Rashad's book for any mention of Kerry, but happy family sounds filled the house before she got anywhere. Smoothing her hair, she hurried to the living room to greet the other Wallises.

Corey, with his fashionable shaven head, was a doctor, Michelle a full-time mother. They were a handsome couple, though Michelle came from a very different milieu from that of the Wallises. She was a Creole, one of the city's elite light-skinned blacks. In a way, Corey's was as much a mixed marriage as if his wife had been white. So far, little Sophia took after the Wallises.

Talba trotted into the room. "Where's that girl?" she said. "Sophia, you here?"

The baby bounced on Michelle's shoulder, reaching out a hand to Talba. Talba greeted the adults quickly, eager to relieve Michelle of her wriggling little burden. Miz Clara went in the kitchen to make some gravy, and in a little bit, Talba returned the baby and followed to make a salad. Miz Clara wasn't big on salads, but Talba and Michelle were, so she sometimes went along with it. In all innocence, Sophia had made everybody more accommodating.

When they were all seated—Sophia in a high chair that Miz Clara had bought for just such occasions—Miz Clara turned to Corey to "ask the blessin'." This sometimes annoyed and embarrassed Talba, but it was one of those accommodations. For one thing, the custom wasn't her own, but she had other objections—first the paternalism of having it done by the ranking male; second, the longwindedness of said male. Unable to confine himself to gratitude for the food, Corey always used the occasion to thank God for everything from good weather to little Sophia's perfect fingers and toes. Talba half expected him one day to express his thanks for the fortuitous illnesses that he treated so lucratively, but it wasn't tonight. Tonight, he was waxing fulsome, if not particularly eloquent, about New Orleans being spared from the hurricane, making much of driving rain and merciless wind, when someone banged on the door.

Not merely knocked, but banged as if they were serving a warrant. Corey stopped in mid-appreciation. Miz Clara exclaimed, "Oh, Lord, it's the po-lice!" and shrank into her chair.

Corey pushed back his own chair, his face grim, but Talba was faster. Whoever it was had to be there for her.

And it couldn't be good news.

Instead of flinging open the door, she mustered as much calm as she could. "Who is it?" she asked quietly.

"Talba? It's Janessa."

Talba opened the door a crack. "What the hell are you doing here?"

"I gotta talk to you."

"Well, now's not the time. And this certainly isn't the place."

"It's an emergency."

"Everything all right?" Corey called.

"It's somebody for me," Talba said. "Y'all go ahead." She slipped out the door and closed it behind her. "Janessa, are you crazy? My family's in there."

Too late, she realized her gaffe. Janessa teared up. "Well, I'm ya sister."

"You're not my mother's daughter. Do you know how much it would hurt her to find out about you like this? What are you thinking of, coming here like this?" Then something occurred to her—her address was deliberately unlisted. "How'd you know where I live, anyhow?"

Janessa stuck out her lip. "I just know."

"You've been following me, haven't you? I didn't know you even had a car."

"Borrowed Coreen's," the girl said.

"They call it stalking. You know that, don't you?"

"You my sister! I got a right."

The door swung open. Corey, who wasn't tall, seemed to loom over the two women. "What's going on out here?"

"This is my business, Corey. Let me handle it." She prayed Janessa would keep her mouth shut. Corey stood rooted in the doorway. Talba turned back to him and raised her voice to her brother, something she'd rarely done in her life: "I said I can handle it myself."

"You don't look to me like you can."

"Corey, you don't know what you're doing. Come on, Janessa." She grabbed her sister's arm and frogmarched her toward her car. A light drizzle was just beginning.

Something in her tone must have finally gotten through to Corey. He slammed the door, furious.

The danger over, Talba slid to a stop, poised to continue dressing down the girl. But Janessa said, "That my brother?" Her face was so pinched with longing that Talba's attention turned abruptly from the other Wallises. Suddenly she felt immeasurably sorry for the girl.

"Yes. That's Corey, and he's a doctor, and he's your brother and you'll love him. Oh, Janessa, I'm so sorry this had to happen! I really want you to know Corey, and my mama and all of us—but we've got to time it right, or everybody'll be hurt."

For the first time, Janessa looked ashamed. "I didn't think. I don't know why I came here. Shoulda *known!*" Her face scrunched up with the effort not to cry.

But Talba knew why she'd come. Janessa wanted in. She wanted to claim the family she'd never known—possibly causing it immeasurable trouble and pain in the process. And who could blame her? It was what Talba wanted for her. But it wasn't something she could deal with right now. She'd have to eventually, but not now. She said, "Talk to me. What's the emergency?"

"Rashad call."

"He did? When?"

"While ago. But that ain' the first time he call. First he call this mornin', cryin' over Cassie. See, he ain' know about Cassie. He saw it on the news, in the paper, somethin', but he don't know much. He think I know more. He call to find out if I do."

Talba writhed with frustration. "Janessa, the point is not what you know, it's what he knows. If he said he didn't know about Cassie, that means he did know about Allyson. Did he say anything about that?"

Her sister looked thoroughly surprised. "Well, no. He didn't."

Talba sighed. "All right then. What'd you tell him?"

"Told him I didn't know any more than he did. Said the police thought maybe I did it, maybe he did. Told all about being arrested."

"You weren't arrested. Did you ask him where he is?"

"He didn't say." She wore a stubborn look that meant even if he had, she wasn't going to admit it.

"What about the second time he called. What'd he say then?"

"Say somebody shot at him."

"Shot *at* him? Or shot him?"

She thought about it. "Don't think they got him. He didn't say nothin' 'bout that. Say he real scared, don't know what to do."

Talba wondered if Rashad had even called. Janessa was quickly revealing herself as a drama queen. Maybe she'd made the whole thing up just as an excuse to bust in on Talba at home. "Did you tell him to go to the nearest police station?"

Janessa had the grace to look guilty. "No'm, I didn't. I say I talk to you, see what you say. He say he call back later. Didn't leave no number or nothin'."

Her sister had never called her "ma'am" before. Talba took it as a sign of good faith. "He's got to turn himself in," she said. "I'll call Eddie. You stay here for a minute. Got that, Janessa? Here. Don't come inside."

Her sister looked at the ground, shamefaced. "That ain' no way to treat family."

It was true and Talba knew it. But this wasn't the time for grand opera on the family front. She put a hand on the girl's shoulder. "Look, we've got an emergency here. Let's deal with that, okay? I didn't look you up at Eve's Weaves so I could treat you badly. We just have to get our timing down. Can you be patient?"

Sullenly, Janessa nodded. Talba really couldn't wait to turn her over to her mother. With a little exposure to Miz Clara, she predicted a rapid improvement in the girl's manners.

Talba went back in the house to get her cell phone. At the sound of the door opening, Miz Clara stood up, put her hands on her hips, and demanded, "Sandra Wallis, what's goin' on here?"

"It's a client, Mama. I'm sorry, y'all, but I've got to take care of business."

She had used the universal masculine phrase for, "Don't bother me. This is more important than petty domestic matters." But apparently it didn't work as well for mere younger sisters. When she started to her room, Corey stood up, too.

"Sandra, this is inexcusable."

Talba saw red. "What, Corey? Exactly *what* is inexcusable?"

"Crazy people invading your mama's peaceful home. We've got a baby in here, girl. What do you think you're doing?"

"I've got a client that's a little upset, Corey. She came here uninvited and for that I apologize, but I will not tolerate your patronizing paternalism." She regretted the alliteration immediately, even before Miz Clara said, "Hmmph. You talkin' just like one o' ya poems." But at least her mother seemed defused.

To Talba's surprise, Michelle stepped in. "Let's eat, shall we? Corey, she's a grown woman." Disgruntled, Corey sat down. Even Miz Clara sat, though not before delivering another loud "Hmmph."

Talba retrieved her phone and a light jacket. Seeing *Laments* lying on her desk, she picked it up, too, stabbed by a pang of guilt at not having thoroughly perused it. "I'm really sorry about this," she said on her way out. "Sophia, Auntie loves you."

Hearing her name, the baby looked up, smiled, rocked in her chair, and banged on her plate.

Talba closed the door and punched Eddie's programmed number as she walked back to the driveway, where Janessa waited meekly.

His wife answered. "Hey, Audrey, it's Talba. Hope I'm not interrupting dinner."

"Eddie just finished. You want him? Take him." It was her little joke. Unlike Eddie, Audrey and Angie seemed to thoroughly approve of Talba.

Eddie came on. "Whatcha got?"

"Janessa heard from Rashad. He said someone's shooting at him."

"Oh, Lord. Where's he at?"

"Neglected to mention."

She didn't say the rest for fear Janessa would hear, but Eddie supplied it. "So the story goes."

"Right. Says she told him she'd consult with us about what to do. I said, tell him to turn himself in."

"You did right. Did you call the police?"

"Not yet."

"Do it—just to get it on the record. Get that book of his—"

"I've already got it."

"Okay, bring it to the office. I'm going to biker bars tonight, but tell ya what . . . I'm gonna try somethin' first. I'll try to meet ya there in a little while, but if I don't make it, don't get upset."

"Okay if I take Janessa to dinner first?"

"Sure."

"The cell phone'll be on." She slipped it in her backpack. "Okay, Janessa, here's where I start acting like a sister. You hungry?"

The girl brightened. "Can we go to Commander's Palace?" The fanciest place in town.

"We're not dressed for it. I know a Jamaican joint that has reggae. Want to check it out?"

"How about Houston's? I never been to Houston's."

"Sure."

Usually Talba avoided restaurants that dealt in the kind of super-size portions notorious for sparking the obesity epidemic. But with its low light and hospitable feel, its familiar goodies like barbecue and burgers, Houston's proved the perfect choice—luxurious enough, but not so alien it made Janessa uncomfortable. She was visibly impressed to be there. Talba congratulated herself; maybe she was making progress in the bonding arena.

They called the police from their booth.

Audrey had made lasagna fit for the gods, but it was going to be a long evening. Eddie figured too much of a good thing would probably make him sleepy.

"More?" she said, automatically passing the dish.

"Naah. Gotta work. Say, ya know any biker bars?"

"*Biker* bars? Me? Talk to ya daughter." She began clearing.

"She probably only knows the dyke ones."

"*Eddee!* Don't be so hard on her, ya hear?"

He was half-convinced his daughter was a lesbian. One thing: She never introduced her parents to any boyfriends. Another: She was the hardest bitch in town; that was one thing Janessa was right about.

"She's an independent woman, that's all," Audrey called from the kitchen.

"Yeah. Too independent." Ever since she was a baby.

"Call her up. Take her with ya."

Now that, Eddie thought, was a terrific idea. With a great-looking babe like Angie, he'd get a lot more action than he would by himself. Not that he didn't have a good pretext—he'd already thought about that—but the idea appealed to him.

He picked up his cell phone and punched in her number.

"An*gie*. Whatcha doin'?"

"Hey, Dad. Same old stuff. Packing for Monte Carlo. Ordering caviar for this party I'm throwing for Eminem. That kind of thing."

"Who's Eminem?"

"Come on, Dad."

"The junior senator from South Dakota, right?"

"Mayor of Detroit."

"Oh, yeah. Mayor Marshall Mathers."

"Dad! You amaze me."

"Look, forget the caviar. How 'bout going out with your old man?"

"Uh . . . well. That's kind of an unusual invitation."

"Hey, I'm hip. I know who Eminem is. Who ya gonna find who's any cooler?"

"What'd you have in mind? Want to take in a rap concert?"

"Thought we'd hit a few biker bars."

"Uh-huh. Pick me up on your hog."

"I'm serious. We found out Austin's a biker. I'm going to ask around."

"Okay. Now it's my turn. Who's Austin?"

"You remember. Allyson Brower's son."

"You gotta be kidding. That woman's son's a biker?"

"Never more serious. Listen, Angie, you could really help me here."

To his amazement, she burst out laughing. "Dad, you're too much—you know that? Swear to God, Talba's a fantastic influence on you."

"I don't know what you're talkin' about."

"Well, think about it. A year ago, would you have asked your innocent daughter to go to a biker bar with you?"

"Since when have I had an innocent daughter?"

She laughed again. "This I've got to see. Eddie Valentino in a biker bar. What you wearin', Dad?"

"Whaddaya mean, what am I wearin'? Who cares what I'm wearin'?"

"Wear those jeans I gave you." He'd never had them on. "T-shirt and baseball cap."

"I don't have any T-shirts."

"Polo shirt then. Pick me up in an hour."

"Sure." He hung up, elated. "Hey, Audrey—she's goin'!"

Audrey came back in, smoothing her apron; beaming. "Now, isn't that dawlin'? A father-daughter night out."

Eddie sighed. At least she wasn't the kind of wife who complained because he had to work.

He was looking for the damned jeans when the phone rang again. It was Ms. Wallis, telling him somebody'd shot at Rashad. Well, that was that. He'd meant to go see the kid's brother, anyhow—it would have to be now. He looked at his watch and figured he could still make his date with Angie.

Since Ms. Wallis was the mistress of the detailed report, Eddie already had Marlon's address. He'd always figured there was more to be had there, and maybe a little ol' gal wasn't the ideal choice to squeeze it out. (Though he'd have worn a dress to work before he'd have used that phrase in his employee's presence—or Angie's or Audrey's, for that matter. Old he might be, but he wasn't stupid.)

He also figured Rashad might have run to his brother's—even if he hadn't done it right away. If he'd really been shot at, he might have decided to become a moving target.

Marlon answered the door with a beer in his hand and from his slightly vague, out-of-focus look, Eddie figured it wasn't his first.

"Yeah?" said his host. Not a good sign. He hoped Marlon wasn't a mean drunk.

"Marlon Daneene? I've got some news about your brother."

He hadn't tried to look particularly grim—no point giving the man a heart attack—but he saw the fear spread over Daneene's face. Okay, so Rashad wasn't with him.

"He's all right so far as I know, but I've to talk to you about him."

"You a cop?"

Shame you couldn't claim to be one, he thought. That would have been the easiest lie. In this case, the next best thing would probably be to tell the truth. "No, I'm working for a friend of his—"

"Wait a minute. Some lady come by; tell me that." Eddie could hear a television blasting out commercials in the background. Funny how you could always tell commercials from regular programming; they sounded even phonier.

"That was Ms. Wallis," Eddie said. "She's my associate. We're very worried about your brother, Mr. Daneene. He called his friend Janessa and told her someone—"

"Well, he ain' call me. I don't b'lieve what ya sayin'. Why he call some gal, not call his own brother?"

Eddie shrugged. "Maybe he thinks the police have your phone tapped. Listen, I've really got to talk to you about this. He told Janessa someone took a shot at him."

But Eddie'd lost him. Daneene had turned sullen. "This some sort of trick? Why I'm s'posed to b'lieve a thing like that?"

"Well, look, he may be in danger. My daughter's his lawyer. Could you just—"

"Why Rashad need a lawyer? How he get one if nobody know where he is?"

Eddie was losing patience. "My daughter is willing to work for him on a *pro bono* basis—meaning she won't charge for her services—if he'll come in and talk to the police. If you'd just tell him—" He held out his card, but Marlon interrupted again.

"I don't need this shit." The black man slammed the door.

Eddie tucked the card under the door and walked quickly back to his car, which he'd parked discreetly half a block away. He got in and hunkered down to wait.

Ten minutes later, about the time it would take to take a whiz, make a couple of calls, explain things to the wife, and find a jacket, Marlon came out and drove away. Eddie followed him to a small, neat bungalow in the Irish Channel and watched him ring the doorbell. After a while he began banging on the door, shouting something. Though a porch light was on, as well as a couple of lights inside, no one answered. Marlon kicked the door and left.

Noting the address, Eddie followed to see where else he'd lead. But he only drove home, slowly—as if he'd suddenly realized he'd drunk too much to be doing this. Eddie extracted his cell phone and called Talba. "Ms. Wallis, you at the office?"

"Sorry—still at dinner."

"I can't meet ya tonight. But go to the office anyway, find out who lives at 4921 Laurel Street, and run a background check on 'em. Then read those poems real carefully and write me another report on anything that could be a clue to where the kid would go."

Chapter Eleven

Talba deliberately kept the conversation away from the two murders and Rashad during dinner. This was another of Eddie's tactics: "Forget the Alamo. Just leave it alone for a while. Catch 'em off guard."

But in the end, she found she didn't have to return to the subject. Janessa kept doing it herself—remembering Allyson and Cassie, fretting about Rashad, speculating as to what had happened. If there was anything to Eddie's theory, this was the mark of an innocent person. A guilty one, according to him, would avoid the subject at all costs.

Still, it gave her a chance to bounce a few things off an insider. "Janessa," she said, "I talked to a few of Rashad's friends today. First, Marlon; then Arnelle, the Montjoys, and Wayne Taylor."

Janessa had barbecue sauce nearly from ear to ear. She applied a napkin to her mouth, looked at the resulting smears, said, "Owweee, this is good! What they say?"

"Allyson got quite a few negative reviews."

Her sister shrugged. "Well, I liked her. She real nice to me and Rashad."

"Did she pay you on time?"

She shrugged again. "She tight with a dollar. But give her time, she pay. I don't mind."

"Some businesswoman you are."

"Who you think you are? My big sister?" Janessa smiled.

"Sorry. It did sound like that." *And probably will again*, Talba thought, amazed at how easily she'd slipped into the role. She changed the subject. "Tell me something. Did Hunt Montjoy ever visit Allyson?"

"Ummm . . . don't think so. He come see Rashad sometime."

"So he was around, right? Did he ever hit on you?"

"Hit on me?" She started laughing so hard Talba could see the half-chewed food in her mouth; she prayed it wouldn't spew out all over the table, but she didn't have her hopes too high. Janessa was braying. "I wouldn't call it hittin' on me, exactly. See, there I am paintin' the mural and he comes in the bathroom, unzips, whips out his dick, and says, 'How you like this, baby?' "

Talba was appalled. "What's the matter with you, girlfriend? You're right—that's not hitting on you—it's practically assault."

"No, it wadn't, it really wadn't. He just messin' around. 'Cause the next thing he does, he turns around like I'm not even there, and takes a leak."

She was still laughing, but Talba was speechless. Finally she said, "And you stood there and watched, or what?"

"You crazy? 'Course I didn't stand there and watch. I ran outta there screamin'—guess tha's what I was supposed to do. Miz Allyson, she come runnin', gets the story, I think she's gon' be real mad. And, really, I think she was a little put out. She make him apologize when he come outta there. He say he don't mean nothin', somethin' like that. Later she tell me how he an 'eccentric genius,' he's not like regular people, and I got to make allowances. When she go 'eccentric genius,' Rashad spin his finger—"

"What?"

"You know." Janessa made the sign for "crazy." "Some reason it struck me funny. That's what I was laughin' at—never did know if he meant Allyson or Hunt. Both of 'em eccentric, you want to know what I think."

It was just the sort of thing Hunt Montjoy was known for, the kind of story men tell on each other, tears flying out of their eyes from laughing so hard. She couldn't imagine why Janessa found it funny, except that her sister had evidently become enmeshed in the rhythms of the household. Bizarre behavior had begun to seem commonplace to her. What Allyson's reaction meant she couldn't imagine—except maybe an impulse to avoid legal action. If there was one good thing about Hunt Montjoy as a person—not a writer—she hadn't heard it yet.

Not even from his buddy Wayne.

She ran the other nutballs by Janessa, but she didn't get much back. It didn't matter—this wasn't a working dinner. It was the first dinner the two sisters had ever shared and they'd gotten through it without tears, sulks, blows, or gunshots—a raging success, in Talba's opinion.

Janessa was contemplating dessert when Eddie called. The girl came alert. "Eddie hear from Rashad?"

"He didn't say, but I don't think so." Janessa wore such a puppy-dog look Talba could remember the desperate, yearning loves of her own younger self.

Given the kid's weight problem, she disapproved of dessert, but she let her have it anyhow. Then she hurried her out of the restaurant, told her to call if Rashad surfaced in any way, and returned to the office, per Eddie's instructions.

She ran the Laurel Street address through a database and found its owner was Felicia Dufresne, a gorgeous name in Talba's opinion. Dufresne was forty-five and had once made news when she was interviewed in connection with a crime in her neighborhood. Talba read the lurid story with satisfaction, reflecting that the best thing she'd ever done was get access to Angie's LexisNexis: The news story said Felicia was a clerk in the assessor's office. From another source, Talba learned she had no liens against her, and owned her modest house. A perfectly ordinary woman, to all appearances. Rashad was twenty-two and Marlon slightly older— Dufresne could be their mother. Or maybe the aunt. Talba wished she had a way of checking her race, but until Louisiana put marriage and birth records online, even she couldn't figure a way to do it.

She put the report on Eddie's desk, and turned her attention to the book of poems. Flipping through it, she found an entire section about a woman the poet had apparently loved. Why hadn't she noticed this before, she thought? And realized it was because they weren't attached to anyone's name, being entitled merely "Street Songs." Some were written from the woman's viewpoint. The woman had been in love, too, but not with Rashad. These were about crack cocaine, about the ritual and the smoke and the high and the crash; about the cravings, and the mess her life had become; about her attempts to love someone who loved her—the poet, Talba imagined—and her failure to love anything at all except her habit.

And some were from the poet's point of view. They were not character studies—they were about the way he loved her. About looking for her in crack houses and bus stations and shelters. About helping her get sober, once even taking her to rehab in another state, only to watch her decline again. The woman had eventually died of an overdose.

In the poems, he called her Celeste, but Talba suspected that wasn't her real name. If the poems were autobiographical, Wayne wasn't kidding about Rashad's penchant for broken wings.

Talba also found a poem entitled "Paw-Paw"—a portrait of a man who faced great odds, but always maintained his dignity, mostly through the sheer strength of his religious faith, something the poet couldn't share—indeed treated with the greatest irony. Clearly, he had tremendous respect for his grandfather, but not a lot for the God who had treated him so badly and who, eventually, had even taken the old man's mind. To Talba, this was one of his best poems—simple and moving; more direct than some of the others. She suspected it had been written more recently, perhaps after studying with Wayne Taylor.

Of special interest, though, were two sections she'd skipped in her earlier effort to find material on Cassie and Janessa. The first was entitled simply "Places," and the second, "Boy on a Bike." The "Places" section contained poems about the lake, about the neighborhood where Rashad had grown up, about City Park, his grandfather's nursing home, the house where he'd lived as a boy ("House of Fear"—that was interesting).

There were eight in all.

And there were a dozen poems about a young boy's bike rides. As Marlon had mentioned, Rashad had grown up on Chippewa Street, near the St. Thomas Project, once the toughest and meanest neighborhood in the city. The project had since been torn down, but it had apparently loomed large in Rashad's consciousness as a kid. Against his mama's wishes, he'd ridden his bike there, as well as all along Tchoupitoulas Street, near the Jackson Street Ferry and the wharves that lined the river. The poem called "Celeste" was the one that caught her eye:

> She say, "Whatever you do, boy,
> Don't go in them projects;
> They got drugs there, and real bad things
> Turn you into a jailbird,
> Maybe a corpse."
>
> So I find me a secret place,
> Down near the old abandoned factory,
> Pretty blue place where no one go.
> But I can
> Turn into a wharf rat.
> Celeste be my tree house,
> My fort,
> Be where I go if I gotta get away.
>
> Later, when I'm grown up,
> Be where I take my true love
> In the dark,
> With all them rats;
> Be our heaven.
> Other side be the river—
> You can look out through the cracks
> And see Algiers,
> See the bridge.
> Own the whole world.

Tchoupitoulas ran from Canal all the way to Audubon Park, and many of the poems had to do with exploring it. What Rashad was talking about here had to be the old Celeste Street Wharf, just off Tchoupitoulas, almost under the bridge. Under "Places," he had one about that area, too, called "Jackson Street Ferry," that mentioned the "sky-blue stretch of the Celeste Street Wharf." And he'd named his "true love" in "Street Songs" Celeste. One of the "Street Songs" had to do with taking her to "a secret place" to detox, a dark place, with rats, where you could see the river.

All this was way too coincidental—almost transparent, it seemed to Talba. Her heart thumped as she wondered if it was ridiculously obvious, therefore couldn't possibly be where he was.

But she thought of the universal writers' dilemma—obscurity. Of the way you could write about your worst enemy or your secret crush in a perfect cocoon of safety—the certain knowledge that he or she would never see your work. The hardest thing about bring a writer—particularly a self-published poet—was getting read. She wondered if the police would think to read *Laments*. And thought not. At any rate it wouldn't be the first thing they'd do—any more than it was the first thing Talba had done. If Rashad had nowhere to go, his old fort would be a natural; that is, if not for the fact that he'd published its existence. No one she'd questioned had mentioned it, though. She had to wonder why.

She got together the report on Dufresne, and then marked the references in the book, along with a note about her theory, put them on Eddie's desk, and went home, hoping to find a dark, quiet house.

She breathed a sigh of relief as she saw that her wish had apparently been granted. Corey's BMW was gone, and the house was dark except for a porch light, left on for Talba. She crept in and turned on a living room lamp, but she nearly screamed when she saw that the room wasn't empty. Her mother, clad in nightgown, robe, and her old blue slippers, was asleep in a rocking chair. That is, she had been asleep. She was now in the process of forcing herself awake.

Her mother's face was drawn, and she had taken her wig off, displaying a near-burr haircut that was actually very becoming. She wore it because she cleaned houses for a living. With a bandanna tied round her head, she was ready for anything. In the dim light, despite the tension on her face, she looked younger than she was, and quite pretty.

"Talba?" she said, and her voice was oddly vulnerable. "Corey say that girl look just like ya, baby."

Her mother almost never called her "baby"—or anything else that passed for an endearment. A half-judgmental "girl" that made Talba wish she were something more acceptable, like maybe a boy, was about as close as she came.

Without warning, Talba felt tears flow. "Oh, Mama!" she sobbed, and went to hug her mother. She had to bend down to do it, and it was awkward with Miz Clara sitting down, but her mother felt soft and comforting; Talba felt a rare surge of love. Most of the time, Miz Clara was just there, more or less a juggernaut. Talba knew that she loved her, but usually, she experienced her as an obstacle to be gotten around. Tonight she felt tender towards her, especially when her mother murmured uncharacteristically, "It's all right, baby. It's all right."

"Mama, you should be in bed."

"Tried that. Couldn't sleep."

"I'm so sorry, Mama—I was trying to protect you."

The old spark flared. "You don't think ya mama's strong enough to know Denman Wallis got a grown-up love-child? How stupid ya think I am? I know he had a woman, I even know he had a baby—you *know* I know that. Stands to reason she gotta grow up, hadn't she? What ya think ya doin'?"

"I know how you hate talking about Daddy." Miz Clara winced at the word—she'd forbidden her children to refer to Wallis as their daddy, a term she maintained he'd never earned, even though he fathered them.

"This ain't about Denman Wallis. This about my deceitful daughter, goin' behind my back!"

"Mama, I said I was sorry. Listen, I'm going to tell you all about it. You want a glass of wine?"

Being a church lady, Miz Clara eschewed alcohol except on special occasions, which usually meant late at night when her daughter brought up the notion of forbidden fruit. As always, she treated the idea as an entirely unexpected and delightful invitation to a rare treat. "Why, I b'lieve I would," she said.

Talba went and poured them both a glass of Chardonnay, gulping down nearly half of hers on the way back to the living room. She handed the other glass to her mother and sat on the sofa.

"The Reverend Clarence Scruggs told me to find her. He told me it was something constructive I could do after—you know." She referred to certain horrifying revelations about her own childhood that came to light about the time she went to work for Eddie. She shrugged. "So I found her—and she didn't want anything to do with me. What was the point of telling you? It would have just upset you."

"Hmmph," Miz Clara said.

"I only saw her once before this week. She called me yesterday—in the middle of Hurricane Carol."

Miz Clara smiled. By now she'd had a few sips of wine herself. "Hurricane Janessa," she said.

"You got that right. She's a handful—did you hear her talk? She's got the worst grammar of anybody I ever heard. But she's a million times better than when I first met her. She was a mess then—fat, sloppy, didn't care about herself; she didn't have any hope, Mama. And she was stubborn! She didn't want me in her life for any reason. Then when she called the other day, she told me I inspired her—that she knew if I was her sister, and I could make it in the world, she could, too. She was doing real well, too—until, uh, something bad happened. She called me to help her with that. So I'm trying to."

Miz Clara rocked for a while, maybe letting it sink in, maybe thinking. Finally, she said, "Ya did right, baby. Miz Clara's prouda ya."

Talba started crying again. This just wasn't the way her mother talked. "Oh, Mama, you really think so?"

Her mother nodded. "I know so." Talba suspected that the mention of the Reverend Clarence Scruggs—an old family friend—had something to do with her sudden approval. "This is a poor, deserted child Denman Wallis left helpless in the world, just like he left you and Corey. Miz Clara wouldn't turn her back on some innocent child."

I hope to hell she's innocent, Talba thought.

"You bring that girl to me."

"What?" Talba wasn't sure she'd heard right.

"You heard me," Miz Clara said, and went to bed.

Chapter Twelve

Angie had her own snug house in the Bywater—not at all a safe neighborhood, in Eddie's opinion, but she insisted the values there were great. She came running out to the car in black jeans, black Harley-Davidson T-shirt, and black bomber jacket. *Now I know she's a dyke*, Eddie thought, but he didn't say it. If it were true, he didn't want to find out by making a stupid joke. And he didn't want the revelation to screw up his focus.

Eddie didn't know every biker bar in town, but he'd figured he could go to one and find out where the others were. There were some on Decatur, in the French Quarter, and that was as good a place to start as any. Austin evidently wasn't local and someone who wasn't would naturally gravitate to the French Quarter.

"I called around," Angie said. "There's this one bar on Decatur Street—"

"Checkpoint Charlie?"

Her mouth pursed in disdain. "That's a pussy bar compared to this one."

"Angie, ya know I hate it when—"

"'Scuse my French," his daughter said. "Let's go there first anyhow. Have a beer, get warmed up. We can park in that lot on Elysian Fields. You like my outfit?"

"Where does a nice girl get a Harley T-shirt?"

"Woke up in it one day."

He winced. "Christ, Angie. Couldn't ya just say ya got it at a yard sale?"

Her laugh trilled in the warm air. "Come on, Dad. Look at it. It fits perfectly." Indeed, it clung to her breasts, though he didn't feel too comfortable looking at them. "I was kidding."

He was too unnerved to say another word till they were in the bar, which was on the corner of Decatur and Esplanade, the border of the French Quarter and the Faubourg Marigny. Maybe that was why it was called Checkpoint Charlie; he'd never thought to ask. The sign outside said it was a bar, grill, "gaming room," and Laundromat. One-stop shopping for your Quarter rats and Faubourg crawlers. Indeed, it did have a few washers and dryers in a side room, a bunch of video poker machines in the bar proper, and a sort of stage with a pool table on it.

A band that didn't seem to have practiced was blaring to a near-empty house. An older couple sat at a table, apparently rapt. Maybe their kid was the guitarist. Two guys played pool on the elevated space to the right. A couple of hard cases sat at the bar. And the bartender was holding his ears. Eddie put him at about fifty, but a rode-hard-put-away-wet kind of fifty. He was skinny and had bad skin. Heroin addict, most likely. His face was scrunched up from the noise.

"Couple drafts," Eddie said, holding up two fingers and pointing. When the man had brought the beers, he winked at the bartender. "Great band."

The man closed his eyes and held his head. "I'd rather be in Fargo."

"You worked here long?"

"What?" the man shouted.

"You want to fuck?" Angie hollered. Eddie felt the blood rush to his cheeks.

"Say again?"

Angie gave her head a "never-mind" shake.

"What the hell ya doin'?" Eddie said.

She laughed again, but he couldn't hear it in the din. She leaned close to his ear. " 'Scuse my French, Dad. Just checking. If he didn't hear that, we're screwed."

He wished he thought it was as funny as she did. But what the hell, he'd bought two beers. Why waste 'em? He pulled out a bogus card he'd brought and showed it to her. It said, E. VALENTINO and on the next line, HEIR HUNTER.

He gave it to the bartender, who looked like he was about to pass out from the pain in his ears. The band seemed to be getting louder and louder. "Looking for somebody," he shouted, and just about then the musical number ended. He'd broadcast the question to the entire assemblage.

It really stole the band's thunder. The rapt couple applauded madly—clearly their son really was in the god-awful band—but everyone else, including the musicians, stared at Eddie. "Uh, sorry," he mumbled.

One of the pool players started over to him. His eyes were wild, like he was on angel dust. "Hey, you guys cops?" he demanded. He had tattoos up and down his arm, a scraggly beard, and matted black hair. Gently, Angie touched his illustrated bicep. "Nice," she cooed.

The guy calmed down. "Always wanted to dance with a cop."

Eddie said, "Hey!" and now Angie touched him as well. "Take it easy, Dad. Things are just getting good."

Bringing her had been a terrible mistake. She had no idea how out of control a guy like this could get. The pool player put an arm around Angie's shoulder, but she wriggled away. "Chill, cutie-pie. My dad's givin' away goodies."

Cutie-pie smiled evilly, and grabbed at her again. "Meanin' you, baby? Tell the old guy *adios*."

She danced away, smiling. "No, really. Look at this." She showed him Eddie's card.

The guy stared at it, so obviously out of his depth Eddie figured he couldn't read. "Ya know what an heir hunter is?"

"I know what an air *head* is. Hey, ya hear about the blonde with the two balloons in her bra?"

"Oh, fuhgeddaboutit." Disgusted, Eddie slid off his bar stool. "Come on, Angie. Let's get outta here."

The bartender said, "Hey, I know what you are. Somebody inherits somethin', you find him, you get a percentage."

"That's right."

Angie winked at the redneck. "Hear that, baby? I'm Angie, by the way." She stuck out her hand to shake. *Don't*, Eddie thought, *you'll prob'ly get AIDS*.

"Chuck," the guy said, and kissed her hand. It was all Eddie could do not to knock his teeth out.

Angie put on a disappointed look. "Well, you aren't him then. Guy's name is Austin."

Chuck was so loaded he couldn't even follow the conversation. "What guy?"

"Guy's gonna get the coins." She turned to the bartender. "What about you, sugar—you Austin?"

"How much money is it?"

Eddie said, "I'll take that as a no." He put a twenty on the counter. "Know any Austins?"

The bartender looked doubtful. "My second cousin—but he lives in Oklahoma."

Eddie shook his head regretfully. "It's not him. I mean— what's his last name?"

"Purcell."

"Uh-uh. Well, thanks for your help."

Chuck said, "Hey, Angie, you aren't leavin', are ya?"

She turned to Eddie, as if all she wanted in the world was to stay and discuss opera with Chuck. "We have to leave?"

Eddie shrugged, kind of getting into it, wondering what she'd pull next.

"Dad's not so young as he used to be." She patted her jacket pocket. "Needs a bodyguard."

Chuck's eyes peeled back. "You packin'?"

The bartender was starting to look slightly panicked. He flicked his eyes at the open door, searching for the beefy dude standing casually on the sidewalk. The bouncer took a step inside. "Well, thanks for all your help," Eddie said again, and this time handed Chuck a twenty. He wondered if he should give the bouncer one, too, decided he didn't really need to.

As Chuck turned happily away, Eddie could see that the back of his T-shirt said, IF YOU CAN READ THIS, THE BITCH FELL OFF.

"What the hell ya tryin' to prove?" he said when he had Angie to himself again. She started to cross Esplanade. "You could have started a riot in there."

"Oh, Dad, you think I've never been to Checkpoint before? Come on—I'm having fun. This other place is right up the street."

"She's having fun," Eddie mouthed, thinking maybe he was, too.

"That place caters to off-duty wait staff. It's nothing."

"That Chuck wasn't no waiter."

"And the occasional drugged-out loser. I think the bikers only come for certain bands. From the look of the bartender, it was his first night—no wonder he didn't know anybody."

"Probably his last," Eddie grumbled, "he don't want to go deaf."

"I'm not sure of the name of this other place. My buddy said I'd know it by the bikes."

They walked a block or two in relative silence, except for Angie's remarks to the various lowlifes who kept hitting on her. "How do you stand this place?" Eddie complained. "One thing I hate, it's the French Quarter. Crime, noise, no parkin' places— and the *stink*. Oh, man, the stink."

Angie inhaled deeply. It was a warm night and the air was particularly redolent. "Beer. Exhaust fumes. Vomit. You gotta love it." He couldn't believe she was the same kid he used to take to get ice cream cones.

"Aren't you hot in that jacket?"

"Very hot. Just ask Chuck."

Eddie thought, *At least he's a guy.*

"Hey, look up there. That must be the place." She pointed to a section of sidewalk heavy with hogs. "Ugh. Yamahas. Another pussy place."

"Angie, ya just *gotta* talk that way?"

She pulled his baseball cap over his eyes. "'Scuse my French."

Eddie looked for a sign announcing the name of the bar, in case he had to tell 911 where to come. It didn't seem to have one.

"Let's go in," Angie said. Mercifully, no band was playing. But the place was a lot livelier than Checkpoint.

All the men seemed to be dressed in black, with greasy jeans and greasy hair. He felt out of place in his never-worn Levi's and polo shirt, but figured it was nothing to the way Angie must feel. The women had on halter tops that barely covered their nipples. Next to them, she looked like a nice kid from out by the lake.

Which in no way prevented her instantly attracting the attention of every male in the place. Eddie could feel a dense cloud of testosterone ooze from their pores and engulf her. She didn't seem to notice.

The bartender was young and thick through the shoulders. Like the last one, he wore a ponytail. Some kind of uniform, maybe. But at least his hair was clean.

"Hey, Joe," Angie shouted. "Whatcha doin' here?"

"Hey, Ange. Long time no see."

"Hey, this is my dad. Dad, Joe. He used to work at Port of Call."

Eddie thought the man blushed, like maybe Angie had had a fling with him. Who the hell was this girl?

"Hey, Mr.—uh—"

"Valentino," Eddie said. For God's sake, she'd taken the guy home and hadn't even mentioned her name. He wondered if it was his shirt she was wearing. Joe shook hands with him, and said, "What can I get for you?"

"The usual," Angie said. "Dad?"

"Draft." He waited to see what Angie's "usual" might be. Joe brought her an Abita Amber, the universal New Orleans yuppie beer. At least that part made sense. Kind of. Joe turned to another customer.

Eddie said, "Nice friends ya got."

"Who, Joe? Used to date a friend of mine. If 'date' is the operative word."

"He's got a crush on ya," Eddie ventured, wondering if "friend" was a euphemism.

She nodded. "Yep. He does. Nice guy. Hey, I see a couple of guys in aloha shirts. I bet Austin wears aloha shirts—what do you think?"

"Sounds right."

"I'll ask Joe if he knows 'em. Hey, Joe, how long have you been here?"

"Couple months."

She pointed out the men in question. "You know those guys?"

"No. Why?"

But she didn't have time to answer—someone yelled for his attention. She leaned back against the bar. "Nice little place," she said.

Eddie looked around and wondered what planet she was from. "If you like beer and puke fumes."

Angie sniffed. "Home, sweet home." He wondered how much of this was an act and how much was real. "Let's just hang awhile before we start asking questions. See if we can make a few friends." She turned to the woman next to her. "I love your outfit. Mind if I ask where you got those earrings?"

Next thing he knew she was embroiled in heavy girl talk. Miserably, Eddie tried to figure out who looked friendly enough to approach. He finally went to the end of the bar, where a guy in a T-shirt much like Angie's was drinking by himself. The guy was burly with the requisite long hair, gray in this case, and a healthy beard—probably a chest and backful, too, Eddie thought, and knew Audrey would say, *You should talk*. The guy's skin was grayish, as if he'd smoked away his color, and he had eyebrows that could intimidate a squad of marines.

Eddie figured the Saints was always a good place to start, and it turned out the guy was a rabid fan, plus his glass was empty. So after a little football chat and another round, Eddie introduced himself.

"Louis," the guy said, offering a handshake like a wrestling hold. "My friends call me Crab Louis. Ya don't want to get me mad."

"Uh-uh," Eddie said. "Oh, no! Think I'm crazy?"

Crab Louis thought that was pretty funny, so Eddie presented him with a card. "Look, I'm a little out of my depth. I'm looking for a guy likes bikes; I saw ya here and thought, 'That looks like a knowledgeable guy.' Wonder if you can help me with somethin'."

Crab Louis brightened. It was amazing how many people responded to a call for help. "Sure, man. What's up?"

Eddie explained what an heir hunter was.

"You gotta be kiddin'," Crab Louis said. "Ya mean that's a *job?*"

"Yeah, but it's hard damned work. Ya gotta search all the records, find out who's got somethin' comin' to 'em; then ya gotta find 'em. I'm not retirin' anytime soon."

Crab Louis looked disappointed. But then he cheered up again. "Yeah, but think how happy ya make people."

"I try. Right now, I don't know—guy I'm lookin' for's named Austin Edwards. Ya know him, by any chance?"

"No, I don't know no Austin. What's he look like?"

"Well, I'm not sure. But what ya bet he's got tattoos?"

Crab Louis got a big laugh out of that one, too. "Look, what kind of biker is he? Outlaw? Old, like Hell's Angels? Does he belong to a club?"

"Like I said, I'm out of my depth here."

"See, different kinds of bikers go to different kinds of bars. Now what age is he? Ya gotta know that."

Eddie couldn't remember, but he took a guess. "'Bout thirty, I guess."

"Oh. Young guy. You could try the Saturn, maybe."

"The Saturn on St. Claude?" It was a pretty famous bar in New Orleans—but not, to Eddie's knowledge, as a biker bar.

"Lot of the young guys hang there—the real hip ones. You know—white punks on hogs. Blacks go there. Ever hear of bikers who'll hang with blacks? These new kids—man! But I been there myself. I'll never go back, but I been there."

"Hey," Eddie said. "Thanks, man."

He laid a twenty on the bar, but Crab Louis pushed it back at him. "Uh-uh. No, man. Glad to help."

Appearances could certainly be deceiving, Eddie thought, as he wandered back to find Angela. She had shed her jacket and acquired a small circle of friends, both male and female. She made the "come here" sign. "Hey, Dad! Over here."

He made it back to her, pointed at the door.

"Gotta go," he heard her say. "That's my dad." He felt a surge of pride—she'd admitted to being related to him. She grabbed her jacket and joined him. "Johnny White's," she said. "Or the Saturn."

"Yeah, I found a guy said the Saturn."

"Well, Johnny White's is in the neighborhood. Why don't we go there first?"

As they walked, he called Janessa on his cell phone. She answered with a rude "Yeah." But Eddie let it go, knowing she hadn't had the benefit of Miz Clara's parenting.

"Hey, sweetheart. It's old Eddie. You all right?"

"Eddie! Ya find Rashad?"

"I'm tryin', honey. Ya sound sleepy. I'm sorry to wake ya, but I got a question—what's Austin look like?"

"Austin? Thought ya was lookin' for Rashad."

"I think Austin might be able to help us. Did you know they were friends?"

"Uh-uh. They ain' friends. You shoulda heard the way Austin talked in front of him."

Eddie gave up on that one. "Well, look. What does he look like?"

"Like a white guy. How'm I s'posed to tell one from another?"

Eddie sighed. "What color hair?"

"Brown, I guess, Kinda long."

"Height and weight?"

"Not too tall. Heavy, kind of."

Typical biker, Eddie thought.

"I mean, not fat like you or anything. Just kinda stocky. Oh, wait. He got a fish on him."

Like she was describing a mole. Eddie waited.

"On his arm, ya know? Real pretty fish. All colors."

A fish tattoo. "The forearm or the bicep? Left or right?"

"Near the hand, kind of. He got other tattoos, too, but can't remember 'em. Colors, though. All around his arms."

"Piercings?" Eddie said, figuring this couldn't be far behind.

"Oooh, yeah. His nose, man. Got this big thing in his nose. Silver, like."

"Okay, dawlin', you go back to sleep now. We'll let ya know if we find Rashad."

He said to Angie, "Real good detective work. We should have been looking for a guy with a fish and a stud in his nose."

His daughter said, "Well, I *figured*. About the stud."

"Hey, Ange—think I'm fat?"

She looked at him carefully. "'Course not. Why would you say that?"

"Just wondering." But maybe he'd lay off the Ferdies for a while.

They worked Johnny White's, using both Austin's name and the body adornments, but only got more suggestions to go to the Saturn—that, and, in Angie's case, certain other suggestions.

When they were in the car, Angie said, "Oh, goody. I haven't been to the Saturn in ages."

"Angie, ya leadin' a secret life or somethin'? Anything ya want to tell me?"

She laughed again. "You and Mom should get out more, you know that?"

"We ain't got the right body art. Say, Ange, ya got any tattoos?"

To his mortification, she pulled her jeans down on the left, exposing an inch or two of white hip. "Check out my dragon."

Eddie kept his eyes on the road. Out of the corner of his eye, he could see something slightly greenish, but he figured he didn't need a better look. "Keep ya pants on, Ange," was all he said. And she laughed again. He didn't know when he'd seen her so happy.

It was a slow night at the Saturn, and Eddie couldn't say he was sorry. Another good thing—his daughter didn't seem to know the bartender.

The Saturn was well known to natives—even the stodgier ones, like Eddie—as one of the more colorful bars in town. He'd heard that, but he'd never been in it. Even though its reputation preceded it, nothing prepared him for the place. It seemed to have once been a corner store and still had characteristics of one, like packages of food piled on the counter, cases of beer on a chair here and there, a refrigerator more or less in the middle of the floor. There were three jukeboxes that he counted, only one of which seemed to work, and a couple of defunct cigarette machines as well. But the place had strange stabs of hipness going for it—leopard covers on inconceivably lumpy furniture, some kind of neon chandelier thing, a ceiling painted with clouds. It also had a lot of paintings, most of which looked to have been done by neighborhood retirees or else kids with more nerve than talent.

Toward the back of the place was a replica of the Statue of Liberty and beside it were three photos—of James Dean, Marilyn Monroe, and Marlon Brando. There was also a crudely painted portrait of the late Princess Di. A back room contained a pool table piled with the kind of thing most people keep in their garages and a sign that said BE NICE OR LEAVE. On one of the beer cases a bumper strip read I'D RATHER BE AT THE OPERA.

A mummy hung from the ceiling.

The night was so slow you couldn't really tell what the regular clientele was, in the event there was one. But one thing Eddie could see—both black and white people came here, some of whom seemed to be from the surrounding neighborhood. There were also preppy-looking folks from Uptown or the 'burbs and people in outfits that ranged from mildly bohemian to outlandish. He didn't see a soul who looked like a biker.

"Probably too early," Angie said. "Or maybe they come on weekends."

One thing—it was a lot less scary here than in those French Quarter dives. He didn't really have a lot of hope, but at least he wasn't afraid of being beaten to death. That is, until some fuzz-faced young punk sidled up to Angie and said, "Hey, babe. Ditch the old guy."

"Forget it, Junior," she answered. "I only need one asshole in my pants."

The guy's face took on a volcanic fury, but Eddie figured he could probably take him. "You heard the lady."

The kid backed away, muttering.

Angie said. "Just like in the movies. Very John Wayne."

Eddie shook his head. "I don't know where ya got that mouth. Talk to the women, okay?"

She turned to her left and started pulling the earring thing again. The bartender didn't look friendly. Eddie looked around for someone who did, and his eyes lit on a woman about his age. She was blond and dressed in black—tiny black tank top with boobs hanging out, upper arms flapping in the wind, little bitty skirt above her knees. Good legs. What the hell, he thought? Angie's idea wasn't bad; women very rarely took a swing at you.

"Quiet night," he said to her.

"How would you know? I never seen you in here."

"There's a reason for that," he said. "My daughter never brought me here before." He pointed to Angie.

"That's ya daughter? Doesn't look like ya."

"Takes after her mother," he said, and realized she'd said it with him.

He started to laugh, but she stopped him. "Next, ya s'posed to say, 'Thank the Lord.'"

"Yeah, I was going to. Buy you a drink?"

"Sure, you can buy me a drink. You a cop?"

He signaled for the drink and smiled. "No, I'm not a cop."

"Ya 'daughter' a cop?" This woman was no Crab Louis.

"No, but you're on the right track. We're investigators." He brought out the card, started to go through the heir hunter spiel, but she wouldn't move on. "Hey, a father-daughter detective team? Really? She really ya daughter?"

"Swear to God." He raised his voice slightly. "Hey, Ange—come here a minute. Tell this lady you're my kid."

Angie finished her conversation and turned back to her father. "I've got what we need."

The blonde said, "Y'all aren't related. No way. This girl's from Uptown."

"Am not," Angie said, and put her arm around her dad. "We're from out by the lake." She put out her hand. "I'm Angela Valentino, and this is my dad, Eddie. Mom's Audrey, brother's Tony."

The woman shook Angie's hand, very ladylike. "Jo Ellen Coulter."

"Dad, I found someone who knows Austin."

"Austin? Austin who? Hey, what's this about?"

Eddie touched her arm. "It's all right. Look at the card. Austin's about to come into some money."

Jo Ellen beamed. "Hey, he is? Well, good for Austin."

Angela said, "You know Austin, too? What Austin?"

"Austin-with-the-fish. Never caught the rest of his name."

The woman Angie'd been talking to joined the conversation. "Austin Edwards. Lives in Venice; comes in on weekends. Cute guy," she said in a proprietary way. Eddie saw that she might have had occasion to know Austin intimately—she was blond, too, and young; very cute in a wholesome kind of way. Like Angie.

"What else do you know about him?" he asked.

"Oh, nothin'. We just talk once in a while."

"Owns a bait shop down there," Jo Ellen said.

That sounded right, Eddie thought. He'd lived in a succession of little fishing towns and he sounded like a notorious underachiever.

"You know the name of it?" Angie asked.

But she didn't. A quick canvass of the bar indicated no one else did either, though most of the regulars had seen the "The Fish Guy" at least once.

"Angela, ya did good," Eddie said when he dropped her off.

Audrey was still up when he got home. "Well? How'd it go?"

"We bonded."

"Aw, Eddie that's wonda'ful! She loves ya, ya know? She just doesn't show it."

"Showed me something, though. You ever seen her tattoo?"

"Oh, sure, Eddie. Angela's got a tattoo, all right. Like I got my nipples pierced."

Eddie grinned. "It might be a thought," he said.

Chapter Thirteen

Talba got to work early and barreled into Eddie's office without even stopping for coffee. She was shocked to see him looking about a hundred and five. Actually, he was just a hair over sixty-six, but he had bags under his eyes the size of her backpack, and on some days, they were the color of raw liver—

on others, cooked liver. She never knew whether the color varied with his degree of fatigue or just with atmospheric conditions. Some days they were even kind of green. Today was a raw liver day.

She said, "You feelin' okay?"

"Never better. Why?"

"You look a little peaked."

"Well, I feel like I'm twenty-five. Spent the evening running down Austin. Turns out he lives in Venice. I need to get down there today, but there's a lot to do first. Good work on Dufresne, by the way."

"How about the poetry? What do you think?" This was the part she was excited about.

He nodded. "You could have something there."

She was a little offended. "You sound pretty underwhelmed. I thought it was a brilliant deduction—Celeste and all that."

He raised a placating hand. "Ya think ya Sherlock Holmes, do ya? Okay, get ya magnifying glass, let's take a ride to the river."

She smiled. In Eddie-speak, it meant she done good. "Your car or mine?"

"Mine. Audrey's, I mean—the port police are less likely to mess with people in a Cadillac than a beat-up old Isuzu." He opened a drawer and took out a handgun. She winced.

"What's that for?"

"The kid could be a murderer. You know that."

"You left your Tee-ball bat at home?" This was Eddie's weapon of choice. It had a nice heft to it, like a blackjack, and it was perfectly legal. His unvarying cover story was that his granddaughter'd left it in the car.

Talba didn't like the gun, and chose to show her disapproval by not speaking until they were in the car. But she couldn't keep it up—her curiosity got the best of her. "What's the deal with Dufresne?"

"I went to see Marlon after you called. Said he didn't know where his brother was, but I think he thought he knew. He rode out to Dufresne's house after I left. Didn't go in, though. I want to know what her connection is. If we don't find the kid at the wharf, I want you to go see her over at the assessor's office. I'm gon' go round up Austin in Venice."

"You're actually sending me out to a New Orleans city office?" Eddie never entered one if he could help it.

"Better you than me," he said as they neared Celeste Street. "I remember when all this was like a beehive."

"See, there's the abandoned factory—from the poem."

Eddie turned onto the service road behind Tchoupitoulas. "Old power plant, I think. Whoops! That wharf's in use. Nobody's hidin' in there." There were a number of roll-down doors on the sky-blue building, the metal corroding away. Some of them were open, revealing piles of lumber currently being removed by a team of workers and heavy machinery. The busy little scene belied a sign saying the wharf was permanently closed.

"I thought it was abandoned," Talba said.

"Let's call the port." Eddie stopped the car and placed a call to the port's information officer. "Hey, I got a question about the old Celeste Street Wharf. What are they using that thing for these days?" No pretext, no identity; just the question. Talba would never have thought of that. Eddie listened for a few minutes and snapped the phone shut.

"They don't berth ships on the other side anymore, but they still warehouse stuff in there."

"Bet anything it's deserted at night. Rashad could still sleep there. Wonder what he does in the daytime?"

"Dream on, Ms. Wallis. He's not there." He started the engine and began to back up. "I'll take ya over to City Hall—I gotta go to Venice."

"City Hall? What for?"

"Felicia Dufresne—you forget already?"

"Trying to."

"Ya want to stop somewhere and get pralines?"

"It wouldn't work for me—I don't have your charm."

Back in the old days, before he had an associate to do his dirty work, Eddie used to arm himself with candy for the bureaucrats, as a kind of low-key bribe. This was because New Orleans civil servants had an even worse reputation than New Orleans cops did before the department clean-up. They were generally considered slow, sullen, rude, uncooperative, and incompetent, for openers. It was common knowledge that every

PI in town would rather hire someone to do a records check in Orleans Parish than face that mess himself.

In Talba's experience, the bad rap was more or less deserved—when she went to get fingerprinted for her PI license, she nearly got arrested because of someone's bad mood. But in her opinion, the bureaucrats probably came by their bad moods honestly: They had to work in the ugliest building in town. In a city of great architecture, citizens have to do their municipal business in the great, flat, beige blight that bears the name City Hall.

"City Cell Block" would have been more appropriate.

The assessor's office was on the fourth floor, and it was all business—a wide pass-through lined with waist-high light gray counters, sections of which were designated for the various wards. Talba had a long wait before anybody bothered to see if anyone was waiting, though once she caught a clerk's eye, opened her mouth to speak, and was told, "I'm on break." Could be understaffing, she thought, unwilling to pass judgment.

Twenty minutes later, when she was finally granted enough of an audience to ask for Dufresne, she was turning into Sandra Day O'Connor.

But when Dufresne herself appeared—in another ten minutes—she seemed as pleasant and cheerful as a hostess. "What can I help you with?" she chirped, in that positive way that indicated she was actually going to help. And she smiled when she said it. Talba was stunned at what a good-looking woman she was. She wore a periwinkle suit and a pair of neat black pumps, and her hair was pulled into a sleek twist. Everything about her said she was a successful woman and happy employee. *Maybe*, Talba thought, *I've lucked out.*

But that was before she said the magic word. As soon as *Rashad* was out of her mouth, Dufresne froze. "And you are . . . ?"

Talba was suddenly so intimidated she almost froze herself. "I'm an investigator working—"

That was as far as she got. "May I see your ID, please?" the woman demanded.

"Sure." Talba popped out her license and badge.

Dufresne studied it carefully. "I don't have to talk to you."

"I'm working for a good friend—"

"Look here, missy, this is my place of work. Who do you think you are, barging in here on non-city business?"

"I thought perhaps—"

"I need you to leave right now."

"But I have some news about—"

"Now!" The woman was yelling and pointing at the door.

Talba figured she'd better get out before Security showed up. But she was about to pop with sentences that hadn't come out. If there was anything she hated, it was someone who interrupted.

However, there was more than one way to skin this cat. Dufresne had to leave the building sometime. Talba looked at her watch. It was nearly eleven o'clock—she was betting she wouldn't have to wait too long. She went out to the little plaza that was one of the few amenities City Hall had to offer and settled down to wait.

It was only about half an hour before Dufresne burst smartly through the door, walking briskly and thankfully alone. Talba simply stepped in front of her, forcing her to skid to a stop. She spat out the words quickly: "Rashad called my sister yesterday. You know he's been shot, don't you?"

Granted, it was a shock tactic, but she was hardly prepared for what happened next: Felicia Dufresne burst into tears. Wasting no time on sympathy, Talba seized the advantage. "Ms. Dufresne, I really am trying to help him."

Dufresne grabbed her by the wrist, snapped, "Come on," and pulled her away from the building. "Where's my baby?"

"Are you his mother?" Talba asked. "My sister's in love with him. I'm trying to help her find him." She wished she'd said that in the first place.

"Tell me who you are and what you know."

Talba told her about Janessa's hiring her, and about the phone call. "What I don't know," she concluded, "is who you are to him. Are you his mother?" she repeated.

"I'm his aunt. He's always been my baby. And he always will be."

It was such a strange answer that Talba was momentarily nonplussed, but this was no time to hesitate. "Here's what I need to know," she said. "Has he called you? Has he been in touch at all?"

Sorrowfully, Dufresne shook her head. "What I know, I know from Marlon. He called last night and said my baby might have been shot, but he didn't know how to reach ya sister. Give me her phone number."

"I can't just give it out. I have to get her permission."

Again, she grabbed Talba's wrist, this time with such force that Talba wondered if she was capable of violence. "You give it to me right now."

Talba snatched her arm away. She reached in her pocket and pulled out a business card. "Write down your phone number. I'll call you when I've talked to Janessa."

Dufresne produced a cell phone. "Call her now."

Talba said, "Look, just keep the card. Let me know if you hear anything."

"I don't need ya damn card. I need Janessa's number."

There didn't seem anything to gain from sticking around. Talba said, "I'm sorry. I have to go now," and walked away. It took all her will power not to look back, so strong—and evidently so volatile—a personality was Felicia Dufresne. She half expected the woman to jump her from behind, but she couldn't show fear; of that much she was sure.

She was shaking when she got to her car. After taking a moment to compose herself, she realized there was a lot wrong with that encounter—a lot more than Dufresne's strangeness and semi-violence. Dufresne hadn't pleaded for Talba to call the minute she knew something.

Which meant she must know something herself. She must want to get to Janessa to call her off.

If Dufresne didn't need her card, fine. She didn't need Dufresne to give her her home number. She had it at the office. She walked back, thinking, deciding what to do next. First, she called the number, just to see what would happen. A man answered.

Rashad, she thought, and hung up. She retrieved her car and set out for Dufresne's house, wondering how long Rashad and Marlon had lived with this woman, and whether it was on Chippewa Street. Dufresne was beautiful, like the mother Rashad painted in the poem he called "Mama," and she said he'd always been her baby. Could he have been writing about her instead of his birth mother? Talba made a mental note to read the poem again.

Dufresne certainly didn't look like someone who'd ever lived a stone's throw from the worst project in town, but a lot could have happened between then and now. Curiously, if she had, she hadn't moved far away from Tchoupitoulas, and she'd never escaped the Irish Channel. Yet the house she occupied now had to be a thousand times better than the one Rashad had grown up in. The neighborhood was nicer by far than the old one and the house itself was the best one on the street. Clearly, Felicia Dufresne had pride and, if not education, at least a healthy respect for it. If she'd raised Rashad—even for a few years—it could explain a lot about the way he was—his love of literature, his ambition, in fact, his brains. She was the sort who'd make a kid do his homework.

Talba banged on the door, which was answered fairly promptly, not by Rashad, as she'd hoped, but by an unkempt man in pajama bottoms. He must be a night worker who hadn't yet gotten up. "Oh," he said. "Thought you were the mailman."

Talba didn't bother introducing herself. This man was half asleep; that could be good. "I'm a friend of Rashad. I mean, a really good friend."

The man smiled. "You Rashad's girlfriend?"

"Yes. Is he here? I've got a whole lot of stuff for him—information, I mean. The po-lice are looking for him."

"No, he ain'."

Talba did her best to look shocked. "But Marlon said—"

"Marlon don't no more know where he is than we do. Came looking for him last night, but Felicia wadn't home. Kept callin' till he got her; she say go to his grandfather. Rashad love his grandfather even more than he love her. Anybody know, she said, it's his grandfather."

"Where does his grandfather live?"

"Place called St. Elmo's. It's a nursing home, like."

"Oh, by the way, is this his mother's father or his father's?"

"Father's, maybe."

"Well, just in case, what's his mother's maiden name?"

He looked at her like she was crazy. "Dufresne. Whatcha think?"

So Felicia was his mother's sister, not his father's.

Talba stopped at a corner store for a sandwich and borrowed a phonebook while she was there. St. Elmo's was on the Chef

Menteur Highway. She went over to Julia Street, bought some flowers, and wended her way to Grandpa.

It was instantly obvious that St. Elmo's was no modern "senior residence" or "assisted living" facility. It was a place where poor people went to die, the old-fashioned kind of nursing home, where withered husks of humans sat around in pajamas, looking as if they'd rather be in bed; where the walls were painted puke green or petunia pink. This one had both colors.

At the front desk, she waited for an attendant, watching the old people nod and pretend to watch television. One couple played cards—a man and a woman who seemed more alert than the others. Finally, a fortyish female attendant appeared, African American and very brisk, wearing a medical smock printed with scythe-like objects that seemed to be faded blue and pink boomerangs. *Who designs these things?* Talba wondered.

"I'm here to see Mr. Daneene," she said.

"Are you a relative?"

She must have guessed right on the name. "I'm his granddaughter. I was supposed to meet my brother, Rashad Daneene. Is he here yet?"

"Oh, yes, we know Rashad. I didn't know he had a sister."

"Did you say yes?" Talba was excited. "My brother's here?"

The woman frowned. "I don't recall saying that. Mr. Daneene hasn't had a visitor in nearly a month." It sounded like a reprimand, and probably was.

"Oh." That was probably all the information Talba needed, but she couldn't think of a graceful way to leave. "May I see my grandfather?" she asked.

The woman smiled. "You're in luck. He's having a good day."

Talba knew that, for Alzheimer's patients, a good day was one on which they were slightly more lucid than others. She hoped the old man didn't realize he didn't know her.

She was relieved to see that he wasn't one of the sad-looking people grouped in the living room, if that was what they called it here. He was sitting up in bed with newspapers all around him.

"He looks at those papers all day," the attendant said. "But when you ax him what the news is, he never knows. You be okay?"

"Yes, thanks." Out of the corner of her eye, she saw the

woman leave. She turned her full attention to the old man in the bed, wondering if he was ever going to look up from the papers.

"Hello," she said. "Do you know me? I brought you some flowers."

He was a thin old man, but despite his thinness he had tiny jowls around his mouth, and his hair was graying—not yet white, but on its way. His eyes were a little sunken, as if he were slowly receding into himself. She suspected that he had long since lost his appetite for food, perhaps for most things.

When he looked at her, she saw something like fear on his face. "Joy?" he said. "No, you ain't Joy. Cain't be Joy."

"No, I'm not Joy," she said, and she was about to introduce herself, but relief appeared so suddenly on his face that she was startled into silence.

"Well, then, you must be Felicia. I get confused. Felicia, you put on weight. I thought Joy done come to see me." He smoothed the newspapers with a hand so thin the skin looked like a scrim of tissue. "The boy come sometime. Tha's about all."

"Rashad?"

He nodded. "My grandbaby. He a *fine* young man. His mama never was no good. *Needed* killin'."

Talba had no concept of how to talk to someone who lived in a different reality. She wanted to follow up on that in the worst kind of way, but she didn't dare risk alienating the old man. He might not have his marbles, but if she threw him off balance, he might figure out she wasn't Felicia. "That's fine talk coming from a nice man like you," she said blandly.

"You live as long as I have, you see most everything. Mmm, mmm. Nothin' ain't black and white no more. Everything happen for a reason."

She sure didn't want him to get on God and it looked as if that was about to happen. "I don't think I remember Joy," she said. "Who was she?"

"What you talkin', girl? You don't remember ya own sister?"

"Oh, Joy. Rashad and Marlon's mother."

"Marlon, yeah. He come see me, too. He gettin' big. Must be nearly grown by now. Pretty soon he'll be down at the hirin' hall like his daddy and his granddaddy before him."

"Marlon's got a painting business, I heard."

The old man shook his head. "He be workin' on the docks. He be down there. You live long enough, you know the way of things."

"Well, Marlon never was the bright one in the family. Rashad got the brains, didn't he?"

At that, the old man started. "They all smart," he said, and there was no mistaking the anger in his voice. "All us Da-neenes, we smart. Cain't get ahead, that's all. Just workin' for the dollar; all we can do."

"I was wondering if Rashad's been here lately." Even as she said it, she realized the futility of looking for him here. Where on earth could he hide in a place like this?

"He here earlier today."

Talba felt a sudden rush of adrenaline. It was possible. The attendant hadn't been there when she arrived. Rashad could have just walked in. "He was here today?" she repeated.

"Umm-hmm. He come most every day."

Well, that couldn't be true. Probably Grandpa's mind was just wandering. "Did he say where he was staying?" she asked.

Daneene looked puzzled. "Don't he live with you?"

"Not anymore. He's been gone a few days. I thought you might know where to find him."

The old man turned back to his papers, apparently ready for the visit to end. "'Spect he be down at the hirin' hall."

"What hiring hall?"

"Down by the docks. You know, where his daddy and I work."

"I don't think his daddy's been there lately."

To her surprise, Daneene laughed. "Nobody seen my son in twenty years. Left ya sister with those two little boys. I always felt responsible."

"It wasn't your fault." She figured she was on safe ground here.

"Shoulda raised him better." Tears appeared in his soft brown eyes; she saw that the whites were faintly tinged with yellow.

This interview wasn't helping her, but she couldn't bear to leave without trying to cheer him up. She scurried around for a vase, something to put the flowers in, glad for the opportunity to check the bathroom (which was empty both of skulking grandsons and vases). "You did the best you could," she said.

"Everybody knows that. He was who he was, that's all. I can't seem to find a vase."

"Shoulda married you instead of Joy. You got a way with kids."

"Well, still, I don't know what you mean when you say Joy needed killing."

"Way she neglected those kids? And drink! Whoa, she could drink. You, too, in those days."

She took a chance. His emphasis—she *needed* killin', not she needed *killin'*—made her think Joy was dead. "What makes you think somebody killed her?" she said. "She ran away, that's all."

"Now, Felicia, you know that's not true. Just because I'm old doesn't mean you can make me believe what's not true. Rashad didn't mean to. He turned out fine—we both know that. It's all that matters."

She couldn't believe what she'd just heard. Rashad had killed his mother? It didn't fit with anything she knew about him. Unless of course you counted the juvenile felony record. And one other thing, maybe—there was something in one of the poems. She struggled to remember it.

"It's all that matters," he said again. "If you hadn't got so drunk and took up with her boyfriend it never woulda happened. It's time for you to go now." He was getting heated up.

"Well, I'll just go get a vase for these."

She went out and asked the attendant for one. As she was arranging the flowers, she said, "Are there any vacancies here? I've got an aunt who's going to need care soon."

The woman shook her head before the words were even out. "We got a two-year waiting list."

So much for Rashad taking over an empty room somewhere in the home. Talba took the flowers back to Mr. Daneene. "We had a nice visit, didn't we?" she said brightly.

He'd forgotten his anger; indeed seemed to have forgotten she was ever there. "Can I do somethin' for you?" he asked politely, as if he'd discovered her trespassing in his living room.

She walked over to the bed and put her hand on his arm. Smiling intently into his face, she said, "You can have a nice day, that's what you can do." She wanted to leave him with a good feeling.

He smiled back at her, for the first time since she'd made his acquaintance.

Talba went back to the office to kill some time till after the work day. She hadn't mentioned it to Eddie, but she was damned well going back to check out that wharf. She just had to bide her time till the boys and their toys had gone for the day. It would still be light between five and seven, say, and maybe a good time to catch Rashad—maybe the time he came back. If he came back.

She tried to find the poem her conversation with Mr. Daneene had reminded her of, but she was shocked at the unreliability of her memory. The "Mama" poem was still all sweet and gooey, just as she remembered, but there was something provocative in it:

> You made up for
> The other one.
> What's done
> Is done—
> But for your beauty
> And your love
> I did my duty
> And maybe above.

And she saw that she was wrong when she told Arnelle Halston that Rashad had written only nice things about his mother. It was the poem entitled "Parents" that struck her now. The poem that started:

> Mama so beautiful, Mother so scary
> Mother with the silver flash,
> Mother with a need to bash.

It was curious that Rashad had changed from "Mama" to "Mother," as if there were two mothers—a good and a bad, perhaps. If the bad one had a need to bash, maybe he had killed her. That silver flash thing bothered Talba.

And so did the end of it:

> I'd like to know
> If I did right

> *By all*
> *Of y'all.*
> *That's what*
> *My fascination is.*

Just what had happened here? Had he stabbed his own mother to protect his aunt? And maybe the rest of the family? If he had, Crockett, the Homicide guy, was already going to know about it—even if juvenile records were supposed to be off limits.

For a couple of hours, she busied herself with employment and prenuptial investigations (which she called "sweetie snoops"), feeling for the first time in days a sense of accomplishment. She and Eddie had worked on hardly anything but Janessa's case all week—and it wasn't worth a penny to the firm. She remembered Eddie's ominous words, "Two days, Ms. Wallis." But he hadn't mentioned the deadline again.

At five sharp, she said good-bye to Eileen Fisher, drove back to the Celeste Street Wharf, parked half a block away, and put her license in her pocket, thinking that if anyone saw her, it might make explaining easier.

The metal doors were closed now, but in some places, they'd separated from the building itself, leaving gaps filled in with pieces of wood more or less just stood on their ends from inside. They'd be easy to shove aside—especially for a young man in his twenties. Talba wondered if she could do it, especially in a skirt. She wished she'd gone home to change.

She looked over the top of one of the wood plinths—which was about chest high. There were wooden boxes inside, and more piles of lumber. With some effort—and quite a bit of trepidation—she jockeyed one of the plinths far enough out of the way to squeeze into the hole it left between the door and the wall. It took maneuvering, but she finally found her footing on solid ground. Her pantyhose had run, but that was about the only damage. Someone like Rashad, she thought, could have just slithered in without moving anything.

Once inside, she closed the hole to hide the tampering. Light came through various holes in the walls, on both sides—levee and river—but it was still semi-dark in the building. Momentarily, she wished she'd brought a flashlight, but her eyes began to adjust immediately.

The space was huge—about as long as a city block—and there were so many piles of stuff, Rashad could slip from one to another as he heard her coming, remaining unnoticed if he wanted to. Best thing was to announce herself as a friend.

"Rashad?" she called. "It's Janessa's sister. Everybody's worried about you."

There was no answer and not only that, Talba felt a stillness in the old building. Her intuition said she was alone.

She walked rapidly towards the bridge and the Central Business District, thinking to turn around and go back toward the Jackson Street Ferry, searching methodically on the way. Every few steps she called quietly to Rashad, but the only answer was an occasional soft rustling, perhaps a rat outraged at the trespass. When she had reached the downtown edge of the building, she slowly picked her way back, searching diligently behind each pile of merchandise and supplies.

She'd gotten only about a quarter of the way when she found Rashad's little nest behind a pile of boxes. She knew instantly it was his. A piece of splotched cardboard had been laid down for a floor, probably something he found in the wharf itself, and on the cardboard were some words written with a felt-tip pen—words that could only have been written by one person. There was also a balled-up shirt, a copy of yesterday's *Times-Picayune* (the one with Cassie's and Allyson's pictures in it) and an empty coffee cup from PJ's—the one on Camp Street, she was willing to bet. She pictured Rashad there, buying coffee and a newspaper, maybe a muffin, looking over his shoulder in case he was recognized, then returning to his nest to read about the death of his friends.

If Janessa's story was true, he might already have known about Allyson—that is, if he'd come back that night. But how could he have felt when he learned of Cassie's death? She shivered, thinking about it.

And realized she was assuming his innocence. If he was guilty, he'd have been reading to find out what the police knew.

Much of the writing on the cardboard had been scratched out, but there was a title that hadn't been: "Celeste Revisited." He'd been writing a poem.

But mostly what he'd written was a lot of false starts:

If I could turn the clock back . . .

Oh, Celeste, that other time was better!

Floating lady, blank-eyed . . .

*This is like that time with mama . . . the nastier the history the
quicker it repeats.*

Each phrase had a line drawn through it, and Talba could see
why. None was a promising beginning. The poet was obviously
suffering, but he hadn't been able to focus well enough to take
refuge in his art. Underneath the crossed-out phrases was a
quote, in huge capital letters:

> POETRY IS EMOTION RECOLLECTED IN TRANQUILLITY!
> —*Wordsworth*

And even after that, he had tried again:

> *Tranquillity just a memory now—*
> *Real life like bad TV*
> *And I gotta find the one-armed man.*

He had crossed that one out, too. She smiled, realizing it was
a reference to *The Fugitive*, the television show in which a one-
armed man frames the hero for murder. She wondered if she
could take it as a sign he was innocent. She could just hear what
Eddie would say: *I wouldn't take it to court, Ms. Wallis.*

She picked up the shirt and gasped as she shook it out. One
arm had been torn off. What was left had big brown splotches on
it. It had to be blood. The splotches on the cardboard did, too.

So perhaps he really had been shot. On the other hand, there
wasn't all that much blood. He could just as easily have hurt
himself in some other way. But she could see that, in a building
as big as this one, with so many hiding places, shooting someone wouldn't be difficult—as long as the shooter was there first.

All he'd have to do would be wait for his prey.

It was starting to get dark, but Talba had no choice except to finish the search—Rashad could be lying somewhere in the vastness of the warehouse, bleeding to death.

She scoured the rest of the building, but found nothing more interesting than a couple of beer cans. She thought of waiting for Rashad to come home, but if he'd been shot here, he wasn't about to return. The combined prospects of pitch dark and rats, no dinner, and probably no luck just didn't add up to a reason to stay.

Excited, she called Eddie as soon as she got back to her car. But for some reason, he didn't answer—maybe he was still in Venice. She left a message detailing what she'd found.

Chapter Fourteen

Eddie put his .38 and one other emergency item in the glove compartment of Audrey's old Cadillac, wishing he had a less conspicuous car. But, against his better judgment, he'd let Ms. Wallis install a Global Positioning System in this one, and it had once come in handy. If Austin had murdered two members of his family, it might again.

It was about a two-hour drive to Venice and Eddie had lots of time to think. Austin was a pretty good candidate, when you got right down to it. At the very least, he might have information that would allow the cops to eliminate his client and get Eddie out from under this money-loser.

He simply could not bring himself to believe that Janessa had done it and, truth to tell, he was rooting for Rashad, too. Everything he knew about the kid made him want him to be innocent; and nothing he knew about Austin made him like him. He was a biker, he'd disappeared after his mother and sister's murders, his other sister hated him—what was left to like?

He drove across the Mississippi River Bridge and took the Belle Chasse Highway towards the Gulf. Venice was the jump-off place for the Louisiana offshore oil and gas industry. It lay at the bottom of a raggedy, narrow peninsula eaten away by erosion from canals built by the oil companies, though the land still retained its eerie marshland beauty, interrupted occasionally by small factories and seafood processing plants. It was big shrimp, oyster, and crab country, as well as a hot spot for sport fishing. Venice itself boasted two marinas and a huge number of support businesses for the oil companies. It was a town where you could easily get a crane or a helicopter, or some great fried seafood. But Eddie doubted you could find an Office Depot or a fresh vegetable other than iceberg lettuce and the random tomato. Stopping at a gas station in a little strip mall, he asked where he could find a bait shop.

The old guy who waited on him looked at least eighty and wore a tattered straw hat against the sun, which was fairly punishing today. It was hard to believe a hurricane had come so close so recently. "Sure," the man said. "There's one right next door."

"Know who owns it?"

"Don't think I do."

But of course he did. Eddie realized he'd encountered small-town America. "Well, thanks, and have a nice day."

"You have a blessed day yaself." He figured the man wasn't Catholic. That was something Baptists said these days. Eddie thought that kind of talk belonged in church. It made him feel itchy, like he'd invaded someone's privacy.

He drove the few feet down the parking lot to Joe's Bait Shop, which Eddie figured had to be owned by a guy named Joe; at least the Baptist could have mentioned that much.

The clerk was a tall, rangy man with blue eyes, dark hair, and that good-natured aura all Cajuns seemed to have. Venice wasn't really Cajun country, but wherever there's fishing, there seem to be Cajuns. "Hey, Joe," Eddie said. "I'm Eddie Valentino. Fellow down at the gas station sent me."

"Good to meet you, Eddie," the Cajun said, thus confirming he was Joe. Eddie asked his question.

"Austin Edwards?" Joe said. "Now that's a *big* fish. We're just small fry here. Mr. Austin don't run no shop, he's got a packin' plant, runs two great big pogie boats—crew of fourteen, each one of 'em—or anyway, he used to. Seems like I heard he had a little bad luck with one of 'em. Got a plane, too. Yep. Austin Edwards is the biggest fish you gonna see in the bait business round here—the Menhaden King of Louisiana, my wife calls him. 'Course she's wrong—guy up in Empire's got a fish meal factory, runs about a dozen boats. But you talkin' bait? Austin is royalty. I mean, he is the *Emperor*—too bad *he* don't operate out of Empire." The guy cackled at his own joke. "'Course, he's more like the wild man of Borneo than your average everyday emperor. Why'd ya think he might be here?"

Eddie shrugged. "I heard he had a bait place in Venice. Got some news for him." He pulled out one of his heir hunter cards.

Joe looked at his card. "Somebody left Mr. Austin some money? Well, if the rich don't get richer. Don't misunderstand me, though—I'm happy for him—Mr. Austin's a real good guy. But you heard wrong, Mr. Eddie. He lives in Venice, but his operation's up around Port Sulphur—'bout a half hour's drive north of here. Ya gonna pass Mr. Gregory's factory first—you can stop there and get directions."

"Mr. Gregory?"

"The one I mentioned with all the pogie boats—little fish-meal factory on a canal you can see from the road—real pretty place. Ya gonna see big old blue boats pulled right up to it."

"And these are pogie boats, you say?" Eddie was hoping Joe would clue him in.

"Menhaden boats. You know what menhaden are?"

Eddie nodded. "They're a kind of trash fish. Good for pet food."

"And bait. Pogie's another name for 'em. Austin calls his operation Great Bait."

Austin was turning out to be a damned interesting character. Eddie wondered about that trouble he'd had with one of his boats—Austin was probably heavily invested and couldn't take a big financial hit. Which might mean he'd asked his mama for money.

Eddie had one final question, though theoretically Joe had already answered it. "Austin's a pretty nice guy, is he?"

"Unless you get him mad," Joe said.

Eddie thanked him and turned his car back around, thinking this was the other side of small-town America—the good, gos-

sipy side dear to a PI's heart. He drove north to Empire, wishing he'd asked which side of the road the fish meal plant would
be on, and eventually spotted it on the right. There was a little
guard house in front. "Say," he said to the guard, "I'm looking
for Great Bait."

"Hey, that's our competition," the guard said.

"Uh-oh. Sounds like bad blood between y'all."

"Naah, I'm just messin' with ya. There's plenty of fish in the
sea. Place is about ten minutes away."

Eddie wrote down the directions and twelve minutes later,
drove into the little parking lot of a compound with a big GREAT
BAIT sign. From what Eddie could see, this one was also on a
canal, as it would have to be, and consisted mostly of a large
loading dock that probably held a freezer. A couple of trailers
joined together and a cinder block building of some sort com-
pleted the compound.

A couple of men were lounging in the parking lot, having a
smoke. Both were black and dressed like fishermen—rubber
boots, baseball hats, jeans, grimy T-shirts—one with the
sleeves cut out—and one wore suspenders. He got out and
hailed them. "Either of y'all Austin Edwards?"

One of the men merely looked indifferent. The other said,
"Ya might try the office. Maybe somebody's seen him."

"Where would I find the office?"

The man pointed to the trailer building, where Eddie found a
well-equipped fake-paneled office staffed by a woman about his
age and at least his weight. She had hips that probably wouldn't
fit in a pirogue, a perm so tight her gray hair looked grizzled,
and a face that had probably never seen more makeup than the
random slash of lipstick, even when she was young. She looked
like she'd raised ten or twelve children singlehandedly. She was
probably what they call "good country folks" in rural parishes,
and just as probably nobody to mess with.

"How ya doin'?" Eddie asked.

She didn't waste time on pleasantries. "Can I help you?"

"Well, I think I've got some good news for somebody ya
know. Austin around?"

"Ya got an appointment?"

"No, ma'am, I don't. I'm not even sure he's the man I want to see, but if he is, he's about to come into some money. Drove down from New Orleans just to find him. Name's Eddie Valentino." He handed her one of his heir hunter cards.

The woman took a long time looking at the card, even rubbed it between her fingers, as if assessing its value. When she made no move to introduce herself, he stuck out his hand and said, "I'm glad to meet ya."

She regarded his hand with the same suspicion as she did the card, finally deciding to risk touching it. "Marie Broussard."

The conversation seemed stalled out. Eddie tried a jump-start. "Like I said, if he's the right Austin Edwards, he might be about to come into some money."

"You could try back around two o'clock." Broussard glanced at her watch. "He might be in about then."

"I was wondering—do you know if he's related to the Edwardses out of Tallahassee?"

For the first time, she looked at him with real interest. "I think his daddy's in Florida. He didn't die, did he?"

"No, ma'am, I don't think so. Another relative did."

"'Cause I know he's been sick," she said cautiously. "Austin runs this place for him."

That would explain why Ms. Wallis hadn't picked it up in her background search. "Oh. I thought he was the owner. Looks to me like you run things."

"Well, I been here a lot longer than the Edwardses. They bought it two years ago, and everything's been downhill since. Weren't for me, this place woulda closed down a long time ago. Austin takes off anytime he wants, leaves me to take care of things but . . ."

This was what Eddie loved, an employee with a grievance. "Let me guess," he said. "But no authority to make decisions."

"That's right." She smiled, showing him a set of nearly brown teeth. "How'd ya know that?"

"It's the way of the world, Ms. Broussard. It's the way of the world." He sighed for emphasis. "Tell me, isn't it unusual to be coming in at two in the afternoon? That the way he manages his daddy's bi'ness?"

"That's nothin'. He's been away. Just radioed this morning to expect him in this afternoon to sign the payroll checks. Sure hope it's a *lotta* money you got for him—or this company's not gon' last another two weeks."

Eddie raised an eyebrow to show he understood the seriousness of the situation. "Any way I can reach him before he comes in?"

She shook her head. "Nope. He's out on his boat. We haven't heard from him since Tuesday."

"He was in Tuesday?" The day after the murders.

"No, uh-uh. That was the day of the storm. Nobody was here that day. Austin left a voicemail sayin' he was goin' fishin' for a day or two."

"Wait a minute—how could he go out in a boat? There'd be storm surge, right?"

She shrugged. "All I know's what he said. For all I know, he's been up in New Orleans, shacked up with some girl. Turned off his cell phone and we didn't hear from him again till this morning. Fishin'! Can you imagine? With the company in this kind of trouble."

Eddie said, "I gotta tell ya the truth. If it were me, I wouldn't be worried."

"That mean it *is* a lotta money?" She showed him brown teeth again.

"Means he probably thought he left the company in good hands. I do."

She kept on smiling, acknowledging the compliment. "Want me to tell him you were looking for him?"

"No, that's okay. I'll catch him."

"All right, then."

He went back to the front of the building, hoping the two smokers had disappeared, and to his relief, found he was alone. Still, his car made a pretty big statement in the little parking lot. He moved it onto the road and parked on the shoulder, out of sight.

Marie Broussard might seem more forthcoming than an employee ought to be, but you never knew. He figured he'd watch the parking lot, just in case. He might as well entertain himself in the meantime. He got out the second emergency item he'd brought along, which was a copy of *The Great Gatsby* he'd found in his own house. When Angela and Tony were growing up, he and Audrey had bought them a library of classics, which had come in handy for school reports, but which he'd never particularly perused himself. However, Ms. Wallis had made him curious the other day. He'd heard that title; he knew he ought to know what was in the book. So he decided to educate himself.

He settled down to read.

By noon, Austin hadn't shown, so he took a chance on a lunch break, and at one sharp, he ambled back into the office. Broussard was eating a tuna fish sandwich. "Austin get back?"

She pointed to her mouth and chewed before she spoke. "When he says two, he usually means three."

"I know what ya mean," Eddie said, and turned to leave, then turned back—his best Colombo imitation. "Did you say he radioed this morning?"

"Yeah, he was on his boat—said he lost his cell phone. Prob'ly he did go fishin', once the weather cleared up."

"Well, thank ya, ma'am." He left again.

This time, however, he made his way to the back of the place, where the fishing boats came in. The air was heavy with a nauseating fish smell. Menhaden, he figured, probably smelled even worse than most fish, especially in quantity.

But on the off-chance Austin really was coming by boat, it was going to be the best place to wait, and it was pleasant here, except for the smell. Apparently, Austin had a little store on the dock, where he sold fuel, a little bait, and a few soft drinks. Now and then a small boat, the kind used for sport fishing, came in and gassed up. Eddie sat in the shadow of the little store. He'd brought the book, and he was nearly halfway through it.

How could such a short book be so famous? he wondered. A schoolchild could read it in a day. Maybe that was why it was popular.

Still, he had to admit the author had something here. He was getting the hang of why Allyson reminded everybody of this Gatsby character, and he was willing to bet, if you found out by the end where Gatsby's money came from, it had something to do with that guy who fixed the World Series. People like that were never on the up-and-up. He was pretty sure Allyson wasn't.

He liked the way the guy wrote. One thing especially reminded him of Allyson, probably explained how she'd ended up like she did: "Dishonesty in a woman is something you never blame deeply."

Until ya do, Eddie thought, *and then the shit hits the fan.*

Gatsby was dead in his pool by two o'clock, and Eddie was pretty impressed. Nice, neat little plot—all those people who were sort of connected, but not really (the Wilsons and the rich folks) coming together at the end. He had to hand it to the guy.

He closed the book and looked out at the horizon. No sign of a boat. He went ahead and read the last couple of chapters. After that, he fell into a mild doze.

The sound of an outboard motor woke him, and he opened his eyes to see a good-sized fishing boat bearing towards the dock—one big enough to have a little cabin. He got up and waved, but he couldn't see anyone on board.

As it drew closer, though, he could see a man on deck. He waved again.

The man threw him a rope. "Hey, could you take this line?"

Eddie was at a loss. "Whaddaya want me to do with it?"

"Cleat it down, could you?"

"Do what?"

"Oh, never mind. Could you just hold it till I get her in?" No question the man was Austin Edwards. He wore shorts, a wife-beater T-shirt, and—Eddie couldn't believe it—a pair of Top-Siders. Pretty good disguise for a biker, Eddie thought.

Except for the tattoos. The shirt let them show in all their glory, especially the red and gold fish swimming on his forearm.

And, except for the tattoos, he was a pretty clean-cut-looking guy, but slightly beefy. Maybe you had to be a certain weight before they'd sell you a Harley. Eddie watched him as he tied up the boat, legs and arms moving as if they'd done this a thousand times. Eddie had half expected a drunk. This guy looked healthy.

When he'd finished the job, he turned to Eddie. "Austin Edwards. Are you the man from New Orleans?"

So Broussard had announced him. "Ms. Broussard say what I came about?"

He shrugged. "Just said you were here."

"Everybody's lookin' for ya, back in New Orleans."

"Who? I don't have a girlfriend. My mother? Surely not my mother."

"Why not?"

He shrugged again. "She never calls me."

"Austin, I got some bad news for ya. Some real bad things have happened. Ya sister passed away." He just couldn't hit the guy with two deaths at once.

All the energy left his face, and much of the color as well. "Arnelle or Cassie?" he asked quietly.

"I'm sorry. It's Cassie."

Sorrow hovered briefly on his features, or dread, perhaps, but anger replaced it in a flicker. "You're lying! My mother would have called me! She would have sent out the Coast Guard. *Somehow*, she would have found me."

Eddie put a hand on his shoulder. "Ya mother's gone, too, son."

"I just saw her!"

"When was that?"

"I just saw her! God, she's a *horrible* driver."

"How's that?" Eddie said, and then realized what he meant. "They didn't die in an accident, Austin."

The rage and disbelief were beginning to ebb in the other man. He was starting to get limp and numb, the way people do when they get bad news. Eddie couldn't have said whether his grief was genuine, but in case it was, the guy's feelings were more important than the damn case.

"Ya want to go in the office? Talk about this?" Eddie said.

"No. Tell me now."

"Somebody shot ya mother."

Suddenly it seemed to occur to him that he didn't have a clue who Eddie was. "Are you a cop?" he asked.

"No, son. I'm a private investigator. I wasn't kidding when I said everybody's looking for ya."

Austin said, "I'm outta here," and leaped back onto the boat before Eddie could stop him.

Damn! This just couldn't happen. Eddie leaped, too, but the boat drifted an inch or so as he did, just enough to make him miss his footing. He fell in the water, the boat in front of him, a shell-covered piling in back. He went under briefly, and came up coughing and snorting salty water, shells digging into his back. The water was surprisingly warm, but the boat was alarmingly close. He had no idea when it might decide to drift back towards him.

"Help!" he yelled, hoping Austin had an ounce of decency. "Austin, help!"

"Fuck!" Austin shouted. "Just fuck!"

But he grabbed a boat hook, flipped it, and fended off the pier with the blunt end of the pole while he reached for a line to throw Eddie. "Grab this, and hang on for a minute."

Gratefully, Eddie took the line and let Austin float him over to the stern, where the fish guy once again fumbled one-handed to get the boarding ladder down. "All right. Come aboard."

Eddie heaved his sopping self up the ladder and onto the deck.

"You all right?" Austin said.

Eddie felt his back for damage. "Yeah, I'm all right. Ya got anything to drink around here?"

The futility of trying to abscond physically, either from Eddie or the news he brought, seemed to dawn on Austin. But Eddie had just brought up another avenue of escape. "Yeah," he said grimly. "I got something to drink. Let's both have one."

He went below, giving Eddie a chance to take off his shoes and socks and sodden, gun-heavy sports jacket. Austin returned with a bottle of bourbon and two glasses. He didn't offer Eddie any dry clothes, just a good half cup of straight-up whiskey.

He drank his own in one swallow. Eddie cheered up. Maybe the worst was over. But he was soggy and he still had a horrible story to tell. "There's no easy way to say this. Someone stabbed Cassie and then shot ya mother. Or maybe it was the other way around. The cops don't even know which happened first."

Austin stared as if he hadn't heard, set his mouth in a line, poured himself another drink, and tossed it down his throat. "They stabbed Cassie?" he said. "Who would kill poor little Cassie?" He sounded like he was talking about a character in a movie.

"The police are tryin' to find out. Surprised they didn't call ya—ya mother must have had ya number."

"Goddamn it to hell! I left in such a hurry I forgot my cell phone. When did it happen? Yesterday?"

"Monday night."

Austin leaned forward, fury in his eyes. "Monday night?" he shouted. "The hell it was Monday night! I was there Monday night."

"Who else was there?"

Austin shrugged. "Just two kids who work for her. A girl who was doing some painting and a poet who lives in the carriage house. My mother and I had a fight—that's why I left." He paused, remembering. "Oh, shit!"

"What?"

"I was drinking that night. I—really said some things I shouldn't have."

"And then what?"

"I went back to my room and tried to watch television. Finally I said, 'Fuck it!' and left. Just came home."

"Hold it a minute. Didn't you know about the hurricane warnings?"

"Oh, hell. Walter Anderson rowed out to Horn Island and lashed himself to a tree in a hurricane—why the fuck would *I* be afraid of a little hurricane?"

"That some crazy biker friend of yours?"

"He was an artist. But you got one thing right—he was crazy."

"I hear ya live in Venice. Goin' there in a storm'd be about the same as bein' out in the Gulf."

"Yeah, well, I might be crazy, but I'm not as crazy as Walter Anderson. I slept here in the bunkhouse." He indicated the cinder block building.

"Anyone else there?"

Edwards made a noise that may have been a laugh, but it was more like a yelp. "Fuck, man! Ain' nobody else that crazy."

Eddie was really interested in one thing only. He asked the crucial question. "When ya left ya mama's, were they all still there? All three of 'em?"

Austin thought about it a minute. "No. Uh-uh. I don't think the girl was. Rashad—he's kind of Mother's bitch—was out with Mother on the patio. Having some kind of serious talk."

Okay, that was it. The thing Eddie had come for. His client wasn't exactly cleared—the police might say Janessa could have killed Cassie and then come back to Allyson's and killed her, too—but at least Eddie had a witness to corroborate her story. If he could just get him back to New Orleans. "Ya gotta come back and talk to the police. They're lookin' for ya."

Another penny dropped. "They think *I* did it?"

"I didn't say that. But they can't eliminate ya as a suspect till ya tell 'em ya story."

Austin tossed down another drink. He was growing calmer by the second, but Eddie could see the sadness starting to spread through his cells. His cheerful face had turned itself inside out, his features seeming now to point downward. Eddie had a long afternoon ahead of him.

For a moment, Austin sat there, trying to put the puzzle together. Finally, he said, "Cassie was there, too? At my mom's?"

"No. She was killed at her apartment. The coroner discovered her body when he went to give Cassie the news."

Tears flowed down Austin's handsome face. "Poor little Cassie. Who would kill poor little Cassie?"

"Was Rashad involved with her?"

"You know Rashad?" Austin asked.

"No, I haven't met him. Janessa found Allyson the next day—both you and Rashad were gone."

"Oh, man. Oh, man!" He picked up the bottle and drank till he gagged. Then he sank back in the cockpit and said, "Rashad killed them? Why would Rashad kill them?"

"Nobody said Rashad killed 'em. Rashad isn't there, that's all. Like you."

"Tell me the whole story, okay?"

So Eddie did, stumbling over the part about the swimming pool, but he managed to spit it out, and noticed that Austin's wince was the first sign he'd cared for his mother at all.

After that, Austin sat there, eyes glazed, while Eddie shivered in his wet clothing. When he finally spoke again, his voice was slurred. "So what are you doing here?"

"I was hired to look into the murders. I want you to come back with me."

"I need you to leave."

"They can't hold the funerals without ya, son." At the "F" word, Austin started sobbing.

"Oh, God, not Cassie! If some bastard could do that to Cassie, there's no good anywhere. D'you understand that?

There's no reason to live, because there's no good left any-where. If Rashad could do this—"

"Ya think Rashad did it?"

"He disappeared, didn't he?"

"So did you."

"But—I didn't know."

"Nobody's gon' know that till ya tell 'em."

Austin picked up the bottle, which was about half-empty now, started to drink, then stopped, his eye caught by something on land. Eddie turned to see Marie Broussard walking toward the dock, a sheaf of paper in her hands—probably the payroll checks.

He called to her. "Ms. Broussard. We need some help here. Need to get Austin off this boat."

And Austin picked that moment to dive off the boat and start swimming.

"Ms. Broussard. Quick! Get somebody."

For a moment, Eddie contemplated jumping in after him, but then he heard the motor of a little fishing boat coming towards the dock. Broussard was trying to flag it down. "Virgil! Fred! Austin's in the water."

One of the men aboard held his hand up to his eyes. "What's he doing?" he shouted.

"He's drunk," Eddie shouted. "I think he's trying to kill himself."

Virgil poured on speed and hurtled toward Austin. Eddie threw a life preserver. "Hey, Austin, grab this!"

The swimming man gave no indication he'd heard. To Eddie, it looked as if he was having a hard time, swimming against the current, maybe. Virgil and Fred drew up close and cut their en-gine. "Hey, Austin. Hey, man! Come on. Get in the boat."

Austin kept swimming.

Broussard had reached the dock by now. She stood there with her checks in her hand, her face screwed up against the sun, and probably against the sight of a man trying to swim to his death. "What's wrong with him?"

"He had some bad news."

"I thought you had good news."

"Turned out the person who died was his mother."

Broussard crossed herself and started to pray. Austin was

still swimming, but it looked to Eddie as if he'd slowed down. The men in the boat had begun to row, just keeping abreast of him, waiting for him to tire enough so they could haul him aboard.

They were a couple of hundred yards out by now, and the boat blocked his view, but Eddie saw one of the men jump overboard and start to grapple with Austin. Finally, the other hit Austin with the paddle, but he fought back. The fisherman hit him again, with so much naked force Eddie feared that, one way or another, Austin wasn't going to make it back to dry land. But finally he went limp. Virgil grabbed him, but he didn't seem able to hold him. "Fred! Fred, I'm losing him."

The other man jumped in the water, and, for a few minutes, they struggled to hold the unconscious man above water, dog-paddling back to their boat, which had begun to drift.

Finally, one of them let go and swam back to the boat. He climbed in, turned on the engine and circled back to his buddy and the dead weight that was Austin. The other pushed from the water, and his buddy pulled, but the boat began rocking so precariously that they had to stop. Abandoning that plan, Virgil or Fred—whichever it was—simply grabbed the boat with one hand and held on, still holding Austin with the other, while his buddy slowly putt-putted in to the dock.

If Austin wanted to drown, it looked as if he was getting his wish. Eddie tucked his gun in his trousers, threw his coat, shoes, and socks onto the dock. Then he scrambled off Austin's boat and helped tie the little one up, then heave the fish guy onto the dock. As Austin rolled to his side, about a quart of water poured from his mouth, and he began to cough.

"Crazy motherfucker!" Virgil offered.

"Shoulda left him there," Fred said in disgust.

Abruptly Austin quit coughing, and looked around him. And just as suddenly, his eyes rolled back in his head, which hit the dock so hard it bounced.

But his chest rose and fell rhythmically. "I've got to get him to a doctor," Eddie said. "Y'all help me get him in the car?"

Virgil was staring at a drowned pack of cigarettes. Disgustedly, he threw it in the water. "Mister, he can die for all I care." He stomped off toward the building.

Fred shrugged. "I'll take his feet."

"I'll help," Broussard said.

"Just grab my things, will ya?" Obediently, she picked up his soaked clothes, her glance straying nervously to the gun he'd stuck in the front of his pants.

"It's okay," Eddie said. "I'm a private investigator."

She nodded as if it that explained things.

When they arrived at the empty parking lot, Fred looked around, puzzled. "Where's your car?"

"Let's put him down. I'll get it."

"Gladly."

Fred was gone when he came back, leaving Eddie and Broussard to hoist the soaking, barely conscious dead weight into the back seat of Audrey's Cadillac. At least it didn't fight.

"Ow!" Broussard groused. "Think I broke my back."

"Bye. Thanks for the help," Eddie said, and took off. Doctor, hell. He turned the car around, negotiated the country roads back to the highway, and lit out for New Orleans.

"Oh, man," Austin moaned. "Oh, man."

Okay, he could talk. The worst that could happen, he'd get pneumonia. Eddie, too. He called Audrey. "Baby, I got a situation."

She'd heard that one before. "Oh, boy."

"I got a half-drowned suicidal wreck in the car. I might have to stay with him all night."

"Aww, Eddie," she said. "I wanted to go to Jack Dempsey's. Get some shrimp."

"Tomorrow."

"*The District*'s on tomorrow."

"Sorry, kid, I'll make it up to you. I'm in Port Sulphur. Call you when I get back."

Next he called Janessa. "You got a key to Allyson's house?"

"Why ya wanna know?"

"I've got Austin. Meet me there in two hours." He figured Janessa was strong enough to help him do what had to be done.

But when they arrived, Austin had sobered up enough to walk, with a little help from his friends. He actually sat up in the back seat when the car stopped. "Where the hell are we?"

"Ya mama's house."

Janessa was already there, waiting on the front porch. She approached the car gingerly, like it might explode. Austin lit up.

"Hey, Janessa. What's shakin'?"

She looked them both over. "Why ya wet?"

"Took a swim. Austin, ya got clothes inside?"

"Yeah, prob'ly. What the hell we doin' here?" He seemed momentarily to have forgotten his troubles.

Eddie gritted his teeth and opened the back door. "Janessa, help me, will ya, honey?"

Austin said, "Hey, I can walk."

He teetered up the front walk, then the steps, then through the house to a room that was obviously a guest room, and that was it for Austin. He fell down on the bed and started snoring.

Eddie said, "We gotta get him out of these clothes."

"Uh-uh. I ain' undressin' no white man."

"Just the shirt. I'll do the pants." He held up Austin's limp torso, cajoled Janessa into slipping off the shirt, then he wrestled the shorts off himself.

After that, he covered Austin up and he and Janessa left.

"He kill 'em?" she asked.

"I don't think so. But he corroborates ya story. Says ya were gone when he left."

All she said was, "What he say about Rashad?"

Chapter Fifteen

Talba was getting ready for work when Eddie called. It was Friday morning, she'd found Rashad's nest, she had a new lead, and she had a reading that night. She was in a great mood. "EdDEE!" she squealed. "You must have found Austin."

"I need ya to pick me up." His voice was grim. "And bring that little laptop of yours."

"Okay. Sure." She took it with her everywhere. "Be there in twenty minutes."

"I'm not home. Come get me at Allyson Brower's house."

"What on earth are you doing there?" He hung up without answering.

He was waiting outside. He picked up the laptop on the shot-gun seat and got in the car, settling it on his lap. "This thing charged up?"

"Sure. Why?"

"I need ya to find my car."

He meant he wanted her to activate the GPS in Audrey's Cadillac. "Uh-oh."

"Bastard stole my wife's car."

Talba asked no more questions. She took the laptop from him, clicked on the GPS program, and showed him what it indi-cated—the Cadillac was traveling down the Belle Chasse High-way toward the Gulf.

"He's goin' back to Port Sulpher. Let's go get him."

"You want to drive?"

"Yeah." That seemed to calm him down a little.

Each of them got out of the car, walked around it, and changed places. When they were traveling south on the other side of the river, Talba said, "You want to tell me what happened?"

"I got him, brought him home, and he stole my car. End of story." His features were set so tight he could have been a statue of himself.

She shut up and wondered if it was safe to change the sub-ject—she was dying to talk about Rashad. But maybe it was better to let Eddie cool down by himself. She waited about an hour before she spoke again. "Looks like Austin's almost there. Could you fill in a detail or two, maybe?"

Eddie shrugged. "Says he went fishin' after he left Monday night—you believe that? Came back in his boat yesterday after-noon."

"Fishing in a *hurricane?*"

"Yeah, right. But he didn't know about his sister and mama, unless he's the best actor since De Niro." Eddie sneaked a look at her computer screen. "Which he could be—he could be. He got real drunk when I told him and leaped overboard—couple of fishermen hadn't been coming in, he coulda drowned. He was more or less unconscious, so I said I'd take him to the hospital. But then he came around, so I took him to his mama's instead."

"You *what?* He could have died of hypothermia."

"Ah, it's October. Water's still pretty warm."

"Okay." She wasn't going to argue—obviously, the man

hadn't died. "So then what? How'd you get in the house?"

"Ya sister. She even helped me undress him. He corroborates her story, by the way. So I stayed with him just in case, let him sleep it off, and when he got up, he couldn't remember who I was. I was in the kitchen making coffee for him, the sono-fabitch. ('Scuse my French.) See, I made the mistake of leaving my keys on the counter. I was tryin' to refresh his recollection, and right in the middle of it, he grabbed 'em up and stole my car. Like I said, end of story."

And a pretty hard story for you to tell, Talba thought. She said, "Makes him look pretty guilty. So why aren't we calling the police?"

"'Cause we got the damn GPS."

Something was bothering Talba. "Eddie, could I ask you something? Was your gun in that car?"

He shook his head vigorously. "Ya think I'm crazy? Hell, no. I got it right in my pocket."

She felt better, but it still didn't make sense. "I just don't get it. This seems like a job for the cops."

Eddie had an odd, stubborn look on his face that she hadn't seen before. "It was my fault, Ms. Wallis, I pressed him too hard. Kinda tried to strongarm him into going down and talkin' to the cops."

"Okay. I get it."

"No ya don't." He looked as grim as she'd ever seen him.

But she was pretty sure she understood what was going on. Eddie prided himself on being the ultimate people person. He was the only PI in town who could tame the bureaucrats at City Hall, who was owed so many favors he could even get a cop to run a list of names through NCIC (a $10,000 fine if the cop ratted him out, plus criminal charges for the cop). Once, he'd even tricked a racist sheriff into letting Talba out of jail.

This was a matter of pride with him. It must have cost him a lot just to tell Talba he'd screwed up. If he'd made a misstep in psyching somebody out, he was going to correct it himself or die trying.

Except that he wasn't stupid. If he really thought there was a chance of dying, he'd call the cops in a heartbeat—and he certainly wouldn't endanger Talba. At least that was what she hoped.

She said, "You don't think he did it, do you?"

"Let's put it this way—the guy's not dangerous. If he did kill his sister and mama, he's not gonna kill anybody else. He's too messed up. And I'm the one who messed him up. He's not angry, he's depressed. It hasn't sunk in what happened yet—what's gotta be done. He's in denial."

Talba almost laughed—Eddie might fancy himself a great manipulator, but psychology wasn't his usual thing.

She glanced at her screen. "He's there! You were right. He got to Port Sulphur and stopped."

They arrived about forty-five minutes behind him, to find Marie Broussard walking toward the parking lot. "Hey, Mr. Valentino. Here's ya keys. I was just gonna return ya car."

"Hey, Ms. Broussard. This is my associate, Ms. Wallis. Austin around?"

"No, uh-uh. He got here a little while ago, signed the payroll checks, and took off on his motorcycle. It was real nice of you to lend him ya car."

"Did he say where he was going?"

She shrugged. "Just said to return ya car—he'd be back when he got here."

"That's *all*?"

"Somethin' wrong?" She was suddenly anxious. "Uh-oh. Ya didn't lend him ya car, did ya?"

"Ms. Broussard, ya gotta help me. He's had a real bad blow, and he did somethin' stupid. Ya want to make sure he stays out of jail?"

Her eyes got watery. "Mr. Valentino, you may not believe this, but I love that boy like my own son. He don't mean no harm. I know him. Look, he came back all this way just to sign those checks. What does that say to you?"

Eddie patted her arm. "I'm not gon' report this. You can rest easy on that. But ya gotta help me." He reached in his pocket and pulled out his wallet. "Ya think ya can give me a call if he shows up again?"

"Uh—sure."

Eddie handed over a couple of twenties. She took them without hesitation, but there was something noncompliant in her face. "I sure would appreciate it," Eddie said. "Say, ya think he went home? Can ya give me his address?"

"Sure. Give me ya card. I'll write it down for you."

"Much obliged." Eddie gave her a business card, and when she'd written the address, took it back from her. "You take care of yourself now." He turned to Talba. "I'll go see him, Ms. Wallis. You go on back to the office."

Talba understood that he didn't want to say more in front of Broussard. "Okay. See you there."

He called her on her cell phone before she was out of the parking lot. "No way that woman's gon' help. She saw my gun yesterday. She'll call his house and warn him, but I'm gon' check it out anyway."

"And then what?"

"If he's not there—and he won't be—I'll check around here for biker bars, see if I can turn him up. Meanwhile, you keep on Rashad."

"Eddie, I need to tell you something. I went back to the wharf." She told him what she'd found.

"Ms. Wallis, Ms. Wallis. Ya shouldn't have gone back by yaself—ya know that, don't ya?" He sighed. "Call the hospitals, see if anybody's got him."

This was what she'd meant to do, anyhow. "How about the cops? I left his stuff at the wharf. Should I tip them?"

"Naah, let me have the pleasure. I'm gon' tell Sergeant Crockett my associate figured it out from poetry—be a lot of fun."

"Should we check it out later—see if Rashad comes back?"

"Whatcha think cops are for?"

"I was hoping you'd say that. Sure you'll be all right?"

"You kiddin' me, Ms. Wallis? This is Eddie Valentino ya talkin' to."

"Just be careful." She pulled into the first fast-food joint she came to, went in, got a Coke, and sat at a table with her computer. No sense wasting the drive time back to New Orleans. She made a list of hospital phone numbers, got back in her car, and started dialing, wishing to hell she could e-mail. At least her pretext was easy—she was the sister of a man she'd seen shot—yep, actually *seen* it, and her brother had fled the scene and he hadn't been home. Did they have a Rashad Daneene with a gunshot wound? Or any other young black male with a lot of curls and a pretty face?

Nope. They didn't. Had she called the police? Of course she had—what the hell did they think she was, crazy?

Rashad might know a doctor somewhere. Or he might not be shot. Or he might be dead. Lots of options.

But no Rashad.

She'd double check the phonebook when she got back, make some more calls, but that was all she could do for now. To stave off boredom, she went over the case in her head.

Okay. Nobody liked Allyson Brower, even her own daughter. Her son might have done it, but Eddie didn't think so. Which left whom?

There was Arnelle, of course. And Janessa. And Rashad. But no one else seemed close enough even to want her dead. She wondered if Allyson had a boyfriend no one knew about. Or an ex.

Maybe Burford Hale was a possibility, the man she'd met at the birthday party for Hunt—the one in the white linen suit. Talba remembered that the invitation had come from Hale, via Mimi Dirr.

Mimi was a doctor's wife, like Arnelle, not to mention Michelle. Come to think of it, that was quite a little profession in New Orleans. Mimi was on the board of one of the literary festivals and was someone Talba knew only from parties. But she had a great sense of humor, she loved to gossip, and she always sought Talba out when they turned up at the same events. And Talba hadn't touched base with her. What *was* her problem?

She got Mimi on the phone. "Hey, girl. Can you keep a secret?"

"No, *ma'am*. Everybody knows that."

"Really. This is important."

"Okay, but don't ever ask me again. One's my limit."

"Well, Eddie and I are working on the Allyson Brower murder. Uh, suicide. Whatever it is."

"Wow. You said 'murder.' Who did it?"

"That's not the secret. I just told you the secret."

"Oh." Mimi made no effort to conceal her disappointment. In her world, it was such poor gossip, she'd probably forget it, which was good.

"I called to get the skinny on Allyson."

"Well, don't ask me. She was your basic Woman of Mystery.

Moved into town, started throwing parties—that's all I know. We called her The Girl Gatsby over at the festival office."

"There's a resemblance."

"I don't think she was a bootlegger, though. Got her money from an ex-husband."

"Don't they all."

"Maybe she killed him."

"The ex-husband?"

"Maybe he was mobbed up, and the mob came and got her. It wouldn't explain Cassie, though." Mimi paused a moment, sobering herself up. "Poor little Cassie."

"Did you hear what you just said—'poor little Cassie'? Wish I had a dime for every time I've heard it. Nobody cared about Allyson—everybody cared about Cassie."

"Honestly, I don't think anyone knew much about Allyson—except maybe Burford Hale."

"Ah. That's what I was wondering. Who is he, anyway?"

"He's in real estate. From Kentucky, I think. He gives fantastic parties, too, but he goes in more for the social crowd. He found Allyson her house; then he kind of took her under his wing—showed her the ropes, I guess. How to meet everybody in town she thought was worth knowing."

"Was he Allyson's boyfriend?"

"Oh, yeah. They were engaged for a while. But here's the weird thing about that—I always thought Burford was gay."

"Oops. There's a man I'd love to talk to."

"I'll give you his number if you promise to tell me absolutely everything you know about all this."

Talba laughed. "Mimi, you're crazy, girlfriend. If he's in real estate, how hard can he be to find?"

"Just thought I'd try." Talba heard her flipping cards. "Here it is. It's his cell phone." She recited seven plump, delicious numbers, which Talba dialed immediately.

The thing about real estate guys, they always answered. Burford didn't disappoint.

"Hey, Burford," she pronounced. "It's the Baroness."

Dead silence, just as she'd suspected. He didn't have a clue who she was. "The Baroness de Pontalba. Remember? You got my picture in the paper."

"Ah. At poor Allyson's."

"Well, I wanted to thank you for that."

He chuckled politely. "You're welcome, Baroness. It was good of you to call." He hung up.

Talba hit redial. "Not so fast, Burf. That wasn't the only reason I called. I need to talk to you about Allyson."

His voice changed subtly. "I'm showing a house right now, but—"

"Afterwards then."

"I'm curious. What's this about?"

"It's about her death. I'm involved with the investigation."

She was well aware it might have sounded more or less nuts coming from the average black female poet, but Talba had had so much publicity that most people who were aware she existed knew she was a PI.

"Oh!" It was the kind of "oh!" that people blurted when they were really, really interested. "Have you had lunch?"

Yes! Talba thought. "Not yet," she said. "I'm on the road, but I ought to be back by two o'clock, latest. Would that work for you?"

"I'll make it work. Where, though? We need somewhere quiet, if you know what I mean."

"How about Hooters?"

He burst out laughing. "You're kidding, right?"

"Uh-uh. What are the chances of running into someone you know at Hooters?"

Hale was still chuckling. "Slim to impossible," he said. "Two it is." He had an accent that was vaguely British, while remaining so Southern you could sop it up with a biscuit. Interesting trick, Talba thought.

Eddie had taught her the Hooters dodge long ago. Nobody local, "black, white or green," to quote the master, would be caught dead there. Talba arrived first and scanned the menu, knowing perfectly well she was going to have a burger in the end. Her previous excursions here had illustrated the wisdom of this—when in Rome and all that. She ordered iced tea and spent a little time feeling sorry for the poor waitresses—in their pantyhose, shorts, and high-riding hooters—before a casually clad Hale slid into the chair across from her.

"Oh, hi. Didn't recognize you without your linen suit." He still looked dapper, though. It was that neat little moustache.

"*You're* the one. I thought you were famous for looking outrageous."

"That's real life. This is my day gig."

The waitress appeared, pad in hand, generous bazongas mounded over a neat white, mostly unbuttoned shirt, tied at the waist for greater neatness still. The management probably made them wear Wonderbras. "Something to drink?" she asked.

"Scotch and water," Hale answered. Talba restrained herself from raising an eyebrow. Even in New Orleans, people went easy on the booze in the daytime. Hale said what she was thinking. "I think I need fortifying."

He took a fortifying gulp. Talba sipped at her iced tea. "Ready to order? The burgers are good here."

"Sure. I've got the strangest feeling this lunch isn't about eating, anyhow." He looked the waitress in the eye, something Talba thought not many men would be able to do. "Two burgers."

"Dressed?" the woman said. She meant with lettuce and tomato, but now Hale did let his glance stray to her chest.

"Preferably," he said. She nodded, not catching the irony, and pirouetted away in her sneakers and pantyhose.

"Fat chance in this place," Talba said.

Hale gave a theatrical shudder. "God, this is a strange country!"

"Yep. A little piece of America, smack in the middle of civilization."

Once again, Hale gulped scotch. "It's no weirder than the rest of my life. For the last year, anyhow."

"I take it you're referring to your relationship with Allyson Brower."

"That woman was . . . was . . ."

"Evil incarnate?"

He considered. "Could have been. Could definitely have been."

"I hear you were engaged to her."

"God! How could I have been so stupid? Who killed her, Baroness? And *who* killed poor little Cassie?"

"Aha, another one."

"Another what?"

"Another of her dear friends who won't miss her at all."

"Oh, I'll miss her. I'll miss her crazy phone calls in the middle of the night; I'll miss her impossible demands and her searing insults. I'll miss her all right. And it's going to hurt so *good.*"

The waitress brought the hamburgers. Talba began pouring ketchup on hers, trying not to seem overeager. She tried for lightness. "You must have a really great alibi for the night she was killed. You're sounding like a hell of a suspect."

"Alibi?" He looked surprised. "I never thought about it. What night was she killed?"

"Monday." Surely he had to know, the whole city did.

"Oh. That's okay then. I was at a hurricane party. What, exactly, did you want from me?"

"I guess, mostly to know if you know who killed her."

"Uh-uh." He applied mustard to his bun. "But I sure know a lot of people who might have wanted to. And, yeah, you can put me at the top of the list."

"I take it your relationship ended badly."

"Ended badly? It started badly, it was always bad, and now I have a lot of bad memories." He bit into the sandwich, chewed once, gulped, and said, "A lot of *stupid* memories. Did anyone mention I'm a homosexual?"

Talba nodded. "That seemed like the consensus."

"So why would I be engaged to a woman, right? Because she *seemed* like a man. She was more like a man than John Wayne."

"Now, he was a particular kind of man. Was Allyson a conquering hero type?"

"God, no. I just meant she had a very masculine mind."

"In what way?"

"Well, that's the problem—I can't really tell you. She was like . . . Svengali. She could hypnotize you into thinking she was anything she wanted you to be. She could make you *believe*. Take me. I am only attracted to men. Men only. See that waitress? She's got about as much appeal for me as this salt shaker." He picked the object up and jiggled it. "How the hell did Allyson convince me I wanted to marry a woman?"

"Well? How did she?"

"Let me think." He drank and ate while he tripped down memory lane. "First of all, she made me admire her. She came into town all effervescent—you know those really upbeat

Southern women? The kind who can make you forget there's anybody else in a room? That you just can't take your eyes off, and you can't hear anything else except her talking?"

"You sound like you're still in love."

"Love! I was never in love. I was in some sort of crazy trance. See, first she came to me to help her find a house. And she chirped and bubbled and *enthused* and just, you know . . . made you want to be around her. She loved everything and if she didn't love it, she could say such scathingly funny things about it, you'd be rolling on the floor."

"Pretty hard on your nice linen suit."

"She even made me buy the damn suit. Do I look like the white suit type to you?"

"Actually . . ."

"Don't say it. Yeah, a lot of people have said it since. She convinced me I didn't really know myself—that she knew me much better than I did . . . that she could somehow see into my soul. Read my mind. I don't know. Sometimes she'd complete sentences for me. When we first met, that is. It stopped after a while. I think now she was just incredibly observant. She figured me out. Watched my reactions, listened to the way I talked, noticed what I liked."

"Like what?"

"My mama, for openers. I was very close to my mother. She was ill when we were together and she needed quite a bit of taking care of. And I took pleasure in taking care of her. Next thing you know, Allyson had me taking care of Allyson. I even painted her *toenails*, for God's sake!"

"I'm surprised. I would have thought she wouldn't be caught dead without a professional pedicure."

An ironic little noise—a smirk maybe—debouched from around a bite of hamburger. "She probably wouldn't. The thing was to get me to take care of her—to make me enjoy it. To portray herself as a poor, put-upon, helpless female at the mercy of her money-grubbing children for the pitiful few cents they allowed her."

Talba was surprised. "Including Cassie?" she asked.

"No, not including Cassie. To hear Allyson tell it, Cassie was a venal little bitch who wanted the money that Austin held in trust for Allyson; and Arnelle had somehow gotten all the money from her father, Allyson's first husband, that should have rightfully been Allyson's. . . ."

"Hold it. Arnelle's father is dead. She probably inherited his money. And Austin doesn't have a penny, according to his big sister."

Hale shook his head. "You're not getting this, are you? It was probably all a fabrication. Every single word of it. The point was to make me feel sorry for her and want to help her. Would you believe I actually lent her part of the down payment on her house?" He nodded. "Yep, I did. And I'm generally considered a good businessman, same as I used to be considered the queen of Queenland. She said she had a big payment coming in the fall—from her trust—and if she lost her opportunity for the house . . ." He paused and drank deeply. "Oh, God. I can't even talk about this without gibbering. She made me feel like I was the world's greatest real estate agent. Pathetic, isn't it? When she got her money, she was going to not only pay me back, but help me buy out my partner, who happened to be my ex-lover— you can imagine how much I wanted to get out of that one—and she'd set me up in her carriage house (rent free, of course) and once we were married, I could leave my apartment and live with her in the Big House."

Talba was shaking her head, not getting it.

"Okay, you think I'm crazy, but you have no idea of the persuasive power of the woman. Part of it was promises—those and sheer exuberance. She was going to throw all these parties for me to make business contacts. And she did give a few. I have to give her that. She did."

"I thought her thing was to give parties for artists and writers."

"Well, that was the payback. She'd give a party for me, and then she'd give one for herself, and I had to get people there that she wanted. In certain circles, I do know everyone. Ever since I helped Hunt and Lynne Montjoy find their house, I've been pretty well connected in that area."

"I heard she actually paid you to introduce her to people."

"Oh, she did. She doled out money in dribs and drabs, but the big payoff never came." He sighed.

"With your repayment," Talba said. "I guess you didn't make her sign a note for the loan."

"Are you kidding? We were engaged by then. I was going to

live in her house, and it was going to be half mine anyway." He wiped his mouth delicately, but let his napkin slip to the floor. "Anyhow, she said the money would come in the fall, as soon as some 'legal complications' got ironed out. And then there was her catalogue business, which was always teetering on the verge of making money. The way she told it."

"I'm just curious. How did she . . . uh . . ." Talba didn't know how to put it.

"Seduce me? The usual thing. Moonlight and roses. Candles and too much booze. It was like anything else. I'm gay; she knew what gay men do."

"Oh. You mean the thing all men want."

"Yeah. Men are men, I guess. She actually convinced me that might be enough. Anything was possible as long as we were together, because we were *meant* to be together. *God*, this is embarrassing!"

"And how did it fall apart?"

"Well, she got crazier and crazier. And also the money never came—the money she owed me, I mean. By the time I got the idea I was being taken for a ride, I was in so deep I didn't know how to get out. It was that thing you hear about men doing to women. That psychological abuse thing, where they cut them off from the herd and just . . . work out on them. She got me at a vulnerable stage. I was just out of a relationship, right? So first she sucked me in, then she started getting abusive. And my mama was dying by that time, just to make things worse. Also, half my friends wouldn't talk to me, they thought what I was doing was so crazy. So I needed her. She was my only friend, I thought. She was my lifeline. And besides, if I made her mad, I was never going to get my money back. I was smart enough to know that. So just when I needed her the most was when she started getting abusive. You know what happened, eventually? My ex-lover persuaded me to go away with him for a weekend, and when I got to Florida, he had all these guys there from my former life and . . . I don't know . . . just being with them made me remember what real life was all about. *My* real life."

He picked up his drink, and this time he sipped, apparently having gotten his blood alcohol level high enough to calm down. "So I broke up with her on the phone—from down in Destin—and after that she never let me have a moment's peace.

She called me all the time, with threats and intimidation, and tears—you name it—but fortunately that was all electronic." He smiled. "Thank God for voicemail."

"Tell me—how did you react when you found out she was dead?"

"You really want to know? I thought, 'What a waste.' But it was about her life, not her death. You know what? I don't think we were ever really engaged at all. I think she was just conning me."

"Out of the money, you mean?"

He nodded. "That was part of it, but only part. I was like a trophy wife. She wanted to show me off—who doesn't want a presentable man around?—and also to mask her real interests."

Talba realized she had a great talker on her hands, and the scotch wasn't hurting. "How about another drink?" she asked.

"No, thanks. I just needed a jump-start."

"Well, then—about her real interests. She had a secret lover? Is that what you're saying?"

"Oh, didn't she wish. She moved here for Hunt Montjoy. She chased him all around the country. I don't even know where she met him—Tallahassee, I think."

Talba's heart picked up speed. Allyson had lived in Tallahassee. And thinking back to Hunt Montjoy's C.V.—had he? She couldn't remember, but Hale supplied the missing piece. "Montjoy taught at Florida State."

"And that's where she got her master's!"

"Oh. Did she? I didn't even know she had one."

"She did. In English lit; can you believe that?"

"Oh. My. God. I'll bet the whole thing was in aid of chasing Montjoy."

Talba considered the implications of that—and there were many. "They were actually having an affair—is that what you're saying?"

"Not to my knowledge they weren't—not in the usual sense. But she did sleep with him at least once, when she first moved to town. Trying to rekindle the old relationship. She told me that."

"So they *had* been involved."

"In Tallahassee. At least that's my understanding. It was like she was stalking him. Moved here for him, got Lynne to do her house. Can you believe that? Hired his own wife."

"And she told you all this? All the while convincing you the two of you were soul mates?"

"She told it like it was in the past. Like I was helping her recover. But you know something? It wasn't in the past. Know how I figured it out? Montjoy was the only person on God's green earth she had a kind word about. She was paranoid as hell. At the time, I believed her lies—I thought she really was being taken for a ride by everyone in her life. But she never said anything like that about Hunt. She acted like he was God on the half shell. That's how she happened to give that Leo party for him. You know—the one where I met you." He winced at the memory. "Possibly the nadir of my life."

Talba said, "There's something really strange about all this."

"If I were a little younger and less imaginative, I'd probably say, 'Well, duh. . . .' God, I hate that expression, don't you?"

The last thing Talba wanted to do was get off the subject. "I understand," she said carefully, "that Cassie was the one having the affair with Hunt Montjoy."

"Cassie! You're kidding."

"I can't prove it. I've just heard it rumored."

"Oh, man! That must have seriously pissed off Gatsby Girl."

"Gatsby Girl? Did you know that's what they call her at the literary festival office? The Girl Gatsby."

"No, I thought I made it up. When you think about it, though, it's kind of obvious, isn't it?" He sipped his drink one last time, found he'd hit bottom, and changed his mind about not having another. With his glass, he signaled for one.

Talba was thinking she'd found a motive at last—one that didn't involve Janessa or Rashad. "Let's get back to this pissed-off thing. Let's say her daughter really was secretly involved with the man she loved, and she found out about it. Could she have killed her in some sort of blind rage? And then gone home and killed herself?"

Burford Hale laughed. "Well, the first part, maybe. She didn't give a tinker's damn for that pretty little girl." He shook his head. "But I don't see her getting all guilty about it. She just wasn't the remorseful type."

"You're not the first person who's said that. Tell me, have you told the police any of this?"

His drink arrived and he swigged without even setting it down first. "The police? No, they haven't talked to me yet. They called; I guess they were going through her Rolodex, or maybe Arnelle told them about our pseudo-engagement. But I'm not scheduled to see them till tomorrow."

"So why'd you agree to talk to me?"

He considered. "I like your voice," he said finally. "You've got a really great voice. There's something soothing about it."

She didn't believe it, but she couldn't wait to tell it to Eddie. "Come on. Really."

"Okay, but that really is part of it. The other part's curiosity, I guess. I thought you might have some stuff to tell *me*."

Talba let it hang there.

"Well. Do you?"

"I just did—that Cassie might have been involved with Montjoy."

"Give me more."

What could it hurt? Talba thought. The man's tongue was wagging like a puppy-dog's tail. "Okay," she said. "Maybe we can figure something out here."

"Like what?"

"Like who'd want to kill her."

He laughed again. "That's easy. Everybody."

"I think the police theory is that Rashad did it."

"Rashad? That kid who lived in the carriage house. *My* carriage house? He was the one who took over when I wised up."

"Somehow I don't think they were engaged."

He shook his head in agreement. "No, it wasn't sexual; that I'm pretty sure of. I mean, she had kids, she wouldn't . . ."

"Rashad's a grown man."

"Barely. I think he was way too callow for her." He took another deep draught. Apparently, this helped him think. "No, it wasn't that. I mean, look—legally grown-up or not, he was a kid; and he was black—excuse me—" He glanced at her to see if she was offended. Deciding she wasn't, he continued "—and poor. There was no percentage in showing him off. She wasn't really interested in sex. She needed men for what they could do for her. And Rashad was a natural for the honey-dos. Plus, she got to look generous for taking care of him."

"Do you see any motive for him to kill her?"

"So far as I know he's a pretty sweet-tempered kid. But she probably did owe him money . . . I guess you never know."

Same old thing, Talba thought. "What about Janessa? The girl who was painting the mural?"

"Same thing, I guess. But why would either of 'em kill Cassie?"

Suddenly Talba had a thought. "Well, what if Rashad was involved with Cassie—and *he* was the one who found out about Montjoy?"

"In that case, why kill Allyson?"

Talba shrugged. "To frame her for murder–suicide."

"Could be. Could be, but I don't buy it. And Janessa I don't see at all—she *couldn't* have been involved with Montjoy."

After Montjoy's unkind remark, Talba tended to agree with him—but what if that was a cover-up? On the other hand, why cover up for Janessa? "Moving right along," she said. "How about Hunt or Lynne?"

"Sure. I could see it. Lynne for obvious reasons; Hunt because he's a mean-tempered sonofabitch. Anything could have set him off. But, again, it doesn't explain Cassie."

"Arnelle or Austin, then. For her money."

Hale shrugged one shoulder only, a dismissive gesture that was over so fast she barely saw it. "Allyson claimed they were the ones controlling the purse strings, but that was probably a lie. Sure, why not? But, then, why Cassie?"

It was getting to be such a refrain, Talba was starting to wonder if the two women had been killed by the same person. And yet, what else made any sense?

"Rosemary now," Hale said. "Let's don't forget Rosemary."

Talba already had. "Rosemary? Refresh my memory."

"Rosemary McLeod, her business partner. If Allyson screwed the rest of us, think what she must have done to that poor woman."

Ah, yes, the business partner. Talba couldn't neglect her if Rashad or Austin couldn't shed any light. She wondered how Eddie was doing down in Port Sulphur.

"Well, what I'm really working on is clearing my client. . . ."

"And who might that be?"

"That part's confidential. But here's what I can tell you—

Rashad and Austin were both at Allyson's the night she was murdered. . . ."

"Before or after?"

"That's the dicey part. They've been missing ever since."

Hale brushed his moustache. "Four days. That's a long time. Do we even know if they're still alive?"

"Austin's been sighted, but we don't know where he is now." She didn't see the point of mentioning Rashad's call. "I was wondering if you have any idea where either one of them might go."

"No," he said. "No idea at all. But it's pretty suspicious. Maybe they're together."

"Could be," Talba said, but in her heart, she was thinking she'd struck out in the missing persons area. The Hunt-and-Allyson connection, though—that was juicy. She signaled for the check. "This is on the firm. Thank you for your time, Mr. Hale. I've got to go home and write a poem."

"I didn't know poets had deadlines."

She looked at her watch. "They do if they're reading in five hours."

Hale lifted his glass. "Write like the wind, Your Grace. May I call you Your Grace?"

"I prefer it, actually," the Baroness said.

Chapter Sixteen

Friday was open-mike night at Reggie and Chaz, the restaurant where Talba was more or less the house star. Whether or not she was billed as "special guest"—which she wasn't tonight—she usually turned up at least once a month. Tonight she intended to wear both her hats. By all accounts Rashad had a lot of friends who were poets, but she had no names—she'd have to use her stage-time to try to contact some.

Though she had plenty of old material, she really needed something new, as she'd told Burford Hale. No sooner had she sat down to write than the title came to her: "I'm Looking for a Man." After that, it flowed. As always—and practically over Miz Clara's dead body—she wrote in the vernacular, though she always spoke in standard English. She couldn't explain it, it was just how the poems came to her. How she heard them. (But she tried not to go there with most people—just to let it be.)

It took her a good two hours to compose and polish the poem, leaving only a few minutes to get a snack, put together an outfit, and get there. Her mama was in the kitchen. "How's my baby?" Miz Clara said.

"I'm fine, Mama." She answered with her head in the refrigerator. "How was your day?"

"My day was the same as always. Scrubbing toilets, cleaning kitchens, listening to cracker trash tryin' to tell me how to clean. What they think my bi'ness is? By the way, you ain't my baby now. Got me a new one."

"Oh, Sophia. Sorry, I don't have the daily report." She found a chicken leg, closed the fridge door, and ate it standing up.

"I don't mean Sophia. I mean Janessa."

"Janessa. Oh. Janessa." That was the last thing she expected. "I think I feel an attack of sibling rivalry coming on."

"Baby, that ain' nothin' new to you. You been competin' with ya brother ya whole life. You ain' answer my question."

"How about, 'contrary as ever'? That good enough for you?" It was what Miz Clara used to say about her children when someone asked after them.

"When ya gon' bring her 'round?"

"Soon. Just as soon as I clear up this case I'm working." *As soon as I'm sure she didn't kill a couple of people.*

"Ya readin' tonight? Whatcha gon' wear?"

"Now that's the question. I'm about to go work on it." She finished her chicken leg, cut herself a chunk of cheddar cheese, and took it back into her room. As she ate it, she checked her e-mail, but there was nothing urgent. She washed her hands and found her new pants. They were black chiffon and cropped just above the ankle, but unlike most cropped pants, they weren't cut straight. They were ruffled bell-bottoms, slit up the legs, with more ruffles in the slits. A chartreuse tunic went with them, with wide sleeves that fluttered when she moved her arms, permitting her the kind of sweeping, regal gestures appropriate to a Baroness.

In the V-neck of the tunic, she fastened a sort of collar made of jet beads, found the matching earrings, and checked the mirror. A hat or not? *Something*, she thought, and rooted out an orange and green scarf, which she folded into a kind of Indian headband trailing long, loose ends. And for funk, a pair of flat burgundy-colored ankle boots cut low enough so you could see their tops inside her side-slits—a look the designer never intended.

She let Miz Clara check her on the way out. "What do you think? Am I a Baroness?"

"Ha! More like you a rummage sale. I'm gon' wrap ya up and take ya over to the church. Ya good for ten dollars, easy." She considered. "Shoes bring down the price, though. Ain'tcha got somethin' better'n those old things?"

"That's my mama! Always right there with the ego boosts."

Miz Clara turned to her *TV Guide*. "Your ego don't need no boostin'."

That was the way she'd raised her children: Spare the praise or spoil the child. It probably made you try harder, Talba figured. Or else just quit trying altogether. Sometimes you just couldn't win. For instance, Talba's clothes were too funky, but Michelle's too straitlaced. Talba's sister-in-law dressed like an Uptown white lady, and Miz Clara was always after her to "try a little color." So far as Talba knew, Michelle didn't have a thing in her closet that wasn't black, white, or gray. Miz Clara went around saying she was afraid Sophia was going to grow up thinking her mama was in mourning for somebody.

"Wish me luck, Mama."

"Break a leg," Miz Clara said, cackling at herself. Talba had taught her to say this, and it never failed to crack her up.

To her chagrin, Talba had found that in New Orleans, poetry readings tended to be either exclusively African American or mostly white. The odd person of color turned up at the white ones, and you never knew who'd be in the audience, but most poets tended to stick with their own. This bored the Baroness. Early in her career, she'd made a point of performing at both kinds of readings and, partly due to extensive press coverage (which she had engineered herself), but mostly due to her ex-

traordinary talent and stage presence (in her own opinion),
she'd gained quite a following. (Of course, a lot of people said
they went just to hear her mellifluous voice, but the Baroness
discounted those fools.) Mostly because of her efforts, she
liked to think, Reggie and Chaz was one of the few venues in
town that attracted a truly mixed crowd. And it was mixed in
more ways than racially. It was a hangout for artists, writers,
musicians, professional Tarot readers, Faubourg fashionistas,
Bywater baristas, even tipped-off *touristas*—just about everybody who thought they were hip except Austin Edwards.

It was decorated in a style that Reggie, one of the owners, described as "cheap and cheerful," its most arresting feature being
the gaudy collection of Guatemalan belts that hung like stream-
ers from the ceiling.

The black readings nearly always started late; the white ones
more or less on time. Reggie and Chaz compromised, starting
time being no more than half an hour after the announced curtain. That worked just fine for the Baroness, providing exactly
the right amount of time for a pre-reading glass of wine. She bel-
lied up to the bar, ordered herself a Chardonnay, chatted lightly
with friends, and looked around to see who was there that she
didn't know. There were many. Good. The place was going to be
packed. Surely there'd be someone there who could help her.

The emcee that night, Lemon Blancaneaux, was the kind of
guy who loved to hear himself talk. When he ran out of things
to say, he'd repeat his opener, "How y'all tonight?" and use the
slight pause to think of some new prattle with which to oppress
his audience.

But everyone was friends here, and enjoying beverages, and
courting the good will of those who'd soon be his or her audience, so no one booed or hissed. Talba was all but asleep when
he called the first poet who'd signed up to read. This was a guy
she knew, someone famous for his drinking, who called himself
Serenity Prayer Jones—Prayer to his friends. Prayer had written what could only be called an ode to his favorite tipple,
vodka and Coke—known to bartenders as a "Black Bitch"—
which was also the name of the poem. Because he was African
American, he completely got away with it, and even the
Baroness herself had to check her dignity and roll on the floor a
bit as the double entendres flew around like confetti. Actually, it

was a pretty hard act to follow, and the next poet wasn't remotely up to it. She was a young white woman disturbed by the recent war in Iraq, and Talba had a feeling she wasn't going to be the last to tackle that subject before the evening was over. She got only polite applause.

The third poet appeared to be Japanese, but evidently identified as black. His subject was his own oppression. After that, a black woman read some very sweet verses about her childhood in rural Louisiana; Talba quite liked her, but the audience was in a more raucous mood. She herself was next, and for once she was actually a little nervous. But the noisy applause caused by the mere mention of her name—finally achieved after a nearly interminable introduction by the loquacious Lemon—went a long way toward restoring her confidence. There was even some foot-stomping.

As she often did, she talked a little about the poem before she read. "This is a poem I wrote about somebody I don't know, but I bet some of y'all do. He's somebody I'd like to meet, somebody I've got some business with, someone who's really well-liked by everybody who knows him, but who might be in a lot of trouble right now. And he's somebody I need to help. If anybody out there knows who I'm talking about, you're going to find the Baroness myself out in the bar waiting to buy you a drink, just after I read my poem, which is called 'I'm Looking for a Man.'"

She unfolded the poem. She'd noticed that white poets actually did read, and usually very badly, in her opinion. What on God's Earth made people want to read poetry in a monotone? She simply did not understand it. Most African American poets memorized and *performed* their poems, and the Baroness herself was no exception—with an old poem. With a new poem, she usually read, but she *always* performed. These people hadn't pried themselves away from their TV sets to be bored to death; the least she could do was give them a show.

She repeated the title before she started: 'I'm Looking for a Man.'

> *I'm lookin' for a man*
> *His Aunt Felicia still call "baby,"*
> *And that's what he might be.*

Could be just some poor soul
Wandering out there lost and homeless,
Nowhere to go,
No friends in hell or Eden,
Pack o' dogs on his trail.

But he might be something else,
Something nobody know about,
Could have a real dark side;
Gotta have demons
Back behind those pretty eyes—
Otherwise, he wouldn't be a poet.
Likes to medic tattered feathers,
Sex therapy, kind'a—
Sleep with baby, ya gon' be all right.
Turn him down, he don' care,
Ya still gon' be all right.
He ain't in it for the pussy.
Somethin' else there.
Somethin' no one knows about.

This man grow up on Chippewa Street,
Right down near the project
They tore down to build theirselves a Wal-Mart—
Now what we need a Wal-Mart for?

(Here the foot-stomping resumed—nobody in this crowd liked that Tchoupitoulas Wal-Mart. Feeling more confident, she forged on.)

Daddy gone; mama gone, too.
Ain' nobody home but On-tee,
(And Marlon and Paw-Paw)
He love to ride that bike of his—
Have adventures, fly like a buzzard,
Glide like an albatross—
Or maybe a vampire.
You tell me.

He want somethin' he ain' never gon' get
On Chippewa Street.
He want the world.
He find somethin' take him to heaven,
Same thing we all find,
But most of us still here.
This man ain't.

He find him a white woman old enough to be his Maw-
Maw,
Give him a house.
He find him a white man, 'most as famous as Elvis Presley,
Just as close to being God in that white world of his,
Just about as dead.
He find his own swimming pool.
With blood in it.
He find him a young white lady friend.
With blood on her.
He find him a second white man.
With a fish on him.
He find him another white man.
With stripes on him

He find him a young black woman-girl,
With a crush on him.

He find my sister.
She be all right,
Just like all them others;
She be just fine.
Maybe.
If he ain' got somethin' ugly in him.

I AM LOOKIN' FOR THIS MAN!
White po-lice lookin' for this man!
My sister lookin' for this man!
Another man lookin' for this man!
And that one got a gun.
We in a race here.

The room was dead quiet. Talba let it be, just for a second, and then she executed a perfect curtsy, announcing as she always did that "The Baroness myself thanks you." And the audience went wild, perhaps at the sheer strangeness of it, though more likely it was her intense performance that got them. She knew she was a good poet—she had some awards to prove it—but she was an even better performer. And even she had to admit she really did have a great voice.

A spotlight followed her as she marched grandly to the bar. She thought of having a Black Bitch, she'd enjoyed Prayer's poem so much, but she couldn't stand the taste of vodka. Settling on a margarita, she daintily licked at the salt, wondering if anyone was going to seek her out. Well, actually, *someone* was going to—someone always did—but would it be someone who could help her find Rashad?

A few people said, "AwRite!" or "Nice, Your Grace!" depending on their race, but it was a while before anyone came to claim a free drink. She knew who it was going to be, as soon as she saw her—she could tell by the purposeful way the woman walked, by the anxious look in her eye. The woman was spaghetti-thin—that vegetarian, green-tea kind of thin that indicated a volatile temperament, perhaps a former drug problem, an obsession with clean living so pervasive you could tell she was trying to shake something.

She wore a camisole top that showed her protuberant collarbone and left bare her matchstick arms, and a sarong from the flea market that wrapped around her nearly twice. She was African American, and fairly dark, but she either spent a fortune at the hair salon or there'd been a white man in the woodpile sometime in the family history. Her hair was thick and long, and definitely African, but it waved rather than crinkled. She had a small face, too small for all that hair, but you couldn't argue that she wasn't beautiful. Her skin glowed the color of coffee beans, and seemed to have been burnished with a chamois. Her nose was tiny, and round, not straight—the only thing about her you might call "cute" rather than beautiful, but somehow it still came down on the side of beauty. Her eyes said she lived in a world of hurt.

She tilted her chin at Talba, and slinked through the crowd.

Her eyes were wet. "What kind of trouble is Rashad in?" she said by way of introduction.

"I'm sorry I upset you," Talba said. "Would you like something to drink?"

"Seven-Up. Thanks." The woman struggled for control.

"I'll try to give it to you in a nutshell. You know about Allyson and Cassie?"

The woman nodded.

"I'm afraid he hasn't been seen since they were killed. I'm Talba, by the way."

"Oh, sorry." The woman extended her hand. "Everyone knows who you are. I'm Charmaine French. Rashad's a real good man. Haven't seen him in a while, but we used to date. The police really think he could have done something like that?"

"They're just looking at everybody who knew Cassie and Allyson. We don't know if he was actually shot, but he did call my sister and say someone shot at him. I'm sorry to deliver the bad news. You know I'm a PI?" Charmaine nodded. "My sister wants me to try to help him. Do you have any idea where he could be?"

The bartender set Charmaine's drink down. She picked it up and drank through the straw. "No, but I sure wish I could do something for him. He was real good to me. That was a beautiful poem, Baroness. Anybody who knew him would know who you were talking about."

"It was all put together from impressions I have from friends of his. I've actually only met him a time or two in passing. I was hoping to find someone tonight who could shed more light."

"Well, I can. He's a good man! He'd *never* do something like that."

"The police think he might have been involved with Cassie."

"No. Uh-uh. They were friends. He took me over to her house once while we were dating. I didn't see any sign they'd ever been involved. He *will* date white chicks, though. That much I know."

Talba took a big sip of her drink. "This is really good. Sure you don't want one?"

Charmaine gave her a regretful smile. "I don't drink anymore. I was a serious pothead, on my way to being a drunk, too—and God knows what else. Rashad got me over it."

"Did you meet here?"

"No, I was in a poetry workshop he gave."

"That's how my sister met him. You know Janessa Wallis?"

Charmaine smiled. "Janessa's your sister? Sure, I know Janessa. She's real good friends with him."

Talba looked at her over the rim of her glass. "Just friends?"

Charmaine nodded vigorously. "Oh, yeah. I'm pretty sure of it. Now Janessa might have a little crush on him—most of the female students did—but we were taking the same course. I kept missing class, and Rashad came to see me. That's how he found out about my problem. With the pot, I mean. I don't know why, but we just started dating." She shrugged, as if she were unaware of her beauty. "He couldn't have been seeing anyone else in the class because he was always with me."

"He was dating a student?"

"Well, actually . . ." She hesitated, took another sip, and dabbed at her forehead with a bar napkin. "It's hot in here. I don't know if I should mention it, but I will, because it gives you an idea of his ethics—we never had sex until the class was over. But he was interested. Oh, yeah, that was obvious. And then we dated for a while after that, and then . . ."

"And then you broke up."

"I don't know if we did. Not exactly. We just sort of stopped seeing each other. I guess you could say we both moved on."

Talba considered. "Charmaine, can I ask you something? I wonder if it coincided with your getting clean? I mean, after you could take care of yourself, maybe he just . . ." She didn't know how to say it. "I mean, you're beautiful, but I get the impression he likes to *fix* things. I mean . . . people."

Charmaine began to play with her napkin, her face betraying distress; hurt feelings, maybe—at the very least, confusion. "I never thought about it like that," she said. "I guess I didn't especially notice because all of a sudden I was so much busier than I had been—I'm a student at Southern, did I say that? And all of a sudden I was going to classes and going to meetings, and actually completing assignments. I don't know, I guess I thought we just didn't have time for each other anymore. But come to think of it, his life didn't change. Maybe you're right—maybe I just didn't interest him if he couldn't help me."

Talba said, "You know what I think? I think sometimes people come into other people's lives, serve a purpose, and then they're gone. I wouldn't go so far as to say they're 'supposed' to play a certain role—I don't think we could presume to know anything like that—but my mama's a church lady, and she probably would. I just notice it happens a lot."

Charmaine played with her hair. She seemed to enjoy flicking it over her shoulder and back again—and who wouldn't? Talba thought. "You know, that's just like Rashad. I thought your poem really nailed him—in a nice way, I mean. He does like to help people. See, Cassie . . . do you know about Cassie?"

Talba shook her head. "I'm not sure what you mean."

"Well, she was having this awful affair with this big-deal writer. Big-deal *married* writer. I mean just horrible. Treated her like shit on a stick."

"You mean Hunt Montjoy? I've heard she might have been seeing him."

"Well, believe it. She was. That's why Rashad took me to see her. She'd called him crying, saying she was going to shoot herself. . . ."

"Omigod!" Talba said, thinking of the gun. "Did she threaten suicide on a regular basis?"

Charmaine shook her head so vigorously her hair swung back and forth, turning itself into a gorgeous heavy curtain. Talba suspected this was something she did often, perhaps for the sensation of it as much as the appearance. "I don't think she did. But Hunt had humiliated her in front of a friend, and when she called him on it, he said she was lucky to have him, she was nothing but a little gutter slut, and a few other lovely things. Rashad had to go over and calm her down—part of his helping thing. He thought another woman might help. Didn't, though. All I could think of to say was, she ought to cut the rat bastard's balls off. She told me to stay out of it." She smiled. "Can't think why."

Good idea, Talba thought, hoping Cassie hadn't belatedly decided to take the advice.

"He'd invite Cassie to a party, be there with some other woman; make dates and stand her up; buy her presents and call her a whore if she took them. I mean, not then—not on the spot. He'd bring it up later."

Talba said, "I just don't understand how she could have had

so little respect for herself And I really don't see how Rashad could stand the bastard. I hear they're good friends."

"Oh, Rashad! He sees the good in everybody. He said Hunt was a great writer and kind to him, but he was just horrible with women, and no woman should ever get mixed up with him. And Cassie! She'd tell these stories, and then say Hunt wasn't so bad when he wasn't drinking. Say sometimes he was real sweet to her, people just didn't understand him. That's some shit, isn't it? I guess she thought she could sober him up all by herself."

"Tell me something. Did you ever hear that Hunt was involved with Allyson—Cassie's mother?"

Charmaine sputtered in her Seven-Up. "Well, if that's not one for the books! No, I never heard that. But I'll tell you one thing—it wouldn't surprise me."

"Look, let's leave the Cassie-and-Hunt show for a minute. What I'm trying to do is find Rashad. One thing I know—he had a girlfriend who was a crack addict. He used to turn up at crack houses and places where she'd go to crash, and pull her out of there."

"Oh, I know about that one. The one he couldn't save. She died."

"What I'm getting at—could he have gone back to any of those places? To hide out?"

Charmaine arranged her hair again; it seemed to be more or less her hobby. "I don't know if I see that. Rashad couldn't stand to even talk about that part of his life. I think he really did love that girl."

"Well, maybe he's staying with an old girlfriend—he must have lots of them."

Charmaine shot her a look. "Not me, if that's what you mean. I haven't heard word one from him."

"But if you dated, he must have told you something about his exes. Was there anyone he mentioned that I could talk to?"

She pulled at her lip. "There was Kerry. What about Kerry?"

Talba remembered the name—Wayne Taylor had given it to her. "Somebody else mentioned a Kerry. Said she was suicidal, and Rashad helped her. But I don't have any other details."

"I don't know much about her, either. Just that she was white. She had some kind of bad home life, maybe her daddy beat her, I don't know—another of Mr. Do-Good's hard luck cases.

What I do know is this—she lives in Mississippi or some place. North Carolina, maybe. Makes sense he'd leave New Orleans—if he's running away, I mean. Maybe he went to see Kerry."

"What's her last name?"

She wasn't surprised when Charmaine said she didn't know.

"Well, maybe he wrote a poem about her—do you happen to know if he did?"

"Hmph." For a moment, the elegant young woman sounded just like Miz Clara. "Never wrote one about me. Guess there were too many of us."

"For heaven's sake, he's only twenty!"

Something mischievous flashed on Charmaine's somber features. "Man's sexual peak, they tell me. But listen, kidding aside, I asked about that—with Kerry, I mean. He said, 'Oh, no, I could never write about it.' Naturally, that got me curious. So I asked him why, and he just said, 'It's not for public consumption.' Kind of mysterious."

Talba wanted to get away to chew on this information morsel, but she felt obliged to stay awhile, keep Charmaine company, see if anyone else came forward. All the same, she excused herself long enough to call Darryl to see if his daughter had gone to bed and he wanted company. She was high from her gig and she didn't want to wait till tomorrow.

Chapter Seventeen

It was a long night. They hadn't seen each other in a while and there was plenty to talk about. And talking was never enough; two or three athletic events ensued as well.

It was just what Talba needed—that and a lazy day just hanging out, and then maybe a Saturday night dinner at some nice restaurant. It occurred to her not to answer when her cell phone rang at eight-thirty.

But there was too much at stake to let it go. Janessa could

have heard from Rashad again, or maybe Charmaine had—
Talba had given her a card. The last person she expected to hear
from was Eddie, considering the wild-goose chase he'd em-
barked on yesterday. "Don't tell me you found Austin," she said
excitedly.

"Uh-uh. He found me. Looked me up in the phonebook." The
name of the agency was officially E.V. Anthony (after Eddie's
son, and also to get in the "A's" in the Yellow Pages), but Eddie
never missed a bet—both he and Talba were listed separately as
well.

"Well, where is he?"

"Allyson's. He asked me to breakfast. Want to come?"

"Oh, man." Talba was half-awake and wholly stunned. "Oh,
man, you have got to be kidding."

"Never more serious. Guess he liked me. You mind picking
up some coffee and bagels or something?"

"Bagels, hell. How 'bout I whip up some cornbread? Maybe
grits and grillades. Won't take but a minute."

"Ms. Wallis, Ms. Wallis. Cranky as usual. Guess ya didn't
make it over to Algiers last night."

"Well, I did, matter of fact—and I was up late, if it's any of
your business."

"That's the last thing it is, Ms. Wallis. Whatever ya do, don't
tell me about it. Allyson's at ten, okay? Better yet, come a little
late. So ya don't scare him to death before I get there. Angie's
comin' too—the both of y'all'd spook a pit bull."

She hung up and broke the news to Darryl, who seemed too
sleepy to figure out what she was saying. And then she dressed
again in her Baroness clothes, thinking, what-the-hell, it would
really annoy Eddie, and that couldn't be bad.

Instead of bagels, she opted for muffins, which she purchased from the PJ's on Camp, thinking maybe, just maybe,
she'd see Rashad there. But two fugitives in one day was way
too much to hope for. She came away with nothing but a bag of
muffins and four cups of coffee.

Being perennially punctual—it was nothing she could help—
she arrived exactly on time, thinking to wait a few minutes if
she didn't see Eddie's car. The house was still marked with yellow crime-scene tape. In New Orleans, crime scenes are rarely
sealed unless there's a good reason for it, but in this case, the

cops apparently had already gathered their evidence. If they hadn't, too bad—Eddie and Austin were inside. Audrey's Cadillac was parked on the curb, Austin's hog inside the yard. Talba figured that one had Allyson spinning in her grave—or would have, if she'd been in it. The autopsy had been done, but Arnelle had decided to postpone scheduling the funeral, in case the prodigal brother turned up.

I guess, Talba thought, *her worst fears have been realized.*

The man who answered the doorbell wasn't exactly the one she was picturing. He was about five-ten with long, lean muscles, and plenty of them, rather than the barrel-chested look she expected from a biker. He had longish, light brown hair, slicked back with water, as if he'd just gotten out of the shower, and he wore khaki shorts, a guayabera shirt, and no shoes or nose ring. If it hadn't been for the tattoos on his arms, she'd have had to say he looked like a preppy with redneck leanings, something on the order of Hunt Montjoy. His face was weather-beaten and a little craggy—attractive, but just short of handsome. The look on it said he'd have been less surprised to find a deb in a ball gown on his porch than the person he was looking for.

She was amused. "Oh, hi," she said. "Eddie didn't mention I was coming? I'm his associate, Talba Wallis." She held up her bag of goodies. "See? I've brought breakfast."

He laughed. "You're Eddie Valentino's associate? I was expecting someone named Sal or Vito."

Eddie walked up behind him. "For Christ's sake, it's the Baroness. I thought Ms. Wallis was coming."

"Had a gig last night. You guys want your coffee or not?"

Austin moved aside. "Sorry. Come in. I thought at first you were a friend of my mother's. I mean—no particular friend. You're her type, that's all."

When Harleys fly, Talba thought. She said, "She did invite me to a party here once—or rather, Burford Hale did. I'm a poet, if that's what you mean."

"A PI poet! Bet Mother loved you."

"Not so far as I could tell, actually. Shall we take this stuff to the patio?" Not waiting for an answer, she headed that way, forcing the men to follow if they wanted coffee. She set it on a table and turned around to face her host, already regretting her flipness. "Mr. Edwards, I'm sorry for your loss."

A cloud passed over his features. "Thank you. I'm still trying to make sense of it."

"We all are."

The bell rang again. Eddie said, "That'll be Angela. Let me get it."

Austin turned to Talba. "Angela?"

"Eddie's daughter. She's a lawyer."

"Oh. Well, I guess I might need one." He unloaded one of the coffees and began adding cream and sugar.

Talba was about to say Angie already had her hands pretty full with Rashad and Janessa, but she figured that could come out in good time. She only smiled as Angie followed Eddie back to the patio, wearing jeans and a pink tank top. It was the first time Talba'd seen her in anything but all black. "Angie, you look fabulous," she blurted. Something about the pink seemed to bring out color in her face that Talba had never seen before. Her hair was in a ponytail, but the short ends at the front hung loose around her face. Today she wouldn't even have scared Janessa.

"You can be my lawyer any day," Austin said. Talba sensed Eddie prickling. And maybe his instincts were working—when Austin and Angie shook hands, Talba could have sworn they locked eyes. "Angela," their host said, "have you had breakfast yet? I was going to make omelets."

"Sure, I'd love one," Angie said, and sat down at the round table where Talba had set her muffins and coffee.

Talba served both Valentinos their coffee and went into the kitchen to find a plate for the muffins. She smelled better, fresher coffee brewing, and saw that Austin had prepared piles of cheese and onions and peppers and was already breaking eggs. Angie followed. "Can I do anything?"

Austin whirled rapidly, almost bumping into her. Again, he seemed to pause a moment, and when he spoke his voice was gentle. "Sure. You can set the table. Let's eat on the patio."

"Okay. Sure."

Talba arranged her muffins and took them back, to find Eddie staring into the pool. "Didn't Janessa say something about a cat?" he said. "I don't see any cat."

"Oh, Koko. Arnelle has her. She offered her to me—along with Cassie's cat."

"Ya gonna take 'em?"

"I'm thinking about it. Sure wish they could talk."

"Naah. If cats could talk, think of the business we'd lose." He grabbed a muffin and began tearing it apart. He picked out a raisin and ate it.

"Strange remark coming from you," Talba said. "This case being such a money-loser and all."

It was an opening for him to say, Okay, absolutely no more time would be spent on it after this weekend, but he only raised an eyebrow. *Good,* Talba thought, *I'm not bringing up the two-day deadline if he isn't.* What he said was, "Ms. Wallis, ya ever read *The Great Gatsby?*"

"Sure. Why?"

"Everybody says Allyson reminded 'em of Gatsby, but ya know what? I think there was a lot of Jordan Baker in her. Nick Carraway's girlfriend, ya know?"

"Huh?" Talba knew she sounded like a junior high kid, but she wasn't expecting literary allusions out of Eddie's mouth.

"Ya remember what Nick said about her? 'Dishonesty in a woman is something you never blame deeply.' Shows how times have changed, huh? People sure as hell mind it now."

Talba looked at him accusingly. "Eddie, you've been to the library."

"Whassamatter, think I'm stupid?"

Angie reappeared with place mats and napkins, and Talba jumped up to help her. "Hey, Ange, did you know your dad's into American lit?"

Either she didn't hear the question, or her mind was elsewhere. She only said, "Y'all just make yourselves comfortable. We've almost got it happening here."

When she had disappeared again, Talba said, "Burford Hale minded. A lot."

"Who the hell's Burford Hale?"

Talba gave him a mini-report while Austin and his new assistant created breakfast. The next time they saw Angie, she was setting down two plates of omelets and home fries. Austin followed with another two.

This is pretty weird, Talba thought. *One minute this guy's a fugitive, the next he's having a brunch party at his dead mama's house.* She was wondering what it was all about when Austin started explaining.

"That's better," he said, and Talba saw that he'd consumed a substantial portion of the food on his plate in approximately forty seconds. "Nothing like a lot of grease and gunk for a hangover."

Eddie said, "I take it that means you imbibed a little yesterday?"

"Uh-uh, brother. You've got me wrong. I imbibed a *lot* yesterday. Sorry about your car, by the way. I wasn't thinking too clearly."

Eddie waved a gracious hand. "Ah, it needed the workout."

Austin had nearly cleaned his plate and was putting apricot jelly on a muffin. His face cracked in one of those self-conscious grins that Talba noticed passed for an apology with certain men. "I guess it was shock. All I could think of was *not* thinking of what I should have been thinking of. You understand what I mean at all?"

Eddie looked a little bewildered, but Angie said, "Totally. It's the broken leg syndrome."

Both Austin and Eddie went blank. "*You* know," she said. "All you can think is, 'Damn! I've got a run in my stocking.'"

"That's it!" Austin shouted, muffin crumbs strewing out of his mouth. "That's it exactly. I had to sign the payroll checks and I had to get my ride. That was all I let myself think of. And then when I'd signed the damn checks, and gotten on the Harley, it hit me. I mean . . . the bad news hit me. I turned right around and came back here and bought a bottle of Jack Daniels on the way. And then I got here and I drank and watched old movies, and . . . ummm . . . cried." He looked back down at his plate, picked up his fork, and searched unsuccessfully for one last morsel of food.

Talba could believe the drinking part, but the crying didn't convince her. Except that, when Austin raised his eyes, they were a little too shiny. "I couldn't believe my little sister was really gone. And my mother. She was like a force of nature. Nothing could hurt her. I fell asleep and finally I woke up and almost called Arnelle. You don't know what a big deal *that* is." He turned up his palms. ". . . Anyway, I finally believed it. So I drank some more and slept some more and this morning I woke up. Really, really, really hungry."

Everybody was embarrassed. Talba decided to change the subject ever so slightly. "Did you know I'm Janessa's sister?"

"No! How the hell could that be?"

Talba shrugged. "Long story. But here's what I'm curious about—she says you insulted Rashad Monday night; other people say you were friends."

"Oh, shit! Goddammit, I'm going to quit drinking. Yeah, Rashad's my friend. Look, I'll tell you the story on that. I don't know how to say this but . . . well, basically, my mom was no mother at all. She always treated us like a big inconvenience—except for Cassie, that is. She more or less treated Cassie like a boil on her behind." Talba winced, but to her amazement, Angie smiled. "So, what can I tell you? I never grew up. When I saw her so happy with Rashad, treating him like *he* was her son . . . this old, ugly junior-high jealousy just bubbled up, and I said mean things to him." He held up apologetic palms again. "I don't like to admit it, but she could make me turn into a six-year-old who wanted his mama. So I act like a six-year-old sometimes. Where is Rashad, anyway?" He did the guilty-grin thing. "The police make him leave? I need to apologize."

Eddie and Talba exchanged glances. Finally, Eddie said, "We don't know where he is. I told you that—you don't remember?"

Austin looked confused. "Uh, no. I guess I don't. What do you mean you don't know?"

"He's been missing since Monday," Talba said.

"Oh, man. He was the last to see her alive, you mean."

"Janessa said Allyson told you she wasn't going to give you a penny of her money," Talba said. "Why would she say something like that?"

"Well, that was specific. It might sound like some empty threat to disinherit me, but it wasn't. I came to get a loan from her. That's what I was here for. One of my boats sank a while ago, and the insurance company's stalling around about it, and the longer they stall, the more money I lose. But that's not the problem—I'm a good fisherman. I could always make a living that way; I did it for a long time. Bet I'm one of the few laborers working in the Gulf who has a degree from Dartmouth." He paused and looked around the table; Talba had a feeling their expressions didn't disappoint him.

"I used to work for that plant in Empire as a pogie boat captain—I'm pretty good friends with the owner, so he tried me out, and what do you know, I was damn good at it. I mean, look, it isn't rocket science. And I got to know the menhaden business, so when the bait company came up for sale, I talked my dad into buying it. But not for me. I don't give a damn. I could be happy just going out on a boat, or working on the oil rigs. I didn't even like the responsibility of being a captain. But Dad's getting on, and I thought it would be a great investment for him. The thing is, it's starting to turn sour on us, and Dad's sick; I mean, really sick. You know what I mean?" He glanced at each of them in turn, holding their eyes until they understood that his dad was dying. "So I asked Mom for a loan, and she pretty much hated Dad. . . ." He got up and left the table, returning in a moment with a glass of water. But his eyes were slightly red. Talba suspected he'd been composing himself. "Anyway, she said she'd think about it and then when I acted badly, she decided to hit below the belt." He looked at Angie when he said it, and Talba could have sworn there were tears in Angie's eyes, but it couldn't be. Angie was the toughest lawyer in the parish. She made a slight movement with her right hand, the hand closest to Austin, as if she wanted to touch him, but caught herself in time. "So that was what that was about," he finished.

Again, they sat quietly, embarrassed. Austin started up again. "That was the state of mind I was in when I rode off into a hurricane. Yeah, it was crazy; I admit that. But *I* was crazy; I didn't care whether I lived through it or died. I just wanted to feel alive. Look, I don't know whether you understand this, but there's something really physical about working on boats, being in storms, battling it out with yourself. Do you understand at all?"

They all nodded.

"I wanted that storm. I just wanted it. It was like, 'Bring it on!' You know?" He shrugged. "Too bad if that makes me a murder suspect."

Up till that point he'd been doing fairly well getting Talba's sympathy, and apparently very well at getting Angie's, but he was lapsing into that six-year-old thing he'd mentioned. Okay, he was capable of acting like a child, Talba thought. Maybe it was a good thing they were actually seeing it.

"But no way I'd hurt one crinkly hair on Cassie's innocent

little head. No way in hell." He made no attempt to hide his tears.

"Ya think Cassie and Rashad were involved?" Eddie said.

"No way," he repeated. "My sister liked older guys. Married, preferably. Rashad was her buddy. For all I know, she told him everything." He brightened. "He didn't kill her, I guarantee you that—but maybe he knows who did."

Maybe that's why somebody took a shot at him, Talba thought. Maybe he'd gone to sleep in the carriage house and then seen something that made him get out of Dodge, to save his own hide.

"How about ya mama?" Eddie said. Talba wondered if he'd made the question deliberately ambiguous.

He shrugged. "Just about anybody could have killed her—I mean, could have had a reason to kill her. And Mother could have killed Cassie," he said, looking again at each of them in turn, making sure they were getting it. "I'm gonna tell you something. She was completely capable of it."

"Why's that?" Eddie asked quietly. Quiet like a snake, Talba thought.

For the moment, Austin ignored him. "But she'd never have killed herself. She was too much of a bitch. She and Cassie, though—they went at it all the time. Fought and fought and fought about everything. She just *destroyed* my sister, man; kept her from being who she could be. Worked her self-esteem down to a little nub, and then worked it down a little more."

"Why didn't she do it to Arnelle?"

"'Cause Arnelle's a bitch, too. That kind of stuff rolls off her; also, Hubby's a buffer. But he's got some bad investments. Arnelle needs money. According to Mother, I mean. Arnelle could have killed her for that."

"Burford Hale says she controlled Allyson's money," Talba said.

"She might have. I don't know because Big Sis and I don't keep in touch. But she doesn't have any herself. Maybe there was something from her dad, but she's probably run through it. All I know is what Mother told me, and what she said was Arnelle was always after her for money. And there was no love lost between those two.

"But I'll tell you what—I don't think Arnelle did it either, if only because it doesn't explain about Cassie. And I've been thinking about this, believe me. Burford Hale, now—there was a man with a motive."

Angie said, "Why are you so sure Rashad didn't do it?"

" 'Cause she was the goose that laid the golden egg, man. He got a lot from her. No percentage in it. And then there's Cassie."

There was always that.

"Y'all want some more coffee?" Without waiting for an answer, Austin left to get some, Angie's eyes following him into the kitchen. Eddie's mouth opened to say something, but either he never got it out or his voice was drowned out by the shrill one that tore through the relative peace of the patio. "What the fuck are you doing here?"

"What the fuck are *you* doing here?" Austin riposted.

As one, the three others rose and raced into the kitchen. Arnelle had arrived. Her neat bob had gone limp, and she was wearing jeans. She looked like she was about to go for a knife.

"You killed Mother, you bastard."

Austin's face turned gray. "Hi, Big Sis, I'm fine. It's great to see you." He was trying for fake heartiness, but his voice sounded thin and forced, a little frightened. "Ever heard of the Prozac Nation? They could use you over there."

"Who are these people? Are you having a party, Austin? Wouldn't that be just like you! Right on the spot where Mother died."

Talba stepped forward. "I'm Talba Wallis, Mrs. Halston. I came to see you the other day."

"Oh. You looked different."

Quickly, hoping to defuse the situation, Talba introduced Eddie and Angie, but Arnelle wasn't up for polite conversation. "Just what are you people doing in my mother's house?"

Austin said, "Funny. I thought it was my mother's house."

"Could you two play nice?" Angie said, and Austin flushed. His shoulders relaxed, and he turned to her.

"Sorry," he said. "I'll just show my sister to the door. We haven't seen each other in a while, but we find the shortest reunions are usually the best. In our family, guests stink after three minutes instead of three days."

"Guests, hell! This is my house," Arnelle said. "All four of you will leave now."

"Why, Arnelle? So you can loot Mother's jewelry box?"

Arnelle turned red, making Talba think Austin had something. "I bought this house for Mother, Austin. It's my name on the deed."

Talba said, "Burford Hale didn't mention that," whereupon she turned redder still.

"Look, if you want to throw me out, call the cops," Austin said. "And by the way, help yourself to the jewelry—I don't want it. I don't want a damn thing that reminds me of her."

Somehow, that cooled her out. Maybe the jewelry was all she really wanted. "You sure?" she said. "Look, we'll divide it up later. I just came to take it to a safe place. I mean, I thought—with the house vacant and all—"

"Sure, Arnelle, you go and take it somewhere for safekeeping. Just don't try to throw me out of my own mother's house."

Arnelle did a one-eighty and disappeared down the hall.

Eddie said, "I'd follow her if I were you. Make sure that's all she takes."

"Naah, the hell with it," Austin said. "She can take everything in the whole damn house for all I care. Let's go back to the patio."

No one moved.

"Look, we were having fun, weren't we? Let's have a Bloody Mary."

Eddie said, "I've got a better idea. How about you and I go over to the cop shop and give 'em your statement?"

"Monday, my man. Monday. You have my word on that. Just let me have the weekend to get used to all this."

"All right, we're out of here."

"Hey! Tell me y'all aren't going to leave me alone with the bitch."

Angie said, "I'll stay and have a Bloody Mary."

"You will?" Austin looked as if a star had just fallen from heaven into his hand.

Eddie said, "Angie."

His daughter patted his hand. "Dad. It'll be okay."

"I'll take real good care of her, Eddie," Austin said. "Arnelle tries to kill her, I'm all over it."

Eddie raised an eyebrow at Angie, and she gave him a little reassuring nod. Talba hurried him out of the house. They walked to the sidewalk in silence, but when they got to Eddie's car, Talba couldn't resist a tiny dig. "So, Eddie, you satisfied? Guess Angie's not a lesbian."

"I'd almost rather she was. He's a murder suspect, for Christ's sake."

"She can handle herself."

"I hope to hell ya right, Ms. Wallis. Can't stop her; she's free, white, and twenty-one."

"Real nice expression."

"You know it doesn't mean nothin', except that I can't do a damn thing about her. I'd like to spank her little behind."

"Look at it this way. If she wants him to go to the cops, he'll go to the cops."

Eddie popped his car lock with the remote, and put one hand on the door handle, as if he were about to go. Without turning back to look at Talba, he said, "Ms. Wallis, tell me somethin'. Ya don't think she's gonna sleep with him, do ya?"

Talba couldn't believe what she was hearing. Having screwed up his courage, he turned around and looked at her. "Eddie, you're asking me? How do I know?"

"You're a woman, aren't ya?"

"Hadn't thought of that. Well, I probably know the answer, then. No. She's not going to sleep with him." At least not today, Talba thought. Definitely not till he's cleared.

Angie was still Angie.

Chapter Eighteen

Talba figured the problem of whether or not Austin actually went to the police was out of her hands—if Eddie and Angie couldn't handle it together, nobody could. And she had something important to do Monday morning. She was haunted by what Rashad's grandfather had told her—about himself and Rashad's father working on the docks.

It was as good a lead as any. She couldn't do twenty-four-hour surveillance at the Celeste Street Wharf, and her gut told her Rashad had left there for good, anyhow. If someone had really shot at him there, the place wasn't safe for him. Besides, whether he was there or not, he'd still need money. The same thing applied if he was hiding out in some crack house. He'd also need money to get to North Carolina or wherever Kerry lived if he planned to stay with her. And something told Talba he wasn't going to get very far with an ATM card. How much could a kid like Rashad—a poet who basically did odd jobs for a living—have in a bank account? Sure, Marlon or Felicia might be slipping him something, but if he was paranoid enough, he might assume the police were watching their homes. And they might be, Talba thought.

The thing was, his grandfather had said where to find him—had *told* her. And no one else had. So why not take a chance? She opened the phonebook to "Employment" and noted several agencies that seemed like they might handle dock workers, or maybe other kinds of temporary help. The truth was, Rashad was a slight man, unused to manual labor. She could see him doing banquet or office work more easily than heavy lifting. Still, he wouldn't have the nerve to go to white collar employment agencies. He'd go where people like him went—the down and out, the rap-sheet encumbered, the drifters, the desperate.

And there was such a place with extremely high visibility. Furthermore, it was near the place Rashad grew up, and near the Celeste Street Wharf. It was a hiring hall on St. Charles Avenue, just upriver from Lee Circle.

She'd never been in it, but she'd been by it many times in the early morning and seen the sidewalk jammed with men, mostly African American men, dressed in work clothes. The overflow from inside, she assumed. She wondered if they placed women, too. Aha—there was her pretext.

She dressed from her orphan third pile of clothes, Miz Clara's famous "somethin' to slop around in." It was a day for what she thought of as the American uniform—jeans and T-shirt. God, what she'd give for stock in Gap. Or maybe Wal-

Mart or Target. Every American, despite age, race, sex, national origin, or religious preference had to have drawers and closets full of jeans and T-shirts. Miz Clara worked in them, and so did the guys down at the hiring hall. Even Eddie probably had a pair of jeans, and Angie probably lived in them when she was off work; Austin had them, Marlon had them, Demetrice had them, Darryl had them, presidents had them, and First Ladies probably had them.

Damn, they were wrong for a Baroness!

But, for anonymity, you couldn't beat them. Today, she was a humble job-seeker. Her own mother wouldn't recognize her. She drove past the hiring hall and parked her car on a side street, then walked back and began looking casually over the crowd of men on the sidewalk. She didn't see anyone she recognized, but she didn't tarry too long, so as not to stand out too much. She elbowed her way into the building, which housed a dreary room somewhat like an old-fashioned bus station, with rows of benches, a counter in front, and a sign announcing what kind of jobs were filled here. She was studying the sign when she became aware of movement somewhere to her right. Glancing casually over her shoulder, she saw that someone had stood and begun to push his way outside. She was almost sure it was Rashad.

"Rashad! It's okay!" she called, and he began to run.

After all this time and effort, here he was. And the little shit was running away from her. Janessa had probably already told him, during one of his calls, that Talba was looking for him. Obviously, he'd recognized her, and he didn't want to be found. Well, the hell with that. To hell with both of them.

She chased him out of the building and through the crowd, her progress impeded by the sea of humanity waiting to be hired to move furniture and wash dishes. "I'm Janessa's sister," she yelled. "We got you a lawyer."

He didn't even glance at her. He took off across Calliope, under Highway 90, and ran across St. Charles to Lee Circle, which was indeed a circle, with a statue of General Robert E. Lee in the center of it. The trouble was, Lee's statue stood on a mound that was more like a small hill. Rashad bolted up the mound and over it.

And once he was beyond the crest, he was out of sight.

Talba puffed after him, turning her ankle slightly and muttering. When she reached the top of the mound, he was gone.

She ran down the far side of it, crossed the street to the front of the Hotel le Cirque, and spied a dark alleyway where he could have easily disappeared. But he could also have run into a building, or behind one, or simply had such a head start that he'd gotten halfway down the block and found a hiding place somewhere in the vicinity. Without much hope, she entered the alleyway—and saw nothing. And nobody.

Her ankle was starting to throb.

Well, hell. Even if he'd gone this way, she'd never be able to catch him with a bum ankle. At least she could stop calling hospitals—obviously, he was in glowing health. Nothing to do but go back to the office and ice her injury.

On the way, she called Janessa, but her sister didn't pick up.

She was good and angry. And disappointed. Even if they found Rashad again, what good was it going to do? If he didn't want to be found by the good guys, she might as well call the cops and let them take over.

Not even counting brunch with Austin, Eddie had a pretty eventful weekend. One thing, he received a call from his daughter Sunday afternoon saying she'd meet him at the Second District at nine A.M. Monday to take Austin in to give his statement. All Eddie had to do was call Crockett and tell him to be there. That, and pick Austin up. "Okay, Ange, thanks," he said. "Hope you didn't have to do anything too compromisin' to set it up."

"Since when's a little blow job going to compromise me?" she said, and hung up, leaving her father staring at the phone. She was getting way too big for her britches. He should never have taken her along to those biker bars. Now she thought she could talk to him like he was her college roommate.

Sighing, he said, "Audrey, what do you think of a girl who says 'blow job' to her father?"

"Ya dreamin', Eddie," she answered. "She probably said 'blow dry' or somethin'."

Shaking his head, he decided to call Theresa Salvatore while he still had the phone in his hand, and a crumb of ambition.

Theresa had been the bartender at Pete's last time he'd been in there, and many years before that—and he'd be pretty surprised if she wasn't still. He didn't have her home number, but he did have Pete's' unlisted one—which was its only number. If you had it, you could call there and tell your old man to come home, but you couldn't get it unless Theresa liked you. You also had to ring the doorbell to get in. The place was like a private club for the neighborhood—as well as for every fireman who lived or worked Uptown. It was in the Irish Channel, coincidentally on Chippewa, Rashad's old street, but far upriver from his old neighborhood. Not that it wasn't in a dicey area—hence the locked door—but it was quite a few steps up from the Chippewa near the old project.

Being a neighborhood bar and a firemen's bar, it was exactly the kind of place a phony-baloney like Hunt Montjoy would go to avoid Yuppie scum—and to convince himself of his own authenticity. How he'd found out about it, Eddie had no idea. He'd have had to be taken there, as Eddie had been himself, by some buddies who lived in the Irish Channel. Eddie still went there now and then, for Monday night football, or just to have a drink with his old buddies. If it wasn't so far from home, he'd probably have brought Audrey so they could hang with Theresa, who was like the Mother Superior of the neighborhood. Probably half the clientele came in just to pass the time of day with her.

Theresa was what Montjoy would probably call a character—but the truth was, she was like all the women Eddie'd grown up with in the Ninth Ward, and she was a lot like Audrey, and half the other women in New Orleans, including plenty who'd been born Uptown and never crossed the Industrial Canal. She was bright as a bauble—though in a street-smart kind of way—sexy at sixty-three, observant as Sherlock Holmes, and about as quiet and ladylike as Joan Rivers on speed. And a lot funnier, in Eddie's opinion. There were other similarities as well—she probably spent as much time and money on grooming and jewelry. Her nails were perfectly painted lethal weapons, the better to show off her many rings, and her ink-black hair was always piled into the kind of up-do invented in the '50s and kept alive in the salons of New Orleans. She was the only woman he knew who could swear all day and all night and it wouldn't even faze him.

She had one kid at Harvard med school, and another at the University of North Carolina.

An unfamiliar male voice answered the phone, probably a customer. "Theresa there?" he asked, not even wasting a "hello."

In turn, the guy didn't waste a "Sure, just a minute." The next voice he heard was Theresa's. "Hey, dawlin'," he said. "Eddie Valentino."

"Eddie Eight-Inch." It was what they called him in Pete's, and it had nothing to do with anyone there having seen him naked, and everything to do with his job. They went in for nicknames there, arrived at after four or more Buds, but unfortunately never forgotten. "Hey, dawlin'" she repeated. "How's the dick business?"

"Can't complain," he lied. He could probably complain three weeks straight about the last week alone. "Might bring me to your place one night this week."

"Oh, yeah? Frank Martzell's wife cheating on him again? Don't bother. If she is, she's not doin' it here."

"Naah, so far as I know, she's behavin' herself. Ya know a guy named Hunt Montjoy?"

"Oh, that guy. Whatcha think of some jerkoff grabs the good-sized behind of a sixty-three-year-old married woman?"

"A real gentleman, is he? Well, don't take it too personally—his reputation precedes him."

"I'm not s'posed to take my own butt personally? Listen, if that asshole and his prissy little Tulane friend never darkened my door again, it'd be about three weeks too soon. He makes *Heather* look good. You know Heather, that skinny little bitch from down the street? Comes in here, wiggles her itty-bitty ass, points at my firemen, who I love like Godiva chocolate, which, by the way, is *always* welcome here, dawlin', and says, 'Can't ya make those guys shut up? I come in for a quiet drink, I want quiet.' I say, 'Heather, this ain't no funeral parlor, and it ain't no Sunday school—this is a *bar room*, in case you didn't happen to notice,' and then I go tell my firemen what she said. This one big guy, Jimmy O'Connor, you know him? Well, Jimmy hollers out, 'What bitch said that?' And Heather turns every color in the Crayon box. Didn't keep her from comin' in again, though." Theresa sighed.

Eddie said, "What little Tulane friend?"

"I don't know, some twerp of a professor wears *pin stripes* meets him here for *story* conferences. They're s'posed to be writin' a screenplay together. You beat that? A screenplay. Like this is the bar at the Beverly Hills Hotel, and they gotta come here to show off their Armani jeans and talk loud on their cell phones and sip Perrier." She snorted. "Not that they do."

"Not that they do what?"

"Any of the above. No Armani, no cell phones, *definitely* no Perrier. Uh-uh. We're talkin' Jack Daniel's, and vodka and cranberry juice. Pink drink! My gay boys, who I loooove like fine champagne, which, by the way, dawlin', is always welcome here, order pink drink. This little twerp ain't gay, though. So tight-assed, if he was, he couldn't even get laid."

Even from Theresa, this was too much for Eddie. "Nice talk, kid."

"Whaddaya want, Eddie? Did I mention this ain't no Sunday school I'm runnin'?"

"The twerp named Wayne, by any chance?"

"Eddie Eight-Inch! Dick of my dreams. Now how the hell did you know that?"

"Trick of the trade, dawlin'. And it's not Tulane, it's UNO."

"Ah, hell, I know it's UNO. He just seems like he *oughta* be from Tulane."

"So when do the tinsel twins come in?"

"Tuesday nights, usually. Sometimes they do Monday night football and then 'work' afterward—more like, play with themselves. I mean anybody can *say* they're a writer, right? Why the hell would you work in a bar?"

"Probably isn't Wayne's choice. It'd be Montjoy's thing, though."

"You got that right. Man's a lush. Now, *he's* here just about every night. Days, too, sometimes."

"Do me a favor, Theresa. If I come in to see him, you don't know me, okay? And you never heard of that Eight-Inch thing."

"Two little words, babe."

Eddie sighed. "Chocolate and champagne."

"Not just any chocolate, dawlin'."

"Right. Godiva." He'd have to have the stuff sent. How was he supposed to be a stranger if he came in with an armload of gifts?

He'd get Eileen Fisher to figure it out.

He got to the office at eight A.M. on Monday, an hour early, and already Ms. Wallis had a bug up her butt. He hadn't even had his coffee when she exploded into his office like one of those Fourth of July starburst things, all shiny and everywhere at once, and a little scary. The good part was, she carried two cups. "Guess who I just saw?"

He wasn't up to caring yet. "One of those for me?"

She set a cup on his desk. "Rashad's who I saw. And let me tell you something—he doesn't want to be found. He made me chase him."

Eddie took a hot, sweet sip. Ahh. Better. "Ya tellin' me ya let him get away?"

"Forgot my Nikes. Also—" She bent down and rubbed her leg. "I twisted my ankle. Otherwise, it would never have happened."

"Yeah, tell me about it. Where was he?"

"Did I mention I saw his grandfather Thursday? Come to think of it, we've got quite a bit of catching up to do. Grandpa's pretty far gone, but he said, go look for Rashad at the hiring halls, so I did. And bingo, there he was."

"Which one? That one on Saint Charles?"

"Yeah. He doesn't have a car, so I thought—"

"Uh-huh. That's why ya got a PI license. He was there, huh?"

" 'Was' is the operative word. He recognized me and hauled gluteus. Another thing—according to Grandpa, he killed his mother."

Eddie set his cup down hard enough to splash coffee—and he needed every drop of it. "That's it. The case is closed, Ms. Wallis. We take Austin in to corroborate Janessa's story, and that's the last move we make. That little pissant doesn't want to hold still for us, let the white po-lice have him."

"I was kind of thinking that, too. I mean, we never did know what the juvenile record was about. History of violence . . . I don't know . . ."

"Ya tell Crockett about Celeste Street?"

"I thought you were going to."

"Forgot. I'll tell him both things when we take Austin in— about that and the hiring hall."

"I doubt Rashad'll go back to either place."

"Hell with it. That's Crockett's problem."

"Look," Talba said. "One other thing, just for the record. What if Cassie and Allyson were both involved with Hunt Montjoy?"

"I'd say they had a pretty dysfunctional family going."

"Well, there's a new insight."

"Don't get smart, Ms. Wallis."

"Sorry, I was just agreeing with you. It kind of sheds a different light on murder–suicide, though."

"Not our problem, Ms. Wallis. Somethin' wrong with ya hearing?"

Chapter Nineteen

Eddie arrived at Allyson's early, about half-worried he'd have to tell Austin he couldn't go to the cop shop wearing an aloha shirt and shorts. But he was pleasantly surprised to find the biker attired in jeans and a polo shirt—not exactly suitable for the White House, but fine for the Second District on a random Monday. *Angela,* Eddie thought. She'd want him looking like a credible witness and wouldn't have been shy about telling him so.

Speaking of which, the first words out of Austin's mouth were, "Where's Angie?" He actually looked in the backseat, as if he expected to find her bound and gagged on the floor.

"She's meeting us there. She'll go in and talk to Crockett with you—I'm just along to make sure this damn thing gets done."

"You don't have to worry. Miss Valentino says 'pogo stick,' I make like a wallaby."

"Don't we all, Mr. Edwards." Eddie couldn't help heaving a deep sigh. "Don't we all."

"Hey, call me Austin, Eddie. We're all family here."

God help us, Eddie thought, wondering if Austin was twitting him, or if it had just slipped out. The latter, he decided—surely you wouldn't deliberately anger the man who was currently driving you to the police station.

Angie was waiting outside the Second in her accustomed all-black lawyer drag, prompting Austin to break into a great big boyish grin. "Ah, the dominatrix look." Apparently, he liked it.

"Hey, Austin. Hey, Dad," she said. "Crockett's waiting for us."

Austin said, "You know I'm doing this for you."

"Ya better do it for yaself," Eddie snapped.

Crockett greeted him with a handshake. "EdDEE! How's the lovely Audrey? Listen, we'll get your statement, too. Boudreaux's gonna interview ya." He cocked his head at the others. "You two come with me."

So Eddie spent an hour telling about his two trips to Port Sulphur, and their subsequent sumptuous brunch with a murder suspect, while Crockett grilled Austin—to whatever extent Angie permitted.

Afterward, Angela came and got him. "Dad, come with me. Austin, you wait for us."

"What's up?"

"I'm going to let Crockett tell you. He wants Janessa to plead out."

She led him to the room she and Austin had recently vacated, where Crockett sat complacently, hands folded on a table. "Tell him, Reuben."

Crockett said, "Y'all have a seat."

They had a seat. Crockett said, "Eddie, it looks pretty bad for your client."

"Yeah, yeah. That's what you guys always say. Whatcha got, Reuben?"

"Look, we've got two witnesses saying the same thing, but that doesn't prove anything—you know as well as I do that your client could have been killing Cassie while Rashad and Allyson were still smoochin' on the patio."

"Objection, Reuben," Angie said. "Nobody was smooching."

"This ain't court, Miss Valentino." Crockett unclasped his hands and leaned forward. "Look, ya know about the glass over at Cassie's with Allyson's prints on it?"

"So?"

"So it came from Allyson's house. That is, it's the same design as her other glasses, and Cassie didn't have any others like it."

"Whatcha gettin' at, Reuben?"

"Wouldn't you infer from that that the glass was planted?"

"Not necessarily, but so what if it was?"

"Well, Allyson's prints weren't the only ones on it—we've got two good ones belong to your client."

"Janessa?"

"Ya got two clients here, Eddie?"

Eddie was trying to assimilate it. What the hell did this mean? He remembered LaBauve saying Crockett had something else, something he was waiting to spring on him. He must have decided now was as good a time as any to squeeze Janessa's side.

"Suppose," Crockett said, "somebody was trying to make this thing look like murder–suicide? And that somebody left her prints on the evidence she was trying to plant?"

"Give me a break, man. That doesn't fly and you know it. There could be a million other explanations for that." But at the moment he could only think of one: Janessa had been dumb enough to leave prints on the glass.

"Tell ya the truth, I like it," Crockett said. "We've gotten convictions on less."

Eddie stood up. "The hell you have. Why don't you go arrest her if you're so sure?"

"Eddie, I'm giving you and ya lovely daughter a chance here—you can still get the kid a good deal."

Eddie looked at his daughter. "Angie? Your call."

She nodded, as if she needed his approval like she needed another ten pounds. "Thanks, Dad." She stood and offered Crockett her hand. "With all due respect, Reuben, you can go to hell."

"Angie, for Christ's sake," Eddie said.

"Ah, relax, Eddie," the cop replied. "Angie and I are old sparring partners. I know she means no offense." He turned toward Angie. "And none taken, good-lookin'." He winked at her.

Eddie knew she wouldn't have permitted either the compliment or the wink if she hadn't been out of line.

"I was just giving y'all a chance," Crockett said again. He walked them to the stairway. "Y'all have a good day now."

At the last minute, Eddie remembered about Rashad. "Oh, Reuben, by the way, I've got something for you. You know my associate, Ms. Wallis? She's spotted Rashad twice—he's been camping out at the Celeste Street Wharf. And he's looking for work at that hiring hall near Lee Circle. Don't say I never gave you anything."

Not giving Crockett a chance to answer, he turned and joined the others.

He and Angie made Austin sit in the car while they hashed it out. "Whaddaya think?" Eddie said.

"I think we'd better get Talba and go see the little bitch."

Eddie winced. "For once, I gotta agree with ya nomenclature. Meet ya at the office? I gotta drop Austin."

Angie looked at her watch and sighed. "The things I do for free."

"Ya got nothin' on me—I'm the resident expert on that one."

Talba was feeling a huge sense of accomplishment, having spent the morning putting ice on her ankle and catching up on routine employment checks and sweetie snoops. She'd taken Eddie seriously about dropping the case; it was good to devote a few moments to clients with the odd coin in their jeans. And her ankle was a whole lot better.

Whatever she expected of Eddie when he came back from the cop shop, it wasn't what she got—which was more or less a fire-spewing dragon. Expletive-spewing, at any rate, and that just wasn't like Eddie. Angie was with him and she wasn't much calmer. Instead of spewing, she withdrew into some tight, grim space like its own little low-pressure area, a storm just waiting to blow.

Talba stood when she saw them, thinking Austin had split on them again. "What's the matter?"

"Get that sister of yours on the phone. Now!"

"Okay. And then what?"

"Tell her ya got somethin' real exciting to tell her and ya'll be right over."

"And will I?"

"Oh, yeah. We all will. Might take all three of us, but we're definitely gon' wring her lyin' little neck."

Talba looked from one Valentino to the other and decided whatever was going down was real—neither of these people was stupid, and they so often disagreed that if they agreed for once, Talba figured she probably did, too. And when all was said and done, she owed Eddie a lot more loyalty than she did her sister, who might indeed be a lying little bitch. In fact, there was very little evidence to the contrary.

Janessa picked up on the first ring.

Talba said, "Hey, I've got news. I'm coming over right away."

"Wait a minute. I'm not home."

"Oh. Then where are you?"

"I'm paintin'—workin' a job with Marlon, Uptown."

"Where Uptown?"

"Jefferson and Magazine. Real nice house we paintin'. Whyn'cha come on over? Maybe you could take me to lunch. I'm gettin' pretty hungry."

"Good idea. Give me the address." Talba felt like a traitor.

"We'll go in my car," Eddie said.

"Uh-uh," Angie replied. "I might need to leave sometime between the flaying and the drawing and quartering."

"Ms. Wallis, you go with her," Eddie said. "I don't trust myself to talk right now."

When they were barreling down Magazine Street, trying to keep up with a furious Eddie, Talba said, "Angie, what's up?"

"Looks like she did it, Baroness. All the time it's been her—or at any rate, there's something very important she forgot to tell us." She told Talba about the prints on the glass.

Janessa and Marlon and some other man—part of the painting crew, Talba surmised—were sitting on the front steps of a big brick house, taking a break. Janessa had on overalls, with a bandanna tied around her head against paint drips. Talba got out of the car and waved from the street. "Hey, Janessa, come on. Let's go to lunch. Hey, Marlon. I won't keep her too long."

Janessa hurled herself happily down the walk and flung herself in the back seat. "Where we goin'?"

"Byblos," Angie said, picking a Mideastern restaurant something like Mona's, but fancier. Lately, these had proliferated in New Orleans, and offered good, fresh food without a lot of deep-frying and sauces—always a good choice, in Talba's opinion.

Janessa was immediately suspicious. "What's that?"

"Mideastern, you'll like it."

"Eeeew. You mean, like with the library paste you scoop up with some kind of round bread, tastes like sawdust?"

"How about Semolina?" retorted the ever-flexible Angie.

"Pasta," Talba said. "Giant portions."

"Okay, yeah," the girl said.

Angie got on her cell phone. "Dad. Meet us at Semolina."

That made Janessa happy. "Mr. Eddie comin', too? What y'all found out?"

"We'll tell you when we get there."

Privately, Talba wondered if a restaurant was really the right place to have this conversation, but then again, it would put them all in better moods. She thought Angie was doing all right, but the minute Eddie walked in, you could see something was wrong—at least she could. He was limping more than usual, his face was slightly red, his pouches looked like something you could buy at Hold Everything—and his eyebrows met in the middle. That was the real tip-off. He scared Talba and he wasn't even mad at her.

But Janessa seemed oblivious. "How ya doin', Mr. Eddie? 'Sup? Y'all found Rashad?"

"Janessa. The cops want to arrest you for murder."

The waitress picked that moment to appear. At the mention of the "M" word, she turned a color somewhere between mauve and magenta. "I, uh, uh . . ." she stammered, but Eddie was unfazed. "We'll have the Malibleu salad," he said. "Bring us four of 'em, four iced teas."

So much for Janessa's pasta. Talba noticed her sister's color wasn't too good, either.

Eddie's face had taken on the wrath of the Old Testament God. He turned his pouches and unibrow frown full on his young client. "What the hell were you doing at Cassie's the night of the murders?" His voice was somewhere between a croak and a growl.

Finally, Janessa had the good sense to look scared. For the whole last week, Eddie had played good cop to Angie's tough one. Janessa swiveled her head, as if seeking the former Mr. Nice Guy, or maybe an exit.

Apparently seeing no way out, she turned her attention to her former protector, tears shining in her eyes. "I wasn't at Cassie's. What you talkin' about?"

"The police say you were, Janessa. They found your fingerprints."

"Well, I *been* to Cassie's. Just not that night."

"That's not gonna fly. They found the prints on one of Allyson's wineglasses."

Janessa looked utterly bewildered. "Y'all ain' makin' no sense."

Talba took pity on her. "They think you took the glass over there."

"Why'd I do a dumb thing like that?"

"Because you didn't think it was dumb," Angie said. "You thought you were being real smart."

Janessa went pouty. "I don't know whatcha talkin' about."

"Why'd ya try to slip one by us, honey?" Eddie said. He was the good cop again.

Frustration was pouring off Janessa like sweat. "I didn't lie to nobody. Look, Austin tol' ya, didn't he? Thought y'all was takin' him to the po-lice."

"We did," Angie said. "And that's when they told us about your fingerprints."

"They believe Austin? They let him go?"

"Janessa. What about the glass?"

Their salads were now being delivered, but the waitress looked ready to run for cover if anyone made a sudden move. Janessa said, "Whoa. That thing's big enough for three people."

"Two, anyway," Eddie said. "Shouldn't have ordered so many. But these are on Angie—you're her client. Or you were. Angie, you firin' her?"

"No, I'm not firing her. If anybody needs a lawyer, it's Janessa here." She took a bite of her salad, which had bits of apple and blue cheese in it. "This is delicious, Dad. I wouldn't have thought it was your thing."

"Yeah, well, I wouldn't have thought butt-dragons were yours."

That seemed to interest Janessa even more than the threat of life imprisonment. "Butt-dragons?" she asked, and Talba could only be grateful. What the hell had Eddie meant?

Angie was wolfing her salad, looking a lot more relaxed than usual, in fact, almost happy, which wasn't her usual expression. Was there something about having a client neck-deep in bean dip that she thrived on? She had an almost dreamy expression. "Not dragons," she said. "That's 'dragon,' singular. Forget about my dragon. Janessa, I want to know why you took that glass over to Cassie's."

"I didn't take no glass to Cassie's."

"Well, were you there? Were you drinking out of it?"

"No, I wasn't drinkin' out of it. I don't even like wine. Hardly ever drink wine. I need to see that waitress."

Scowling, Eddie signaled the poor woman, who arrived in about a millisecond, eager to avoid offending Janessa. Janessa pointed to the rest of her salad. "I need a go-cup for this."

"A go-cup?" The waitress looked like she'd rather die than disobey.

"She means a doggie bag," Eddie said, and the woman disappeared with a swish. He turned back to Janessa and saw that she had started to cry. "What is it, honey?"

"I thought y'all were my friends. Thought ya were tryin' to help me." She turned on Talba. "And you! You my sister. Come here callin' me a liar and a murderer. I don't need this kind of shit. Listen, I did it, okay? I killed Cassie and I killed Miz Allyson. Y'all satisfied?"

The waitress, who'd just returned with the packaged-up salad, gasped and dropped it like a bomb on the table. Eddie gave her a benign smile. "Pretty good, isn't she? We're rehearsing for a play."

"Oh." The woman's teeth showed, but her cheeks were tight, the smile not quite coming off, her face more or less saying, "Too late. I just wet my pants."

Turning back to his client, Eddie said, "Great, Janessa, that's just great. Now we've got a witness who heard ya confess, and she's *not* ya friend—what ya want to do something like that for? And what in the name of God do ya mean ya killed Cassie and Allyson?"

"That must be how my fingerprints got there, right? Ain't that what y'all are sayin'?"

"No, we are asking you how your prints got there." Angie's relaxed mood was as dead as the plants on her plate. "We're saying that's what the police are going to say—in court. And furthermore, we're saying you better come up with the real explanation."

"It was like they said—I was jealous of Cassie, 'cause Rashad, he couldn't leave her alone. And I killed Miz Allyson 'cause she come in and caught me. She brought her own wineglass. She was drinking wine, and she come in and—"

"Right, kid," Eddie said. "You were busy killing Cassie with a knife, but you happened to have a gun handy for Allyson. That the way it went down?"

"No, she had the gun and I got it away from her."

"Uh-huh. How'd you get her body back to her house?"

"I, uh—I made her drive back and I shot her over there."

"What'd you do that for?" Eddie asked quietly.

"Um . . . I don't know, I wasn't thinkin' straight. See, I was so nervous, I drank Miz Allyson's wine after I shot her, and after that—"

Talba was in mild shock, but nothing Janessa said surprised her anymore. Angie had gone dead-white at first, but her color had come back a little bit at a time—and then some. She was getting redder and redder. Eddie was laughing.

Angie said, "Janessa, hear me! You may not say anything like that to any police officer or *anyone* else—anyone at all, do you hear me? They will throw your ass in jail so fast you'll time-travel—you'll get there before you left home, you know what I mean? And once you're there, do you have any idea how hard it's going to be to get you clear of this? They have enough evidence to arrest you right now—do you *get* that? They could arrest you for murder. The only reason they haven't already is, they aren't sure you did it. They still need to talk to Rashad, and also check out Austin's story—though I wish them good luck on that one—but they *could* arrest you. And if you walk into a police station and tell them you did it, they will. And that's the last thing you want, do you understand?"

Eddie said, "Ah, let her go, Angie. Her story's so full of holes, it's the best thing she could do for herself."

"Dad, keep out of this!"

"Janessa, ya full of it, aren't ya? Why'd ya go and tell us a stupid story like that?"

But Janessa was starting to cry again. "Y'all are *hateful*. Cain't tell who ya are, what ya want. Y'all just hateful!"

She picked up her parcel and left the restaurant. In a great gust of sympathy, Talba went after her. But by the time she reached the door, Janessa was halfway down the block.

"JanessAAAAA! Wait up!" Talba wasn't sure whether she would or not. But the girl stopped and let Talba catch up.

"Don't be mad. We're all trying to help, the best way we can." *If you only knew,* she thought.

"Don't seem like it to me. Seem like ya' gangin' up on me, maybe settin' me up."

"What was that confession thing about, Janessa?"

The girl shrugged. "Maybe I did do it."

"Uh-huh. Well, I've got something for you."

"What is it?"

"An invitation. My mama wants to meet you." She knew this had a truly excellent chance of backfiring; but on the other hand, she couldn't think of any other way to get Janessa's trust back.

"Ya mama?"

"Uh-huh. You want to be part of the family, don't you? Mama says to bring you home."

Janessa said, "Forget that shit," whirled, and walked toward the bus stop.

"I saw Rashad this morning," she called, and Janessa turned around.

"Ya pitiful, ya know that?" she said.

I think, Talba muttered to herself, *she might be right.* She went back into the restaurant and said, "*Why* are we working so hard for this girl? I thought we were going to give her up because we couldn't get a response out of Rashad. Now we're all over her again."

Eddie said, "She didn't do it. And Crockett wants to fry her."

Angie locked her hands behind her head. "Well, I've got two reasons. One is, I'm not doing it for Janessa—I'm doing it for you, Talba. But I'm also doing it for Allyson and Cassie. This thing's getting to me."

"I know what's *gettin'* to you," Eddie said, but Angie chose to ignore him. "You're her sister," he said to Talba. "And you're the one who's giving up?"

"Oh, hell. No. Of course not. But she's such a pain, with all that drama. And I feel so bad because—"

"She's *in* pain, Ms. Wallis."

She was hugely relieved, but she spoke lightly. "I'm not used to being the older sibling. This is giving me a new respect for Corey." But there was quite a bit more to it. She was embarrassed for her sister, and hugely guilty on her account. She'd been about to say she felt bad because the case was such a drain on the firm. She was frustrated, sure, but deep down, she'd also wanted to give Eddie an out. She wouldn't have blamed him for taking it, but he'd come through like a champ.

"Also," he said, "she's scared out of her mind. Question is, why the hell's the kid so scared?"

Chapter Twenty

The answer to that was simple, in Talba's mind. If Janessa didn't do it herself—and Talba had to admit, the least a murderer should know about her crime is how she did it—then she had to be afraid for Rashad. The same Rashad who wouldn't even talk to Talba after she'd spent days tracking him down.

Talba was starting to think he had done it.

She recognized that Janessa, with her manipulating and whining, was still a child in many ways (Talba really couldn't wait till Janessa met Miz Clara), but she also sensed that her sister was lying about something. Certainly she was lying about having killed Cassie and Allyson—unless she was much more clever than Talba thought—but there was something else. She smelled it. And it wasn't about when she left Allyson's Monday night, unless Austin was lying, too.

Talba was thoroughly sick of the whole tangled mess, and felt worse because Angie and Eddie were in so deep.

She thought about how to approach the case in a new way. What if she looked at it like a homicide cop would? As simply a case to be solved, not a client to be cleared?

In her haste to find Rashad, she'd left a few leads unfollowed. There was one person who'd been close to Allyson, for instance, whom she hadn't yet interviewed. Maybe she'd go see Rosemary McLeod, then try to find out names of close friends of Cassie's and track them down, too.

But the truth was still the same—they needed to find Rashad. The only two witnesses said he was the last person who'd seen Allyson alive.

For today, though, she decided to let it go.

She got online, looked up Rosemary McLeod, and found that she lived on Upperline Street. This kind of thing really was sinfully easy these days, she thought, only briefly flirting with the idea of calling first. Surprise was always better, she figured.

The thing she failed to consider was the possibility of her being the surprised one. Rosemary was home, all right. And she was ensconced in a bed in her front parlor, dressed in a pink nightgown with some lacy thing over it. And she was completely bald.

Talba was admitted after a maid carried a couple of messages to Rosemary, a uniformed employee who clearly thought Talba had no business visiting her boss. Which, probably, she didn't. She now remembered something Lynne Montjoy had said about Rosemary being ill. She really seemed to have dropped the ball on this—first forgetting Rosemary entirely, and then forgetting she probably shouldn't be dropping in unexpectedly.

But apparently, in the long run, she was welcome, because she'd been ushered in and Rosemary was heaving herself up to a sitting position. "Miss Wallis. If I'd known you were coming, I'd have put on my wig." She extended a papery hand. "I've never met a real private investigator."

She had as sugary an accent as any Talba had ever heard. Usually these Uptown magnolias put her off—they sounded to her like someone doing a bad accent in a movie set in the South. But Rosemary possessed a gentleness that seemed real. Perhaps she was really a terror momentarily beaten down by chemo, but Talba decided to go ahead and like her anyhow. She smiled. "I'm afraid you'll find PI's an ill-mannered bunch—I should have called first. I do apologize."

Rosemary waved her fragile little hand. "I welcome the company. Sit down, Miss Wallis. Would you like some iced tea?"

"Thanks. Just some water." A compromise between Eddie's rule about taking what you were offered and a guilty need not to put the maid to too much trouble.

"You want to talk to me about poor Allyson, I understand." She touched a hand to her bald head. "My problems seem absurd when I think that in two days we'll be burying my oldest friend, and her daughter."

"They've scheduled the funeral, then?" Talba asked.

"Sorry, I misspoke. I believe they've decided on cremation. They're having a memorial service at Allyson's house. I don't suppose Arnelle and Austin managed to agree on it—probably Arnelle just went ahead and did it—but they *have* scheduled it." Rosemary dabbed at her eyes and it occurred to Talba that she might finally have met someone who actually liked Allyson.

"Your oldest friend," Talba said. "Mmm. Mmm."

"Oh, we go all the way back to when we both lived in Tallahassee—we were both young, bored divorcées in those days. Always trying to find some new way to get in trouble."

It was all Talba could do not to gasp, given what she'd been told about Hunt and Allyson. She said, "Allyson studied poetry, I believe."

Rosemary nodded. "Very smart woman. Yes, indeed, she did. She was getting her master's. And she had the most adorable little shop. She was quite a good designer, you know. Even now—I mean up till her death—she designed most of her own clothes. Back in Tallahassee, I worked for her for a while. I was divorced and had a teenaged son. And ambition." She played with the soft pink cotton blanket between the white sheet and the wine satin duvet cover. When she finished pleating it, she looked up at Talba almost defiantly. "Lots of ambition, Miss Wallis. I was definitely going to set the world on fire, with my amazing handmade jewelry. Can you imagine? I actually thought I was going to make money designing jewelry." She laughed. "Fortunately for me, I met Johnny McLeod. And Allyson married as well, of course—twice, in fact."

"I take it Allyson sold your jewelry in her shop?"

"Oh, yes, she was very supportive. But, truthfully, if it hadn't been for spousal support, I'd never have made it—until I met Johnny, that is. Anyway, I did meet him, and we moved here, and Allyson and I kind of lost touch for a while.

"But then one day out of the blue she called to say she was moving to town and she had a great idea for a business. She wanted to start a catalogue company that would sell New Orleans art—isn't that terrific? I jumped at it, naturally. Think of all the great local designers we have here, of just about everything—furniture to metalwork, to jewelry (that's still my first love)—to Mardi Gras masks, wall clocks, art glass. Anything you can name, some artist does it here. We sold everything from JazzFest posters to one-of-a-kind works by fine artists—absolutely everything. And we carried books—those count as art, don't you think?"

Talba smiled again. "Especially poetry."

"It was absolutely a fantastic business. If it hadn't been so capital-intensive, I'm sure we would have developed a devoted clientele. We might not have been rolling in money, but it was always partly for the fun of it—and the pleasure of doing something for our artists."

Talba seriously doubted that was the way Allyson saw it. "I'm curious," she said. "How did it work as a business? I mean, who had what job?"

"Well, I was CEO and Allyson was president." Rosemary laughed. "Isn't that grandiose? We had a lot of fun with that part of it."

"But how did you actually divide the labor?"

"We both found the artists—that was the fun part—but neither of us had any experience producing a catalogue, so we had to hire an agency. They did an absolutely gorgeous job."

"It sounds expensive."

"It was ruinous. I'd never have sunk the money into it if I hadn't been absolutely convinced it would pay off handsomely." She looked out the window, for a moment not meeting Talba's eyes, or perhaps she was genuinely interested in a bird on a nearby branch. "But it didn't," she said at last.

"I'm sorry. But at least you were in it together."

Rosemary's mouth twisted, as if she were trying to control it. "In a sort of a way, yes."

"Uh-oh. Sounds like it wasn't that great a partnership."

"No! Allyson was wonderful. I knew what I was doing when I got into it. My husband's gone now and my son told me not to do it, but I thought, I don't care what happens, I want this chance to succeed in business. But of course I didn't know I was going to get sick." Once more, she touched her head, rubbing it a little; Talba wondered if she'd shaved it when her hair got sparse. "Sometimes I think I gave myself cancer, just worrying about the business." She sighed. "I really don't know what went wrong. All Allyson's projections indicated we'd break even in the first six months. We thought people would kill to buy this stuff.

"And a lot of people did buy it. We actually took in a couple of hundred thousand dollars in no time at all. But we never dreamed it was going to be so expensive to produce the catalogue. And the postage! We forgot about that entirely."

The pronouns weren't lost on Talba—Allyson had made the projections, but "we" had forgotten and miscalculated and screwed up. Either Rosemary had to be the world's worst businesswoman, or Allyson had conned her so completely she didn't even know she'd been conned.

"Something like that must have been pretty tough on the friendship," Talba said.

"Oh, no. Allyson was a force of nature, that's all. You just had to accept her for who she was."

Talba figured Rosemary was in for several hundred thousand dollars, at least—that was a whole lot of acceptance.

"So that was our relationship," Rosemary concluded, folding her hands on the duvet cover. Rather than tired out by the interview, she seemed invigorated. "I loved her, and I'll miss her. And that poor little Cassie—such a shame about her."

"About her death? Horrible, yes."

"Not just her death. Her life. She just never could seem to do anything right. Her mother was always so worried about her."

Now here was a very different view from the prevailing one. Talba wondered if there was some shadow cast of friends who'd adored Allyson and condemned Cassie. "How was that?" Talba asked. "What kinds of things did she do wrong?"

Rosemary laughed. "Well, wanting to be an actress—what more can I say?"

"But . . . I don't understand. Her mother was a poet, or a student of poetry, at any rate. That's not usually considered a lucrative career, either."

"I don't think it was about the money," Rosemary said gently. "I think it had to do with motivation. No matter what, Cassie just couldn't seem to—you know—up and *do* anything."

"But she was pursuing her career as an actress, and working for a caterer as well. That's what most aspiring actors do, isn't it?"

"I don't know." Rosemary made a peacemaking gesture. "All I know is, she was a disappointment to her mother."

Talba considered asking about Hunt Montjoy, but something told her not to go there—probably the fact that she couldn't think of a way to ask the question she wanted to without being downright offensive. Inwardly, she laughed at herself. Something about Rosemary's exaggerated gentility had gotten to her.

"I guess I should ask you the important stuff," Talba said. "About her death."

Rosemary visibly took a breath.

"Are you all right with this?" Talba asked.

Rosemary nodded, reaching for a glass of water beside the bed. "I want to help."

"Okay, then, Can you think of anyone who'd want to kill Allyson?"

Tears leaked into the corners of Rosemary's eyes. "I've thought and I've thought about that. I can truthfully say that Allyson Brower was one of the finest human beings I ever met. I never in my life ever met anyone so generous and kind and so *loved*. I wracked my brain for days on this, and I honestly couldn't think of a soul who'd want to hurt her."

Talba absolutely couldn't believe what she was hearing. "What about her children?"

Rosemary nodded. "They had their differences. But in the end, Allyson loved them, and they loved her."

"Old boyfriends? Anyone like that?"

"Of course that terrible Burford Hale disappointed her so horribly. Cheated her out of all that money, and then refused to marry her. But, honestly, I can't see a motive in that. Can you?"

"He cheated *Allyson?*"

"Oh, yes." Rosemary's expression clearly said, *Some detective.* "He lived in her carriage house, or had his office there or something, for months, and took advantage of her so abysmally. Never paid her a cent of rent."

Two sides to everything, Talba thought. She said, "Surely you must have a theory, Mrs. McLeod. The killer had to be someone who knew her—do you have any thoughts at all?"

"I should think it would be obvious. It was that boy, Rashad something. You know how Allyson collected strays—or perhaps you don't. But Burford Hale was one, I guess. And then that boy. There was always someone hanging around looking for a free lunch. She didn't know anything about Rashad—anything at all. I'll bet if you looked into it, you'd find he has a history of violence."

He might, Talba thought. *He just might.*

"I'm actually surprised the police haven't made an arrest."

"Maybe they will soon," she said. *Thanks to my superior sleuthing.* She rose and extended her hand. "Mrs. McLeod—"

"Rosemary."

"Rosemary, I've so much enjoyed meeting you. It's a privilege to see someone so fine-spirited in the face of—" Talba was floundering, wishing she hadn't started the damn sentence. It sounded pompous and wasn't the sort of thing she usually said, but something about Rosemary McLeod had touched her—perhaps it was her baby-pink innocence, encased in a baby-pink gown and blanket.

"Why thank you, Miss Wallis," Rosemary said, "I've enjoyed your company."

Talba left thinking it was too bad Allyson and Rosemary couldn't have been lesbian lovers—it would certainly bolster the theory of someone for everyone. Or perhaps they had been. If she put her mind to it, Allyson could evidently seduce almost anyone.

Chapter Twenty-one

Eddie thought it might be a good idea to give the whole Rashad thing a rest for a day or two—let the kid settle down after being chased by an avenging goddess, which is what Ms. Wallis must have looked like. He pictured her flying up that hill at Lee Circle, and chuckled to himself.

What he needed was a new perspective, and he wondered if he could get it at Monday night football. Whatehehell. He could just go, and if the tinsel twins weren't there, he could come back the next night. And it didn't matter if he arrived empty-handed—Theresa wasn't going to burn him, so long as he got the goodies to her before he asked for the next favor.

Having had only salad for lunch, he figured he could have as much dinner as he wanted, and Audrey had bought steak—steak and spaghetti being a specialty of hers. In fact, she specialized in spaghetti and anything. But the trouble with steak was, it made you sleepy. So Eddie didn't get to Pete's till after a little nap, which put him there in about the middle of the third quarter.

What they did on Monday nights at Pete's was set up a wide-screen TV in a back room, but tonight the Saints were playing the Falcons, and the Saints were trailing, 28–0. People were so demoralized they were filtering out of the back and beginning to drown their sorrows in the bar proper, where the jukebox bawled out "Unchain My Heart" and four silent televisions provided partial escape from the Saints' humiliation. Eddie figured he might as well establish a command post at the bar before it got boisterous and crowded. The place was the size of the average home living room, and who cared about the game at this point?

The first thing he noticed was that Theresa wasn't behind the bar. The guy who was, big guy with glasses, was one of the

owners. He knew Eddie, but with luck, Theresa had spread the
word to forget the Eight-Inch thing.

"Eddie Eight-Inch!" the guy said. "Long time, no see."

So much for being undercover. "Hey, Jackie. No joy in
Mudville, huh?"

"Thought that was baseball."

"Yeah, maybe it was."

To signal that he wasn't up for conversation, he glued his
eyes to one of the silent televisions that were always on, for
some reason. Gradually, he began to inspect the rest of the
room. A more ordinary watering hole you couldn't imagine.
Originally dubbed the Out in the Cold Bar, Pete's was dark,
with the dark, fake paneled walls of a million gin joints in a
thousand towns. It had about five or six tables and a regular old
beat-up bar, with a couple of firemen's hats hanging behind it.
But there was something about the place—something beyond
the sum of its parts. It had great ambience, even with Theresa's
absence.

It took a few minutes to take everything in, but Eddie gradually realized that the guys he wanted were seated at a small
round table by the front window. Both of them, only the twerp
wasn't in pin stripes. Eddie figured him for the one in the blue
button-down. In here, that was like wearing a tux. The other one
had on an orange Auburn T-shirt that covered a well-formed
bourbon belly, and a baseball hat. The clincher was the big
mess of papers they had on the table. That was definitive. No
one, but no one had ever brought work into Pete's before—he'd
have staked his life on it. So it had to be Taylor and Montjoy.

He moved down a couple of seats, to get a little closer. If he
really paid attention, he could just hear.

"I don't buy it," Taylor said. "The guy's wife just died, and
he's going out prowling the night after the funeral? Uh-uh. Totally out of character."

"What does a hack like you know about character?" Montjoy
sneered.

Hoo-boy, Eddie thought. *Is my timing good or what?*

"Look, Hunt," Taylor said, "they brought me into the project
because I know how to write a screenplay. Sure, it's your gig;
sure they want your name. You don't have to remind me every
ten seconds. I think by now I'm pretty well aware of it. But you

might want to remember that they asked for another writer because the average poet doesn't write screenplays."

"Novelist."

"What?"

"You forget I'm a novelist, Taylor?"

"Look. Let's cut to the chase, as we say in El Lame. You pay almost ten bucks for a movie, you don't want to see Harrison Ford acting like an asshole."

"He's not an asshole, he's trying to forget."

"It's not going to play that way."

"Shit! That's hack thinkin'. What the fuck do I care how it plays? Are we aiming for quality here or are we pandering to the masses?"

"Hunt, they're paying us to write a *movie*."

"The goddamn thing's supposed to be noir. The guy can't be a candy-ass." Eddie noticed that Montjoy's S's were getting fuzzy.

"Look," Taylor said, "let's go back to the master on that. 'Down these mean streets a man must go, a man who is not himself mean, who is neither tarnished nor afraid.' He's untarnished, see? He's a better man than you or I."

Montjoy boomed out a laugh. "Wouldn't take much, would it?"

"Guess not." Taylor chuckled a little as well, but tentatively.

"Sure wouldn't take much, would it, Wayne, my man?" He got up and grabbed his buddy's shoulder, possibly to steady himself, and then he lurched over to the bar. "Let's see what ol' Eddie Eight-Inch has to say about it."

Shit, Eddie thought. *What's Theresa done? Spread the word a PI's coming in tonight?*

"Hey, Eddie! Hunt Montjoy. How ya doin'?" He clapped Eddie on the shoulder as if they'd been buddies since high school.

"Yeah, I know who you are. The question is, how do you know me?"

"Whaddaya mean?" Montjoy looked at him as if he were speaking pig Latin. "I heard Jackie call ya Eddie Eight-Inch. Whole place did. Said to myself, I gotta meet a guy named Eddie Eight-Inch. Now, why they call ya that, Eddie?" He winked, and it made Eddie feel dirty. He got an inkling why women hated that kind of thing.

There was a scraping of chairs and a general chorus of

"shit"'s from the other room. The game was over, and people were starting to melt back into the front bar. Almost the first one out was Theresa. Seeing Eddie, she glanced quickly away.

This was getting to be a mess. Now he really needed her, to give him legitimacy. "Theresa!" he hollered. "Hey, it's Eddie—don't ya remember me?"

It took her about a nanosecond to get his drift. "Eddie, babe! Ya lost weight or somethin'—lookin' like a million, dawlin'." She came over and hugged his neck.

"Hey, ya know my good friend, Hunt? He wants to know why they call me Eddie Eight-Inch."

She smirked. "Ax him what he *thinks*."

Eddie turned triumphantly back to Montjoy. "Some things a gentleman just don't mention."

"You sound like Wayne over there. Hey, Taylor, come meet Eddie Eight-Inch."

Taylor joined them. "Heard of both of y'all," Eddie said. He'd decided to go for broke. "What's ya movie about?"

Montjoy grabbed the floor. "There's this PI, see, who's having an affair with this woman—I see her as, like, Catherine Zeta-Jones; real sensual babe. Well, our guy's wife gets murdered, you follow? While he's with the babe—"

"—And the cops think he did it," Eddie finished, "but he's got no alibi because she's his best friend's wife."

Montjoy looked disgusted. "Eddie, Eddie. Give us a little credit. We're professionals here."

"Okay, what really happens?"

"Well, after he leaves the babe, she gets murdered, too."

"Hold it. I thought it was Catherine Zeta-Jones."

"So what?"

"Well, you can't kill off the star at the beginning of the movie."

Taylor started guffawing like Eddie was Chris Rock. "Oh, yeah. Man's a professional."

He looked at his pal. "See? Every guy on a bar stool knows more about movies than you do. What'd I tell you? This ain't art, buddy—it's a money-making machine."

A nasty glint shone in Montjoy's eyes. "If it's got your name on it, already it ain't art. Goes without sayin'."

Eddie said, "Oh, I don't know, Mr. Taylor. My associate's a

poet and she's been readin' your novel. Says it's good stuff. And she's got an MFA." (To his knowledge, she didn't.)

Taylor was starting to be amused. Eddie had an idea he knew exactly who he meant. "Oh, yeah? What does she think of Montjoy's stuff? He's got a Pulitzer."

"Says it's sexist."

"She's mistaken," Montjoy said. "My work's not sexist. *I'm* sexist."

"Ya proud of that?"

"Listen to him. 'Proud o' dat.' You teach at UNO with my buddy here?"

"Touché," Taylor said, and he took a good swig of something that looked decidedly pink, exactly as Theresa had predicted. "Hunt, I believe our friend is having us on a bit. I think possibly his associate paid me a visit last week." He stood and stuck out his hand, which Eddie shook reluctantly. "Mr. Valentino, I presume?"

Eddie said, "Dr. Valentino to you," to show that he got the joke. "At your service."

But Montjoy was drunk enough to take him literally. "Oh, shit. Since when did they start giving Ph.D.'s to yats to teach 'popular literature'? Now, there's an oxymoron for you. Popular fuckin' literature! You get your degree from Diplomas-R-Us or what?"

For once, Eddie wished he had one of those official-looking badges Ms. Wallis was so crazy about—flashing it might give Montjoy a minor heart attack, or maybe a stroke, which he would really enjoy about now. Failing that, he figured he'd have to grovel. "Naah." He looked at his beer, and laid on the accent as thick as he could. "I ain't no professor, Mr. Montjoy. But I am at ya service. Ya writin' about a PI, right? Well, ya lookin' at one. Step right up and get ya free information. I'm in a helluva mood. Never have been a Saints fan."

He made sure he delivered the last line low enough that no one else heard. In these parts, knocking the Saints was like knocking Catholicism. But he'd guessed right about Montjoy, who promptly gave him five. "My man! Never could stand those wusses. You really a PI?"

"Thirty years' worth," Eddie replied.

"Hey, Wayne! We got us a gold mine, here. What you drinking, Eight-Inch? Say, how do you find out if somebody's got a criminal record?"

"Ya mean ya don't know?"

"I know it's illegal; I also know there's tricks of the trade."

"Yeah, we got 'em, all right. But they might disappoint ya."

"You bribe a cop, right? What's the right amount to offer?"

Eddie was starting to have fun. "What century you guys livin' in? Hey, Theresa, bring me a Heineken, will ya?"

Theresa said, "Sure thing, dawlin'."

Taylor eyed him. "Figured you for a draft man."

"I'm a consultant, right? So, whatcha waitin' for? Bring on the good stuff."

Montjoy clapped him on the shoulder. "You're all right, Eight-Inch. Hey, Taylor, you takin' notes? That's a pretty good line."

"Yessuh, Mr. Montjoy. Whatever you, need, suh."

"So, Eddie. How much ya gotta pay for a rap sheet?"

"Nothin'."

"Whaddaya mean, nothin'? Oh, I get it—you gotta save some cop's ass somewhere along the line, and after that, he's your faithful servant. Well, hell, even Taylor here coulda figured that out."

"Actually," Taylor said, "I think I did suggest it."

This was so close to home Eddie was inwardly wincing. He said, "This is the twenty-first century, ya heard? Ninety percent of a PI's bi'ness is done online these days."

"Right. Hey, Taylor, let's just have the guy go to rapsheets.com, okay? Everybody under twelve'll probably buy it."

Eddie shrugged. "You asked."

"You trying to tell me that's what you actually do? There really is a site like that?"

Eddie prayed Ms. Wallis hadn't been putting him on. He gaped at Montjoy. "Why'd ya ax if ya already knew?"

"Knew what, Eight-Inch? What in God's name are you talking about?"

Theresa brought the beer, and, to Eddie's relief, Montjoy fished out some money for it. He took a long pull. "I'm talkin' about rapsheets.com. If ya already knew about it, why'd ya buy me the beer? Thanks, by the way."

Taylor started laughing, saying, "rapsheets.com" over and

over again, unable to stop. Eddie realized he must be as drunk as Montjoy, who joined in after a while, and so did Eddie. Montjoy clapped him on the back again. "You're all right, Eight-Inch. Hey, Taylor, why don't we have a scene like this in the picture? I mean *just* like this—you know, with Zeta-Jones. She asks how to get a rap sheet and they go through this whole misunderstanding thing, with Ford doing this deadpan routine? Whaddaya say, huh?"

Eddie said, "I thought Zeta-Jones was dead."

"Naah, you talked me out of that. Let's keep her alive—we're in this for the filthy lucre, right?"

"Now you're talkin'," Eddie said. "But a whole scene, ya know, I gotta charge ya a little more than a beer."

"Right," Taylor said disgustedly. "I knew there was going to be a price tag."

"Now, hold on. Hold on a minute. I'm a PI, ya know? Information's money to me. All I need's a little four-one-one." Here he dredged up a term he'd heard Eileen Fisher use when talking to her friends. He figured it might sound like PI talk to these bozos.

"Sure, Eight-Inch. Anything you need. If it's about literature, ask me. Some kind of *pop* crap, Taylor's your man." He drank, spilling about a dollar's worth of Jack Daniel's, and wiped his mouth with the back of his hand.

"I'm lookin' for this kid, Rashad Daneene. Little bird told me he was a friend of y'all's."

"Little bird calls herself a Baroness," Taylor said. "Pretty good poet, by the way. You could pick up some pointers, Montjoy."

What was happening finally filtered through the poet's alcoholic haze. "That black chick? *She's* your assistant? Hey, Eight-Inch, I had you figured for a racist."

"Back at ya, Hunt-man. But I got it on good authority ya pals with Daneene."

"Yeah, Eight-Inch, Rashad and I used to be friends—till he murdered a couple of people."

"Naah, he didn't kill those women. Way I see it, Brower stabbed her daughter and then offed herself."

"That the way the police see it?" Taylor asked.

Eddie shrugged. "I think they're comin' around to it. I'll tell you frankly, I'm kind of worried maybe she whacked Rashad while she was at it." He turned up his palms. "Kid's disappeared into thin air."

"Probably with one of his little girlfriends," Montjoy offered.

Taylor nodded. "Kerry, maybe. There was this girl named Kerry. . . ."

"Who the hell's that?" Montjoy said, and shot Taylor a dangerous glance. "Taylor, what the fuck you talking about?"

Taylor looked his buddy in the eye. "Give the man a break, Hunt. He needs to find the kid. You know her last name."

"I don't know who the fuck you're talking about."

Taylor shrugged and said to Eddie, "Well, I only knew her by Kerry. She's a little girl Rashad hung out with."

"Oh. Well, any other ideas?"

"Ya know what? I'm sick and damn tired of this crap," Montjoy said. "We come in here to have a quiet drink, get a little work done, and next thing you know, some two-bit private dick horns in on our conversation. Man, this is like our second home. I've never seen you in here, Eight-Inch. Who the hell you think you are, comin' here like this, with some clumsy ruse about helpin' us with our picture? Taylor, I'll tell you one goddamn thing—the PI in the picture's gotta be a damn sight slicker'n this one. Better dressed, better lookin', with a third-grade education, at least. This guy couldn't detect his way out of a shot glass." By now, his voice was so loud the whole bar could hear him.

Taylor looked at Montjoy's empty glass. "Well, *you* probably could."

Eddie set his bottle down. "Nice talkin' to ya, gentlemen. Theree-saah! Gimme a kiss, dawlin'." He went over and kissed her on the cheek. "You'll be gettin' a package from me."

She shook her head. "Forget about it, dawlin'. I feel real bad about this. You're what this place is all about." She flicked her chin at the screenwriters. "Those guys are just passin' through." She raised her voice. "Hey, Hollywood boys! Whatcha mean insultin' my regulars? Ya eighty-sixed."

Taylor said, "Huh?"

Montjoy turned red, as if he were either going to have a heart attack or hit somebody.

"I mean it. Get on outta here."

The room erupted in applause. Someone yelled, "Hey, the

Saints mightta lost, but we got our bar back!" People started cheering and clinking glasses.

A woman hollered, "Drinks for the house! On my old man," and Eddie left before Taylor and Montjoy could get it together to follow.

What the hell, he figured. The night wasn't a total loss. He'd made Theresa happier than chocolate or champagne ever could have. But he was going to send some anyhow.

Chapter Twenty-two

Usually, Talba was the one who found her way first thing in the morning into Eddie's office, if only to check on the ever-changing color of his eye bags. But she'd barely gotten her computer booted Tuesday morning when he slouched into her office, coffee in hand, bags more or less green. "Well, if it isn't Little Merry Sunshine," she said.

Wearily, he sank into her extra chair. "Got a new respect for ya, Ms. Wallis. I thought maybe Hunt Montjoy was so surly with ya, because you're, uh . . ."

"Black and female."

"Uh-uh. Young and female. But I met him last night. I'm real proud o' ya for not deckin' him just for bein' an asshole. And notice I'm not even excusin' my French. Sometimes there's only one good description."

"Oh, boy. No wonder you look like you've been tied down and tortured."

"Yeah, well, I managed to get him eighty-sixed from his favorite bar. Least I accomplished something."

She was awestruck. "There is a God! Tell me everything."

So he did, the whole story, which wasn't like him at all. When he got to the part about rapsheets.com, he said, "Gotta thank ya for that one. Say, is that a real thing or not?"

"It's a real thing. I've got it in my 'favorites' folder—want to see?"

"Ah, that's your department."

"Well, it's only semi-useful. Just works for some states—Louisiana isn't one of them. But, anyway, that's so funny, the way you put those guys on."

"What a coupla assholes."

"I didn't think Taylor was that bad. He's a fan of mine."

"Or he pretended to be. Wait, I take that back—he told Montjoy he could pick up some pointers from you. As a poet, I mean."

She laughed. "He didn't!"

"Those two are like a couple of twelve-year-old brothers—fightin' all the time, needlin' each other—I got no time for it. Listen, I probably didn't get anything out of the interview at all, if ya want to call it that, but Taylor did mention a girl named Kerry, used to hang with Rashad. Ring a bell with you?"

She nodded. "He mentioned her to me, too—one of Montjoy's castoffs. And so did Charmaine French, this poet I met who's—"

"Wait a minute—she's a castoff of Montjoy's?"

"Yeah. Rashad's M.O.'s healing broken hearts. Hunt cracks 'em, Rashad cures 'em. They're a tag team."

"Montjoy said he didn't know her."

"One of them's lying, then."

"Find her, Ms. Wallis. Somethin's funny here."

"Even the Baroness can't find a person with no last name."

He stood up. "Ya asked Austin about her? He was pals with Rashad."

She shook her head. "It didn't come up while he and your lovely daughter were courting."

"Don't remind me."

"I'll go see him." She had a couple of other things to ask him, anyhow.

"You do that. After ya tend to that stack on ya desk." He indicated her usual quota of background checks. "Me, I'm gonna work on the Jackson insurance thing."

So she waited till a decent hour—which coincided with having finished twelve employment checks for one of their biggest clients—before calling to see if Austin was home.

"Baroness! Just the woman I want to talk to. I've been dealing with Arnelle—I need to see someone I can stand."

"I'm flattered."

"Get over here, will you? I'm putting coffee on." After a beat, he said, "Forget that, It'll be eleven-thirty by the time you get here. How about an early lunch? I'll make you an omelet or something."

"Tell you what. I'll pick up sandwiches on the way. What's your pleasure?"

She could have sworn he said, "Make mine Angela."

"I beg your pardon?"

"Egg salad, if you can find it."

The guy was an egg freak. And unusually friendly under the circumstances—but she figured that had something to do with his lawyer.

By the time she got there, he'd laid the table on the patio and made a pitcher of iced tea "Couldn't get egg salad," she said. "Tuna fish okay?"

"Perfect. Hey, I've got chips." He transferred the sandwiches to a pair of Italian ceramic plates, and added a mound of greasy discs to each one. "Zapp's," he said, munching one and letting his eyes roll back in ecstasy. "One of the great things in life."

Keeping up a running yammer, he carried the plates to the patio. "Hey, Baroness, I've gotta ask you something. I've really been wondering, who's your favorite poet? I mean, do you read only, like Langston Hughes, or do you go in for any of the dead white guys? Sit down, why don't you?"

She followed instructions. "I've been known to check out some white guys—that's who mostly wrote in English. Oh, yeah, and women. They've composed a poem or two."

"Yeah, man." He took a healthy bite of his sandwich. "You absolutely can't beat Sylvia Plath. Anne Sexton's good, too. Oh, and Emily Dickinson—can't forget the oldies but goodies. You want to know the truth, though—I'm a Wallace Stevens guy."

Talba more or less worshipped Wallace Stevens, but she wasn't up for bonding with Austin over "The Idea of Order at Key West." She said, "You know what? You could be the weirdest biker I ever met."

"Yeah, but how many bikers *have* you met?"

"Touché, Mr. Edwards. Let's just say you don't fit the stereotype."

"I'm not kidding. I read the guy when I'm out on my boat."

Talba saw an opening. "Have you read Rashad?"

"Sure. He's my buddy. Some of his stuff's pretty good."

"And the rest?"

Austin winced. "Reads like something a schoolkid scribbled."

"That's what I think, too. Well, who knows? Maybe it is."

"His book's damned uneven. I think he probably got a lot better after he met Wayne Taylor—and my buddy Hunt, of course."

Talba almost choked on her sandwich. "You're friends with Hunt Montjoy?"

Austin put his hands in his lap and gave her his full attention. The truth was, he was an extremely attractive man. She could see what Angie liked about him. "Sure, why not?" he asked, giving her a kind of tough-guy half smile.

"Jesus! Where to start?"

"You mean that redneck routine of his? Yeah, it's a little wearing, but I'm a biker, remember? And a fisherman and a laborer. He goes in for that kind of thing. He doesn't know I run a company—that would probably destroy me in his estimation." He did the smile thing again. "But, you want to know the truth, we're really only acquaintances. He was Mother's friend, actually—he was just around, so I talked to him."

Talba took a breath. "Was your mother involved with him?"

"Are you kidding? My mother and Hunt Montjoy? She probably *wished*. But not a chance. No way. I'd have known."

"Some people think she was. Or had been."

He didn't answer for a moment. Deliberately, he took a sip of tea, thinking it over. Finally, he said. "Had been. Now, you might have something there. She very well might have been. In Tallahassee, when I was a little kid, I saw something one night. I never was sure, but I thought I saw them kissing. They moved apart real quick when they realized I was there."

"Uh-huh. I was afraid of that. What about Cassie?"

"What do you mean, what about Cassie?"

She didn't answer, figuring he'd get it soon enough.

He drank more tea, and his demeanor, she noticed, was decidedly heavier; almost somber. "You mean, was she involved with Hunt?" His fists clenched. "I swear to God . . ."

Talba shrugged quickly, realizing she'd gone too far. "It's a rumor, that's all. I can't believe it either. I just thought I'd ask."

He didn't answer, but he attacked his sandwich as if it were Montjoy himself, tearing off bites with a predator's teeth and masticating fiercely, a warrior stoking up on fuel for the battle. Talba devoutly wished she could stop what she'd inadvertently started. "Hey, listen, pay no attention to me. It's my job to ask dumb questions. Let's talk about something pleasant, why don't we?"

"Like what?" His voice was a rumble. His eyes had taken on a feral look, and she was aware of the power of his body. This was a man who could probably pull in a few hundred pounds of fish without breaking a sweat. Dartmouth or not, Wallace Stevens notwithstanding, a man who did the work Austin did, who got tattooed, rode a Harley, and ran a bait company, was probably perfectly at home in a world where violence was a Saturday night sport. He was no Hunt Montjoy—he was the kind of man Montjoy wanted to be.

She said, "You're not thinking of confronting Montjoy, are you? Listen, I'm sure I'm wrong. No way I could be right about something like that. Besides, think of your lawyer. She'd kill you if you messed yourself up with the cops."

"Angie?" At the sound of her name, the sun came out on his face. "She would, wouldn't she?" He munched a chip, this time a lot more delicately. It was like a violent squall had passed over the landscape, leaving a cool breeze in its wake. "Hey, what's the deal with Angie, anyhow? She married?"

"You mean you didn't ask her when you had the Bloody Marys?"

"Are you kidding? She's my lawyer. We just talked about Mother. And Arnelle. Like what my rights are—you know, whether I can stay here. Stuff like that."

Talba smiled. This was kind of fun to watch. "No, Angie's not married."

"Involved with anybody?"

"Now that I don't know. Why don't you ask her yourself? She looked like she'd be open to it."

"Open to what?" That cute half smile played around his lips.

Talba smiled back at him, aware that they were flirting. "To a question like that."

"I don't know. She seemed kind of all business to me."

"She likes you."

"She said something?"

"I could just tell."

"You could? I couldn't."

"Good God, were you asleep or what? I thought Eddie was going to skin you alive. All I could do to get him out of here without throwing a punch."

"Think I could take Eddie?"

"Not a chance. You'd have to take me, too."

"Oh, God! Not that."

"He's an irascible old coot, but he's my old coot."

"You really like him, huh? Good boss?"

"Now and then. Main thing, Eddie's an honorable man. How many of those do you see these days?"

"Funny. He seems like the kind of guy who'd be a racist. Best case, a sexist."

"Oh, he is. But he fights it, and that's something. Well, anyhow, Angie and Audrey fight it for him. They made him hire me. And it turned out all right."

"I got a feeling you're the one turned out all right."

"Well, so did Eddie." She was feeling a lot more relaxed, now that her host had mellowed out. "But I'm a pretty good detective when it comes down to it. Which reminds me, I came over here to ask you a question."

"Seems to me you already have."

"What? Oh, you mean about Hunt. No, that was idle speculation. I was wondering something else. Regarding Rashad."

"Oh, yeah, Rashad. I feel really bad about what I said to him. I mean, *really* bad. You have no idea."

"He liked to take care of women, apparently. Women like Cassie. Maybe like my sister. I'm wondering if he's with one of them now. You know any of his ex-girlfriends?"

"No. Rashad didn't talk about his private life."

"He ever mention a girl named Kerry to you?"

"Kerry? That rings some kind of bell. Somehow or other, I've heard that name."

"Maybe from Cassie? Maybe she knew her."

"No, not from Cassie. From somebody else. Oh, yeah. I've got it. I've definitely got it. It wasn't either one of them—it was Montjoy."

"Him again. It makes sense, now that you mention it. Wayne

Taylor told me Rashad used to, well, the way he put it was 'clean up Hunt's messes.' Montjoy would trample all over them, and Rashad would come along and dress their wounds. He said Kerry was one of the casualties."

"Yeah. Yeah, it's coming back to me. We were at a party, and they served mojitos. Hunt was drinking one, and, just for something to say, I said, 'I thought you were a bourbon man.' And he said, 'I am, but I knew a girl named Kerry once. She liked mojitos. So this one's for her.' Like she was dead."

With my luck, she is, Talba thought. She said, "Damn! I was hoping for a last name."

His chair scraped on the concrete as he pushed it back. "Let's go ask Hunt."

"Forget it. Eddie already asked him. He wouldn't talk about her."

"Well, he'll talk to me about her." Talba saw that his jaw was set with a determination that wasn't there before, not even when he seemed in the throes of murderous rage.

And the rage was there, too. It had been crouching like a leopard, under the surface, waiting for any excuse to spring.

"Austin, we can't just . . ."

He interrupted her. "I can." He left her sitting at the table and strode into the house.

It happened so fast it took her a moment to realize what was really going on. By the time she'd followed, he'd already left through the front door and mounted his Harley. "Hey, listen," she called, as the great machine kicked into action, signaled by a roar that drowned her out. Austin waved good-bye.

"Shit!" she said to no one in particular, and went back in to get her car keys, reaching for her cell phone as she walked. She punched in Angela's number.

"Angie? Talba. I've got an emergency. How fast can you be at Hunt Montjoy's house?"

"That," the lawyer replied, "would depend on where Hunt Montjoy lives."

"Damn." Talba was aware they were losing precious seconds. "Hang on, let me look it up."

While she fumbled with the phonebook, Angie said, "What's the emergency?"

"That ape Austin's just gone over there to beat the truth out of Montjoy. I've got a feeling you're the only person who can calm him down."

"I'm on my way. Call me back with the address. Just give me a neighborhood."

"Garden District. Really near here, unfortunately—I'm at Allyson's."

The line went dead, Talba found the address, ran for her own car, and relayed the address en route. It was only a few blocks away.

When she arrived, she saw the hog in the driveway, but no sign of a person. Maybe Austin and Hunt had decided to have a nice cup of tea instead of busting each other up. She parked, not sure what to do next—wait for Angie, probably. So she was sitting in her car when the Montjoy door opened to discharge two extremely red-faced, shouting men, followed by Lynne with a broom, literally sweeping them out, which she achieved by holding the broom upside down and smacking them about the shoulders. *Why in hell*, Talba thought, *does she stay married to that animal?*

The two amateur pugilists squared off in the gorgeous garden, dukes up, breath ragged, eyes like wolves. But it was obvious even to Talba that Hunt had absolutely no chance against Austin, who was younger, stronger, bigger, and altogether more sober. Maybe, she thought, Lynne had shooed them out because she smelled freedom.

Like to do it for you, sweetheart, Talba thought, *but I don't need the karma.*

She left the car and walked over to the little fence around the yard. At first, the men just circled one another, Hunt's face getting redder and redder, Austin's breathing perceptibly slowing. He was visibly gathering his strength. In a few moments, if Angie didn't get here, there was going to be mayhem.

She saw Austin's lips move, but she couldn't make out what he said. But Hunt's reply was completely audible: "Get off my property, you piece of shit."

Austin swung at him, but he ducked. Montjoy was sweating. *Probably terrified,* Talba thought. *Maybe this isn't all bad.*

She might have really enjoyed herself if the two of them had merely continued dancing, Austin growing increasingly menacing, Hunt cringing more by the second. But Austin swung again, this time catching Hunt on the right jaw, knocking his head back so hard Talba heard his teeth click together.

It had just gotten very unfunny.

When Austin spoke again, she heard him clearly. "Who's Kerry?"

Hunt replied in a growl. "You ever mention that name again, I swear to God I'll break every bone in your body."

"How you gonna do that, you tub of lard?" Austin punched him in the gut. Then he cuffed him lightly about the face, with first one fist, then the other. Hunt's head bobbled like a puppet's.

Talba yelled, "Austin, for God's sake, leave him alone."

Austin responded by bending over and butting his head brutally into Hunt's squishy midsection. The poet fell over backward; Austin simply kicked out his legs and fell gracefully on top of him, grabbing his wrists and holding them with one hand. He doubled up the other fist and held it in the older man's face. "Who the fuck is fucking Kerry?"

Hunt spat at him, catching him on the nose. Talba had to give him points for heart, even if he wasn't much of a fighter. Reluctantly, she reached for her phone to dial 911, thinking she'd put it off far too long, and wondered vaguely what Lynne was doing while her husband was being pounded to powder. Rejoicing, probably.

Just as she was about to dial, Angie's car descended like a spaceship and landed with a squeal of brakes. The lawyer leaped out the door, the ignition still on, waving her cell phone and shouting, "Austin Edwards, you get off of that man before I call the cops and get your ass thrown in jail and let them throw away the key."

Still holding Hunt's wrists, Austin twisted his head to look at her. "Hey, Ange. How you doing, babe?" he said, almost happily, and turned back around to Hunt. "Give it up or I'll kill you in front of two women."

Hunt seemed suddenly a lot calmer now that the cavalry had arrived. "Just for the record, I don't know what the fuck you're talking about."

"Okay, this is it," Angie yelled. "I'm pressing the button."

With one athletic pop of his body, Austin sprang to a standing position, and reached down a hand to help Hunt. "Nice match, old buddy."

To Talba's utter amazement, Hunt took the hand, smiled, and struggled to his feet. "You know your way around the ring, kid."

"Years of Saturday nights in bars."

Hunt made a fist again, and cuffed Austin on the shoulder. "Next time I ream your thirty-year-old ass."

Austin held out his hand. "Call me any time you want a rematch."

Hunt took the hand and shook it.

Talba looked on in something resembling shock.

Hunt coaxed his battered face into a smile. "So what's with this Kerry chick? Why are you looking for her?"

"We know you know her, Montjoy." Austin spoke so softly Talba could barely hear, but she had no trouble detecting the menace in his voice.

"Seriously—you must have a good reason for coming over here and assaulting me in my own home."

Figuring they could go in circles for hours, Talba interrupted. "We think Rashad might be with her."

How he mustered it, Talba would never know, but at that moment, Hunt let loose with a big old roar of a laugh. "Hey, Baroness, you and Eddie Eight-Inch ain't even found Rashad yet? Swear to God, it's the Keystone Dicks. Know where I'd look if I was you?"

Talba barely heard him. She was thinking, *Eddie Eight-Inch?*

"I'd look right in my own backyard. Y'all know what Robert Johnson used to do whenever he came into a town?"

Talba searched her memory—Robert Johnson, Robert Johnson—yes! The early Delta blues man, the one who'd supposedly been poisoned.

"He'd find himself the ugliest bitch on the street and shack up with her. Figured she'd do any goddamn thing for him."

Nobody said anything for a minute, having not a clue where Montjoy was going with this. "Rashad's probably pullin' a Robert Johnson. Check out your sister, Baroness—ugliest bitch *I've* seen on the street."

Austin tensed like a tiger, but Angie sprang before he did. She had let herself quietly in the gate, and she now launched herself at Austin, probably saving Hunt Montjoy's life. The rage in Austin's face had multiplied exponentially, and it hadn't been pretty before.

But it disappeared as suddenly as it had gathered. He put an arm around his lawyer to keep his balance. "*Hello* there," he said, his face about two inches from hers. "Have you dreamed of this moment as long as I have?"

Angrily, she wriggled away, pivoted, and called over her shoulder, "See you in court, Edwards."

He trotted after her. "Hey, what's that mean? You turning me in for fighting or something?"

"I don't have to. With that temper of yours, one day you're going to need a lawyer the worst kind of way."

"Aw, don't be like that. Tell you what, I'll go to Anger Management."

"'Bye, Austin."

Chapter Twenty-three

Hunt Montjoy was a loathsome human being, but his thoroughly disgusting remark smacked Talba in the face like a pie—or maybe a lightning bolt. Vivid as a film, she saw a pattern she couldn't believe she'd missed—Janessa's changed behavior. Her sister had been way too calm lately—not nearly as concerned about Rashad as she had the first few days. Yesterday, when they'd had lunch with her, she'd barely asked about him. And, before they sprang the prints on her, she'd actually been happy. There could be only one reason for that. She knew more than they did, and what she knew was fine with her. Much as Talba hated to admit it, Hunt was probably right.

As soon as she'd said good-bye to Angie, Talba drove straight to Mystery Street, fueled by a fury she hadn't felt in a long time. She shot up the stairs to Janessa's apartment and began banging on the door and shouting. "Janessa! Open up or I swear I'm calling the police!"

No one answered.

She banged some more, yelling louder if that was possible, not caring who heard, just hoping Janessa did.

Still no answer.

She took out her cell phone and yelled again. "I've got nine-one-one on auto-dial and I'm punching it now."

The door flew open. A flustered Janessa stood at the entrance. "What's up, goddammit? Whatcha mean, comin' here like this?"

Talba spoke quietly, trying to get back in control. "Let me in, Janessa."

"Why the hell should I let you in?"

"Because you don't want me calling the police on Rashad. I know he's here."

"Ya crazy. Go on and call 'em. He ain' here."

"Show me."

That threw her for a loop. "Whaddaya mean, show ya?"

"Let me in to search the place." Even as she said it, she knew it didn't mean anything even if Rashad wasn't there. He could be coming and going, just using the place to sleep.

But Janessa stood firm. "I ain' lettin' nobody in." Her lip stuck out like a kid's. She was putting up a brave front, but Talba had never seen her so upset, not even at Allyson's the rainy morning when she'd found a body.

And then a hand appeared on her shoulder. Talba looked up to see Rashad standing behind her. He said, "Janessa, we gotta do it." And Janessa started crying, more from the strain of keeping up the front, Talba sensed, than from defeat. She pivoted and flung her arms around Rashad, who held and patted her, just as he must have soothed a dozen young women before her. "It's all right, honey, you did the best you could. Everything's all right now."

Talba was still fuming. "Can I come in, please?"

Rashad eased Janessa aside so that Talba could enter. The first thing she noticed was that the room was surprisingly neat, partly because there was so little in it—a futon and a sort of black-painted wide wooden bench that served as a makeshift coffee table, a TV that sat on the floor, a few oversized pillows, plastic cartons containing clothes, a thrift store lamp or two—that was about it. A single book lay facedown and open on the coffee table—a copy of *The Great Gatsby*. Behind the main room was a little kitchen, and on a counter were two salad plates covered with crumbs, which had probably recently held sandwiches, and two Coke cans. "Very nice, Janessa," she said, glad her sister wasn't a slob on top of everything else. Also glad she saw no drug paraphernalia, smelled no pot smoke. She fixed Rashad with as mean a frown as she could muster. "You're in trouble, my man."

"I know," he said, and she saw that he had a quiet dignity. "I was going to call you today, anyhow."

Janessa broke away from the clinch. "Why you didn't tell me that? Here I am, doin' everything I can to keep the po-lice outta here, and you was gon' *call* 'em? Jus' like that?"

"I wasn't going to call the cops. I was going to call Talba. My aunt talked me into it."

Janessa sniffed. "Same thing," which set Talba off again.

"Janessa, do you have the tiniest understanding what three full-time professionals, two of whom don't even know you, have been doing for you for a week? You asked us to find Rashad, we've been chasing our tails all over hell and gone trying to find him, neglecting our other work, losing hundreds and hundreds of dollars, and he's been here with you all this time, you little bitch! I swear to God, I'm gonna wring your neck." She realized she'd almost said "your fat neck," and stopped, startled that she'd been able to control herself as far as she had. "Bitch" could be forgiven, but "fat" could not.

The look of horror on Janessa's face told her for the first time that, no, the girl really had had no idea what kind of sacrifices they'd made for her, what her deceit had meant to anyone other than herself. She'd caught herself a handsome guy and shacked up with him and that was probably all she'd been aware was happening that week. "Oh, my God!" Janessa fell apart again. "Oh my God, what have I done? I thought I was protectin' him—I knew I done wrong, comin' to ya in the first place—I tried to tell ya, but ya just wouldn't be fired!"

"Oh, great, it's my fault." Talba was so thoroughly pissed she was thinking again of calling the police.

Rashad sat down on the futon, his head in his hands. Talba fumed quietly, trying to get up another head of steam to tell him off, too. But after a moment, he raised his face and said, "This is my fault. Talba, I'm sorry. I should have never got Janessa into this. But could I tell you one thing up front? Just one thing?"

"This better be good."

"I didn't kill anybody. I loved those women. Both of 'em. They were two of the best friends I ever had. I asked Janessa to help me, just till I could find out what happened . . ."

Talba felt her anger rising again. "Are you telling me you've been playing detective? With two full-time professional PI's and a lawyer working on this, you've been running around like the Hardy Boys?"

"Hardy Boys! That's cold. More like Morgan Freeman, you know, in that movie where—"

Talba couldn't stand to listen to it. "You two are *children!*"

Rashad stood, apparently thinking height might reinforce his adult status. "I know how serious this thing is. They took a shot at me, didn't they?"

Talba remembered the bloody shirt. "I found your shirt. But you don't look to me like somebody who's been shot."

For a moment, he looked puzzled, and then he showed her a scrape on his arm. "Oh, I know what you're talkin' about. They didn't get me, but I got hurt runnin' away. Went back and got my backpack, but I sure couldn't stay at Celeste after that."

"Who was it, Rashad?"

He shook his head. "Couldn't see. It was night." He looked at his injured arm. "That's how come I fell."

Talba was starting to get over her anger. "Okay, let's move on. We're about to have a meeting with Eddie and Angie. Are you two going to go get in that car with me, or am I calling the po-lice?"

Janessa looked at Rashad, who nodded. "We're coming." The girl was still weeping quietly. It was amazing how thoroughly she seemed under Rashad's spell. Talba hoped to God he hadn't killed two women.

"Just a minute. Let me call Eddie." Turning on her cell phone, she saw that she had a message from him. Not bothering to listen to it, she auto-dialed the office. "EdDEE, guess who I'm bringin' in?"

He sighed. "Gotta be Rashad. I don't know how the hell ya got him, Ms. Wallis, but I got his aunt right here in this office, saying he wants to see ya."

"Oh, really?" So he hadn't lied when he said he was going to call her. "Well, he's seeing me. And I'm about to bring him over to see you. Can you keep her there? And let's get Angie in on this."

"If she ain't shacked up with Evel Knievel."

"I think she's over that for a while. And thereon hangs a tale." She hung up in time to see Rashad stuffing something into his backpack. "Hey! That's not a gun, is it?"

Rashad smiled. "No. It's not a gun."

"Okay, then, everybody ready? By the way, Rashad, your aunt's with Eddie."

He seemed to brighten. "For real? I'm really going to see my aunt?"

"If you don't disappear on me."

"You don't have to worry about *that*," he said, so sincerely that she was pretty sure another chase was about to ensue. But to her surprise, he was a perfect little gentleman on the way over, during which no one spoke a word. Talba was actually dying to question the two miscreants, but she wanted them in a properly sober mood when they got to the office.

But when they entered, wild laughter was spewing from Eddie's office. She raised an eyebrow at Eileen Fisher, the receptionist, who only shrugged. "Angie's in there."

Eddie was wiping tears. "Come in, come in. How ya doin', honey?" he said to Janessa, after which he shook hands with Rashad, as if he hadn't been the cause of nearly a week's worth of grief. Rashad hugged his aunt, who wiped away tears.

"Angela's just been tellin' me about Hunt Montjoy getting his ass kicked."

Rashad looked concerned. "What happened?"

Eddie was suddenly serious. "Tell you what, young man—we'll ax the questions for a while, all right? Ms. Wallis, get us a couple of chairs, will ya?"

"I'll do it," Rashad said, and Talba didn't protest.

"Hello, Ms. Dufresne," she said, and Dufresne gave her the first smile she had since Talba had first said Rashad's name to her.

"Felicia. I apologize for the other day."

"Actually, I think these two had better do the apologizing."

Janessa took one of the chairs Rashad had brought in, started to say something, then thought better of it. Rashad gave the other chair to Talba, and stood beside it. "Not Janessa. Me. I've only been at her house a day or two. Before that, she didn't know where I was any more than anybody else did."

"Well?" said his aunt. "Where were you?"

"You didn't know either?" Angie asked.

Dufresne shook her head. "He called once to let me know he was all right. That was all till today. I left a million messages, but he never called back."

Rashad cleared his throat. "Look, y'all, I went a little crazy, all right? Aunt Felicia knows why. I got somethin' real bad on my juvenile record. And by the way, I'm black, in case ya haven't noticed. And I was staying with Miz Allyson for free— like I was a drifter or somethin'. So I come home, find her floatin' like that, think I don't know how it's gon' look?"

Talba noticed that, under pressure, he'd lapsed into the vernacular. Dufresne frowned at him, and Talba had a glimpse of what it must have been like, growing up in her house— something like living with Miz Clara, who couldn't have used standard English if you'd told her the winning lottery numbers, but who knew it when she heard it.

Rashad caught the frown, too. "Sorry, Aunt Felicia."

Eddie said, "Why don't you start from the beginning?"

He shrugged. "You know most of it, from Janessa. Austin left, she left, Miz Allyson and I talked for a while, then I told her I was going out."

"Why?" asked Eddie.

"I just had to get out of there. Be by myself. Think. I was real disappointed, you know? I just walked down, got on the streetcar, and rode to River Bend. Found a bar and went in. Had a drink and went to another one. Then I came home and found her."

Eddie said, "So you went to two bars. Thought you weren't twenty-one yet."

"I haven't been carded in two years."

"Okay. What two bars?"

"I don't know. How the hell am I supposed to remember that?"

Eddie made the pipe-down sign. "Would you recognize them again?"

"Maybe. Who the hell knows?"

"Talk to anyone?" Eddie was firing questions like bullets.

"No."

"See anybody who might remember you?"

He shrugged. "Maybe the bartender at the first one. It was a white chick. Flirted with me a little. I was the only brother in there; same at the second, now that I think of it."

Eddie made a note. "Go on."

"So when I found Allyson, I freaked, that's all. Picked up my backpack, went to Celeste. But you know about that."

"The wharf."

"Yeah. I had some pot with me, and I stayed there two nights, smoking and writing poems, reading. Had a little money, went out in the day time. That's how I found out about Cassie. Nearly killed me, man. I loved that girl."

Janessa gave him an anxious look, but he didn't respond. Talba got the feeling the relationship—if it was one—was as one-sided as Montjoy apparently thought it was.

"Then somebody shot at me, and I had to get out of there. I was running out of money, too. So I went to this place where I used to go to find Monica."

Janessa interrupted. "That's the girl he calls 'Celeste' in the book."

"Oh." Eddie raised an eyebrow. "Crack house?"

"Sort of. Crash pad, more or less. But you had to pay to stay there. That's how come I went out to get work—when *you* saw me." He pointed with his chin at Talba.

"But I didn't get any work that day on account of having to leave in a hurry." He shot a wry look at Talba. "I was just about at the end of my rope, so I called Janessa, asked if I could stay with her a day or two."

No one said anything for a moment. "Wanted to think about things for a while."

Angie said, "Seemed to me you'd had more than adequate time to think about things."

"I was stoned a lot of that time."

"Well, that's just great," Felicia said.

"Aunt Felicia, I'm sorry. It's just—" He stopped in mid-sentence. "I was sad. Real sad. And I was real scared. Still am."

Talba was thinking the story more or less hung together. In his situation, given his background, she might have done something similar herself. It wasn't smart, but it made a kind of hopeless sense. Except for one thing. "What about the Hardy Boys action?"

Eddie, Angela, and Felicia stared at her. "What are you talking about?" Felicia said.

"Well." He took a breath. "I got a theory. Kind of half a one, anyhow. I started thinking about it while I was at Celeste, after I heard about Cassie. It just . . . wouldn't leave me alone."

Eddie said, "We're listening."

"See, I had to read this." He struggled with his backpack, finally pulled out the copy of *The Great Gatsby* Talba had seen at Janessa's apartment—the thing he'd stuffed in his pack at the last minute. "You know how everyone always said Allyson reminded them of Gatsby? They even used to call her The Girl Gatsby at the literary festival office. Well, Hunt used to laugh about it—he said he was Daisy to Allyson's Gatsby."

Talba looked at Eddie to see if he was following, and saw that he was nodding. "Gotcha so far. Where ya going with it?"

"Well, then he laughed and said if anything ever happened to Cassie, Allyson would have to take the rap for it. I didn't understand, see, because I hadn't read the book. Then when something did happen, I got curious."

Janessa said, "What the hell ya talkin' about?" And Felicia shot her a grateful look.

Rashad turned to her. "See, Gatsby's this character that's kind of like Allyson, and he's in love with Daisy, who's married to Tom. But Tom's got a mistress named, uh . . ."

"Myrtle Wilson," Eddie supplied.

"Yeah, Myrtle. Well, see, Daisy accidentally kills Myrtle and Gatsby takes the rap for it—"

Janessa interrupted. "Why he do that?"

"To protect Daisy—because he's in love with her. But then Myrtle's husband kills Gatsby for killing his wife. Ya understand?"

Eddie said, "I'm sure they'd be real proud of ya for that over at UNO. But would ya mind explainin' what it's got to do with real life?"

"I think Hunt did it," Rashad said.

Janessa looked utterly mystified. "Why ya think that?"

"Well, he *said* it. Maybe he set it up."

"Like the lady said," Eddie interrupted. "What makes ya think that?"

"Because I'm Nick."

"Wait a minute," Janessa said. "Who's Nick?"

"He's Gatsby's friend—and also Daisy's cousin—but the main thing is, he's the guy who tells the story. See, Hunt knows I know what he said. I *could* tell the story. Somebody took a shot at me, so it must have been Hunt. 'Cause I know too much. Y'all get what I'm sayin'? Allyson's been after Hunt for years, which makes him Daisy, like he said. But the *main* idea is that Gatsby takes the rap—that's the idea I think he gave himself with that stupid joke of his. He was involved with Cassie, so if he kills her, then Allyson's got to get blamed. So he frames her for killing Cassie, then takes her out and makes it look like she got remorseful and killed herself."

Rashad wore the earnest expression of a student trying to make himself understood to a professor who wanted to flunk him.

"Son," Eddie said seriously, "didn't you mention you were smokin' a lot of pot while you were workin' this thing out?"

Rashad's shoulders went down, and he bowed his head slightly, taking the news of his "F" as much like a man as he could. "All I know is, somebody shot at me. Has to mean something."

"Aren't you forgetting something?" Eddie said. "It was Janessa's prints on that glass over at Cassie's house. Not Hunt's."

"Well, if he was setting it up, he'd have wiped the glass."

"So how'd it get Janessa's prints on it?"

"I've been thinkin' about that," Janessa said. "I washed the glasses before I went home that night. I don't know, force of habit."

Rashad nodded. "That's right. She came and got my glass and Allyson's. I remember that."

"Still don't explain the prints—if ya washed 'em, they'd be clean."

"I didn't just wash 'em. I put 'em away."

The room went silent for a minute.

Finally, Eddie said, "Well, why didn't ya say so, honey?"

"I forgot."

Rashad was getting excited again. "So Hunt kills Cassie—"

"Why'd he do that?"

"Lover's quarrel." Rashad shrugged. "You *know* that had to be what it was."

"Yeah, well," Eddie said. "The police think you're the lover."

"I wasn't! Cassie and I were nothing but friends. I'd take a polygraph on it."

No one said anything, so he continued. "He kills Cassie, then he goes over to Allyson's and has a drink with her—he was the one person she'd *always* open the door to. She was crazy about him. So he gets her to drink, shoots her to make it look like suicide, and then goes back to plant the glass, just to sew things up."

"Doesn't explain why it didn't have his prints on it."

"Maybe he wiped the glass, but he missed Janessa's prints."

"Thin," Eddie said. "Thin. Downright anorexic. Besides which, I just don't think that's enough reason to kill somebody."

"What? To save yourself? Best reason there is."

Eddie was shaking his head. "I don't buy it. That takes some real meanness. Sure, he might have killed Cassie in a fight. But why not just clean up the scene? Why go and frame somebody else for it?"

Talba wasn't exactly on Rashad's side so far as logic went, but one thing seemed obvious: "Well, if anybody's that mean, it's Hunt Montjoy."

Eddie's head was still moving. "Nice try, son, but I don't think the state board's gonna be issuin' ya PI license any time soon." He shrugged, showing his palms to the heavens. "Just don't make no sense. That's all. And it makes me wonder, young man—cock-and-bull story like this just makes me wonder."

Felicia Dufresne looked alarmed. Talba could see she'd been thinking of Eddie as an ally, and she was starting to have doubts.

"Let's try out another theory." Talba could have sworn his eye bags actually jiggled. "You say you weren't Cassie's boyfriend, but maybe you were."

"No! I swear."

"Or maybe you just hated to see Montjoy treat her so bad. Either case, you fight with her, you kill her—"

Felicia screamed, "Rashad wouldn't hurt anybody!"

Eddie looked dead-on into her eyes. "We know he's got a bad juvenile record, Ms. Dufresne. So maybe he stabs her, and then he remembers this stupid joke of Montjoy's. Or maybe he made it up himself."

Rashad reached for his backpack, which he had placed on the floor. "I don't have to listen to this shit."

"Now hold ya horses, son. Tell me somethin'—did Montjoy ever say this to anybody else—this Daisy and Tom thing?"

Rashad, now halfway to the door, stopped in his tracks and pivoted. "Yeah. Sure he did. Said it to Wayne. You can check it out—Wayne knows about this. He thinks I'm right."

"Ya been in contact with Taylor?"

"Sure I have. He's my best friend."

"This is just great," Talba said. "Wayne's *Hunt*'s best friend. Why would he accuse him of murder?"

"Well, things have been a little tense lately—ever since Hunt started dating Cassie."

"Why's that?" Eddie asked.

"What do you mean, why's that?"

"Last I looked ya understood English."

Rashad walked back into the room and put his backpack down again, slowly and carefully. "There's something funny going on here. Are you telling me none of you know Wayne and Cassie were together for two years?"

A shocked silence ricocheted off the walls. *How could that be?* Talba thought. *I'd have found out about it.*

"Some detectives," Rashad said. "How come you don't know this? Allyson and Cassie fought about it all the time."

"Allyson's ghost didn't mention it."

Rashad considered. "Wait a minute. Austin didn't know—Cassie never talked about her boyfriends with him. I mean, he knew she dated married men, but . . . well, you know Austin. She sure wasn't going to name names. And she wasn't close to Arnelle. I don't know who else knew. Maybe no one."

Talba was kicking herself. Cassie must have had a best girlfriend—maybe if she'd tried to find out who that was . . .

Rashad was still talking. "I think I was her best friend. She didn't hang with women much. Maybe no one else did know," he said again.

Talba thought, *These people, these people*.

Eddie looked at her slyly. "Mamas, don't let ya babies grow up to be writers."

Angie smiled, but Felicia and Janessa just looked blank.

Janessa said, "This don't make no sense. Hunt and Wayne still friends. Why's that?"

"Money," Rashad said. "They're writing a screenplay together."

Eddie looked weary. "Sheds a whole new light on ya theory, doesn't it?"

Rashad only looked confused.

"I want ya to think about that. Look, Rashad, you're gon' have to talk to the cops tomorrow. Meanwhile, tell ya what we're gonna do. First of all, we're all going home. Rashad, ya stayin' at Janessa's again. Janessa, he leaves, ya call me immediately. Is that clear? *Immediately*. Or this firm is outta this so fast ya gon' feel the breeze. Ms. Wallis, ya gon' pick him up tomorrow, see if you can find those bars he says he went to that night. Even streetcar conductors. Let's see if we can prove even part of his story before we go in and talk to Crockett. Lot goin' against ya, son. A whole lot."

Felicia said, "I want to say one thing before we leave." She stood up, as if about to give a speech.

Eddie looked up at her, and must have hated it, Talba thought. But he only said, "Yes?" in the same weary tone he'd been using ever since he found out about Taylor.

"I want to tell you what's on Rashad's juvenile record."

Rashad said, "Aunt Felicia, don't!"

Looking straight at Eddie, she said, "It says he stabbed his mother with a kitchen knife."

Janessa looked at him in horror.

"He didn't," Felicia said. "*He's* Gatsby. He took the blame for me."

Chapter Twenty-four.

Talba's head felt as if somebody had squeezed it. *Aspirin*, she thought. *And Darryl*. Fortunately, the latter was already on the program—they were going to have one of their short dates. But, much as she wanted to tell him everything, she wanted even more just to let her mind hang loose and sway in the wind, rocked by any gentle breezes she could summon.

She called him. "You up for a movie?"

He hesitated, but not for long. "Sure. What do you want to see?"

"I don't care. As long as it's really, really silly. I absolutely cannot handle anything resembling thought."

"I'm looking at the paper now—*Daddy Day Care*?"

"Ideal. I'll meet you there."

And so they had sat happily at the Palace on the West Bank for almost two hours, holding hands, laughing, and, in Talba's case, unwrinkling her head. Afterward, he said, "Asian?"

"You read my mind. Nine Roses."

Actually, reading her mind hadn't been too hard. The best food on the West Bank was Asian and Nine Roses was their personal favorite. She was drinking beer and munching on spring rolls before she felt ready to talk about the case. "The good news is, we finally found Rashad."

"Uh-oh. What's the bad?"

"He was staying with Janessa."

"No! Why, that little—"

"Go ahead and say it."

"—bitch."

Talba raised her beer. "I'll drink to that." She managed to tell the story more or less coherently, something she didn't think she could have done without a little cinematic help. She finished with Felicia's story. "According to her, Rashad's mother was a raging bitch and also a drunk, which his poems more or less indicate. Says the two of them were drinking quite a bit in those days, and they got in a fight over a man and . . ." She shrugged.

"Felicia just happened to stab her?"

"Could have happened that way. In a crazy way, it makes more sense than the kid doing it. He was upstairs, came running down when he heard his mother's screams, and held her while Felicia called nine-one-one. They both say it was *her* idea for the kid to take the rap."

"What? The mother's? You believe that?"

Talba shrugged again. "*Could* have happened. You know

what they say on flights? Put on your own mask first. If the mother died and the aunt was in the joint, what would have happened to the kid? So Felicia agreed to it, and then they were all stuck with it."

"Did she die?"

"Not then. She passed away two years later, of natural causes, apparently."

"Overdose, I bet. So Felicia wants everyone to think the kid's really some kind of low-flying angel who's shouldered this burden all these years."

"You couldn't take it to court, but if you read the poems carefully, it makes sense. There's a lot of soul-searching, 'did I do right' kind of stuff."

"Somehow, I don't think the cops are going to buy it."

"Goes without saying—but Eddie and Angie and I are the kid's only hope. Felicia was trying to convince *us*, that was all."

The waitress arrived with more beers and more food—they'd ordered three appetizers to be brought in three courses. It was their favorite way to eat. Greedily, they applied themselves to potstickers. "Well?" Darryl asked. "Did it work?"

"Oh, who cares. None of us want it to be Rashad. He's a good kid and the two white guys are more or less scum."

"Little Miss Politically Correct."

Talba savored a greasy, meaty, doughy bite. "Nothing to do with race. They both cheat on their wives, they both treated Cassie horribly, they even treat each other like dirt. Of course, Wayne Taylor does have one sterling characteristic—he claims to be a fan of mine. On the other hand, that probably means he's just a manipulator. But here's the interesting thing—that crazy Gatsby theory of Rashad's doesn't fit Hunt at all, but it fits Taylor almost perfectly. He's the real Wilson character—if Cassie's Myrtle, I mean. Also, he's the only one in the entire cast of clowns and screwballs who has an actual motive for murdering either one of them—he could have fought with Cassie because of Hunt, or he could have fought with Allyson because she didn't want Cassie seeing him. Only problem is, he doesn't have a motive for whacking the other one."

"Sure he does. The time-honored frame-up to save his own skin."

"Yeah, but Eddie's right. He pointed out you don't need

someone else to take the fall—all you need is no evidence against you. And if one was a crime of passion, it doesn't make sense that you'd then get smart and premeditate the other."

"Unless you wanted the second one dead even more than the first one."

"Yeah, that's what we're missing—a motive for that. But someone did shoot at Rashad—and we know he'd talked the theory over with Taylor."

"Yeah, but on the phone, presumably. How would Taylor find him?"

"How'd I find him? It'd be easier for Taylor—he knew about Celeste all along."

"Wait a minute." Darryl set down his beer so hard it sloshed. "This is way too good a case against Taylor. Don't you think it's pretty weird no one else knew about him and Cassie? How do we know they were really involved?"

She shrugged. "I haven't really talked to Cassie's friends—I was trying to find Rashad, remember? Anyway, Hunt knew, according to Rashad. But that's a good point."

"That's the thing—it's all 'according to Rashad.' Do we really have any evidence that somebody shot at him? Or only his story?"

Suddenly, Talba saw a possibility she'd missed. "Oh my God! The kid looks guiltier than ever—his story's got more holes than a window screen. As Eddie would say."

Darryl smiled, extremely pleased with himself. "My money's on Rashad."

"Oh, yeah! The half-ass theory, the trumped-up stories—not one, not two, but *three* of 'em. Taylor and Cassie being an item, he himself getting shot at, and last but not least, Felicia being the fiend who stabbed his mother and made him pay for it. Oh, man! Why didn't I see it?"

"'Cause you needed a movie. And . . ." He eyed her critically. "Let me see, maybe something else. Your brain still seems kind of worn out to me. I think you need a little more relaxing."

She smiled. "Not a half-bad idea. So much for a short evening."

"You want short and sweet, you got the wrong guy."

"Who said anything about sweet?"

* * *

She went straight to Janessa's in the morning, intending to go through the motions, no matter what she really thought, and pick up Rashad to check out his semi-alibi. But a numb Janessa opened the door, wearing only a T-shirt and underpants. The girl looked terrified.

"What is it?" Talba pushed past her, wondering if Rashad had done something violent. But he was only standing in the middle of the apartment, fully dressed, and clutching his cell phone. He was looking down at the floor where the futon was still unfurled and un-made up. But he was unmistakably crying.

For a moment, Talba merely stood and stared in shock while he pulled himself together. He brushed his face with his hands, but when he finally raised his eyes to her, they were brimming again. "Hunt's dead."

"Hunt Montjoy?" she said stupidly, as if she knew as many Hunts as Bills. "How could he be dead?"

Rashad shook his head, signifying ignorance. "Lynne found him in the garage. In his car. Wayne just called."

Her first thought was suicide, that Hunt had asphyxiated himself. "He killed himself?"

Rashad looked even more stricken. "I just don't think he would. He's not the type."

He sure wasn't the type, Talba thought. Rashad was right about that. She had no doubt Montjoy was capable of killing someone, but the idea that he'd actually be remorseful seemed preposterous.

"What else did Wayne say?"

"Lynne said he had a fight with someone yesterday—"

"Austin."

"He took off afterwards. Didn't say where he was going, didn't come home last night. She found him this morning."

"Let me call Eddie." She stepped outside and speed-dialed him.

"Ms. Wallis, this better be good. I haven't had coffee yet."

"Hunt Montjoy's dead." She gave him the details.

"Now that," he said, "is one hell of a coincidence."

"Coincidence? You're kidding, right?"

"Got it in one, Ms. Wallis. It ain't no coincidence. I'm callin' Crockett."

"Are you going to tell him about Rashad?"

"Got to now. Least maybe the kid's got an alibi for this one. That is, if ya sister counts. 'Course Crockett'll probably think they did it together."

"You don't think Hunt killed himself?"

"That's what I'm gon' find out. Bring the kids over, will ya?"

Janessa had used the interval to get dressed and was now making up the futon. Rashad was in the little kitchen, holding a mug and staring out the window. "Plan's changed," Talba said. "We're going to Eddie's office."

Rashad nodded. "Good."

But Janessa balked. "Why we doin' that? Y'all gon' turn Rashad in, aren't ya?"

Talba opened her mouth to speak, but Rashad barked from the kitchen, "Shut up, girl. Just go."

Janessa looked at him as if he'd hit her. Her eyes filled briefly, but she picked up her backpack. No one spoke during most of the short ride to the CBD, but when they were almost there, Rashad said, "Funny thing. Yesterday I could have killed him myself, I was so sure he'd killed Cassie and Allyson."

"And now?" Talba asked.

"Now, I just think it's a horrible waste."

I think I smell a poem coming on, she thought, but she kept it to herself.

Eddie was on his second cup of coffee, and a lot more alert than he'd been on the phone. "Morning, everybody. I talked to Crockett."

"Did he kill hisself?" Janessa blurted.

"Not yet, but he's under psychiatric care—three deaths in a row, it's kind of got him down."

Rashad snickered, but Janessa looked hurt. "I meant Hunt."

Eddie looked at her over greeny-violet eye bags. "They don't think he did, no. They've got to do an autopsy, but there was one thing that argued against asphyxiation—Lynne says the car was off when she found it."

"Maybe she kill him," Janessa said.

"She had good reason, I'm sure," Eddie replied. "For that matter, she had good reason to kill the other two. But that's neither here nor there right now. Where were you model citizens last night?"

"Home watchin' TV," Janessa answered. Rashad was distinctly subdued.

"Together?"

They nodded.

"All night?"

"Yeah." Janessa slid a shifty peek at Talba.

Eddie stood up. "Okay. Let's go. Crockett wants you over there right away. Botha ya."

"Hey!" Janessa wasn't going quietly. "What about the bartenders? How 'bout the streetcar guys? Ya sellin' us out!"

"Janessa, be quiet!" Rashad said. "I just want this over with."

The room went quiet. Talba glanced at Janessa, worried she was going to tear up again—if she'd had a crush on Rashad before, she'd now become his slave.

"Look," Rashad said, "ya think they gon' lock me up?"

Eddie shrugged. "Depends on whether Crockett believes ya—my guess is not; still too many loose ends. And don't worry about those bartenders. The cops can fix a time of death between about two hours, usually. We'd have to find one to swear you were there for the whole period in which both women could have been killed, and, frankly, we already know you weren't, right? How long were you in those bars?"

"Not long. Half hour, forty-five minutes."

Eddie nodded. "So it might help, but it's not going to stop him locking you up. Anyway, it's really Crockett's job to find 'em, not ours."

"Ya sellin' us out!" Janessa screamed. Her eyes were painful to look at, they were so scared; but whether for Rashad or herself, Talba had no idea.

Rashad said, "Shut up, Janessa! Look, I gotta talk to Eddie and Talba by myself."

"Ya what? Ya want *me* to leave?"

"Just for a minute, all right?" He was so obviously trying to be patient with her that Talba felt momentarily sorry for him; she figured living in close quarters with her clingy, tempestuous sister would try anyone's patience. "I need to explain somethin' to 'em. Don't worry—it's somethin' you already know about."

Janessa sulked her way to the waiting room.

"Look, there's just one thing I want to do, okay? I want to go to the memorial service."

Talba wondered if Eddie was as baffled as she was. "For Hunt?" she said, unbelieving.

"No." Rashad shook his head vigorously. "For Allyson and Cassie. It's tonight at Allyson's. I, uh—I called Austin. He invited me. If they lock me up, promise you'll get me out in time."

"Well, son," Eddie said, "I see why you'd want to be there for Cassie if Crockett wants to hold ya, but—"

Rashad interrupted him. "Not Cassie so much. I want to be there for Allyson. It's like the book, you know? I'm Nick, I've got to be there for her." He paused. "Because maybe nobody else will be."

Talba had read the book so long ago she could barely remember what he was talking about, but Eddie said, "Owl Eyes went to the funeral."

"And that's exactly what I'm talking about! Maybe some of the freeloaders will come, those assholes who came to her parties because it was the place to be, but you and I both know Allyson didn't have that many real friends. Even Austin and Arnelle more or less hated her." He beat the air with the flats of his hands. "I just want to be there for her. That's why I came in this morning. Could have left again, right? But then they'd pick me up at the service. This way, I've got a chance, anyhow. Miz Allyson was good to me. I owe it to her." His eyes were shiny with tears. He lowered them quickly.

"Well, son, ya got a good lawyer." Eddie sounded uncharacteristically hearty. Talba could tell he was moved. "Is that all?"

"I just want to get sprung by tonight. You gotta bail me out if they keep me. Or get Aunt Felicia." The enormity of his naïveté swept over Talba like a garment.

Eddie stood up. "We're gonna hope for the best, son. Let's go see Crockett; Angie's meeting us there. Ms. Wallis, meanwhile, get a picture from Felicia and check out those bartenders."

"Okay, sure."

"You go to that thing tonight, too. And Rashad—one word to Crockett about that Gatsby garbage, and you're the next to die. Ya hear?"

Chapter Twenty-five

The morning had barely begun, and already Talba was boggled. She didn't know whether to believe the kid or not, but it had been a very pretty speech. First, she called Austin to see if she'd be welcome that evening, and having done that, she called Felicia and secured a picture of a much younger Rashad, one who barely resembled the young man who'd stood in the office that morning. Without much hope, she went out to look for bars near the River Bend.

She found a couple, but of course no one on duty had been working two Monday nights ago, which meant she'd have to come back later—with Rashad in tow, if he wasn't in jail.

Next, she phoned the RTA to see if she could find out who'd been driving a streetcar around ten P.M. two Mondays before, but nobody wanted to tell her. Eddie was right—this was Crockett's job, and it would be a lot easier with his clout. But she could always invent a pretext and try again later.

In the end, she wasn't too disappointed—she hadn't really hoped for much. She thought she could do better trying to confirm whether Taylor and Cassie had really been involved. Lynne Montjoy might know, but the day of her husband's death didn't seem the right time to ask.

Briefly, she considered Taylor himself. She tried Mimi Dirr instead.

Mimi was mystified. "Wayne Taylor?" she said. "Wayne and *Cassie?* I've never heard that. He and his wife just had a baby."

"Well, look, did Cassie have any close women friends?"

"Yeah." Mimi sounded like she was in shock. "Janet Taylor."

"Wayne's wife?"

"Yeah."

"Oh, boy. Guess she didn't confide in *her*. Anybody else?"

"She was really close with Raoul Fernandez. He's almost the

same as a girlfriend. She used to turn up with him at parties—which would make sense if she was dating a married man."

"Especially that one. I hear she dated Hunt Montjoy, too."

"Come on!"

"Maybe they didn't go out in public." Talba felt reasonably confident about Hunt—she'd gotten the story from several sources. But thinking about the difference in Cassie's public and private lives depressed her. She wondered briefly whether Austin knew about Cassie and Taylor—but after yesterday's fight, asking him was out of the question. Fernandez was probably as good a place to start as any. He was someone whose name Talba knew well—a local stage director whom Cassie must have worked with.

"Know where to find Raoul?" she asked.

"You could try the phone book."

And so she did, wishing she'd thought of this before wasting her time calling on bartenders—no way Fernandez was going to be home in the middle of the day. She dialed his number, thinking to hang up and race right over if he answered. He didn't, and worse, his voicemail said he was out of the country.

Burford Hale? she wondered. He and Allyson had been close, and supposedly Allyson knew about Taylor. She might have told him.

"You know," he said, "I always wondered about that. Those two spent a lot of time together at parties. But, no, Allyson didn't mention it."

Cassie must have had plenty of friends in the theater, but without Fernandez, it would take time to find out who they were.

In some ways, Cassie was coming clearer to her—a beautiful woman who dated married men and befriended gay or otherwise nonthreatening ones, like Rashad; who probably didn't like women much because they reminded her of her mother; who didn't have enough self-confidence to date available men.

She must have been hugely depressed, Talba thought. And possibly angry. She wondered if Cassie herself could have started the fight in which she was killed. She sighed, and buckled down to sweetie snoops. Eddie popped his head in about one-thirty. "Ms. Wallis, ya sister's still free."

"Oh. Good. How about Rashad?"

"Him, too. You'll probably see 'em both tonight. What'd ya think of that speech of his?"

She shrugged. "Could have been true. What about Hunt—do they have a cause of death yet?"

He shook his head. "Nope. And they won't for days. Cops think it's an overdose—and you know how long toxicology takes."

"Maybe it was just a coincidence after all."

"And maybe I'm F. Scott Fitzgerald."

They got two new clients that day—a funny thing how time filled up once it was freed. One was a doctor from Baton Rouge who didn't want to hire a local detective to spy on his wife. (Talba smelled bucks there.) The other was an insurance company that didn't buy someone's back injury story. This was Eddie's kind of case—he loved to go out with his video camera, spy on the guy for days on end, and catch him moving furniture if he got lucky. And she had to admit, he nearly always did.

She spent the rest of the day contentedly backgrounding the doctor and doing employment checks.

The memorial service, which she gathered was really something more like a cocktail party, was set for seven. By seven-fifteen, only a handful of people had arrived, two of them Rashad, in a white shirt and sport coat, and Janessa, in a slightly inappropriate skin-tight dress with cleavage. The Baroness herself had opted for something halfway between the daytime wage slave and the poet who ruled the night—she had on the same ruffled bells she'd worn to her last reading with a simple white shirt. Austin met her at the door in one of his surfer shirts, incongruously paired with a tie. "Mother hated these," he said, "but I think she'd have liked the tie, don't you?"

She couldn't help rolling her eyes. "Angie might like you if you'd grow up a little bit."

"Angie? Oh, she likes me. Count on it." He was smiling so broadly Talba could almost believe he knew something she didn't.

Except for the sparse turn-out, the gathering in some ways resembled the Leo party that had so amused her and Darryl before everyone died.

Before everyone died.

The phrase shocked her, came to her before she could choke it off. She felt a momentary eye-watering, tears more about the fleeting quality of life than any of the missing cast members. It had been a night of utter absurdity, a night to reflect on the follies of human natures, a silly time when death was something that happened to people who had fully lived their lives.

Arnelle, who was fluttering about in a black cocktail dress, had evidently pulled out all the stops. A bar was set up, along with a lavish buffet catered by Food for Thought, which gave Talba an idea. She asked a passing waitress if she'd been friends with Cassie. "No, actually." The girl blushed. "I'm the one who was hired to replace her."

Talba tried again with a waiter, who smiled. "Yeah, I knew her. Great girl, shame." He looked uneasy.

"Were you close?"

"No, uh . . ."

"I'm looking for someone who really knew her well."

"Oh. Simon. The redhead. He's probably around some-where." And he disappeared, looking glad to get away. Talba went in search of the redhead, whom she found arranging trays in the kitchen.

"Hi, I'm told you were a good friend of Cassie's."

"Yeah. God, I miss her!"

"Could I ask you a personal question?"

"Depends."

"I was just wondering . . . did she talk to you about her per-sonal life?"

He looked at her suspiciously. She wondered, too late, if he'd been involved with Cassie, or maybe wished he had. Perhaps a man wasn't the best person to ask. This one was attractive, with curly auburn hair, but he gave off no signals that said overtly gay or straight. "Why do you want to know?" he asked.

She opened her purse and pulled out her official-looking badge. "I'm an investigator looking into her death."

He barely glanced at the badge, just looked much relieved, and said, "I'll do anything I can to help catch that bastard." His square jaw set angrily.

"Any particular bastard?" Talba said. "Are you saying you have some idea who it was?"

"Jealous wife—that'd be my first thought. Cassie had a way of getting into situations that weren't good for her."

Talba nodded. "So I hear. Do you happen to know who she was involved with?"

He ground his teeth. "That bastard, Hunt Montjoy." He was openly showing so much hatred Talba wondered if he even knew Montjoy was dead.

"And you think Montjoy's wife killed her?"

"Naah, but she probably should have. You know what I really think? I think he got drunk, had a fight with her, and things got out of hand." He shrugged. "I think that's why he killed himself."

"I just wonder, though . . . if they fought, it must have been over something. Was she seeing anyone else?" *Like you?*

"Not that I know of."

"Well, how about the guy she dumped for Hunt?"

"No idea who that was." Simon shook his head. "Wasn't me, that's all I can tell you. She never gave me a look—just wanted me for a pal. You had to be married or violent or both to get her attention. God, she was self-destructive!"

"That's what I hear. But Hunt's is the only name I've got."

"Maybe that's because he did it."

Talba thanked him and went back to the public rooms. Everybody'd had a drink by now, and the place was buzzing. The size of the crowd had more than doubled, and most of the people looked young. They were probably mostly Cassie's friends, as Rashad had predicted. Since Talba recognized hardly anyone, she was reluctant to go around asking about Cassie's exes.

She ran into Austin again, even now relishing his bad-boy role. "Arnelle wants to start the speeches," he said. "But I said no. I'm still trying to think of something good to say about Mother."

"Austin, listen, didn't you tell me Cassie had a habit of dating married men?"

"I wouldn't call it dating, exactly."

"Can you give me names?"

"She didn't share that stuff with me. I just know what Arnelle told me. Why don't you ask her? Hey, Arnelle!" He called so loudly that a few people stared. Arnelle, twenty feet away, whirled around looking furious. It probably cost her, but she joined them to avoid a scene. "What is it?" she hissed.

Talba decided not to pussyfoot. "Do you know the names of any of Cassie's ex-boyfriends?"

"That bastard, Hunt Montjoy."

Funny, everybody had the same opinion of him. Talba wondered what *his* memorial service was going to be like.

"Anybody else?"

"No." She whirled again, and left them.

This was going nowhere. Maybe it was best just to leave it alone. The good news was that Janessa and Rashad weren't in jail—maybe she'd gone far enough; maybe there was no need to pursue the thing any further.

She saw Burford Hale in the crowd, and decided he must have come for Cassie, not Allyson. She noticed an older woman she was sure she knew, but couldn't place—a very chic woman in slate blue silk that was fabulous with chestnut hair that must, at her age, have cost a mint to keep up. Wayne Taylor was talking to her, his back to Talba. She was weighing the pros and cons of confronting him directly when a plump, round-faced woman touched her on the shoulder. She was holding a baby.

"Aren't you the Baroness Pontalba? I'm Janet Taylor. Wayne was thrilled you caught his Frankenstein class the other day."

Oops, Talba thought, *abort mission*. She was thoroughly disconcerted. "Hi. Cute baby," she said, aware that she was so nervous she was more or less chirping.

Janet held the kid up to be admired. "This is Georgia. Isn't she adorable? Is she not the cutest baby you ever saw?"

Talba laughed. She liked this woman, liked her pretty, wholesome face, liked her enthusiasm for her child, liked her general exuberance. She was a model of positive energy whereas Cassie, by all accounts, had been lovely, but wildly neurotic. Interesting contrast, Talba mused, reflecting that poor mental health often seemed, for a certain kind of man, a prerequisite to romance.

Janet was still talking. "We couldn't get a baby-sitter, and we adored Cassie so much, we really, really had to come say goodbye to her. I figured, what the hell, Georgia has to learn about death sometime and she'll be among friends. She's not going to be warped, do you think?"

Talba laughed again. Coming from another woman, Janet's words might have seemed ditsy, but Janet spoke them with a certain irony—you could tell there was a piece of her that really did worry that her daughter would pick up the sadness in the room, yet another that told her not to be an idiot.

Talba touched the infant's face. "Hi, Georgia. You're just gonna sleep through this, aren't you? You wouldn't dream of being warped."

"Wayne is inordinately proud of that Frankenstein routine, you know. He's always doing something off the wall, but that's really one of his favorites. And he's such a fan of yours! He was so pleased you caught his act."

"It was a kick," Talba said, but the conversation, under the circumstances, was starting to make her decidedly uncomfortable. Fortunately, she was saved by Austin, banging a gong for attention.

To Talba's surprise, he delivered a moving, near-tearful eulogy to both his mother and Cassie. So much for the bad boy.

Eight or nine people spoke about Cassie, including Burford Hale, which she suspected was his revenge on Allyson—death by snubbing. And Rashad read two new poems—one for Cassie and one for Allyson.

After that, one other person spoke for Allyson—the older woman in the slate blue dress, whose gorgeous hair proved to be a wig. She introduced herself as Allyson's oldest friend, Rosemary McLeod, and proceeded to paint her friend as a saint, exactly as she had in private. Talba was so uncomfortable with the naked naïveté of it—which more or less convicted Allyson while purporting to praise her—that she distracted herself by looking around again, and saw that she wasn't the only one. People were shifting their weight and changing position, in that way they do when they smell something wrong. She did notice one thing—Wayne's face was bruised and swollen. She wondered vaguely if Janet had found out about his affair and beaten him up.

More and more people contributed a story or two about Cassie, here a tear, there a laugh, but no one else rose to say how much they'd miss Allyson—not one single person—until it was clear the ceremony was winding down. Austin as master of ceremonies called one last time for speakers, and Janessa, looking like she might cry, came to the microphone. Her hands were shaking.

"I didn't know Miz Allyson well," she said. "But what I did know, she was good to me, and she was good to my friend. And I think she was good to some of y'all, too. Y'all came here and you ate her food and ya drank her liquor, and now ya just doin' the same thing all over again. Shame on y'all. Shame on ya!" And she stumbled back out of sight, crying.

Talba found her and tried to touch her, but the girl shook her off. Rashad was standing nearby, the picture of helpless distress.

"Janessa, I'm proud of you," Talba managed. "That was really a brave thing to do." Janessa turned her back and walked away.

Chapter Twenty-six

World's biggest anticlimax," she reported in the morning. "Couldn't even find out if it's true about Cassie and Taylor, although Rashad's prediction came true—it *was* mostly Cassie's friends. Not a soul spoke for Allyson except Austin, the big hypocrite, and her friend, Rosemary McLeod, and Rashad, who wrote her a poem. Oh, yeah, and Janessa. But there was a guest book—I could check out the Cassie thing that way."

Eddie shook his head. "Not worth it. And don't even mess with Rashad's bartenders. We found the cops two witnesses, our client's still out of jail, and so's her boyfriend—let's give the damn thing a rest. I got an insurance case to do, and the Lord only knows what you got on ya plate."

"Fine with me," Talba said. "I've got plenty to do." Not only that, she was heartily sick of the case. She did have a couple of regrets, but they weren't big enough to make her argue. One thing, she still felt bad about Cassie. Another, she didn't want to take Janessa home to Mama till she was sure the girl wasn't a murderer.

And there was one other thing—the Hunt Montjoy connection. She'd sure like to know what had happened there. Something told her he could have killed both the other victims, but he'd had far too high an opinion of himself to nip such greatness in the bud.

Still, life went on, and one way or another, Janessa had to grow up. Talba applied herself to other cases and probably would never have given Montjoy another thought if Mimi Dirr, in her role as designated gossip for the literary set, hadn't called to find out if Talba'd turned up anything on Cassie and Wayne Taylor.

"Naah," she said. "It's probably just one of those rumors."

"Oh. Well. Never say I don't check out my rumors. Are you going to Hunt Montjoy's memorial service?"

Talba leaned back in her chair, shoulders aching from hours bending over her computer. "Hadn't planned on it. When is it?"

"Tonight. Why aren't you going?"

"Couldn't stand the man, for one thing."

Mimi giggled. "Well, who could? But listen, this is the literary event of the decade. Wayne Taylor and some of his buds have booked Café Brasil."

"*Café Brasil?* Isn't that a little funky for a memorial service?" It was a dance club.

"You know, celebration-of-his-life kind of thing. There's a bar, and a microphone there—that's half the battle. The Praline Connection's doing the food."

"That's convenient." The Praline Connection was right across the street.

"It isn't that. It's because they have fried chicken livers and fried dill pickles—his two favorite foods."

"Oh my God. Lynne can't be in on this." Talba couldn't see the elegant designer ordering up a mess of fried pickles.

"No, there's a family funeral for him next week in Alabama—or wherever he's from. This is just his writing pals."

"God, he would have hated that! So far as I could tell he prided himself on not being friends with writers. Unless you count Wayne, of course."

"Listen, you've really got to pop in, check out hypocrisy in action."

She still wouldn't have gone if Austin hadn't called and

asked her to be his date, a proposition which caused her to laugh in his face. "Are you kidding? I've got a boyfriend. Take Angie."

"I hate to insult you, Baroness, but I'm only trying to make her jealous. She won't go with me."

"Why not?"

"Thinks I killed Hunt."

"And did you?"

"Well, I tried. You saw me. Pick you up at six-thirty?"

"Forget it. I'll meet you there." That way she could just not show up if she so decided. But the more she thought about it, the more she thought she couldn't afford to miss it. She and Eddie might have suspended the case, but you never knew when it was going to come back and bite them in the butt. Besides, Austin didn't need a date—he could go alone. She wanted to find out why he'd bothered to call her.

The minute she walked in, she was struck by the sense of celebration in the air. She thought that, if it had been her own memorial service, she might have preferred people to treat it slightly more seriously. A bluegrass band was playing, something Talba had never in her life heard in New Orleans. Leave it to the redneck poet crowd to come up with one.

Her "date" found her mulling over the question of turnip greens versus crowder peas. "Like the band? I found 'em myself."

"Austin, you're full of surprises. Why'd you want me to come to this?"

"Baroness, I didn't give a rat's ass if you came to this or not. I just wanted to see you."

She decided on turnip greens, but no rice; cornbread on the side. She placed her order and turned back to him. "Why's that?"

"Angie tells me you've stopped your investigation."

"We thought the police could take it from here. We found you and Rashad for them—they might as well earn their salaries somehow." Accepting a plate, she said, "This is great cornbread—have you tried it?"

"How about if I hire you to continue?"

She almost choked on her greens. "What for?"

"I need to know who killed Cassie."

She studied him, trying to figure out what the hell was up.

The look on his face was serious enough, but this was one volatile guy. She had no idea how trustworthy he was—or how deep the animosity ran between him and his older sister. "Are you trying to nail Arnelle?" She gave him the helpless sign. "Because I can't do it. I couldn't do it even if I wanted to. I don't see a shred of evidence that she did it."

He grinned. "Arnie? No, we're bonding." Seeing her skeptical look, he said, "Seriously. She's in it with me. We both want to hire you."

"Arnie. That does it, I'm not buying a word of this."

"I swear. Well, technically, I'd be paying, but she's all for it. Listen, I'll prove she knew I'd be talking to you."

"How?"

"She asked me not to forget to ask you which cat you want— Koko or Blanche."

Talba still wasn't buying it. "Austin, what's behind this?"

He stared at the band as if he'd never seen a banjo in his life, and he just had to memorize what it looked like. "Look, I don't expect you to understand this. But something happens to you when someone dies like this." He paused, his jaw set hard. "When someone is murdered. You know how they talk about 'closure'? God, I hate that word! But I get it now. I completely get it. Sure my mother was difficult, but she was still my mother. No way she deserved to die like that." Tears weren't exactly flowing, but his jaw was working now and his brow was furrowed. He wasn't finished. "And Cassie was my baby sister." He gasped the words, barely able to talk.

Talba decided, for the moment, to take him at face value. The world was full of great actors, even fuller of gifted liars, but maybe he wasn't one. "Okay, okay. But I've got to run it by Eddie—I'm not sure we don't have a conflict. I told Arnelle that."

"Yeah, but that was when you had another client. Now you don't."

"Technically, we do, but—"

She was interrupted by Peter James, the distinguished and much honored writer of humor who'd apparently been chosen to serve as master of ceremonies. The band had lapsed into respectful silence.

James was from South Carolina, but she'd met him a number of times at the local literary festival. He was a member in very good standing—if not the acknowledged leader—of the good ol' boy literary network. So he and Montjoy had been friends, that went without saying.

James was something of a poet himself, though his poetic bailiwick was self-acknowledged doggerel. Still, it was extremely witty doggerel. He began the evening with a poem to his old buddy, Hunt, whom, one line went, "We won't forget, no matter how much he might wish we would." And which went on from there to describe a few choice moments from the great man's life that might have been better off forgotten.

Just when Talba thought the event was beginning to resemble a roast more than a wake, James got to the "but seriously" part of the speech, which he then turned into a graceful tribute to Montjoy's literary achievements. As he spoke, the band struck up "Amazing Grace," and played it very softly under his voice. When he was finished, there was barely a dry eye in the house, certainly not in Austin's head. Talba was stunned to see him weeping, as he hadn't at his own family's service.

He pulled out a handkerchief. "Delayed reaction," he said, attempting a smile. "And the music."

Embarrassed, she turned away, and for the first time, scanned the crowd. Since she hadn't really come in her professional capacity, she'd focused on Austin rather than the bigger picture. She wasn't surprised to see Rashad, though Janessa wasn't in sight. Mimi Dirr was there, with a bunch of people from the literary festival. Protocol demanded that one of them would have to speak, Talba thought, though Hunt had been famous for accepting their invitations, turning up at their parties, and insulting half the women while hitting on the other half. They'd probably drawn lots, with the loser getting the honor.

Most people were standing, but about thirty chairs had been set up, and on one of these, near the front, sat Lynne Montjoy, her blond hair clipped into a low-slung ponytail, her skinny body in a black suit that looked absurdly formal in this crowd of fashion villains. Most of the men looked as if they'd gotten their clothes at Goodwill, then slept in them a few times to break them in; the women, suffice it to say, had left their panty-hose in their hosiery drawers (in the event they actually owned any). Talba herself was wearing flowing purple pants and knee-

length matching jacket—for her, almost conservative except for
her orange tank top.

All she could tell about Lynne was that she looked drawn—
and who, under the circumstances, wouldn't? *Me*, Talba
thought. *I'd be dancing in the streets.* Lynne was sitting with
Wayne Taylor, whose back was really all she could see of him.
Rosemary McLeod, whom she recognized by her lustrous wig,
was sitting on his other side. Talba figured she must be feeling a
ton better, out two nights in a row.

A celebrated historian who taught at Tulane followed Peter
James, offering a much more sober view of Montjoy's work
and influence, frequently and sadly mentioning the "gaping
hole" he was going to leave in the "intellectual community."

A young woman who'd had Hunt as a writing teacher spoke
painfully of the influence he had had "over me," an image that
caused titters among the standees; and Mimi Dirr, who'd
clearly lost the draw, was forced to eulogize him on behalf of
the festival—which she cleverly managed to avoid by reading
one of his own poems, about death and how unimportant we really are in the scheme of things. She kept a straight face—and
her black dress helped—but Talba was terrified she was going
to giggle aloud at the knowledge that she'd managed to pull off
calling Hunt Montjoy unimportant at his own memorial service. Talba sincerely hoped he wouldn't haunt the poor
woman—she could hardly imagine a worse fate.

Unlike Cassie's and Allyson's service, this one could easily
have gone on all night if they hadn't run out of alcohol. After
about forty-five minutes, Lynne Montjoy rose and, instead of
offering her own eulogy, only thanked all those who had spoken, announced a short break, and invited everyone else to have
at it as soon as they'd wet their whistles—though she put it a bit
more delicately.

Delighted with the invitation, Talba and Austin bolted for the
bar, which, fortunately, was quite near. "Now this," Austin said,
"is my idea of a funeral."

Noticing that Lynne had taken the opportunity to duck out,
Talba said, "It might be about to get better—or worse, depending on how you look at it. Look, there's Wayne Taylor." Taylor
was coming toward them—or more specifically, toward the bar.
His face was so battered, Talba suspected he had a broken nose.

He was walking with a limp. "Hey, Austin. Baroness. Janet enjoyed meeting you last night."

Talba made no attempt to control herself. "My God, Wayne. What on earth happened to you?"

He looked sheepish. "Tripped over a toy, and fell down my own front steps."

They both made sympathetic noises, and let him through to order two glasses of white wine. Talba watched him take one back to Rosemary McLeod, thinking well of him for taking care of her.

The evening may not, as Talba had predicted, have gotten better after that, but at any rate, it got more embarrassing. Fueled by the plentiful supplies, more and more people were moved to recount their own experiences with the wild man—some of which were unsuitable for the widow's hearing, and some pretty much unsuitable for anyone. Far from being properly appalled, Austin was having the time of his life. "Aren't you glad you came?" he whispered. "You'd have had to commit suicide if you'd missed this."

"It might have been preferable," Talba answered nervously, and as she glanced back at the stage, she happened to see Rosemary McLeod whispering familiarly into Wayne Taylor's ear. She had wrapped one hand around his neck and insinuated the other into his hand. It wasn't sexual, necessarily, but it was certainly intimate, the kind of thing you did with someone you knew well if you really needed to get their attention. Or maybe, given the bizarreness of this crowd, it was sexual.

She grabbed Austin. "What the hell is that?"

"What the hell is what?"

"Taylor and McLeod—they're acting like lovers."

He snorted. "Are you kidding? She's his mother."

"She's his *mother?* Why didn't anyone tell me?"

He stared as if she were crazy. "Uh . . . well . . . why would you need to know?"

He was right. There was no reason to have told her, no reason for anybody except Burford Hale—who had sent her to Rosemary—even to know Talba knew her. She saw Taylor help Rosemary up and out of there, which was undoubtedly what the desperate little clinch had been about. She probably couldn't handle this tasteless circus for one more second.

Remembering the story about Allyson's shop in Tallahassee, and the friends and their two sons, she suddenly realized something. "You've known Wayne Taylor all your life!"

Automatically, Austin shook his head. "No, I haven't. I only met him when—oh! Wait a minute, Tallahassee. Well, that didn't exactly count. I was four and he was sixteen or seventeen." He shrugged. "A grown-up to me, anyhow. I didn't remember him at all when Mother moved here a couple of years ago. Of course, Cassie'd already been here awhile—she went to Tulane, you know, and then she just stayed. Somewhere along the line, I guess Mother got her to look up Wayne and Janet. All I know is, she was friends with them by the time Mother moved here. She introduced me to them, not Mother."

Peter James got up again and tried to send people home, but they were having none of it. The stories were getting increasingly unflattering, revealing more and more of Hunt's dark side, and quite a few people were getting off on it. Less subtly than Mimi Dirr had, they were insulting him at his own service, and James was visibly distressed.

Maybe, Talba thought, Hunt, like Allyson, also had only one true friend. Rashad, pushing his way out, came by to say hello. "You aren't going to speak?" Talba asked.

Rashad shook his head. "I was, but seems like people just want to hear themselves talk." He sounded profoundly disappointed. "I'm getting out of here."

"Good idea," Talba said, and followed.

Chapter Twenty-seven

There was Ms. Wallis, first thing in the morning, as usual, eyes bright as a couple of diamonds, messing up his schedule again. He didn't even wait for her to open her mouth, which meant he had to be quick as a lizard. "Don't even think about it unless you've got coffee."

She smiled, and held up a paper bag. "Not only have I got coffee, I've got *good* coffee."

"Gimme." He held out a greedy paw, wondering if there was such a thing as an employee who was just a little *too* eager, and quickly dismissed the thought: *Eddie, ya just old. Ya hate it when she makes ya notice.*

She was eyeing him critically. "Good color today."

He touched a hand to his cheek, wondering what on God's earth could have elicited such a peculiar comment. "Uh—really? What color am I usually?"

"Not your skin. Your eye bags."

"What eye bags?" He was putting her on—she'd once roasted him by composing a sonnet to his bags; he knew perfectly well they were his most distinguishing characteristic. His best feature, in his opinion.

"Those tan-lookin' hampers you've got—bags isn't right, really. They're more like lunch boxes. Tan's not bad, by the way." She handed him his coffee and plopped herself in his other chair. "I went to Hunt Montjoy's memorial service."

That gave him a bad feeling. "Think I'd rather talk about my facial flaws."

"Hey. I love your bags."

"Uh-huh. I thought we were off this case."

"Well, here's the good news. Angie wasn't with Austin. I was."

Not sure what she meant, he supported his face in his hand. "Give me strength."

"He asked me, so I went with him. Seems he wants us to re-open the case for real—meaning, for our usual hourly rate."

For a moment, Eddie brightened, but on consideration, he couldn't see a way. "Probably a conflict," he said. "This is good coffee."

"Don't say I don't take care of you. Here's the thing—I told him he'd have to talk to you, but then something happened that made me think we should reopen it anyway."

Eddie was liking the whole conversation less and less. "What kind of something?"

"You know how you were talking about some kind of real motive for killing Allyson? That self-preservation wasn't good enough?"

He nodded.

"Wayne Taylor's got one. Allyson duped his mother into investing in her company and then dug her in deeper and deeper, out of sheer incompetence and arrogance." She shrugged. "For all I know, it may even affect Taylor's inheritance—that part I can't research. What I do know is, she's oblivious about what happened to her—apparently has no idea in hell. But anybody she tells the story to kind of gets mad on her account—it's that transparent. So if it makes me mad, how mad do you think it would make Wayne? The same Wayne, by the way, who was having an affair with Allyson's daughter that Allyson had been trying to break up." She paused, which gave him a little time to connect the dots. She was talking fast, but she was making sense. "And his mother has cancer. He might even blame Allyson for that. You know how people are."

Despite himself, Eddie was getting interested. "Go on."

"Well, I've thought about this quite a bit. If Taylor really was involved with Cassie, they kept it pretty quiet, and I think I know why. First of all, Cassie was friends with his wife."

Eddie shook his head. "Women are bitches, 'scuse my French."

"Yeah, well, it kind of balances things. Taylor and Montjoy being such saints and all."

"All right. Touché."

"And second, Wifey just had a baby. Maybe that was why they broke up. In fact, maybe Cassie was the one who did it, because now she could see Taylor was never leaving, etcetera, etcetera."

"Same old story."

"Either that or the guilt got to her. So she dumps him, and then starts seeing his buddy, which makes him mad. He wants her back, she won't play, they fight, he stabs her."

Eddie was getting into it. "Or Taylor dumps her and then she dates Montjoy to make him jealous. But it doesn't work, he's happily back with his wife and child, so she threatens him, maybe calls him names . . ."

Ms. Wallis's eyes got even shinier, if that was possible—but maybe it was from the caffeine. "I like that one even better. He loses his temper big-time. And then, when he sees what he's done, and he's trying to figure out what to do next, he remembers that remark of Hunt's—about Allyson having to take the blame if anything happens to Cassie. And he thinks he can kill two birds with one stone."

Eddie was thinking. "Only no one quite buys the murder–suicide thing."

"When I really think about it," Ms. Wallis said, "the way the crime scene was cleaned up points to Taylor more than anybody else. He writes these kind of . . . thrillers. I never read the book about the Nazis, but I kind of think that's what it was. The other one was. And his one movie was about a cop. He was probably into all that procedural stuff. And getting that glass with the fingerprints—it's exactly what a writer would do."

Eddie set down his cup and folded his hands. Now was the fun part—the part where he got to tweak her. "Ya got a perfect little psychological case, Ms. Wallis. Only thing is, it's all in ya mind."

"Hold on a minute." She was so excited she was spilling coffee. "I've got somewhere to go with this. There's one little thing I didn't mention."

He pressed his lips together in frustration. Of course there was. Surprises were the woman's middle name. He waited, not about to give her the satisfaction of asking.

"Wayne's all banged up," she said. "Got a broken nose and he limps. Like he's been in a fight."

"So?"

She shrugged. "I wonder if he fought with Hunt Montjoy."

"I don't see whatcha gettin' at."

"Lynne said when her husband left that last time she saw him, he told her he was going to see somebody. And it happened right after that fight with Austin. So I'm thinking maybe it was Wayne he went to see. See, the fight with Austin was about who this girl was—this girl named Kerry that Taylor said Hunt had treated really horribly."

Eddie's brain was starting to feel like spaghetti. "Slow down, Sherlock Holmes. Ya leavin' the rest of us behind."

"All I'm saying is, when Austin went over there, he reminded Hunt that Taylor had ratted him out about Kerry, and maybe that made him mad enough to go over and attack him."

"And what would the significance of that be?"

She smiled at him. "Hunt's dead, right?"

He looked at his watch. "I'd kinda like to know what this is all about sometime before lunch."

"I figure the cops have probably talked to Taylor about Hunt, don't you? Why don't we just ask them if Taylor says they had a fight?"

Suddenly Eddie saw the point of the whole conversation. Ms. Wallis conducted her investigations as she thought best—until she hit a snag and needed him for something. "You mean, why don't I call my buddy in Major Case Homicide."

"I was kind of thinking that, yeah." She was leaning back in her chair, all smug and smiling. It was annoying, being played this way, but on the other hand he thought she was onto something. "I'll think about it, Ms. Wallis."

"I'd appreciate it." She got up and eased out of the room, her ears pricked, he knew, for the sound of him reaching for the phone. He let her get too far away to hear before he called LaBauve. Waiting for a return call, he reflected that Rashad might have been onto something with that Gatsby thing. If Wayne Taylor was involved with Cassie, whom Eddie saw as the mistress character, Myrtle Wilson, then Taylor was the closest thing to a husband she had—which would make him the Wilson character, Gatsby's murderer. Eddie liked that. As theories went, it was neater and more symmetrical than Hunt-as-murderer.

It took a couple of backs and forths, but he had what Ms. Wallis wanted by midmorning.

His associate, hunched over her computer, barely heard him when he entered her office. "Yeah, they fought," he told her. "Over what ya said. Where ya goin' with that?"

"Let's try Rashad. He knows her." She dialed her sister's number.

Eddie stood and listened to the ensuing conversation for five or six minutes, but in the end, he couldn't stick it out. So far as he could tell, Rashad had left Janessa, and Ms. Wallis was doing the Big Sis polka.

Rashad was back at Allyson's, at Austin's invitation, and Talba, for one, didn't blame him. Janessa threw out a few phrases about giving him space, but she was much more into crying and moaning and accusing. Once again, without Rashad to cling to, she was all over Talba, nagging about being let into the family. It took twelve minutes to shake her off—Talba timed it.

She had a bad feeling about what Rashad and Austin might do, just the two of them, in what amounted to a bachelor pad—bad enough to make her pay a visit instead of calling.

They were sitting around the pool in shorts, no shirts, no shoes, drinking Bloody Marys and smoking pot. Which made them extremely expansive and thrilled to see her. After hugs and "lookin' goods" and could they get her a drink and would she like a toke, she finally joined Austin at the table on the patio and confronted Rashad while he sprawled on a chaise longue. "Rashad, who's Kerry?"

The answer was less than dramatic. First he made a face. And then he blew out some smoke. Finally, he said, almost in a whisper, "Who?"

Damned if he was getting away with the innocent act. "You heard me. Who the hell's Kerry?"

"Kerry," he said. "This is weird."

"Look, I know you're stoned, but you're not stupid—and by the way, neither am I. I know she was your girlfriend. What's weird about asking about her?"

He shook his head. "Kerry wasn't my girlfriend. She was jailbait, man. She's just a girl I helped. Hunt put her through the wringer like nothin' you ever saw. Jesus, he could be a bastard! Always good to me, though. Yep. Always good to me. See, what's weird is, I hadn't seen Kerry in a year. Until yesterday." He pulled himself to a sitting position. "I went to pay my respects to Lynne, you know? At the house. And she was there. She's some kind of relative of Lynne's. I don't think I ever knew that." He took another toke, as if that were going to help him think. "Her niece, maybe?"

Austin raised an eyebrow at her, but she was too way too preoccupied to respond. She kept on Rashad. "*That's* who Kerry is? Lynne's niece? Jesus, man. His own wife's *niece*."

"Some kind of shit like that. Known that a few years ago, mighta killed Hunt myself. Now . . ." He didn't even attempt to complete the sentence, but Talba knew all too well what he was

trying to say. Something along the lines of "Now, I'm just trying to forget." She realized he probably didn't even know about
the fight between Hunt and Austin.

She stood up. "Exactly how early do I have to get up to find
anyone sober enough to answer a simple question? Austin, what
the hell's going on here?"

He had the grace to look ashamed. "Yeah, you're right, you're
right." He nodded briskly every time he said "right." "We're just
taking the day off, that's all—in memory of old Hunt. Tomorrow, it's business as usual. I'm going back to run the fucking
bait hut, and Rashad's taking over here as poet-in-residence."

Rashad laughed. "Caretaker. Arnelle's hiring me to keep
Austin out of here."

"Problem is," Talba said, "I'm here today. Think you could
summon up a lucid three seconds?"

Rashad snapped his fingers. "Madison. Hey, man—Madison!" He was lapsing into the kind of talk his Aunt Felicia'd
probably washed his mouth out with soap for. "Don't say I
never did nothin' for ya. It's Madison, man."

"What, exactly, is Madison?"

"Kerry's name. Name's Madison, man."

Talba rolled her eyes at Austin. "I'm calling his aunt and your
sister."

"Oh, Lord," Rashad said, and started laughing uncontrollably.

Austin stared at him and shrugged. He seemed perfectly in
control. "It was pretty high-quality shit," he said apologetically.

"Forget Arnelle, I'm calling Angie. Rashad, Janessa sends
her love."

"Yeah, man, I love her, too."

As she always did, Talba had made a formal file when she
backgrounded Lynne and Hunt Montjoy, which she now hurried back to consult. Though it wouldn't include Lynne's
maiden name, it would include her full name, and "Madison"
might be in it.

It wasn't, though. But that didn't mean anything.

She could have stopped to background Kerry, but she was in
way too much of a hurry. She simply thought up a quick pretext, dialed the Montjoy home, and asked if Kerry Madison was
staying there.

"This is Kerry," said a dubious-sounding young voice.

Talba forgot about the pretext. "Kerry, my name's Talba Wallis and I'm a private investigator. I have evidence your uncle may have been murdered. I wonder if you could give me a few minutes?"

"Uh, shouldn't the police . . . um . . ."

Talba could have kicked herself. "Look, Kerry, it's a whole long story. I work for E.V. Anthony Investigations—if you've got a phone book, turn to it, okay? See us there? Old, distinguished firm. And you can meet me at the office, so you'll know I'm legitimate."

She spoke without confidence. Even as the words poured out, she knew she was leaving out the thing Eddie had always taught her she needed most—a good reason to help her, a motive, so to speak. She took a chance. "I know the guy was an asshole, and I know something bad went down between you. But there might be somebody worse out there, that's what I'm worried about." *Like maybe your aunt.* "We really need to talk."

"How do you know . . . ? Um . . . I'm leaving in about an hour."

"Perfect. I'll take you to the airport." *And you can be grateful and spill your guts.*

"Um . . ."

The girl wasn't too quick, that was obvious. "I'm on my way."

"Wait! My mother's here. I can't just . . ."

"Right. Say Rashad's coming to get you. She'll buy that."

"Oh, Lord, if she ever hated anybody . . ."

"Doesn't matter. She'll buy it." Talba looked at her watch. "Noon straight up."

The girl who came out the door carried a blue duffel that looked only about half-full. She must have come just for the memorial service, though Talba hadn't seen her there. She was average height, maybe a little heavy, and pale. A white, white, white chick, saved from total blandness by magenta-colored hair and purple lipstick that, unfortunately, bleached her out even further. She looked scared to death, which was good. Scared, Talba could deal with.

She got out of the car and reached for the duffel. "Hey, girlfriend, this all you got?"

The girl stopped dead in her tracks. "I know who you are!"

"Uh-oh. Caught me peeping at a keyhole?"

"You're the Baroness de Pontalba."

Talba executed her Baroness curtsy. "The Baroness myself thanks you for flying Air Poetica. Our cruising altitude will be roughly sea level, or a little below, with a complimentary stop for coffee if you should so desire." She opened the door and ushered in the passenger.

The girl slid in and turned to her, staring. "I've heard you read three times."

Talba fired up the Isuzu. "Oh, really? I'm surprised your uncle allowed it. But then, why not? He pretty much thought I didn't exist."

"No, he didn't. He thought you were probably the worst poet in America."

Talba smiled. "Sounds right."

"But then that's what he said about everybody. As long as they were female."

"Or black."

The girl shrugged. "He never complained about Langston Hughes."

Talba laughed and Kerry, once she was sure how Talba was going to take it, joined in.

Evidently, she wasn't half as dumb as she'd appeared on the phone.

"Listen, I'm sorry I didn't recognize your name on the phone. I'm not sure I ever even knew it."

"And why should you? For that matter, why should you have even heard me read?"

"Oh, I'm . . . well, I'm doing my dissertation on contemporary African American female poets and the spoken idiom, that . . . oh, never mind. My boyfriend calls it 'Black Chicks with Chops.' You get the idea."

Talba was getting more than one idea, and it was amusing her no end. "Are you saying what I think you're saying? Am I in somebody's dissertation?"

The purple-lipped girl turned to her in astonishment. "You're in lots of people's dissertations—didn't you know that? You're a cultural icon."

It was true that Talba had had a small volume published by a hip-lit press a few years ago, but it was so supremely obscure, the first and only printing so minuscule, that she could no longer even find used copies. If she was a cultural icon, the culture that had elevated her had to be as obscure and attenuated as the volume itself.

"Little *moi?*" she said. "Surely you jest."

That sent Kerry into a fit of the giggles. "Some tough black babe."

"*I,*" said Talba grandly, "am a Baroness. In case you haven't heard. Are you a poet, too? Is that why you chose that subject?" They were approaching I-10 and the last thing Talba wanted was for Kerry to get over the novelty of having a subject of her dissertation drive her to the airport.

The girl colored, creating a Barbie-pink flush that clashed with her hair and lips, which fought with each other as well. "Hunt didn't think so," Kerry said. "Bastard! But I *hate* his kind of poet. I can't stand those whitey snots who just move their cracker mouths in a phony-ass monotone. Like they all think they're T. S. Eliot or something. What I like about black poetry is the performance. The vigor! The passion!

"By the way . . ." her flush deepened ". . . you're a fantastic performer."

"Thanks." Talba gave her her Baroness smile, mostly generous and gracious, yet slightly condescending due to her rank. "I mean it's a little . . . with your uncle and all . . . he never even noticed poets like me. . . ."

"Oh, he noticed. Believe me, he noticed. He was just a small-minded, jealous, supremely insecure, pathetic asshole bastard sonofabitch. Couldn't even get it up most of the time."

Talba raised an eyebrow. "And you would know, I hear."

The girl sighed. "Why do you want to hear my story?"

"Listen, have you got time for coffee?"

Kerry looked at her watch. "Maybe at the airport. Let's just get there first." She pulled out a pair of blue-purple sunglasses and put them on. Talba wasn't sure why.

Wanting to get Kerry into the position of owing her one, Talba steered the conversation to poetry until they were safely at the airport, even taking the unusual step—once they were in the terminal—of offering to critique some of Kerry's poetry. The offering part was unusual, but being asked wasn't. She wondered why this was the first she'd heard of Kerry. "Why didn't you get in touch before?" she asked. "If you wanted to meet me?"

"I don't know, I . . . well, actually, Hunt convinced me that would be gauche. That it was beneath a poet's dignity to, uh . . ."

"Wait a minute! He must have mentored people. Like Rashad, for instance."

"Rashad? 'Mentor' isn't really the word I'd use. Rashad was more like Hunt's favorite bird dog. Oh, hell, what would I know about Hunt? We hadn't been close in a long time. I, uh . . ." She took off her glasses and looked at Talba through tragic dark blue eyes. "I had an affair with him. I know, I know . . ."

"Kerry, I already know that. Nobody's going to judge you for being young and stupid. We all were at one time."

"I was sixteen." Her eyes overflowed.

"Omigod." Quickly, Talba found a restaurant, sat the girl down, and ordered coffee, regretting, under the circumstances, that it couldn't be morphine. *Sixteen*, she was thinking; *the daughter of his wife's sister. What a maggot-infested rat turd. What a rare and vital specimen of the virulent evil-virus.*

But the girl wasn't finished. "He got me pregnant."

"Shit!"

She shrugged. "Well, it could have been worse. At least he paid for my abortion. Mostly."

Talba was getting the hang of the sunglasses. Kerry had them on now, and, although she dabbed constantly at her cheeks, at the tears flowing freely beneath them, no one could actually see her eyes. A good thing, Talba thought. She didn't want to.

"I don't like the sound of that 'mostly,' " she said.

"When he gave me the money, he took it out of his wallet and counted it, and then he looked at his watch, said, 'Almost lunchtime—I'm gonna need a few bucks,' and put one of the twenties back in his wallet. I was standing on the sidewalk and he was in the car. He . . . just left. And all I had was a ten."

"He left you ten dollars short?" Talba really couldn't believe it. "What on earth did you do?"

"I went inside and tried to make a deal with the clinic. Somebody in the waiting room heard the whole thing and tossed in the other ten." The last couple of lines took her a long time to deliver. She was fighting sobs, but quite a few were escaping.

"My God. Have you had therapy?"

Blowing her nose, the girl nodded. "I started once I got to college and out on my own. I never told my parents—either they wouldn't have believed me, or my dad would have killed Hunt. And poor Aunt Lynne! I didn't—I just—I mean, I did a terrible thing to her. . . ."

"For Christ's sake, you weren't the one who did it."

"Believe me, my family would have seen it that way. They thought Rashad was the cause of my trouble. And he was the only thing holding me together, man. He was all there was! My parents are Bible beaters, see. They knew I was depressed, but they thought I just needed to get away from 'that black boy' and come to Jesus. You know why I came here? I didn't have to. Know why I did?"

Talba nodded. "Sure. I'd have done the same. You wanted to see him dead."

"They cremated him, goddammit!"

"Bad break." Talba smiled, which provoked a smile from Kerry.

"Okay. I know what that sounded like."

"No, really. I'd have felt exactly the same." She wasn't lying. "So Lynne never found out?"

"Not unless he told her. What do you think the chances are of that?"

"Zip and none, frankly. How about Wayne Taylor?"

"Wayne Taylor?" Her nose wrinkled in puzzlement. "Who's he?"

Chapter Twenty-eight

It was Taylor. It had to be Taylor. Everything pointed to it, including the absurd notion of trying to make Hunt look guiltier by revealing what he'd done to Kerry. It had to be him and he had to be falling apart, maybe getting more dangerous and reckless every day. He could have killed Hunt, and Hunt might not be the last.

The question was, what to do next. She couldn't very well go to Crockett and tell him Taylor had a good motive, so he must be guilty.

Her phone rang as she was simultaneously thinking that thought and getting close to the Superdome exit, which would take her back to the Central Business District. Maybe Eddie hadn't had lunch yet and she could snag him to chew the thing over. "Hello," she said, her mind already on what to order for lunch.

"Hey, Baroness, we solved the case." It was Austin, even more wasted than two hours before.

She wasn't sure if this was a joke or what. "Congratulations," she said tentatively.

"It's Wayne Taylor, man! Has to be. A ten-year-old could see it. Hell, *Arnelle* could have figured this one out."

Because she had just come to exactly those two conclusions herself, her guard was a bit down. "Yeah," she said, "but the question is, what to do about it."

For the next few hours, she kicked herself for those words, but in the end, it was Darryl who convinced her that by the time she talked to Austin, events had already spun so far out of control she had no way of stopping them.

"We're *doing* something about it," Austin said. "We are in that very process right this minute. We are very much aware that Wayne Taylor killed my mother and my sister, and maybe Rashad's buddy, Hunt. In addition, he shot at Rashad and set him up to rat out his own friend, and maybe kill him. We are at this moment on our way to Wayne Taylor's one o'clock class, formerly known as Writing the Novel: A Seminar."

"*Formerly* known as?"

"We're about to rename it—thought you might like to join us. Liberal Arts Building, room four hundred and three." He rang off.

Talba listened to the dial tone for a long time before she snapped out of the paralysis she'd gone into. She was aware of her skin cooling, as if the temperature had suddenly dropped, and of goose bumps popping out on her body, of her mouth going dry, and a certain lightheadedness, which made her shake her head to clear it and drive past the dome, to take the Elysian Fields exit, the fastest way to UNO.

She tried to think. Call Eddie? Call 911? No. Call Austin. Find out if they had weapons. But she didn't have his cell phone number.

Rashad then. Janessa would have that one. She dialed, fingers shaking. "I need Rashad's cell phone number."

"Why? What's goin' on?"

"Give it to me, Janessa. I've got an emergency."

"What kinda emergency? Rashad's not gon' be arrested, is he?"

Talba thought about it. "Not if I can stop him."

"Why? Whassup?"

"Give me the *number*, Janessa."

Janessa surrendered the number, which Talba punched in with shaking fingers. It rang seven times before she got a voice-mail message. She wanted to throw the phone.

Back to square one: What to do? She didn't think she could call the cops—even Skip Langdon—on the basis of somebody saying they were about to rename a class. What kind of a threat was that? And why the hell hadn't she asked more? Then she remembered she hadn't had a chance—Austin had hung up on her.

Wayne. She could call Wayne. She tried his office, then his home, but she didn't have his cell phone number. Not that he'd answer it, anyway. It was quarter of one. He might be on his way to class, perhaps already there. She wondered if Austin and Rashad were, too.

She did the only three things she could think of: She got the number of the UNO campus police, she put it on speed-dial, and she kept driving. She would have prayed, too, if she'd been a church lady.

Her spirits lifted when she got to the parking lot—there was no Harley in sight. And none parked illegally on the grounds of the building. So far, so good. As she neared the classroom, she could hear Taylor talking to someone. And then a woman answered back. That had to be good. Even better, music was wafting out of the room, something upbeat and vaguely familiar.

The door of the classroom was open, and Talba could see that several students had already drifted in. The woman Taylor was talking to was Janet, his wife, dressed in one of those shapeless linen bags that a certain kind of New Orleans woman wore almost as a uniform—the young married, young mother kind of Uptown woman. Whoever made those dresses must be a jillionaire, Talba thought, just on the basis of sales in Orleans Parish alone. They had huge pockets that seemed never to be used and they seemed to come only in beige. They doubled as sundresses in hot weather and jumpers in the fall. Janet wore a peach-colored T-shirt under hers. Her light brown hair was slightly untidy, her round face a little flushed. She looked rather like an amiable cherub, and Talba strongly, strongly felt this was no place for her at the moment. She looked around for Georgia, the baby, but saw no sign of her.

There was no sign of Rashad and Austin, either.

What Janet and Wayne seemed to be doing was tacking photos all over the walls of the classroom. For some reason, they had also set up a little café table in front of the desks, with a tablecloth and candle.

Two more students entered the classroom. "*Cabaret*," one said. "What's happening?"

The music, Talba thought, finally recognizing it. *He means the music.*

"We're in pre-war Berlin today," Wayne answered, throwing an arm at the wall of pictures. "As you may know, my wife Janet's the official 'setting' photographer."

"Ah," the student said, "This must be the class on 'setting.'"

Wayne looked at his watch and then at the door, where he spotted Talba. "Baroness. To what do I owe this honor?"

"I need to talk to you. Would you mind . . ."

But he didn't even hear her. He was completely full of himself and the performance he was about to give. Two more students slipped in, bringing the number up to about a dozen. Talba wondered how many more there could be. Janet waved at her.

"Students, we have a rare treat today. This is one of our finest contemporary local poets, the Baroness de Pontalba."

"Listen, I . . ."

But she never finished the rest of the sentence, having become distracted by the stomp of motorcycle boots. "Wayne, close the door and lock it!"

But of course he didn't. Instead, he walked to the doorway and looked down the hall. For some reason, it didn't occur to him to be nervous. Merely puzzled, Talba thought. "Hi, guys," he said. "What's up?"

They were smiling. And why not, considering the morning's systematic substance abuse? "Hey, Wayne," Austin said. "Thought we'd help you teach your class today." He was wearing jeans, a T-shirt that showed off his torso, and one of those oversized belt buckles that look like they'd work fine if you forgot your brass knuckles. And then there were the boots, actually cowboy boots; but nonetheless the whole effect was threatening. Rashad was . . . well, he was still a skinny poet, but in Austin's shadow, he might, just barely, have passed for an outlaw.

Wayne showed no sign of alarm, but he did grab for the door and step over the sill, attempting to close it for what he probably imagined would be a man-to-man talk of some description.

Austin stuck out one beefy hand and slammed it open, striding past the startled professor and into the room. He was strutting like a rooster. Rashad herded Wayne and Talba back into the room: "Have a seat, Professor. Baroness. We're teaching the class today."

Austin said, "This is the lecture on plot you've all been looking forward to."

It was a simple statement, but Talba realized, in retrospect, that it was brilliant. At the moment she was just dazed.

"Y'all heard of Murder One? Today we're doing Murder 101. Come on up here, Professor, and sit down at this nice little table. Might as well be comfortable."

Taylor said, "You can't—"

But before he got any further, Austin grabbed him by his lapels and manhandled him to his feet and over to the table, Taylor resisting hardly at all as Austin shoved him into one of the chairs, so that he now faced the class like somebody on the witness stand.

Talba glanced nervously at Janet and saw that she was smiling, a faint blush of excitement tinting her cheeks. Far from being nervous, most of the students looked excited, anticipatory—in fact, as if they were enjoying themselves very much.

Austin said, "How many of y'all are working on detective novels?"

About half the class raised their hands.

"Well, we're gonna plot one today."

With a shiver, she saw what they had done—they had turned Wayne Taylor's own strategy against him. He was the professor who invited monsters to class—to his students, this looked like business as usual. The class was completely up for whatever was happening. Even his wife was.

Truth to tell, Talba was herself. This could definitely get interesting. There was just one thing that worried her. Where these nutballs were going with it.

Austin began to write on the chalk board, simple words and phrases like THWARTED LOVE, REVENGE, GAIN, BETRAYAL, KNEW TOO MUCH. "What do you think these are, class? Murder motives; that's right. Okay, here's our story. Professor Taylor here has a lover—let's call her Goldilocks. But she dumps him because the wife's pregnant and she knows he'll never leave her. Or maybe Wayne gets an ounce of conscience himself, and he dumps *her*. So she moves on. And whom do you think she moves on to? Why the professor's best friend, that's who—the Second Bear, shall we say. How'm I doing, class?"

Almost everyone was smiling. A couple of kids were giving the thumbs-up sign. Talba thought Janet was looking a little ambivalent, but she couldn't be sure.

"But that doesn't work out, and Goldilocks wants him back. Or maybe he wants her back. Which is it—shall we vote?"

A white kid in the front row, a guy whose legs must be six feet long and stuck straight out in front of him, said, "He wants her." A chorus of "yeahs" backed him up.

"Okay, that's what starts the argument. But things get out of hand, and he realizes just how mad he is, just how mad at *everything*—Goldilocks, his wife, his kid, his so-called best friend, the stinking university—and he stabs her and stabs her, and stabs her, and he can't stop. But then he does stop. And she's dead. He can't believe it—he's killed his lover! But, like her, he moves on. So—what does he do next? Call the police?"

"Hell, no," said a female voice.

"Good. What does he do instead?"

"He cleans up the evidence," the girl said. She wore glasses and a halo of dark, airy curls.

Austin actually prodded Wayne with his forefinger. "Yeah, that's a start. But there might be more. What else?"

The girl with the curls was on a roll. "How about framing somebody?"

Rashad said, "Good idea. But it would have to be just the right person. Maybe somebody he wants to kill anyhow."

"And as luck would have it, he knows just the right person. So he does it," Austin said. "He makes it look like murder–suicide. He is unbelievably cold-blooded. He goes to this woman's house and he has a drink with her, and he shoots her. And then, he takes the glass she has just drunk out of—with her fingerprints on it—back to the first victim's house. How am I doing so far, Wayne?"

Wayne's smile was thin. He looked distracted, as if his mind was on something—like a way out.

"I like it," said the girl with the curls. "Very noir."

Wayne bowed his head. "Thank you, Miss Weatherby."

"But he overlooks one thing," Rashad said. "It doesn't work because there are already prints on the glass—the prints of the person who washed it and put it away."

Wayne started. Talba realized he hadn't known about that part.

A kid in the back raised his hand, one of two African American students in the class. This one was heavyset, with a big, round, jowly face, baggy jeans, and short hair. "Somethin' funny here," he said. "How does he keep from getting his own prints on the glass?"

"Easy," Miss Weatherby said. "He wears gloves."

"Which he just happens to have handy?"

"He rifles the first victim's drawers," Weatherby said. "And maybe he finds some. If, not, maybe she colors her hair—and she's got some of those latex gloves like the dentist wears." She paused a moment. "Hey, we're plotting, right? Could go either way."

Talba was getting increasingly nervous. As long as Wayne went along with the game, he was fine (which made you wonder what on Earth Butch and Sundance were trying to accomplish)—but she couldn't help wondering about Janet. Had she ever suspected something about Cassie? Maybe even known? She might believe for a while that this was some kind of skit, but she had to wonder why Wayne had gotten her down there to put up the Berlin photos if he'd scheduled something else. And she had to know Rashad and Austin were talking about two real murders. Talba tried to shrug it off, hoping the worst that happened was she'd learn about the affair the hard way.

"Right," Austin said. "It's just a story. So he goes through all these machinations to get the police to think it's murder–suicide, but that extra set of prints throws everything off—along with other stuff that doesn't add up. So what does Wayne do next?"

A boy with a bad case of acne looked up long enough to say, "Maybe he lies low."

The other black student, a girl with straight, neat hair disagreed. "I don't see him as that kind of guy. He's an action player."

"And not only that, he sees another opportunity," Austin said. "There's something else you gotta know. Rashad here's a tenant of the second victim. He comes home and finds her dead, and he's got a little something in his background, so he splits, thinking he might be a suspect. But here's the kicker." Austin held up a finger. "Rashad's the Third Bear. He's a real good friend of Goldilocks, and also Wayne, the First Bear, and also the Second Bear, Goldilocks's new man. So Rashad doesn't know where to go or what to do, and he calls his buddy Wayne for advice. And what do you think Wayne does next?"

Miss Weatherby's eyes were shining. "He sets Rashad up."

"Yeah," Rashad said, and his voice was surprisingly calm. "Yeah. My best buddy sets me up. But he doesn't set me up to take the fall for the murders, because I'm not the one he hates. The one he hates is the one he thinks took Goldilocks away from him. He sets me up to set that guy up."

A chorus of near "boo"s went round the room. "Uh-uh," Miss Weatherby said. "He does not do that. It's way too complicated."

"It's worse than you think, Miss Weatherby," Rashad said. "He makes me think the Second Bear did it, but I don't think he wanted me to rat him out. Uh-uh." He looked Wayne full in the face. "He wanted me to kill him. Because he knew the shit he was telling me was just garbage—that the Second Bear could easily shoot it down if he got arrested. But, see, he knows I'm a killer. Remember that little thing in my past? Wayne figured it out because of something I wrote."

"And he knew one other thing about Rashad," Austin said. "He knew Rashad couldn't stand to see women in trouble. So he started a rumor about the Second Bear that was guaranteed to make Rashad so mad he'd come after him. Only it wasn't a rumor—it was true."

"And I found out what he'd done," Rashad said, "and now I'm here."

A blonde in the first row spoke for the first time. "Oh my God! What happens next? It's like we're living the story! This is fantastic, Dr. Taylor. I've never had such a sense of how plot and character fit together so perfectly, how they're really one and the same, mirror images of each . . ."

Wayne wiped sweat off his face. "What happens next," he said, "is we applaud." He stood. "Very nice, gentlemen," he said to his tormentors.

Rashad put a hand on his shoulder and shoved him back into the chair. "Sit down, Papa Bear. The story's not over yet."

Talba heard a rustling in the back of the room. "You sonofabitching bastard asshole douchebag." Janet was standing, her face twitching, spittle flying, almost as if she were foaming at the mouth. She wasn't sweating, but her face was red, much redder than when she blushed; she looked as if she were burning up, powered by a heat that came from inside and had barely begun to crackle. Her hands were shaking, which terrified Talba: She was holding a gun.

She held it in both hands, like detectives do on television, and she was pointing it at her husband. Probably he had given it to her. Half the men in New Orleans had bought guns for their loved ones, so they'd feel safe coming and going on the two-foot section of mean street between car and house.

Automatically, Talba's hand went to her phone, to her speed-dial button for the campus police. She punched it, but what to do next? Did she dare take the phone out of her pocket and talk? No way she wouldn't be overheard. And might a sudden action of any kind set Janet off? Her heart stuck in her windpipe.

But she saw that a lot of the students were smiling, some outright laughing, thinking it was all part of the show. Wayne had gone white; his face and neck glistened with sweat. Rashad looked bemused, as if he himself half thought it was fake. But Austin was beginning to wake up a little. He actually looked slightly alarmed. Talba half hoped Janet would shoot *him*, she was so angry at the whole performance.

But what she mostly was, was scared. What if this woman started shooting up the classroom? Janet walked to the front of the room, never taking her eyes off Wayne. "I found the fucking gloves."

Talba thought, *Oh, shit,* and Wayne actually said it.

The black kid from the back hollered, "Great acting, Dr. Taylor," but Talba noticed that Miss Weatherby's jaw had begun to twitch. The curly-haired girl's eyes were as bright as before, but earlier they had been flashlights, soft and large and searching; now they were lasers.

"You left them in the pocket of your jacket," Janet said. She was now in front of the class, but far enough away from the Hardy Boys and her husband that they couldn't make a sudden grab for her. Talba wondered if *she* could, but decided she'd have to run a few steps, which would give Janet time to whirl and shoot her.

"Cassie was my friend," Janet said. "How could you kill Cassie? And that poor mother of hers. She was just an old lady. Just a harmless old lady. You bastard! How could you? All this time, you and Cassie . . . and then . . . you killed her."

Austin picked that inauspicious moment to say, "He killed Hunt Montjoy, too."

Wayne turned on him. "You don't know what you're talking about! Hunt beat the shit out of me, and all I did was give him a few drinks to calm him down."

"All this time," Janet said, still telling herself the story, "you were a sonofabitchin' lying bastard."

"Put the gun down," Miss Weatherby said. She was standing now, and holding her own gun, much more steadily than Janet was holding hers.

Oh, SHIT! Talba felt sweat running down her back. Janet said, "Shoot me, I don't care." Talba's blood curdled. "My husband is going to tell me exactly why, and how he killed those two women, or I am going to shoot him dead. And I'll do it too, because I just don't give a fuck!" Her voice, slow and deliberate in the first part of the speech, got louder and louder on the last part.

Talba was thinking, *She just can't shoot him—she has a baby! She just can't.* A movie was running in her head, images, sounds, smells . . . far, far from the scene unfolding in front of her.

Wayne was shaking, and sweating, paler still if that was possible, and visibly shrinking—unconsciously trying to make himself a smaller target. "Janet, please! Honey, I can't even remember. I just couldn't stand to see Cassie throwing herself away on that asshole, I just couldn't, uh . . ."

She was going to shoot him. Talba could see her eyes squinching up, her arms tensing. And if she shot him, good riddance, but, oh, God, how could she do that to herself?

She heard herself shouting, not even believing she was doing it, barely recognizing the words, shocked at the volume: *"I smell pine disinfectant!"*

It was so incongruous—and so insanely loud—that every head turned to her. She kept shouting:

> *And the floor of my cell is painted stone.*
> *And the walls are cinder blocks.*
> *And from that concrete wall*
> *Georgia looks at me,*
> *Her blue, baby eyes*
> *As big and innocent as*
> *Forget-me-nots—*

She was bellowing as if she were training to be an opera singer, and walking forward, forward, holding out her hand for the gun . . .

> *And I wonder how she is*
> *And I wonder where she is,*
> *And I wonder if she misses her mama . . .*

Janet whirled, and fired on "mama." Talba winced and dodged, late, automatically, knowing the bullet had been for her, but she kept her eyes on Janet, kept shouting the improvised poem, which was pouring out of her almost without thought. . . .

> *Oh, Georgia, Georgia,*
> *Child of murder,*
> *Child of violence . . .*

She heard Miss Weatherby say, "Drop the gun, or I'll blow your fucking head off," and saw Janet's face fold in on itself, perhaps at the repeated sound of her daughter's name, perhaps at the shock of actually having shot at someone. She let the gun dangle uselessly, though she didn't drop it.

At that moment, the hubbub of what sounded like an entire army unit boomed and clattered down the hall. The door burst open, to a good part of the campus police force.

And Janet did drop the gun.

Miss Weatherby dropped hers, too, piling her hands on her head as if she did it every day.

Chapter Twenty-nine

This was not a caffeine story. The further Ms. Wallis got into it, the more jangled Eddie felt. He wasn't sure why that was, but he was pretty sure the coffee wasn't helping. He put up a hand to stop the disturbing flow of words. "Eileen!"

Ms. Wallis looked a little affronted, but Eileen Fisher was only her usual eager self when she appeared in the doorway. "Yeah, Eddie?"

"Don't we have a bottle of wine left over from Christmas or something? You mind gettin' that open and findin' us a couple of glasses? One for yourself, too, if you like." He really didn't want Eileen drinking in the daytime, but he couldn't see a way around offering.

"No, that's okay," she said, and Ms. Wallis began, "I don't know, Eddie . . ." but he cut her off.

"It'll calm us both down," he said, wondering how to describe the peculiar jumpy feeling that was on him like an animal, wriggling and jiggling and itching and generally making him want to get up and run like hell. Part of it was fear, he thought. He absolutely could not believe the inconceivably dumb thing Rashad and Austin had done, which would have given him the willies in concept alone—but considering the various near-misses, his brain (as well as his knees) had pretty much liquefied in the hearing. And part of it was something else. He didn't really like thinking about it, but it could be envy. It could very well be that. Ms. Wallis had a way of being where the action was. He could remember being like that.

Eileen came back with the bottle and two wineglasses. "Talba?" she offered.

"Sure, why not? Here's to you, Eddie."

"Here's to everybody being in one piece. Would you mind just tellin' me what those two orangutans thought they were up to?"

"First of all, you've got to remember they were seriously

wasted at the time. I can't even believe they made it all the way over on Austin's Harley. They spent the morning drinking and smoking pot, and anything seemed possible to them. They thought they were going to pull some Agatha Christie thing and make him confess."

"Oh, boy."

"Guess you're going to have a pretty hard time accepting Austin as a son-in-law."

"Christ, I liked it better when I thought Angie was a dyke."

"Well, anyhow, it worked, in a sort of a way—I mean, Wayne would never have broken. He was sweating like a can of beer in the sun, but he wasn't about to 'fess up. Pure luck Janet was there." She took a sip of wine. "Bad luck for her and Wayne— good luck for the cops. They got him on the gloves."

"The gloves don't prove anything."

"It turned out they *were* Cassie's gloves—a few sizes too small for Wayne, and the wrong season, anyhow."

"Oh."

"Eddie, I felt so sorry for that woman. Oh, my God! What if she'd shot him? What would have become of that poor child?" She made fists and hit the knuckles together. "When I think about it I could just kill those two fools! God, I'm mad. And that *poem*—it just came out of me. I actually thought I could stop a murder with a poem. I'm the one who could have gotten killed. Do you realize that? She shot at *me*."

"So much," Eddie said, "for the pen bein' mightier than the sword."

"But you know what, I couldn't stop myself. I didn't even think, I just . . . started yelling." Ms. Wallis took a deep sip, and leaned back, apparently reliving the event. "But in the end it worked out, because the cops heard the shot—that's how they knew where to go. See, I forgot to tell you that part. I had them on auto-dial and when things turned bad, I called them—but I couldn't talk. It turned out they answered the phone, which was in my pocket—so they heard some of what was happening, they just didn't know where it was. You know what I'm getting first chance I get?"

He nodded. He was way ahead of her here. "A cell phone with a GPS in it." He was surprised she hadn't already gotten herself one.

"Yeah, well, they were searching all over and some of them were close enough to hear the shot. Good thing that Miss Weatherby didn't start shooting. You will never in a million years guess who she turned out to be."

It was a vaguely familiar name. "Weatherby. I know a Neil Weatherby—worked with him a few times. PI out of Bay St. Louis."

"That's where she's from. She's got to be his daughter. Well, guess what, she joined the family firm—got a permit for the gun and everything. That woman was a PI taking Wayne's class because she wants to write PI novels. You believe that?"

"Ms. Wallis," he said wryly, "that's not exactly the most arrestin' part of this narrative." He wasn't sure what part was. "So tell me," he said, "did Wayne do his buddy, Hunt?"

She shook her head. "Jury's still out on that one."

T alba knew she owed it to Eddie to give him a report the minute the police turned her loose. But what she'd really wanted to do was go over to Allyson Brower's and tear Batman and Robin limb from limb. She'd hesitated on the wine, lest it weaken her resolve, and sure enough, it had. She went home and slept instead.

She awoke to find Miz Clara arranging two dozen red roses in the kitchen. "Look what somebody sent ya. Wasn't Darryl Boucree, neither."

Talba snatched up the card—*"Have renounced Satan, found Jesus, joined AA, shaved heads, and donned sackcloth. Can you find it in your heart to speak to us ever again? Love, Dumb Daneene and Dumber Edwards."*

In spite of herself, her lips twitched, wondering how they'd look with shaved heads, but knowing she wasn't about to find out—because everything in the note was undoubtedly a lie.

"Who they is?" Miz Clara said. "And what'd they do that's dumber'n the next thing? What's all that sacrilegious mess?"

"Mama, you have no idea. But 'mess' works fine. They made a big fat mess. But at least a few things got cleared up. You ready to meet Janessa?"

Miz Clara didn't look up from the vase, but Talba could see that her jaw muscles softened a bit. "Tol' ya I was."

"Okay. Shall I invite her over or what?"

"Tonight be okay. I'll make chicken."

Talba got her sister on the phone. "Janessa, I got a hell of a deal for you. You want to try the best fried chicken in New Orleans? Mama wants you to come over tonight."

"For real?"

"She said it herself."

"Whoa! I can't believe it. Can I bring Rashad?"

Talba hesitated. "Rashad is certainly welcome here, but maybe the first time, just you and Miz Clara—what do you think?"

"You call ya Mama 'Miz' somethin'? What's up with that?"

"Everybody calls her that—it's what she calls herself."

"That ain't why *you* said it. You were tellin' me what ya want me to call her—'cause ya think I'm not smart enough to figure it out."

"Janessa, when I'm talking to my own brother, we call her 'Miz Clara.'"

"Ya own brother. I love *that*. Like I'm not ya own sister."

"Wait a minute—how'd we end up in a fight? I just called to invite you to dinner. I thought that's what you wanted."

"I don't want no part of your fancy-ass family, Ms. Talba Wallis. You can just forget about it."

She left Talba listening to a dial tone, thinking it was the first time she'd ever been told off for asking someone to dinner. Not to mention the first time anybody'd called her family fancy. She wondered how Janessa was going to react to Michelle—because she was pretty sure she was going to get the chance. No way had she seen the last of this kid, as tempting a thought as it was.

She went in to give Miz Clara the news that Janessa seemed to have a previous commitment.

"I ain' surprised," her mama said. "Gon' take her awhile."

One thing, Talba decided—her own conscience was clear. She'd done what Janessa had asked, the girl had rejected it, and the ball was now in her sister's court.

It was a week before she got the e-mail: *"Dear Talba—I am sorry I lost my temper with you. I have been under a lot of pressure lately. Please thank Ms. Clara for the invitation and tell her I would be very happy to accept if I am ever invited again. Sincerely, Janessa Wallis."*

"*It's 'Miz' Clara,*" Talba answered. "*Come to my reading at Reggie and Chaz on the 18th. It's open mike, so Rashad can read, too. Talba.*"

Of course, that meant mobilizing Miz Clara, so she invited Darryl and all three Valentinos to dinner at the restaurant before the reading. Both Eddie and Miz Clara more or less hated poetry (though they wouldn't admit it), but they were crazy about each other. She figured she could get Eddie to come for Miz Clara, and Miz Clara would get a bonus—Eddie and Darryl both.

If Janessa came, she was set.

That night Angie had a special glow to her, Talba thought—and Eddie had news. "My buddy LaBauve called with the dirt on Hunt Montjoy. Autopsy showed enough Tylenol in him to kill a moose. And guess what? Taylor told the cops he gave it to him."

"You're telling me he confessed to Hunt Montjoy's murder?"

"Not exactly. Said he just handed him the bottle and paid no attention to how many Hunt took. Claimed Montjoy begged for it, his hand hurt so much from beating up his best buddy."

"Oh, right. Regular good Samaritan. Well, hell. I guess once you've killed two people, what's three?"

"Hold ya horses, Ms. Wallis. There's more. Montjoy *coulda* died from all that Tylenol—mixed up with alcohol, of course— a fact Wayne Taylor couldn't help but know. But there's a cute little wrinkle here. Looks like somebody might've helped Mr. Montjoy along. He had a little tiny fiber in his nose. Like maybe somebody found him drunk in his car and tried to smother him. And here's the kicker—that selfsame little bit of cotton matched up with pillowcases in old Hunt's own house."

Talba was thunderstruck. "Lynne? You mean Lynne finally had enough?" She knew something else about Lynne.

Eddie shrugged. "They questioned her, but she was cool as a mule. And face it, Hunt was a drunk—he could have slept with his face in the pillow the night before and gotten a thread up his nose."

"Come on!"

"Point is, they couldn't prove anything. But guess what else? Lynne Montjoy left town right after they turned her loose and nobody's seen her since."

"I know where she is. Her niece Kerry called me."

"Well? Ya gon' tell me or not?"

"It's in my poem."

After dinner, when they went in for the reading, the cause of Angie's heightened complexion became obvious. Austin was waiting for her—an Austin who looked terrific bald as an eagle. "My God!" she said to Angie. "He really did shave his head. Don't tell me he really found Jesus."

Angie gave her a smug look. "He's been known to invoke that name."

"Oooh." Talba held her ears. "Don't tell me about it, whatever you do."

Her eyes swept the room. So far, no Janessa. She watched Eddie shake hands with Austin, almost as if he didn't want to kill him. From the look Audrey was giving him, she thought he was hot. Maybe Eddie *would* kill him.

Talba was third on the program that night, a place she liked. The audience was already warmed up, but they weren't yet tired. When her name was called, she took the mike confidently, feeling properly aristocratic in head-to-toe fuchsia, the pants tight-fitting bells (not that different from those black ones she had), the top low in the front with loose, wafting sleeves that ended in graceful little points.

"Poetry," she said, "is what I do to make sense of my life. Yes, I write it, but I live it, too, and we all live it, whether or not we see it. Sometimes life is rhythmic and nuanced, just like a poem, but it's hard to hear the rhythms unless you consciously sit down and try to make art out of it. Always, it's a blank page before it begins to form into patterns, and it's easy to think the blankness is all there is. So the Baroness myself goes in for poem therapy. I hope y'all will indulge me. This poem is called: *The Story of My Life After Hurricane Carol.*"

She opened her poem and began to read, once more repeating the title, as was her custom: "*The Story of My Life After Hurricane Carol.*"

> *The town was wet*
> *And the town was mean.*
> *And Hurricane Carol was on her way,*
> *When my damn phone rang.*

Nothing good could come of it,
Nothing good could follow it,
But I answered my phone when it rang that day.

And two weeks later I was in a classroom,
In a highly respected institution
Of higher learning
When two students whipped out their guns.

This was not no high school.
This was not no Columbine.
These were grown-up middle class
White ladies
Ready to shoot up a university
Classroom.

Y'all mighta read about it.

It turned out that somebody's husband,
A highly respected professeur
Of higher learning
Had up and killed his girlfriend and then
Her mama, just to round things out,
And finally he got beat up by his best friend
For trying to set him up for his crimes.

After the friend beat him up,
He turned up dead himself.
Now, did our professeur *kill his lifelong pal?*

Coulda.
Coulda done that thing.

But so could the best pal's
Cheated-on wife—
Tight, pinch-faced,
Troubled lady.
Left town last week
To marry an Episcopal priest

> *She'd known for twenty years.*
> *And hers ain't the only*
> *Happy ending.*
>
> *The Baroness myself got two new cats,*
> *Used to live with*
> *The ill-fated victims.*
> *But they ain't got*
> *Nothin' to say.*
> *Nothin' much, nohow.*
> *"Blanche and Koko, start talkin',"*
> *I say,*
> *And they do.*
>
> *Say, "feed us."*
>
> *Y'all think I am makin' this up,*
> *And usually I do.*
> *But this poem is true,*
> *And is dedicated to my sister who*
> *May or not be here with you.*
> *And me.*
>
> *Stand up if you are, Janessa.*

Here, she paused, just in case. No one stood, but no problem—she'd written two endings. She recited the alternate:

> *Well, she ain't here, but*
> *Y'all are, and the Baroness myself*
> *Has this to say:*
>
> *Never, ever, whatever you do,*
> *Answer the phone in a hurricane.*
> *Unless ya want to live some poetry.*

She had delivered the poem in her usual melodramatic, sing-
songy style, almost yelling it, and winding down as she reached
the end. She was about to take her bow when Janessa came in
with Rashad, now as bald as her brother, Corey. She wondered

if the James boys had shaved their heads just before the reading. She said, "Well, hey there, Janessa, baby. Hey, everybody, that's my little sister!"

The crowd broke into wild applause. *There*, Talba thought. *Never say I didn't claim you. Fool that I am.*

To the audience, she said, "Y'all beware of ringing phones now. The Baroness myself thanks you."

Turn the page for a preview of

P. I. On a
Hot Tin Roof

JULIE SMITH

Now Available in Hardcover
From Tom Doherty Associates

Chapter One

It was one of those robot voices, a male one: "You have a collect call from Orleans Parish Prison."

Uh-uh. She didn't.

Talba Wallis was already crying and she didn't need any more grief, but she didn't give it a thought. This one wasn't for her. She got those calls about every three months. Something happened to people's dialing fingers in Central Lockup, maybe from the drugs or alcohol that got them in there in the first place. She clicked off her cell phone and went back to chopping onions. Her mama, Miz Clara, was slow-cooking ribs in the oven, and Talba was making potato salad for a family meal: Her brother Corey, his wife Michelle, and the adorable Sophia Pontalba (partially named for her aunt, and now talking a blue streak) were coming over soon. Talba still had to make greens, too—her way, not Miz Clara's. Her mother was inclined to cook them for hours, with lots of pork. Talba and Michelle liked them just barely wilted. Dessert was king cake, a present from one of Miz Clara's housecleaning clients, so no worries there.

She had time, if she put her mind to it.

By the time the phone rang again, she had the salad together and had begun washing the greens. The same voice again. She sighed. May as well tell the poor bastard he had the wrong number. She reached for the phone, nearly tripping over two cats currently trying to wrap themselves around her legs to get her mind off her cooking and on their dinner. She waited for the prisoner's name.

"Talba, it's Angie. I need you."

Angie? Angela Valentino? Angie was about as likely to be in Central Lockup as Sister Helen Prejean. Angie neither relieved herself on the street nor smoked pot in public. She avoided bar fights and had no domestic partner to chase with a cleaver. She was a lawyer in good standing. What the hell was this?

"Angie, hang on; I've got to dry my hands." Talba set the phone down for a moment and found a paper towel. "What the hell did you do?"

"Listen, I'm not the problem, they popped Alabama, too—planted drugs on us."

Big Chief Alabama Bandana, one of Angie's most celebrated clients, a musician and Mardi Gras personality famous for his drug problem.

Somebody *could* have planted drugs on him—or maybe that was just what Angie wanted to believe. "But . . . your parents . . . ," Talba said. She couldn't figure out why Angie was calling her instead of them. Talba's boss was Angela's father, Eddie Valentino, one of the best-connected people in town. If anyone could spring his daughter, Eddie could.

"They went to the Gulf Coast for the weekend. Dad's got his cell phone off."

I'll just bet he has, Talba thought. Eddie was nothing if not discreet, but you didn't have to be a genius to figure out that the Gulf Coast had an aphrodisiac effect on his wife, Audrey. He took her there whenever he could and was always unavailable until they got back.

"You know what it's like in Central Lockup? God forbid you should ever find out. You get access to a phone, but no phone book. You can only call numbers you know by heart."

"Oh. Maybe that's why I get so many wrong numbers." Talba heard herself babbling, aware that she was in shock.

Angie said, "Huh? Listen, it doesn't matter. You've got to get us out of here."

"Obviously. Where do I start?"

"We've got to find a judge who'll set bond on a Saturday night."

"Give me a name and I'll call it."

"No, let my lawyer do it. Jimmy Houlihan. Problem is, I don't know his home number. See if he's in the book, will you?"

"*Your* lawyer? Lawyers have lawyers?"

"Jimmy's a friend."

Uh-huh, Talba thought. *Ex-boyfriend.* Fingers shaking, she looked him up. "Not here—only his office. But I could call his answering service. Or better yet, let me go online. I can't call you back, right?"

"No, but I can call you next time the phone's free."

"Forget it. You've made contact—I'll do the rest. You okay, by the way?"

"I'm making lots of new friends, none of them deputies. No problem, I'll live. I'm just worried about Al."

"Want me to call his family?"

"You can try, but I don't know his number by heart. His real name's Albert Brazil; he might be in the phone book."

"Okay, I'll take it from here. Hang in there, okay?"

"Thanks." Talba heard the relief in her voice. "Listen, one last thing. Tell Jimmy it can't be Buddy Champagne."

"What can't be?"

"The judge. Anybody but Buddy. Whatever happens, not Buddy. Even if we have to spend a week in jail."

"Got it. Not Buddy."

When Talba put down the phone, she noticed that her palm was damp, along with her temples. Whew. This was a blow.

Well, so much for Michelle's health-food greens. She went in search of Miz Clara, who was taking a preprandial snooze, secure in the knowledge that her daughter had dinner under control. "Mama? Can you wake up?"

Miz Clara started. She was wearing a pair of old sweats and a T-shirt, the kind of thing she wore to work; no wig, and she probably wouldn't put one on, either—this was just family. "Sandra, whassup, for heaven's sake? I jus' barely drop off and you come in here shakin' me like somethin' on fire." She called her daughter a different name from the one Talba called herself, and thereon hung a tale—no one in the family ever mentioned Talba's birth name, which was neither Sandra nor Talba.

"Mama, Angie's in jail."

"*Angie?* What she do, insult a judge?"

"Says she was framed. Listen, I've got to get her out. The potato salad's done; you mind fixing the greens?"

Miz Clara looked at her watch. "Take two hours to make greens—I got thirty minutes."

"Mama, it doesn't. Just put them in a steamer for awhile."

"Mmph."

"Michelle likes them that way."

"She would." Michelle came from a much fancier family than the Wallises ever thought about being.

Talba could feel the minutes ticking away. Every second she wasn't working on the problem was a second Angie and Alabama would have to spend in jail. "Go on," Miz Clara said. "Do what ya gotta do. I'll feed ya rats." Cats, she meant. Blanche and Koko were more her cats than Talba's.

First, Talba thought, the musician's family. An Albert Brazil was listed on Villere Street. That would be him. Most Mardi Gras Indians lived in Tremé. A woman answered. "Mrs. Brazil?"

"Ain' no Miz Brazil."

"I'm looking for the family of Albert Brazil."

The woman's voice changed. "Somethin' happen to Albert? Yeah, I'm Miz Brazil." *Just not legally,* Talba thought.

"Listen, Albert's fine. But there's been a mix-up, and I'm working on it. I work with his lawyer, Angela Valentino. . . ."

"Oh, Lord, don't tell me he in jail again!"

"Not for long, if I can help it."

"Who you? Why you callin' 'steada Miss Angela? I ain' know who you is."

"My name's Talba Wallis. I'm a P.I. who works with her father, Eddie Valentino. We do a lot of work for Angie's firm."

"Well, why ain't Miss Angela callin'?"

"She's—uh—" Something told Talba to dissemble. "We're both working on it. She's trying to get a judge to set bond. Asked me to call you; set your mind at ease."

"Swear to God, this the last time! Albert done swore on the Big Book he clean, he stayin' clean. He barely out of jail, and now he back in. You get him out, tell him he better not come home."

Talba knew she shouldn't give out any more information than she had to, but she wanted to ease the woman's pain if she could. "Angela says the drugs were planted."

"Oh, yeah! Uh-huh. That what he always say. They all say that; don't you know nothin'?" She hung up in a fury, leaving Talba with uncomfortable nigglings. Everybody in jail said they were framed. She was well aware of that. She knew Angie well enough to know she wasn't a druggie, but surely the lawyer was being naïve where the Chief was concerned. Talba was inclined to agree with the self-styled Mrs. Brazil—there were probably very few innocent people moldering in Central Lockup.

Finding Jimmy Houlihan's number was a piece of cake, given Talba's computer skills. And after no more than twelve or thirteen rings, a man answered. "Mr. Houlihan?" Talba asked.

"Jimmy? You want Jimmy?" The man sounded as if he wasn't sure he'd heard correctly. In the background she could hear the buzz of conversation, the clinking of glasses, and two different kinds of loud music, one involving drums. "Think he went to the parade."

Talba thanked him and hung up, surmising that since Houlihan lived on St. Charles Avenue itself—the main artery of almost every parade of Carnival—a parade party was in progress. Technically speaking, it wasn't the first weekend of parades— Krewe Du Vieux had rolled the weekend before in the French Quarter.

But it was the second day of the twelve days of almost constant parading that mesmerized the city while paralyzing its traffic every year at this time. The only break would come on the following Monday. Otherwise, there would be at least two parades a day in New Orleans itself, plus many more in the suburbs until Ash Wednesday. No one who lived on St. Charles or near it escaped entertaining. People with college-age children found themselves running impromptu dormitories and soup kitchens; those with out-of-town friends who had the price of airline tickets became instant B&B proprietors; and anyone who was left who knew anyone at all pretty much held open house—whether they wanted to or not.

Since it was only the second day, spirits would be high; nobody'd yet be burned out. No wonder you couldn't hear yourself think at the Houlihan house. Talba was going to have to pay the lawyer a visit, and that wasn't going to be easy, given the traffic. Still, she knew she could do it if she followed Eddie Valentino's Foolproof Carnival Driving Formula, which involved staying on I-10 whenever she could and avoiding Magazine and Prytania as if they were St. Charles itself—in other words, sticking to the lake side of the parade route. (It got more complicated the night of the Endymion Parade, which rolled in another neighborhood entirely, but there were ways, and Eddie knew them.)

Talba followed the Valentino blueprint, ending up on Baronne and wondering where she was going to park. But as it turned out, she needn't have—many of Central City's most enterprising entrepreneurs had set up temporary lots at twenty dollars a spot. This had to be a place where they just couldn't wait for Mardi Gras to come around. It was a dicey neighborhood, the kind where, on a normal night, you might not be all that surprised to find a car window broken or a lock smashed when you returned. Talba figured that tonight the twenty dollars not only paid for the spot, but ought to cover protection as well. Best of both worlds, she thought, admiring capitalism in action, and, despite herself, catching the festive feeling of the neighborhood. Carnival might be a pain, but once you broke down and gave in to it, it sucked you in like a purple, green, and gold patch of quicksand. She certainly hoped Jimmy Houlihan was a good enough friend of Angie's to resist the irresistible.

The Houlihan house was overrun. It was a big brick edifice with columns, decked out with Mardi Gras garlands that failed to make a good showing against the red brick, but a Mardi Gras wreath on the white door took up the slack. The door was open now, and the porch was jammed with white people, glasses and go-cups in their hands. A pale guy in a pinstriped shirt, obviously thinking Talba didn't belong, asked if he could help her.

"Happy Mardi Gras," she said. "Jimmy said to pop by if I could."

He planted a big one on her. "Happy Mardi Gras," he rejoined. "Bar's inside."

Talba grinned at him, dying to wipe off the slobbery kiss, but thinking it might be rude. "Jimmy around?"

He shrugged. "Saw him awhile ago. Look for a Mardi Gras rugby shirt."

She checked out the crowd. Half the men in the crowd wore green, gold, and purple shirts. "Thanks a lot."

She left him guffawing, obviously having had a beer or two, and made her way inside the house. A woman in jeans, smooth hair in one of those neat pageboys favored in this neck of the woods, spotted her and snaked her way through the crush, probably wondering if Talba was someone off the streets, attracted by the crowd. Talba waved as if she knew her. "Hiii! You must be Patsy Houlihan." She'd found the name on an opera Web site. "I'm Talba Wallis."

"Oh, uh, hi. Uh. Talba. You must work with Jimmy." She looked a little confused.

Good. Talba must have guessed right. "I'm a client." She let it hang there awkwardly, forcing the other woman to make some kind of move.

"Well. Let's get you a drink." She turned, expecting Talba to follow her to the bar, which Talba did.

The bartender was African-American, like Talba herself, wearing a white waiter's jacket. "Just water, please."

The guy didn't smile at her, didn't seem to be enjoying his work. She tried Patsy again. "I was hoping to say hello to Jimmy."

Patsy swiveled her head. "Oh. Jimmy. He may have gone out to the street."

Better fess up, Talba decided. "Actually, I'm kind of a client by proxy. I've got an emergency, but unfortunately I don't know Jimmy by sight."

The white woman's features froze. She was one of those bird-like, gym rat types whose day was probably all about getting her fingers and toes painted. The kind who had a garage that opened with a remote and never parked on the street for fear of getting mugged. She might not be a racist, but Talba had a feeling this was the first time an African-American who wasn't on staff had ever been to one of her parties. And she wasn't adjusting any too quickly.

Talba had a feeling mentioning Angie's name wasn't the way to go. "I'm a P.I.," she said. "My firm works with his firm." It might even be true. Eddie'd been around so long he'd probably worked with every lawyer in town at some point.

"But I . . . but it's Mardi Gras!" In some other context it might have sounded shallow, but in New Orleans, everything stops for Mardi Gras. Talba could grasp Patsy's displeasure. This was like appearing at someone's house on Christmas morning.

She was almost out of ideas, but at that moment a man in a Mardi Gras rugby shirt danced up. "Hey, darlin', you're missing the parade." He put a well-shaped hand on Patsy's shoulders, and was rewarded with a scathing look.

"Jimmy?" Talba said, before Patsy could recover. *Can this marriage be saved?* she thought.

The man removed his hand from his wife's shoulder and offered it to Talba. "I don't believe I've had the pleasure."

There were a lot of different ways you could say that phrase. This man said it gently, sincerely, as if, despite its stiffness, it came naturally to him. Talba saw that he was tall, with good shoulders and a big chest. He had silky brown hair—quintessential white-dude hair—and small, stylish spectacles; one of those pinkish Irish faces; a rounded nose, but an oval face, an open one. An attractive man, someone Angie could be friends with.

She gave him a broad smile. "Sorry to barge in like this. One of your clients asked me to get in touch, but when I called . . ."

"Oh, God, no telling who answered the phone."

"It was someone who didn't seem to know where you were." She glanced nervously at Patsy. "I wouldn't have come, but your client's got a sort of emergency."

He laughed. "Don't tell me he called from Central Lockup."

Talba lifted a wry eyebrow. "Guess it's happened before."

Houlihan seemed to be uncomfortably aware that his wife was taking in every word, and doing a slow burn at the same time.

"Patsy, you go on and have fun. Let me see what I can do for this lady."

Patsy drifted away, apparently determined to keep up appearances, but Talba surmised that her house at Mardi Gras had the same rules as an exclusive men's club—no business was to be transacted on the premises.

Talba smelled a spat in the making. She felt sorry for him. "It's Angela Valentino," she said.

"Geddouttahere!"

"She was with Al Brazil when they got popped. You know, Chief of the Poison Oleanders?"

"Sure. Everybody knows Big Chief Alabama. By reputation, anyhow. What happened?"

"She says somebody planted drugs on the Chief."

"That Angie. What a little Pollyanna."

Talba was getting impatient. "I work with her dad, so she called me. Said to get you to get a judge to set bond for both of them."

He nodded. "I can do that. Hey, no problem whatsoever. We got a couple judges soakin' up the suds right out on the porch."

"Well, one thing. She said anybody but Buddy Champagne."

This time he was the one speaking eyebrow language. "Well, that do make it harder."

"Champagne's here?"

Houlihan shrugged. "He's a neighbor. Easiest thing in the world to set it up."

"Loosely translated, she said she'd rather rot in jail."

He laughed. The judges weren't the only ones soaking up suds. "Hey, you're a pretty sharp cookie. Who are you, anyway?"

"Talba Wallis. I work with Angie's dad. He was away, so she called me."

His face clouded. "But why didn't she just call me directly?"

"They don't give you a phone book and she didn't have your number memorized."

"Well . . . she used to." She could see the regret in his face and thought that anyone married to Patsy Houlihan could be forgiven for having a wandering eye. "Angie's really in jail? Little Angie?"

"Last I looked, little Angie could take ten men about your size." It was true, though it had a great deal more to do with attitude than Angie's own size—she was a perfect size eight, maybe even a six.

"Woo. 'Tain't it the truth." Houlihan sighed. "Okay, let me go do the honors. Make yourself at home. I'll find you when it's done."

"Shouldn't be hard." Talba waved at the sea of white faces. "I kind of stick out in this crowd."

"Yeah, well," he muttered, "Patsy's in charge of the guest list." He melted into the melee. If he and Angie had been an item once, he seemed nostalgic for old times.

Making herself at home was a good trick, Talba thought, when your hostess hates you, but she set about making friends with the sour bartender. "Long night, huh?"

The man sighed. "Long as a piece of balin' wire."

"I heard that," she said, rolling her eyes. Evidently she wasn't the only one who had her differences with Patsy.

"Sure you wouldn't like a little something in that water?"

Talba handed him her glass. "Little more ice, maybe. I've got to be alert—got to go bail someone out in a while."

"I'm sure sorry to hear that."

Talba raised her freshened glass. "Happy Mardi Gras," she said.

Turner said, "You can't—"